BRANWELL BRONTË'S BARBER'S TALE
Chris Firth © 2005

Published By
East Coast Books 108 Church Street Whitby

For my Mum
(Barbara Joan Godfrey re Berriman, re Firth, nee Boswell, deceased),
and all the sisters.

Of all the books, archives, periodicals and publications consulted in the journey of preparation for this book – too numerous to list or mention here – 'Brother In The Shadow' by Mary Butterfield, 'The Infernal World Of Branwell Brontë' by Daphne Du Maurier and the secret world of 'The Bradford Observer' on microfiche have been especially useful, entertaining and engaging companions.

Thanks to Sheila Sloan for textual assistance, Michael Wray of East Coast Books for encouragement and support, and to Deborah for her help, tolerance, beauty, forbearance etc.

Cover illustration courtesy of The Tap and Spile, Whitby, Yorkshire.

CHAPTER 1

Maquire, cutter and ornamental hair manufacturer, repairer of periwigs and perruques, just returned from London via Paris thus acquainted with latest, most fashionable styles and latest perfumery. Preparer of beneficial and invigorating remedies. Painless extractor of teeth. Family homes and reputable establishments attended by appointment.
Maquire's Hair Emporium, off Ivegate, Bradford.

Bradford, February 1861

Typical, this February, Bradford evening. Grey and dismal. Fog descending. A slashing filth of rain obliterating any decent view of the hills which cocoon this huddle of a town. The air outside MacCraw's establishment is thick and stinking with the sulphurous spew from a forest of blackened mill chimneys.

In these conditions of the weather and season, the pretty landscape painting that could be knocked out and offered up for inspection is just not possible. No artists have their easels set up out there today. Yet just a few months ago, on this very street corner, upon a summer's evening, at about this time of day, a gorgeous swell of heather-purpled hill tops and sky-capped moorland framing the scene would have made this jumble of streets a sheer lovely place to be loitering and watching the world roll by from. The noises of summer would be up for the hearing too - the soft murmur of leafy trees stirred by some pleasant breeze; twittering larks and trilling blackbirds blending top notes into the gentle clack of hoof and cart wheel upon the cobbles. Of course, more discordant sounds would break through this aural pleasantry - the bickering, guttural voices of the hawkers and street vendors; the perpetual complaints and exclamations of penny-rubbing shoppers; the grating of cellar-poisoned wool combers coughing and raking up the Devil's filth from their very lungs. From across Westgate and the midst of the bustling fruit market would drift the strains of a black and tragic ballad, full-belted out by a tenor voiced patterer who'd sell sheet copies of the songs for a penny apiece. Hardly the sweetest voice you've ever heard, but pleasant enough to tempt you to linger and listen a while in the soft sunshine.

Sure, there can be a lovely view knocked up there from the top of Ivegate, but not in February, and not when it's raining ice.

This town, Bradford, like most places in these days of industrial growth and calamitous progress, is prone to be a place of extremes and opposites. Such ugliness, you'll find, hob-nobbing along with real beauty. The old, familiar, utter grind of poverty limping along beside waltzing new-wealth. Success riding along astride the old mule of dismal Failure. True *genius* striding cock-sure along with strut-footed, shirt-puffing, preening, posturing *minor talent*. Understand that, the happy-go-lucky coexistence of extremes and opposites, and you'll have the gist of this place these days.

On a grim evening like this though, with business slack and the streets fair empty, the patterers and whistlers huddled away in the ale-hovels of the rookery, most young fellows would give anything to be away in summer time and out upon the moor, out amidst the curlew and the butterfly, the summer blooms and the warm-glancing rays of sunshine. Away from hellish chimney fumes and these clouds which blossom up like blackened fungi from the basement workshops where the wool combers toil and dwell. Away from the petty squabbling and life scrabbling of the desperate poor, who cluster in the stinking cellars just up the hill beyond Westgate there. Best of all, away from the damned, eternal snip-snippety-snip of scissoring, the rasping of a razor upon stubble, the staccato chitchat forced upon MacCraw by his coarse haired, grease-slippery customers.

The wealthy and the dandies, the intellectual upstarts, bright mushrumps, the local men of worth - they do not visit him now. Not these days. Not like in the old times, when 'Maquire's Hair Emporium' was fashionable with the young men about town; when he could truly boast in his weekly newspaper advertisement that he was a practitioner of the latest London and Paris styles, having recently been working in a popular West End salon, and right there in the vibrant heart of Paris just the year before that. Those great old days, back in the thirties, when with coin enough to back him up and the nerve to set up a business in whatever town he took a fancy to, he could feign a French ring to his name then fake the very accent without a worry or care. Back before all the great changing and upheaval of the world, the days when Mad Branwell, Lusty-Joe Leyland, Grinning-Billy Drearden, Francis Grundy, Bob Storey, Roving Robinson and Black-Spider Walton, along with the rest of the flame-eyed, spark-minded *'Worldes End Rhymers'* would call in upon the place. They'd sit there gossiping, gassing, sipping on tea, while MacCraw attended and pampered his customers, all dissecting news from journals and the weekly Observer, penning rhymes to each other, generally entertaining the shop. Once upon a while they'd even get themselves a decent haircut. Maquire's was a real beautifying establishment then; a veritable *salon*; a meeting place for gentlemen and dandies of all classes. Certainly, it was not the three-penny cut-hole it's degenerated into now. The place is off the main track these days, thanks to the damned foolish erection of Queen's Mill, which has elbowed the shop aside into back streets while at the same time casting a shadow and pall of fumes all over it. MacCraw's Barber Shop now. No more fancy French intonations or flowery descriptions of hair-cuttery splendour. Back to the basics of the matter and trade. Well, there's the true face of progress for you - from gentlemen's delicate pandering, wig-repairs and ailments of health to three-penny snips and shavings of the mill labourers who dare afford the luxury. Not even teeth extractions or minor snippets of surgery these days - the doctors and the new town hospitals have taken the last illicit dregs of that ancient trade away from MacCraw. Of course, there are a few old faithfuls who stand by him as though he's the last barber in the world, but these are thinning in number, as well as on the head, as the years grind by.

Up at the very top of the winding hill they call Ivegate you'll find MacCraw's place, though these days you might have to make a bit of a search. He's on Millergate, to be precise, which means you take the left turn at the brow of the hill then into the grubby, dark ginnel that winds down beside the new mill there, looking out for the red and white pole that marks out the business of the place.

From outside MacCraw's shop on this February evening, the packet crowded and bottle-cluttered window gleams with gas-lamp. MacCraw, glancing up from his customer, spots the pale, bobbling face of a window-shopper poring over the wares there. He stocks cures and reliefs for all known ailments - Pearson's Neroline for chapped hands; Sarsaparilla drink for just about everything; Dr. King's Camomile Pills for the stomach; Johnson Guthery's Dandelion and Quinine Pills for the liver; Lewis's smokers' bonbons for the breath, and a hundred other brand of potions beside. Peek through this discreetly screening and highly profitable clutter, nose right up to the ice-cold glass, and there in the dingy interior the fellow snip-snippety-snips with apparent intense, peering concentration, as though making a master-work of his job in hand. He's working at the best chair and is jacketless despite the cold, shirtsleeves rolled to the elbow and his ever immaculately clean apron freshly laundered. To be truthful, with age and thickening waistline now upon him, his old eyesight is not what it was, and there's a joke written upon many a tavern toilet wall that if you want a straight fringe then don't go to 'Zigzag MacCraw'. His eyes are on the hairline all right, but this evening his mind is busy elsewhere. A problem has popped up out of his past like a pale, swollen fish surfacing from a dark pond. A problem which like an itching scab or an aching tooth cannot be left alone by fingernail or tongue tip. A twist of history exists that has to be addressed by MacCraw. There are records to be put straight and details to be corrected. The Truth of the past has to be rearranged in its right and actual order. Thus, he'll be closing very soon, half an hour earlier than usual.

It's now the last customer of the day he's busy with. Far more important, this problem resolving, than another shave or trim. Beside the morality of it all, an old friendship is involved. As MacCraw sees it, he owes it to the honour and memory of his good, but sadly long extinguished, friend and drinking companion, *Madness* Branwell. Patrick Branwell Brontë, that is. The very Brontë lad from Haworth way who passed on in the most bitter and self-destructive circumstances a dozen years ago or more now. A tragic loss of a blazing life. A tragic loss of hair too. As a maker of hairpieces MacCraw had a great appreciation of Branwell's insane red sprawl of sky-clambering locks. On more than one occasion, MacCraw had offered him a good price for his crop, it being of that colour and texture that was rare, and thus valuable, to any artful constructor of the toupee, peruke and periwig. He'd had the offer accepted too, and had paid for those curls on more than one occasion, though he'd never actually managed to get his fingers upon a single loose strand of the stuff.

This flame of hair, and all the past associations with it, MacCraw dwells on as he snips and grunts chatter to old Fish David. David is grinning at him in the gilt-framed mirror, slabs of hands clamped on his great flabby knees which seem set to erupt through the tight fabric of his work breeches. David's hardly the slenderest customer in the world. The great lump of the man is set there on the leather cutting-seat, as comfortable as a pork pie in a butcher's shop window, secretive smiles twinkling in his old blue eyes. This is not the most pleasant of haircuts of the day for MacCraw. As his very name might suggest, hoary old David trades daily in fish, and he reeks to the scalp of the stuff. Plenty of lavender-water spray, frequent pinches of self-concocted peppermint snuff and furtive tots of his back room grog are necessary for MacCraw to help blot out David's odour and ease the process along. MacCraw nips at David's nose, pulls his head back and drags aside beard hair so he can see the throat's stubble grain in the fading light, then drags his expert blade over the soap.

'You won't have been too busy today then, eh, MacCraw? Not in this weather, like,' Fish David wheezes, his Adam's-apple bobbling dangerously upon the blade.

'Oh, steady, you know. Not too busy, but busy enough. Keep still, now. I don't want to nick you.'

'I reckon not many'd want an 'aircut in this weather. It's too cold to shear a sheep.'

'Well, I wouldn't be saying that, David.'

'You need all the hair you can keep in this wind. Only the desperate in here now, eh? An' the bored.'

'Aye, maybe so David. And those on a sure certainty with some delightful specimen of our parallel species, hey? Now, which category would that put your good self in? Desperate, bored, or onto a certainty with one of the women folk?'

Here MacCraw winks in the sud-crusted mirror at his customer. Fish David's eyes widen, glittering full of lamps. He seems quite pleased to have been found out.

'I wouldn't lay missen' alongside the bored and desperate, man. I've a date with a lady this evening, if that's what you mean.'

'Ah, a date, is it? That's what they're calling such liaisons these days, is it? A rendezvous, I believe the French say, or so they did in my time in that fair land. And pray, sir, may I be so bold as to inquire after the identity of the lucky maiden who you're blessing your own fair sunshine and rendezvousing with on this bleak, dismal evening?'

'Aye, 'appen you might inquire, MacCraw. Of course you may. But I'll be sayin' nowt.'

'Ah, like that, is it?'

They exchange mirrored smiles, with a wink from MacCraw. The two go far back together, and indeed were great friends in their younger days, when both had more time on their hands, and spare money in their pockets to cast upon it. They know each other too well to pursue the conversation. Anyway, MacCraw is aware of the identity of the poor unfortunate woman, his days normally being spent in the exchange of gossip and trivial speculation that goes on around the cropping and the shaving of a man. Pot Mary, she's called, David's lucky lass. A lustrous, Latin, dark-haired raven, Italian running hot in her blood. Pot Mary, teller of fortunes from the picture-cards and teacups, and a tongue with a razor edged cursing ability. Gorgeous hair that still shines black to the curves of her desirable waist. The same Pot Mary who is perpetually unhappy with her shrivel-pod of a balding husband, Apple Martin, though they've stayed bound together through the changes of the years. There was always somebody interloping between their marital happiness though, and now it seemed to be David's turn. She'd come to stoop that low. Ah, what a waste. Her and David. That night. In the lounge room of The Old Star Inn up on John Street. And her a good ten years younger than him too. Chalk and cheese. Fish and fowl. A scandalous outrage. And thus, suitable meat for the stew of barbershop talking. MacCraw knew all about it, and having always had a soft spot for Pot Mary, even since before his own wife's tragic passing, he was not without envy.

'You'll be wanting this off then, if it's a damsel you're chasing?' he suggests, flicking scissors toward the grey fin of David's stomach-length beard. This is a jest from MacCraw. Nobody has seen the bare skin of David's face since he was fourteen and sprouting, when just setting out as a huckster in the oyster trade. He was of the clean throat but a well-covered chin, with decent, shaggy sideburns style. He'd as soon lose his head as his beard.

'I will not, sir. Just the throat and a trim at the top, as I asked.'

'Well, remember this, they're never worth it David. Cost you an arm, a leg, an aching heart, and a sore head too in the morning. And not to mention the weight loss.'

'Weight loss?' David, snug and secure with his own great bulk, seems concerned by this.

'Aye man, pounds of silver and ounces of gold. Loss of weight in the purse and pocket region of an honest, upright fellow.'

'Ah, quit the blarney and just keep trimming, MacCraw. I'm a full-grown man, in case you hadn't noticed. I'll take aboard all consequences of my actions.'

In this teasing vein the conversation continues until the throat-shave and hair trimming is done. The collar is deftly brushed; coins change hands. A little packet of Godfrey's Elderflower Cordial exchanges hands also, after a furtive amount of hinting innuendo from David. A little remedy and tonic in the powdered form that is said to improve the stamina and inclination in a man. This little packet is passed over without a wink or joke from MacCraw though - half of his income comes from such tonics, cures, creams and potions. A joke around a haircut is fine, but he'd not insult a man by jesting upon his weaknesses of body or lack of inclination.

'I'll be closing now,' MacCraw informs David, once the sachet is safely pocketed. 'I've important business to set to. Literary business.'

MacCraw too likes his secret business to be mulled and gossiped over. He leans forward slightly, placing his weight in his toes, awaiting David's inevitable question.

'Oh aye. What business is that then, MacCraw?'

A subtle pause of silence passes, each man looking at the other.

'Ah, I see,' sneers David. 'So you're not telling, either.'

'No, I'll be telling you all right, if you've a mind to listen. It might even be of interest, seen as it concerns you, in a round-a-bout way.'

David stiffens in his reeking, fish-smudged frock coat. His face flickers, red blob of nose twitching; he's on the defensive now, feeling implicated in some business not of his own concern or making.

'Aye up,' he sniffs. 'What's this then, MacCraw?'

'Relax, man. Nothing sinister. I'm talking about some business back in the old days. Years ago. Nothing that'll touch you now. You'll recall, I'm sure, The Worldes End Tavern out on Manningham Lane? Those days there of the debating society. The time when you were selling oysters and I was just setting up in this trade. You were a regular up at The Worldes End, remember?'

David still looks perplexed and suspicious, keen to forget as much as he can remember of those times.

'Maybe I do. A long time ago, all that though. Can't say you'd find me supping up that way these days. Too rough, man.'

'Well, I was thinking back. The Rhymers. Them debates, and all. Something I've read just lately. If you've half a minute I'll show it to you. It's just an article from last year that an old customer dropped in for me.'

MacCraw scurries around the best chair, rustling through old journals and broadsheets that sprawl in haphazard piles upon the low table before the waiting-bench. His search shifts to his cluttered drawers of brushes and scissors; he goes clacking and banging through the tools of his trade. Still he fails to locate the document and curses aloud that for the life of him he can't remember where on Earth he last put the damned thing. David takes the opportunity to edge toward the street door, wanting to be off about his own business, lingering there with one hand sneaking toward the latch while MacCraw retreats into his snuff and gin hole. Before David can lift the latch and make good his escape, MacCraw is back, emerging triumphantly in flurry of unfolding newspaper.

'Here it is. Here, in the Guardian. You'll remember Joseph Leyland. The sculptor fellow. Big, good looking fellow who died a good while ago.'

'Aye, I do remember him. Died in my debt. Owed me for fish, as well as ale.'

'Aye, that'll be him. Always in debt. And his friend then, that young Brontë fellow. Patrick. Branwell Brontë. Madness Patrick, we called him. Red hair. Real little fella...'

' I do recall him. But he never liked fish. Sad business though, his death and all that.'

'It was. But cast your mind back now. Those nights after the debating was over, when we'd sit around spinning yarns or singing and the like. The tales that fellow would weave us when we were all just this far off the floor...'

MacCraw motions a gap between his forefinger and thumb, an inch or so, indicating their state of past intoxication.

'Well, it's a good while ago you're talking of now. Couldn't tell you a tale of his word for word, but he were a good yarn spinner, that's true.'

'Read this thing then, will you. Read it. Go on. It won't take but a minute of your time.'

MacCraw thrusts the copy of his Halifax Guardian toward David's face, his forefinger jabbing at the article which is causing him such offence and disconcertion. David lowers his hand from the latch, takes the offered news sheets, coughs and grumbles about having better things to be doing with his time, but with MacCraw standing there enthusing on, he feels obliged to read the jabbed at piece. He sighs, shakes the paper straight, squints down and reads:

The Halifax Guardian
15th June 1860

WHO WROTE 'WUTHERING HEIGHTS?'
TO THE EDITORS OF THE HALIFAX GUARDIAN

Sirs,

This question suggested itself to me when I read the extract from a communication in the People's Magazine, published in the Guardian last week. The writer of the article says, 'Who would suppose that 'Heathcliffe, a man who never swerved from his arrow-straight course to perdition' from his cradle to his grave, &c., had been conceived by a timid and retiring female? But this was the case.' and he comes to this conclusion on the published authority of Charlotte Brontë. I think it will be seen from an extract I am about to make from the preface of a MS drama entitled The Demon Queen; or the Victim of Predestination, written a long time ago, but not yet published, that Emily Brontë's claim to Wuthering Heights is somewhat apocryphal.

Here then sir, THE EXTRACT I refer to:

'Many years ago, Patrick Branwell Brontë and I agreed that each should write a drama or a poem, the principle character in which was to have a real or imaginary existence before the Deluge; and that, in a month's time, we should meet at the Cross Roads Inn, which is about half way between Keighley and Haworth, and produce the result of our lucubrations. We met at the time and place appointed, and in the presence of a mutual friend, the late J.B. Leyland, the promising sculptor, plus other spectators of both our acquaintance. I read the 1st act of the Demon Queen; but when Branwell dived into his hat - the usual receptacle of his fugitive scraps - where he supposed he had deposited his MS poem, he found he had by mistake placed there a number of stray leaves of a novel on which he had been trying his 'prentice hand.' Chagrined at the disappointment he had caused, he was about to return the papers to his hat, when friends earnestly pressed him to read them, as they felt a curiosity to see how he could wield the pen of a novelist. After some hesitation, he complied with the request, and riveted our attention for about an hour, dropping each sheet, when read, into his hat. The story broke off abruptly in the middle of a sentence, and he gave us the sequel, viva voce, together with the real names of the prototypes of his characters; but as some of these personages are still living, I refrain from pointing them out to the public. He said he had not yet fixed upon a title for his production, and was afraid he should never be able to meet with a publisher who would have the hardihood to usher it into the world. The scene of the fragment which Branwell read, and the characters introduced in it - so far as then developed - were the same as those in Wuthering Heights, which Charlotte Brontë confidently asserts was the production of her sister Emily. One thing is certain, that Branwell's MS was in existence many years before the three sisters became known to the public under their respective pseudonyms, Currer, Ellis and Acton Bell; and Wuthering Heights appeared but a short time before Branwell was laid in his grave. An intimate friend of the latter (the late Edward Sloan) declared that he had no sooner begun to read Wuthering Heights than he anticipated all the characters and incidents of the story; because Branwell's MS which he had heard read portion by portion as the author produced it, had familiarised them to his mind. There is besides, I think, internal evidence, notwithstanding Charlotte's positive assertion to the contrary, that the novel in question never could have emanated from the pen of a young female. A character so utterly revolting as the principle personage in that strange work, it is beyond the imagination of an inexperienced girl to conceive.

Whatever may be the merits of that work, I believe them to be Branwell's; and it is but right that they should be added to the few laudatory waifs which the biographer of his sister has hung as funeral wreath over his untimely grave. Thus much have I thought it necessary to say in vindication of his memory. Fiat Justitia, ruat coelum.

This proves that 'Heathcliffe', at least, if not all the other characters in Wuthering Heights, had a prior existence in Branwell's manuscript to that given him in the novel ascribed to his sister, Emily.

WILLIAM OAKENDALE
Warley Grammar School, June 12th, 1860.

David struggled over the words and cumbersome sentences, himself not being a master of the reading art. He understood the gist of it though. There followed the letter a lengthy poem by the same pen, dramatising the Cross Roads Inn incident the writer had referred to, but as he was no lover of verse, he skipped this. He remembered Patrick Branwell now that he read about him, but he really did not care about the matter a jot.

'Well, it's interesting that they're still talking about the man, but what of it, MacCraw?'

'What of it, sir? Why, it's the truth, that's what.'

'Happen it is. Can't say I ever got round to reading the book myself. Well, not beyond first page or so. Not what you'd call a right riveting read, in my estimation. But then I'm no great reader.'

'Aye, well that's the crux of the matter, David. I did read the thing. Over and over, several times. Then again, recently too. And this here's the truth. I was there at that very gathering. I heard him read from that book years before it ever came to print. I swear to it, sir. Not only did Branwell tell that tale, or near as damn it, and a dozen times in a dozen different versions too, but I was there, at this very event.'

Again his finger went jabbing upon the newspaper, as though he was angry with the page itself.

'And what's more, I saw him working on it when he lived there up on Fountain Street. I swear it man, the lamp burning, the nib upon the paper, the words flowing. And then she had the audacity... that Charlotte. It was her doing, not the little one's. She stole it from him, that's what. When he was in no fit state to look after himself, she took that book and put it about under other names.'

MacCraw was passionate now, spitting as he babbled, arms flapping, fingers slapping upon the offending page. David was inching toward the door again, keen to be on his way and away from these rantings.

'It was all her doing, and I could have put it right years ago. I felt sorry for them all, you see. Tragic little waifs, the lot of 'em, Branwell included. But I'm going to do now what I should have done back then. I'm going to put pen to paper on the matter. Before I die, I swear on my Caroline's blessed soul in Heaven, I'll put the record straight on this one matter.'

MacCraw, his colour up, folded the news-sheet away, shaking his head, looking very much saddened and maligned. David himself was a practical man, day in day out dealing with practical matters. Buy this, sell that, make a profit, look after yourself first, then your home and family, if you're fortunate to still have them. None of this who-wrote-what-when mattered to him, nor interested him. He felt uncomfortable watching someone he knew get so passionate about nonsense.

'Listen, MacCraw, happen Mad Pat did pen the thing, but what of it? They're all dead and buried now. Let sleeping dogs stay put, they say, and I'd agree with that.

14

Leave the past well alone and get on with your own life.'

MacCraw shook his head grimly.

'But there's more to it. There's another old saw, David - the dog returns to its vomit, and a fool to his folly. It's a matter of honour, you see. He wrote the book, Branwell did. Or most of it. And a curse there is upon it, as I've found to my own great loss. That heathen tale, Branwell dreamed it up, wrote it down, and put it away again. I know that much as sure as I'm standing here talking to you. And there it suddenly is, years later, out upon the world, earning fame and money, under the name of his little sister. That girl, David, she was practically a half-wit. She never stepped much further than her own front door. You know yourself, all poor Branwell ever wanted was to earn fame as an author. His soul up there, God bless it, it must be spinning in a frenzy. So close and still so far, just for the want of the change of a forename. They kept him like a prisoner there in his last days, I tell you. I know it. I went up there on a visit with Grundy. That poor, foolish lad, all he ever wanted was to be seen for what he was. A great big, ridiculous idiot of a genius. And what is it they remember him for now, David? For his drunken raving, that's what. For drunkenness, debauchery and damned lechery too. Well, I tell you, I'm going to put the record straight, David. That I am.'

David finally opened the door, a cold wind slinging drizzle over them and into the shop

'Well, like I say MacCraw, it's very interesting, but I wouldn't bother with it myself. It were a long time ago. No point in digging over old dirt, I say. But I'll be seeing you, anyway. Let me know how you get on with it.'

'I will, David, I will.'

With deft fingertips MacCraw brushed some final, imaginary hairs from his customer's collar, then they exchanged their farewells. David, hat donned, waddled away into the darkness and drizzle of the evening.

MacCraw locked his shop door, drew down the blinds then ventured out to close the shutters. Back in, shivering in his shirt sleeves, he cleared away his brushes and scissors, dimming the lamps until the objects in the shop were just edged with a shape retaining gleam of yellow. Leaving the cleaning of the place for the shop lads in the morning, he collected up the day's feeble takings from the box, and with a candle to guide his way ascended to his living area above the shop. Up the gloomy staircase he went, shading the chamber candle with his hand to protect it from the currents of air which moaned their way about the draughty house. There in his little drawing room he lit the gas lamps, set a candle upon his writing table, then stoked the hearth until the fire was up dancing. After off-putting the task with a dozen other minor jobs - straightening his papers and letters, dusting down the table, cleaning it of snuff and brandy stains, checking his quill nibs and ink supplies, stoking up the fire again, re-reading the offending news article, picking at the cold chop leftover from dinner time - MacCraw eventually felt almost ready to set about his penning. He took a great pinch of snuff to clear the wool-stuffiness within his head, downed a generous tot of brandy to warm his finger-tips, then he was off. There he sat, chasing on his letter-writing venture, trying to catch at his emotion before that passion for righting old-wrongs and correcting mistruths waned on him, or ran to a stutter of dry nonsense upon the page.

CHAPTER 2

Ruth

If grief for grief can touch thee,
If answering woe for woe,
If any ruth can melt thee,
Come to me now!

I cannot be more lonely,
More drear I cannot be!
My worn heart throbs so wildly
'Twill break for thee.

And when the world despises,
When Heaven repels my prayer,
Will not mine angel comfort?
Mine idol hear?

Yes, by the tears I've poured thee,
By all my hours of pain,
O I shall surely win thee,
Beloved, again!

P.B.B 1838

Mister George MacCraw,
MacCraw's Establishment,
Millergate,
Bradford.
February 14th, 1861

Mister William Byles Esquire,
The Bradford Observer,
Lower Cheapside,
Bradford,

Dear Sir,
I have important news, facts and documentary evidence in my possession which I strongly feel will be of interest and perhaps a source of great excitement to you. Should you deign to meet me, as here I request you do, if you'll pardon my directness, you'll realise I'm not at all from these parts. That, you'll realise, is why I don't talk, nor perhaps write, much like the folk around here. Where I originate from is not too important, as I've been to enough and more places to rid myself of all traces and connections with the little town where I was raised, a place to which I swear I'll never return to again even if the devil's own mares try to drag me back there. There's nothing of me and my family there now, myself being the last of a line who have all but been hounded out of the place. But that's not what I write of. Having been widely travelled, I've become a jack of many trades, but only true master of one. That trade I'm employed in at this moment, though not literally - I give a decent haircut, a close shave and have knowledge of many an ailment shifting potion. In short, sir, I'm an expert barber, of the ancient checkered-apron school, trained by my venerable master instructor, a Parisian Mussleman of Turkey way, as he was trained by his master before him, in certain medical and surgical arts, as well as all manner of wig-makery and hair cutting - indeed your own good publication, under a previous editor, printed a series of essays by myself upon the art of my trade several years ago now, as a look back through your own past pages will prove, should you be so moved to examine my credentials and sincerity. I'm no common crocus sir, no quack or street-doctor, the medical side of my trade being outlawed to me now, as you well know, though I've made a fair penny out of that, as well as my legitimate trade. I wander from the point, though, good sir, for it is none of myself that I want to write about to you here, although it is important that I establish myself as an honourable, decent man, and no charlatan, so that you can feel secure in trusting the words enclosed here.

　　　　Had I had the fortune to be born in a different place, or class of our society, I'd perhaps have mastered another trade - the very one which I fumble about in here - that of crafting and penning letters. I daresay, sir, I could have made a great writer, perhaps even a good journalist like yourself, for I've always had a good flow of words out of my mouth, and at times channelled them down a pen, making clumsy prints upon the snow-blank paper. Some, who should by rights be famous, have considered me a good spinner of the oral yarn, and when out of my apron a good poet too, in my day, though I don't get time or inclination to bother with the luxury of that occupation so much these days. I tell you, sir, had I been given the time and resources - that is the money to feed myself and a solitary place to work away from the snuff and brandy - I would have made a fine craftsman of the appropriate word and cannily structured sentence. And it's on this subject sir, that of the writer, that I seek to address you here. In

17

particular, I write upon a matter concerning three sisters, whom you yourself had recourse to mention in the very last edition of your newspaper with reference to a previous article from last year in your fellow journal, the Halifax Guardian. I refer to those sad sisters of the wild hills, the Brontës, and moreover, their brother, Patrick Branwell. Against this man, many years ago, an insidious crime was committed. It was with dismay that I read in your pages such high praise of _Emily_ Brontë and _her_ book, 'Wuthering Heights', but with some gladness and relief that I read your account of the anecdote relating to the true authorship of that aforementioned novel. I know, in person sir, that the anecdote you recount is true and historical fact. I know that it was not little Emily who had recourse to pen that tome, leastwise not solely, and that the main greatness of the work was forged within the heated inferno of another, greater mind. Indeed, as your article indicated, it was the brother of these sisters who wrote the bulk of that book. Moreover, and my point of interest to you sir, I have direct proof of this in my own possession. Patrick Branwell Brontë was not only a valued customer of my establishment, but also a great and dear friend of mine. Sir, hear me out in full before you dash this letter away into your fireplace, discounting it as the stuff and nonsense rambling of a mad-man. I have, in my possession, material and written proof that the aforementioned brother, Patrick Branwell of the Brontë family of the village of Haworth, was the actual and main author of the great novel known as 'Wuthering Heights'. Meet me, sir, and see my proof - but be warned! It is dangerous evidence I have - so much so that I strongly believe it has cost me dear and tragic in a time past, when before I attempted to bring this matter to light in the world. I believe in all sincerity that my own, sweet wife was cruelly yanked from my bosom, and this Earthly life, directly due to contact with the manuscript to which I refer (or indeed another hand-written copy that was then in my possession also, but that vanished without trace upon the cruel event of her death).

Sir, should you consent to meet me, you'll not be lacking for a fascinating tale of local intrigue and interest that would have every reader of your honourable newspaper popping out their eyes upon strings of sheer amazement and disbelief.

I await your swift and prompt reply, and can meet you with the documents at your earliest convenience,

Your willing and humble servant

George MacCraw,
Poet - Master Barber.

Post Script

As proof of my word I here enclose a hand-written copy of a poem by Patrick Branwell Brontë that has but once seen the light of day in print, and that was under a pseudonym in your own newspaper. Compare this written draft to your own print, and then to other known manuscripts of Branwell's, of which I understand there are many. Compare the handwriting sir, and the structure of the phrasing, and you'll know that I am being true to my word. This is but a tiny fragment of what I have to offer up to you, should you be willing to receive it.

Yours once again

George MacCraw
Poet - Master Barber.

Now poor MacCraw, the muse was upon him as in the old days of The Rhymers, and many versions of the self same letter he wrote that night, until his work-table was awash with sheaths and leaves of paper, like a garden full of fallen leaves after a great autumn wind-storm. Each newly begun letter was accompanied by a generous, warming tot of brandy and a head-clearing blast of his best snuff. Each version became unsatisfactory upon re-reading, not ever approaching what he intended to say or correctly expressing the matter clearly enough to satisfy himself. For one thing, over and over, despite his intention to be balanced and unbiased, he found himself being cruel to the memory of the sad little sisters. Indeed, he'd only met them a few times, usually round at Branwell's lodgings. He'd never had a liking for the sharp-tongued eldest, Charlotte, but the other two were little, skinny gentle things, like frail, frightened birds, too young to fly but tipped from a nest, fluttering here and there in over-sized, rustling dresses.

In other versions of the letter he read himself to be too pompous, blowing his own trumpet far too loudly and that of Branwell's with not enough articulate breath, so that it sounded as though he, MacCraw, was the subject or main thrust of the letter, and not the abused genius of his old friend. Nine versions of that letter he had scratched out by ten o'clock that evening, with the fire flickering low in the grate and the fume of the lamps stinging at his ink-strained eyes. Between these versions he'd fed himself on heated up Sunday-broth, and swept the floor of the shop.

Back at the table, exasperated with himself, he poohed and pahed and slapped the wood, before uttering aloud in frustration, "Tis the damned language that's at fault, not myself. I can't shape the gist with it. It hasn't got the words to express the thing!'

And thus, muttering oaths in his fading glimmerings of Gaelic, he signed each of the letters with a dashing, swirling signature, then piled them up on the table before him. Brain now quite brandy-fuddled, he shuffled the lot together without further re-reading, placed one randomly plucked version alone in the envelope he had prepared and addressed earlier, and at last sealed the thing. He had no strong desire to step out into the bitterness of the night. He placed the envelope beside the clock upon the room's mantelpiece. The remaining letters he slid into other envelopes and set in a drawer at the table, intending to address and post them to various places over the coming week. All done, table cleared, he had a final glass of brandy to keep the night-airs at bay, then set about preparing himself for retiring. After his wash and toilet he placed a hot brick in his bed. While waiting for the sheets to warm through he was drawn to the bedding box set at the foot of his old bed. Kneeling there before the box, he bowed his head and, as was his nightly custom, uttered a little prayer for his lost wife. Although MacCraw was ten years widowed from a childless marriage, and had no real faith in the Christian God, he had never lapsed in the love of his darling Caroline. Upon his Amen, he shook his head clear of all thoughts of her, for he cared little to reflect further upon that tragic episode on this already gloomy night. There before him, inside the trunk, hidden beneath the blankets and bed-pans, was the package he had referred to in his letter, wrapped around in sheaths of newspaper, tied within brown paper and ribbon to make a neat and hefty parcel. One parcel, where once there had lain two. The very thought of the loss of the other parcel drew him back toward memories of Caroline, and the circumstances of her death. He felt shameful, knowing that he had avoided blaming those people whom he now felt sure were responsible for her demise. The surviving parcel he eased up out from the box, lifting it gently as though raising a slumbering infant from its crib. With quick strokes of dry fingertips he brushed the paper for dust that was not even there. It was a long time since he had set eyes on the package, let alone taken it out for a leaf through the contents. He set a reading candle on the bedside table, then clambered into his bed with the package. His trembling fingers rustled over the loose leaves and scraps of notebooks, searching for a particular piece. He began to pull out papers, reading through the tiny, wobbling scrawl there, his head swimming with memories of those years the cramped words referred to.

From *'The Journal of Patrick Branwell Brontë'*
Fountain Street
Bradford
Thursday May 24th of 1838

Dear Maria,
My beloved sister, to whom I dedicate this phase of my weekly journal, which I here now begin afresh, having these last days moved from our father's parish. Oh my sister, how I now wish your own shining eyes could be blessed with the sensation of all that I am seeing and experiencing in this busy little town. My new place of location (I'll refrain from calling it home, for I am far from established here as yet) is a cramped and poky jostling of buildings (small factories, wool-warehouses, fat church spires, inns, a chaos of housing and such like) located around the black, frothing sludge of a river so narrow it is in actuality more of a beck. There is a miasmic canal also, such aflow with human filth, vegetable waste and animal offal that it is said any unfortunate who falls into the waters perishes upon the instant, and none will even venture in to rescue the corpse. Do you not wonder, dear sister, that water, such an element of purity and essential refreshment, can be so neglected, polluted and corrupted by human influence? Indeed, there is something divinely retributional in the way the canal-water here, suffering from a build up of waste and foul gasses, has been known to ignite and explode, killing people forced to work upon the barges or walking along the tow-path. Water into fire, you see, sister - I am sure dear Papa would have much to make upon that.
*   The streets of the town itself are pleasantly teeming with all the vibrancy and spice and colour and scents of Real Life. No longer now do I feel penned in lamb-like by the scowling visage of crag and moorland, or oppressed by that damned torture of sky that seems to seek to stamp each crawling human form beneath its mocking, indifferent foot. Haworth, you see dear sister, is no good place for one such as I, who needs the company, joviality, good humour and philosophy of fellows with a broader aspect. Haworth folk, as I've often told you, are a grim and taciturn lot, all God Fearing, bar one or two of them from my little crowd there at The Bull. But here - all's a jumble, rag-bag, mixed-up tumble of a folk. Why, a man does not have to tip-toe around in fear of his neighbours, making pledges of abstinence and vows before the Good Lord - he can come and go as he pleases in his own gait, and if he wants to enjoy a glass of porter or two, then his neighbours think nothing of it, and he does not suffer their clucking and sighs and scorn.*
*   There is society of here of many strata, with little-gentry and starving beggar folk and all in-between flung together in the pot of its streets. We have the busy, pious mercantile class, like my honest hosts here, the Kirkbys (more of whom later, good sister). They have their Ale and Porter Merchants and Shop-Keeping circle - all teetotal, pledged hypocrites, with one eye on their penny-pile and the other on a couch in the Good Lord's Heaven. Good enough to their own (such as, I suppose, myself included), full of charitable intent for society at large, yet I doubt a single one of them*

would toss a penny into the cap of a shoeless, half-perished beggar who'd just footed it all the way from Limerick with wife and brood behind him.

While on the subject, they hate the Irish here, openly sometimes in the streets, and in a more reserved, polite and logical way behind the closed doors of good homes, which is somewhat awkward for a fellow like me, though I can lilt the brogue, chat Cornish, or clack-and-clatter local, as I please, being, as you know, a great imitator. In truth, the bog-folk (as here in the taverns I've heard them called) are coming over aflood in search of sustenance and jobs in the new mills and factories that are cropping up all over the country around, turning their back on their own land, though I daresay their hearts, like our good father's, remain there. I'm no politician, Maria, as you well know - my own aspirations and philosophy displace me from such social concerns other than commenting upon them in some Eternal aspect - but the strata and structure here is plainly visible to one with a clarity of vision such as we possess. Simply, it goes thus. There's royalty, who we all love fine enough, especially the sisters in Haworth now. Of them there's none about here - nothing but portraits displayed upon walls. Then the aristocracy, who remain afar from here also; the nobility, a couple of whom are scattered throughout the region; the gentry, who our family have some small contact with; there's the New Wealth who own the factories and the mills; the merchants; the middle classes; the traders and shop keepers; the artists and artisans; the impoverished hand-to-mouth workers displaced from their own pieces of land or the spinning trade to the new and cruel factory work. Below this come the street traders, the poor jobless, then all classes of beggars and thieves. Then, beneath all the whole lot of that, and holding it all up on its shoulders like some invisible Atlas, there's the Irish. They're a class apart, with their pigs sharing their filthy cellars (for it's true, Maria, our lot have been driven back to less than caves!) and their potatoes and their damned filthy wrap-around of ragging. Oh, it's a pity to see them, in the main, and if I were driven by the fire of Revolution instead of the furnace of Poetry, it's to that cause I'd wield my sword. As it is, perhaps one day I'll address the matter through the pen, as is best fitting for one of my stature. Of course, some do well and not all are blighted by this society, perhaps those like ourselves whose parents came here in a previous generation and have settled to the ways of the land. If anything, Maria, the Irish here add colour and life to this crookedly little hill-spill of a town. Sweet fiddle spills out of all the best inns and taverns, there's a hundred new songs a week added to the local stock, and there's some places you can go to and hear (or tell) a great yarn around the lovely warmth of a roaring fireplace, reminding me much of the days when Papa would collect all us little ones together, sit us in a little cluster before the hearth, then weave us out tales of Granddad Hugh and Gypsy Welsh, and those feuding Cornish and Irish days of his and Mama's ancient families. I'm well in with these story-telling places, for I've a stock of yarns we've picked up or created through the years, and like yourself and our Charlotte I seem to have a natural talent for it. I think I'll be a great local favourite in that field.

Of characters about town, there are too many to mention at present, my political rant having taken up too much page-space already. All sorts of strange, interesting and bizarre folk enliven the street corners and crannies of the markets - beggars, wanderers, hucksters, singers, magicians, thieves, ladies (little more than girls) of low morals and less virtue, and as I pass and look upon them my heart is lifted with excitement, for each of them seems like a storybook just waiting there for the opening. And some of these 'storybooks' I will present you with later, but tonight I will conclude for you with a painting. A little portrait, for that's what I'm become here now - Patrick Branwell Brontë, artist and executor of fine oil portraits, well established, taught in the London Style, private or family sittings at own studio or in the home. Thus reads my business card, sister, though in truth you know that the sentence and the word are my medium. So, my portrait for you here will be one etched of the word.

He's a personage of noble Irish ancestry, the man I paint here, who I encountered while leering and lurching my way around the taverns of the town - doing research, you understand, on my future material, for now in my opinion there's no better research for a bard than the living of life itself. A barber he is, by trade, though he calls himself numerous other things relating to that business. Like every young upstart around town (and especially those of Celtic root) he also declares himself to be a poet. It was while stumbling through the lounge bar of The Worldes End Tavern, Joe Leyland and myself, posturing at being poets of great and famous stature, that I came across the fellow. Through the smoke and grog haze of that room I became aware of a flaming light of true beauty. Ah yes, Maria, I was struck dumb by the absolute physical beauty of this man, in a most assuredly aesthetic manner. He is a true looker, as though Byron himself had glimpsed forward in time and modeled all his greatest heroes, in looks and form at least, on this one singular barber-bard. The sisters would just pale, flush and swoon upon the sight of him. His eyes, set under arches of thick brows, pierce forth bright blue like shafts of starlight seen from the depths of a black cave. Deep and luring, those eyes, all seeing, stripping away the veneer of a man and seeing him true to the core in a mere glance. Uncomfortable, and then exposed, that glance would make you feel, if it were not for the laughing, friendly set of a perpetual grin that settles all around him at ease, and spreads a jovial warmth through those who choose to place themselves in his presence. His brow is high, arched, noble; his nose straight, with wide nostrils having a proud flare that would make a lesser man fear to set about him or treat him ungraciously. His mouth falls fine and firm, yet sensuous, oft curling to that pleasant grin. The chin strong, bordering on the square. His stature is tall, muscular shouldered, loose- legged, giving him a quick and supple movement, lithe as the fabled panther. Surely he is the ancestor of some ancient Irish prince – Eochaid Airem or Cuchulainn himself - for though worldly and flesh now, debased through circumstance into the cutting of hair and wig-doctoring, there's something of that Divine and Eternal spark about him. For a barber, perhaps naturally, his own locks are unkempt, though they look well around the set of his handsome face, framing it in black, unruly coils that cascade down toward his broad shoulders, tied back and pony-tailed in the dated, piratical fashion. He dresses well, though not over expensively – tight black breeches, black boots, black top-coat spotless, shirt exceedingly white, the red neckerchief tied impeccably to add a dash of scarlet danger to his overall appearance. In short, Maria, he's an utter, real Alexander Rogue Percy, that felon of my own mental creation who haunts the Angrian tales that Charlotte and I still indulge in. He's Northangerland, transformed from page to flesh as if by some magical coincidence, resembling those characters of our imaginations even more so than the sculptor Leyland, who I also painted on these pages before you some weeks ago.

Well, we were introduced and he took to our band like a bird to wing, and a great evening we had of it, and a night too, with song, tale and general merriment, though you'll be glad to know, no wenching! Sadly, I must confess, I was ill this morning again, and breakfast with the good Kirkby family was an endurance of purgatorial dimensions.

Do not fret, dearest sister - I will take myself back along the road of my pledge soon, as soon as my research in this field is completed and I am satisfied that I have something to write about, and some experience to set it against. Again will I dwell saintly in the purity of abstinence. I will drink tea quaintly and chat upon the scriptures with aging uncles and maiden aunts. I will retire early to bed with a prayer to cleanse my soul, and plenty of plain water to cleanse my husk. One day, Maria, one day soon. Until then I pray you will forgive me for my indulgences.

Goodnight, beloved, much-missed sister,

PBB

CHAPTER 3

There are no sewers in Haworth; a few covered drains have been made in some of the streets to carry away the surface water, as, for instance, in the upper part of the main street and down Back-lane, but generally the drainage runs along in open channels and gutters. As a necessary consequence of the want of sewerage there is contiguous to each privy a receptacle for the night soil, in some cases walled round, in other cases fenced in with upright stones on edge; into these midden-steads are thrown the house-hold refuse and the offal from the slaughter-houses, where, mixed with the night soil, and occasionally with the drainage from pigsties, the whole lies exposed for months together, decomposition goes on, and offensive smells and putrid gases are given out.

Benjamin Herschel Babbage
General Board of Health
Haworth
1850

Haworth, Friday September 22nd, 1848

MacCraw could read for no longer. The little words were buckling and slithering on the yellow pages before him, his head a haze of brandy, snuff and tiny writing. After a good yawn and rub of his tired eyes, he gathered up the leaves, loosely bound them in their wrapper, then placed the package under his own pillows for safety. He extinguished the candle, and at last shuffled himself deep down into his bedding, searching there for warmth and comfort. He wanted to try recall, in all its bright clarity of detail, his own memory of that first meeting with the man whose reputation he was trying to rescue from the quagmire of History. Yet as he drifted toward sleep it was his last meeting with poor Branwell that his fuddled mind began to weave over. And what a tragic scene that one had been, though not entirely uncomical.

On a Thursday, it had been, back in '48, the late September of that year of Revolutions. A long time, it was, since MacCraw had seen or had anything to do with The Worldes End Rhymers; he had little now to do with the literary set, though he still did scribble the odd verse here and there, when the mood and time came together. Occupied with the upkeep of his business, and with his wife who was suffering a mysterious, ailing sickness, MacCraw was constant enough to remain a contact point for the scattered Rhymers, and it was to him they came whenever they wanted to know news or the whereabouts of any of the old gang. Even so, it was a surprise to see the portly, upright figure of Francis Grundy come striding into his establishment, worries and woes of the world etched deep on his pale, tired face. He was dressed well, a true gentleman, in a navy, brushed frock-coat; single breasted, tightly-buttoned up tartan waistcoat of a bright red check; neatly striped grey and black breeches, and a well made pair of black travelling boots. In his hand he carried a large leather luggage bag and a black, silver-handled umbrella. Clearly he was heading somewhere important enough to demand that he dress for the occasion. The only things about him that could have used a tidy were the grey coils of hair that billowed down from his hat around his coat collar, and the chin-length whiskers that were frizzing out of control, and fashion, along the sides of his jaw. MacCraw had been busy on a beard trim at the time, but he broke off to take Grundy's bag and coat, then sit his old companion down in his most comfortable chair with a glass of good brandy. They chatted around the customer, saying how nice it was to see the other, and tittle-tattling about the weather, recent bankrupts, market fluctuations, and the like. As MacCraw brushed down the gent and discreetly slipped him the earlier requested packet of Howquas Mixture, Grundy came out, blunt and as direct as ever, with the purpose of his visit.

'George, I know you're a busy fellow, but I've a favour to ask of you.'

MacCraw collected his payment for services along with a threepenny tip, thinking to himself that Grundy was perhaps after a monetary loan, for as any decent barber knew, the best dressed appearances often fronted the least means.

'If at all possible, I'd like you to accompany me to Haworth. Tomorrow. It's grave and urgent business I've to attend.'

'Grave business?' muttered MacCraw, punning straight in, as in the habit of the Rhymers' days. 'I trust there, God forbid, that you don't mean of the interring kind?'

He showed and good-byed his customer out through the jangling door, ashamed with himself for his previous, crude presumption about Grundy requiring money. He closed and latched the door, turning to gaze on his old friend, trying to assess more of him. With just the two of them in the shop it was easier to talk more openly.

'No, friend, it's no burial I'm talking of. Leastwise, not yet, though I fear it may well come to that.'

'Haworth, you say? What on earth do you want me up in that hole for?'

'The one and only reason two Rhymers would venture up that far.'

'Branwell, is it? But I thought he was working over York way. Isn't he making his fortune on the railways and due to marry some lady of the aristocracy, or something of the like? So I've heard.'

'Branwell it is, and no, he is certainly not due to be married. Nor is he on the railways these days. You know what he's like for bolstering up his fortunes with a bit of exaggeration. The truth of the matter is, he got himself into something of a dilemma. He's been dismissed from his last two posts in strange, well, let's say dubious, circumstances. Theft at the railways, and a complicated love tangle with the Robinson family over in York.'

Here MacCraw gasped, then whistled, almost bowled wordless with surprise.

'Truly... why, the little...'

' So I gather, reading between his lines. Anyhow, he's fallen sick with the worry of it all. He's been ill a while now, and I fear he needs our help. He wrote to me requesting assistance. Moral assistance, you understand. And perhaps a small loan. I'd do it alone, but - well, confound it, he is so difficult, George. You know how he goes. I fear the poor man's at the end of his tether, and may do some harm to himself.'

'That bad, is he? I'd heard he was having some health problems, back to his old fainting ways, but...'

'More than health, I fear,' cut in Grundy, wringing the rim of his hat in his hands. 'The fellow's sick to the root of his soul. I need a companion, MacCraw. He's begged me up there, but I fear to go alone. I need someone straight and solid at the helm. Somebody safe and reliable to steer the matter through. I could think of nobody but you...'

MacCraw breathed himself up to his full, straightened height at this great and genuine compliment.

'Well, you flatter me sir, but you know I'd not let the old team down. However, I'm afraid if it's just a supping companion you're looking for...'

'No, no - not that, MacCraw. Nothing could be further from needed. In all sincerity, what I really need is that which we used to call a 'safe-head'. Somebody stout-natured and not prone to excesses of passion or nerves, or at least able to control them if they happen to seize upon him.'

Grundy placed his hat on the seat of the cutting-chair then went fingering into the inner pocket of his coat, drawing out a crisp, recently received envelope.

'Here, read this. Perhaps you'll understand the better then.'

In a steady, pale hand he held out the missive. MacCraw took it, turned about his shop sign and drew down the door blind, shutting up his shop for the time being. He slipped out of his work apron, then fished a letter out of the envelope. Instantly, like some long unseen friend, he recognised the old spider-scrawl of his fellow Rhymer's handwriting.

'It's from him then?'

'Yes. It's not long, but read it, and then tell me... and I've seen him of late, remember... tell me if this is the workings of healthy and sane mind.'

Grundy seated himself in the best barbering chair, surveying his old friend through the shop-mirror. He continued to talk as MacCraw struggled over the scrawl upon the page before him.

'And I can't face the family alone - you must appreciate that, George. Why man, those sisters. All the warmth and gladness is gone from them now. They chill me, I tell you. Their eyes are grown cold and stony, full of suspicion. They whisper all the time. It's like sitting in on a scene from Bedlam itself. I swear, I can't face it up there alone.'

MacCraw drifted from the voice of Grundy and could hear the plaintive pleas of their good old friend for himself:

Patrick Branwell Brontë,
Haworth,
September 10th 1848.

My Good Dear Francis,

Begging forgiveness - I was not intoxicated when I saw you last in Halifax, dear sir, but I was so much broken down and embittered in heart that it did not need much extra stimulus to make me experience the fainting fit I had, after you left, at the Talbot Inn, and another, more severe, at Mister Crowthers at The Commercial.

When you return me the manuscript volume which I placed in your hands, will you (if you can easily lay your hands on it) enclose the manuscript called 'Caroline' - left with you many months since - and which I should not care about anymore than about the volume, only now I have no copies of either, my own copies along with numerous others of my jottings having vanished, and I fear, to the eternal flame.

Life is all a turmoil. My very life has been threatened (by the shooting of it!) under circumstances that I will not indulge you with here. Needless to say, such a threat, and a sincere one, keeps the frayed nerves on edge. Further to this, I am threatened with the sheriff and bailiffs at my own Father's door. Could you favour me by informing that infernal landlord, Nicholson of the Old Cock, that payment will be settled on him soon and he has no need to advance with his legal proceedings? And the same message, if you could, to the good Mrs Sugden of The Talbot? If Nicholson refuses my offer I am RUINED. I have had five months of such utter sleeplessness, a violent cough and such frightful agony of mind that gaol would destroy me forever.

When I feel a little better than I do at present, I will write to you a better letter, telling you more of my mind and circumstances than I dare at present do, and leaving you to notice it or destroy it as you choose. I am, sir, degraded and defiled in my own heart, and broken too in my spirit. How I long and yearn to see some of those bright and shining faces of the old days - of Bradford, and The Cross Roads and the Halifax studios. Such a golden time, it seems now, don't you ever think? Though really we were just living our lives from one day to the next, never paying them any significance, never realising how important to us they would become. Come and see me, if the feeling should ever take you. Come up here, or perhaps venture to Halifax, bringing some of the old faces so that we can laugh and play again, and remember the Golden Days.

Excuse this madness of a scrawl. Long have I resolved to write to you a letter of five or six pages, but intolerable mental wretchedness and corporeal weakness have utterly prevented me.

For mercy's sake, come and see me, sir. In truth now, I have sought for you round the inns and yards of all Halifax till I dare not risk my knee and eyesight anymore, and that this very evening. There - it's out. I have searched for you in person, so desperate am I for the confidence of a trusted friend. Please come sir, if at all possible. I write and beg no more.
Yours in all sincerity
PBB

MacCraw folded the letter, slid it back into the envelope, and with grim, knowing nods handed it back to his old friend.

'So you see,' Grundy murmured. ' I'll be needing a solid companion up there. Even if you just linger in the background. Sanity is needed, George. And I'll cover all expenses. Coaches, board, everything. It'll just be for the night. I understand that your good wife is not so well, but it would just be the night.'

MacCraw, of course, had already decided to go with Grundy, and was working on what to say to Caroline, who was upstairs resting, surrounded by her cordials and novels. He had noted the frenzied, gibbering nature of the missive. They were words from a man on the brink, and he knew he owed his old friend some assistance and solidarity.

'Of course I'll come,' he simply said. 'We'll go up the stairs to square things with Caroline, then we'll sort out the arrangements. The poor fellow sounds in a bad way. I know Caroline won't have objections – she well knows the nature of the fellow.'

He drew down the remaining shop shutters, and they ascended quietly, a dignified gloom running between them.

'Caroline...' MacCraw called ahead as he opened the door of the living area. 'Darling – guess who's called by to see us...'

The next morning, Grundy and MacCraw walked down to The Commercial Inn. Somewhat hazily, for as long parted friends in their prime of manhood are wont to do the pair had supped, remembered, talked politics and philosophy far too long into the small hours, they clambered aboard the eleven o'clock coach bound for Keighley. This was the nearest coaching stop to their actual destination, though they were confident of getting some kind of transport further on into the hills. Having had occasion to visit Haworth with Branwell a couple of times over the years, MacCraw knew the place to be a miserable, midden-ridden little village tumbled upon a hillside, buried in dreary moors, moss-bogs and marshland. He was not looking forward with any pleasure to set eyes upon the place again, not even in the good, solid company of Francis Grundy. Not in the dreary late of September when the winter seemed premature, the wind already rattling with ice at the windows. There being no ladies present for the Keighley run, and with an eye on the changeable sky out northward, they had chosen to pay to sit within the carriage. Their fellow passengers in the coach were dour and tight-lipped, as the dwellers of the Pennine fringes tended to be. When there were little chunks of conversation it was all of the grim weather, workers' strikes, the state of France, diseased sheep and the desperate, life-ruining fluctuations in industry of late. Occasionally, filling a lull, MacCraw and Grundy would exchange snippets of what each had been up to over the last years, but this talk did not amount to much. Of poor Branwell they said little, for apparently indifferent ears within the coach burned upon their words, twitching for snippets of news or gossip to pad out paltried conversations back home. They did not want to blacken the name of their good friend further in the locality where he was already undoubtedly infamous for his strange ways and misdeeds. Thus, in veiled, guarded code they chatted, changing the names of the people they referred to, placing them in Manchester and Liverpool or other such more distant places. It emerged that Grundy, along with others of the old crowd, had received several similar rant-filled, debt-laden, begging letters from Branwell, all telling of a self-loathing existence, further marred by sleepless, demon-littered nights. Both men knew of Branwell's capacity for excess - for good and ill - and it was not a pretty picture of their once glorious, flamboyant friend that they were expecting to see up in Haworth.

'Of course, the grim elder won't allow us to set foot in the house there,' Grundy explained. 'None of his old friends are welcome there now, and you can be certain that in his present condition he has no new comrades to mingle his wild thoughts with.'

'Aye sir, it must be a lonely existence the fellow leads. All the more so for being right there in the midst of his own home and family.'

'That's true. He told me in one letter that not one of them except his old father will bless him with a warm word. It's all clucks and tuts and fierce glances from his sisters now especially since his misdeeds down in the valleys. According to him, he's virtually a prisoner in his own home, kept without coin, comfort or company.'

'Ah, well...' MacCraw sniffed down a dose of snuff to keep the cold air from his lungs, then sneezed loudly out of the carriage window. 'Excuse me, sir. Well, you know yourself, our man did always tend to stretch out the wool of truth when spinning a yarn. It could be anything we find up there, with all due respect to the old bard.'

Grundy nodded, then signalled for the conversation to cease as all there were listening to nothing else. A sullen silence now fell between the inhabitants of the coach, all eyes glazed out upon the dismal scenery. A mile or so before the market town of Keighley the rain set in. MacCraw was sorely wishing that he had never agreed to accompany Grundy on this outing. He felt a solemn, pressing weight upon his very soul, something as solid and real as the dense slopes, which glowered around the town up ahead along the valley road. His thoughts flickered around Caroline, who herself lay still sick at home in bed. She had been delighted to see Grundy again, and dismayed when she read herself the letter he'd received from Branwell. There could be no doubt, she had insisted, that her husband must accompany Grundy to try offer their old friend some hope and comfort. She was more than happy for him to spend the few days away, insisting that she could cope with the help of their friends and neighbours.

'Go,' she had said. 'Go, go, go. Try rescue your friend. Why, there is nothing else for it – you must. You don't even need to ask!'

He knew though, that she would miss his attentions, his little calls up and down the stairs when there was a lull between customers; their chat on a night once the shop was closed, when he passed on the gossip from the shop; their meal together in the lamp-glow, still smiling and little-touching of each other as they passed backward and forward, still very much in love after all their years of marriage. Sure, they took each other for granted from time to time, like any long wed couple might do, but there was still the spark of romance between them. He was missing her already, he realised, even though they were barely half a day apart. One night away, he decided. That's all it would be. He couldn't leave her at home alone for more than one night, Branwell or no Branwell.

The coach set them down at the Coach and Horses, in the very heart of Keighley. The whole town itself was no more than a miserable, dirty watering hole and fleece market, four or so miles from their destination. To MacCraw, upon stepping down from the coach, it seemed that they had been set down on the fringes of Hell itself, for the town was a good deal changed since his last visit there. Withered and loom-bent vagabonds and hunched midget-children, dressed in grimy sack-cloth ragging, glowered and scowled at them as they stood waiting for Grundy's leather travel bag. They had been informed at the start of their journey that there would be no more coaches or gigs out from the Coach and Horses that day other than one final afternoon omnibus back to Bradford. While Grundy tipped the driver and booked their return on the Saturday noon coach, MacCraw asked a cluster of the nearest, drenched gargoyles how he might go about hiring a cart to take them to Haworth. They stood still, sullen and silent, grimacing, spitting down into the street in turn as he addressed them. The Keighley welcome. Every time he had been through they had proved a morbid lot, even in bright summer sunshine, but this surpassed even their standards of brash-rudeness. One of them did speak eventually, or rather muttered begrudgingly through the side of his clenched mouth; a lad of about fifteen, with warped knees, his face thin and pinched, as though he was already bent and greying to premature old age.

'Tha'll not get an 'os or cart this side 't day. Not fer 'aworth, anyroad.'

'Surely there's a cart to be had somewhere, man. I'm no gentleman, but we'll pay a fair price.'

The lad shrugged and shuffled back closer to the scant shelter of the yard wall. The lot of them shivering there, lined up, looked like a row of bent and dripping scarecrows. MacCraw tipped him a sixpence, hoping that a coin would further oil his words.

'Ta, mister.' The coin vanished into the rags of the lad's coat and a brief grin flickered over his ashen face. 'Tha' might get wind o' one in t' Packhorse, o'er there.' He sniffed and nodded up the hill toward a blackened stone, lean-to of an alehouse, where the lamps were already glowing in the windows.

'But take care mind, and watch tha' purse. They're a right rough lot in there.'

The lad shuffled away into the rain, MacCraw and Grundy following him before he turned off away from the main street and vanished down a stinking ginnel. In need of sustenance anyway, and well accustomed with the ways of every spectrum of hostelry, ale-house and drinking-den, they gladly made their way through the doors of the Packhorse. The dingy exterior did not betray what lay beyond the door. The tiny place was little more than a cave, a dark, smoke-filled grotto, about the size of MacCraw's own living room above his shop. A tiny hatchway set in the blackened wall opposite the entrance served as a bar. A dozen or so burly men were grouped about the place, hunched around ramshackle tables, all sullen looking, each with a pipe smoking and a well-dinted pewter tankard set on the wood before him. The place, being so small, seemed crowded with just these few groups, and there was a definite air of menace about the place. Not a face turned toward the door as MacCraw and Grundy stepped in, but the muttering of conversation halted, and each face, already dirt-smeared from a morning's labouring, ducked until screened with hat-shadow. There was no serving maid or potboy in the room, nor a barman, or so it appeared.

'Put wood in t' 'ole,' somebody growled.

MacCraw obliged, pushing the door closed behind him, shutting out the wind and rain. They glanced about the place, took in the situation, and knew that the only recourse here was direct and assertive action. Grundy strode the few paces through the room to the hatchway bar, through which he could just about make out barrels and pot bottles, though in the lamp-gloom he could not make out any labels without leaning through and peering beyond, thus possibly appearing rude. He stood squinting through, MacCraw joining him.

'Yes, gents, what can I do for yer?' a cockney bass-voice warbled. There looking up at them from the other side of the counter was the bar-man, a little fellow, as small as a dwarf, his head barely at the level of the hatch. He was well proportioned with a cheery, good looking face, and though tiny was of a strong build, broader than he was tall, his arms thick and ribbed with muscle. He had an amiable, almost handsome face, with a twinkle in the blueness of his eyes that suggested mischief, merriment and much laugher in his company. MacCraw recognised him instantly, having seen him at various Rhymers' reading and story telling evenings about the Riding, though he couldn't put a name to him, and it seemed that the fellow had no recollection of MacCraw. The dwarf had briefly been a cohort of Branwell's, on the fringes of The Worldes End Rhymers, though never really one of them. MacCraw recalled that he had a brusque but captivating manner of telling a tale, and the tales he told, of a life of crime and desperation in his youth in London, he always swore were true to the word. It had been years since MacCraw had clapped eyes on the little fellow, but he'd not changed as much as a hair. Smiling up now at his two unexpected customers, he wiped his huge hands into the fabric of his filthy apron.

'What would you care for, gentlemen? Can I get you anything?'

'I'll have two pints of porter, if you please. Is that in agreement with you, George?'

Grundy did not want to address his friend by his usual tag in here, for at this particular time men of this country breed were likely to be loathing of the Irish. MacCraw nodded, aware of the game afoot.

'That'll do nice,' he clucked in his Riding twang, aware through experience of the hatred that a lilting brogue could stir up in these out of town drink-hovels.

As the dwarf drew their porter into his best pots, he chatted amicably, force of the habit of his trade and his own affable nature getting the better of him despite the usual taciturn clientele. He prattled on with great enthusiasm about the quality and strength of his ales, the mumble of lowered conversations resuming up around them as the room realised that the strangers were not police officers or customs agents.

'You'll have to sit with this ugly band in here, gents, I'm afraid,' he informed them, placing the pots on the platform of the hatchway. 'Unfortunately, our snug room is closed at the moment, as is the lounge.'

He nodded toward a door at the far left of the room, boarded up and covered over with dusty cobwebs, looking as though it was sealed off some centuries ago.

'We're refurbishing. Raising our standards, you know, to take advantage of the more sophisticated clientele that the railway is bringing into town these days. People like yourselves, sirs. From Leeds, I take it? Though it's a bad day for you foreigners to come visiting the town, this weather being what it is.'

They bantered thus a while at the bar, MacCraw and Grundy careful not to state their business, well aware that Branwell would be known in every drinking den in these parts, and probably in debt to all of them. Grundy paid for their drinks, ensuring that he gave the barman a healthy tip as he broached their real business.

'Good sir, I'm sure you have great knowledge of these parts. Would you happen to know where we could hire a carriage, or some such transportation up to Haworth? We need to get up there this afternoon.'

'I don't know if I can help you there, mister,' the dwarf said. He hauled himself higher over the hatchway, inquiring loudly if anyone in the room had a horse and cart for hire, although he need not have wasted his breath, as every single person in the room had heard the request.

'Tha'll not get a cart up that 'ill today,' an ancient yellow-skinned stick of a fellow at the table nearest muttered, clacking out the words around his pipe stem. Most of the others in the room shook their heads in a grave, well practised, manner.

'Aye, not Friday after dinner,' a voice from the far corner offered.

Grundy and MacCraw shrugged, not really understanding.

'The weather is it then?' Grundy pushed. 'Wet roads and trackways?'

'Aye, 'appen t' roads are awash wi' rain water. It's another excess o' liquid that 'll stop tha getting a cart up there today,' the old stick cackled.

The whole bar laughed uproariously at this, as though the fellow had made a great jest.

'These parts, Friday's pay day, gentlemen,' the dwarf kindly explained. 'This whole town will be awash with ale by now. It's sort of traditional, like. Anyone earning stops work Friday bang on midday, then it's a great scrum into the nearest ale-hole. Damn to the rain, that'll not stop you getting to Haworth. But I dare say a tide of beer will.'

This provoked more laughter in the room. Pots were drained, pipes rekindled, the whole atmosphere now transformed to something much more congenial, as though a few good drinking jokes had raised up the good spirits of the whole gathering. MacCraw nodded sagely at the explanation, and Grundy lifted his pot, offering up a toast in acceptance of defeat on the matter of getting some transportation up the hill.

'Oh, well. Legs were made for walking,' he conceded. 'Another for the road, George, and when the rain eases we'll start out afoot.'

'That's wise,' the dwarf said. 'You've a good few hours of daylight yet. No point in wasting them looking on Haworth. Get a few drinks down you, lads, and I'll sort you out with some meat and gravy to warm you for the trek.'

They made their way to the only empty table, a rickety, wobbling thing, set beside the fire, which flickered and spluttered in a dirty grate. There they sat, quenching their thirst and putting away a surprisingly good dinner of pudding, beef and vegetables, served up by the dwarf himself, for it seemed he was without employees or assistants in the place. They had another drink to wash down the food, then another because it tasted so good, and as it goes, the more they drank so the better the company around them became. Once more than two pots had passed by his tonsils, MacCraw succumbed to his natural bent for talking, making no effort by this point to mask his brogue. Fortunately, the fellows of the room had thawed toward them, and the Packhorse crew, a hard-hearted mix of begrudging labourers and professional criminals as it emerged, insisted that they didn't give a damn if a man was Irish or Jewish or black or the devil himself, as long as he was true to himself and decent company to sup with.

Thus it was, several pots and a good few hours later, married and warmed through, with cheery good-byes and hard-handshakes all around, they stepped out doors to find the rain abated, the sky brighter, the grim town looking much more amenable. With riddles of directions for shortcuts and time-saving trails across obscure fields from the men of the Packhorse, they headed on up the hill in a much heartier frame of mind. They cut through a stile at the top of Church Street, and thus out on foot along the muddy track that led along the valley, then struck away upwards toward the distant clutter of buildings that was Haworth.

CHAPTER 4

O, fickle is the powerful grace that lies
In plants, herbs, stones, and their true qualities;
For naught so vile that on the earth do live
But to the earth some special good doth give;
Nor aught so good but, strained from that fair use,
Revolts from true birth, stumbling on abuse.
Virtue itself turns vice, being misapplied,
And vice sometimes by action dignified.
Within the infant rind of this weak flower
Poison hath residence and medicine power;
For this, being smelt, with that part cheers each part;
Being tasted, stays all senses with the heart.
Two such opposed kings encamp them still
In man as well as herbs - grace and rude will;
And where the worser is predominant,
Full soon the canker death eats up that plant.

Friar Lawrence
Romeo and Juliet
William Shakespeare

Interwoven within the fabric of his grim, sustained memory (for despite his night-caps, the depths of sleep evaded MacCraw on this night) flecked strands of happier, earlier recollections. They unribboned in brief, effervescent whispings. They were not the deliberate workings of his mind, but emerged as unbidden intrusions from some submarine world of the brain, like bubbles rising and popping to the dark green surface of a mental, inner lake. And the memory, MacCraw realised, is a fickle thing, playing tricks upon aging people and the young alike. What one man would swear to as the truth, *as he remembers it,* others know in their own hearts that his is a mistaken and confused recollection of events. Over time - that strange, evasive fabric with all its folds and creases, its long and short kinks, its pulled threads and loose stitches - people and places of the past blur or merge to become knitted in a new image upon the mind's bright tapestry. MacCraw began to imagine the inside of his skull as a marquee tent in a summer fete or travelling fun-show. By a trickery of the inner, magic-lantern and that irresistible rack of distorting mirrors, a projection of the mind from present to past and then back again juggles together a new intermingling of times and truths, but rarely throws forward the true picture of that time or event exact and intact in its concrete actuality. Colours change, faces alter, shapes and sounds distort. Even dreams and past fantasies, themselves valid sparkings of the mind's light and electricity, somersault in and out of these so called *memories*, to the extent that no single individual's description of a particular time, person, place or event is to be trusted or accredited as any form of truth. And if this is the case with each and every individual of the species, living, dead and yet to come (or so mused *Metaphysical* MacCraw) then what chance is there for a general, collective authoritative *history* of events? As he lay thus reflecting, the wise saw, Historia Escribium Victor, adequately seemed to sum up his realisation. Now MacCraw's own mind, around this sleep-frayed philosophisation, wove up these memories that he felt to be *real* and *true*, but to prove them thus, he realised, would have been utterly impossible. Any other people present at the events, including the human subjects of the memories themselves, would perhaps have recalled things in a totally different way, or as occurring in some other place, or even at another time. In short, MacCraw saw that his memories and perceptions, like anybody else's, were not to be trusted. Nevertheless, still cast adrift and insomniac in his large and lonely bed upon this fickle lake of memory, he allowed his mind to weave its pictures and flicker those tinted lantern images.

MacCraw's mind unfurled his first, most fateful meeting with *Madness* Patrick Branwell Brontë and his merry band of Rhymers. A great and glorious event, this, to MacCraw, partly because he knew that it had also been of some note to Branwell himself. Up in The Worldes End Tavern they'd first met, sometime in the dog days of the miserable summer of 1838. MacCraw, business finished for the afternoon, it being a Saturday, had gone up that Manor Row and Manningham way in search of good cheer and vibrant, artistic company. The Worldes End, a grand and spacious hostelry of ancient repute, was set amidst a cluster of theatre halls, sordid cellar-inns serving dangerous gin or house-brewed ales, and grotty penny gaffs where the lowest street conjurers performed. Being at the hub of the thriving, thespian centre, The Worldes End was well attended by all manner and nationality of actors, travelling showmen, magicians, clowns, comedians, dancers, musicians, painters and many other of the creative intelligentsia. Along with those came folks of a lesser repute. Gamblers, hucksters, tricksters and whores came peppered in with the colourful crowd, and as the old saw went, where there are whores you'll find gentlemen. That more estimable class tended to be travelling through on their 'business', though one or two would linger afterwards to sup in the old tavern. There was always a lively and colourful crowd guaranteed in The Worldes End on a Saturday afternoon, with fiddles and accordions lilting from all corners. The windows of the high-beamed place were ancient, stained glass affairs that depicted all manner of hunting scenes, the sunshine beaming in through fleeing stags and pursuing hounds with red jacketed huntsmen in the green thickets and forests. The windows cast a kaleidoscope of colour over the dark wooden panels and velvet interior of the southern facing rooms, so it was a beautiful place to be sitting in, whether humming-full of life or just gently quiet for an afternoon's read and personal contemplation.

This particular busy Saturday, MacCraw had been set there by the door-side corner with a travelling trio of Italian acrobats (whose hair he had clipped short and oiled the day previously). Spider Walton was also with him, a famous local boxer of dusky skin and exotic origin (Zanzibar, or so he claimed - though there were many who'd swear that he and his father before him and been born and brought up in the very crooked streets of the old rookery). Discussing hairstyles and beauty treatments of the Italian gentry, MacCraw was astounded to be told that the acrobats themselves regularly used a treatment of the berries of that toxic plant, here called *deadly nightshade*, to enhance their own physical appearance.

'So they use it still, and you too?' he said, leaning over the table to peer more closely at they eyes of a man who called himself Luzio, who of the Italians there spoke the best English.

'We do, my friend, for a growing of the black piece - what is it you say... the centre portion?'

'The pupil, friend...'

'Yes. A tiny droplet only, just dropped in the eye pupil... makes good... beauty... how you say?'

'It beautifies the eyeball,' finished MacCraw, and now he did notice that all three of them had huge moons of dilated pupils, which increased the natural attractiveness of their handsome Latin faces.

'Belladonna,' shrugged Luzio. 'Certainly, taken in the wrong it is a poison. But with the know how... well, all poisons are remedies, they say. Women love us.'

His fellows laughed, and indeed all their eyes had a brightness and attractiveness that MacCraw found most agreeable.

'Look in,' Lucio invited. 'The pupil never closes, not even on the sun's brightness.'

MacCraw was, in a most fascinated, professional manner peering into the convex mirrors of Luzio's eyes, in which he could see most of the whole room in clear miniature form, when he saw the tavern door behind him come swinging inward. Through the doorway tumbled a wild-haired, hatless fellow, followed by a black haired giant who, although wealthy enough in appearance, wore no topcoat. Into MacCraw's own life came hurtling *Madness* Patrick Branwell Brontë and his cohort in song, supping and wenching, the very beautiful *Lusty* Joe Leyland. Whenever these two entered a room it was always Leyland who attracted the gaze first, his electrifying stature and looks being enviously remarkable. Joseph Bentley Leyland, a mere twenty six years of age at this time, and already a sculptor of some fame for his breathtaking *Spartacus* and nerve-jangling, ghastly *Satan,* works so life-like that critics agreed, to see the bronzes stretch up and amble out of the room would have been no great shocking surprise. 'Apollo' Leyland, curly-maned captor of Spiritual Truth, of Angel, Saint and Bloodhound, in wood or stone or whatever other material would come to hand. Not only thus gifted, this blessed carver, but with the stature, charismatic presence and muscular frame of a Greek hero. Unorthodoxly coatless come winter wind or summer sun, his shirt sleeves were rolled up to reveal the sinew and muscle of those stone-wrenching, hammer-moulded forearms which flexed like ropes with every movement, demanding the eye's attention. Wherever Leyland was, the most modern of women (that being those of the least virtues and loosest morals) were not far behind. Upon the sight of this god-man some would actually topple and swoon at his feet, or more than likely, if they were the cunning ones, directly into his arms. Arms ever-willing they were too, for there was no material Leyland preferred moulding and shaping with his wonderful, dexterous, hands than that of the flesh of the human female.

In Joe Leyland's femme-quaking wake, like a happy pet dog at a feast, picking merrily at the scraps and left-overs, trotted young Branwell Brontë, eyes bright, tongue lolling, slavering, barking off with his sharp witticisms. So it was, seen reflected in the scrine-black pupils of an Italian acrobat, into The Worldes End Tavern, these two tumbled, already brandy-married, eyes blazing fire, headlong into the life of George MacCraw.

MacCraw, on this day with still only twenty three years upon him, was himself no bad-looker. Having travelled two years through southern Europe, his skin and complexion still retained a healthy pallor, his black curls a glossy sheen. He was already considered a man of the most modern style and taste, for though he dressed simply, it was with great aesthetic effect. He had studied minutely the fashionable tricks, traits and details of the strutting dandies of London, Paris, Madrid and Rome. Added to this, he was a young man of some wealth (or so he led people to believe), having inherited a good portion of a small but healthy fortune amassed by his late father, albeit, so the rumour went, under dark, mysterious and dubious circumstances. He had his trade too, along with his *Emporium* and two other small properties bought outright in the town's little centre. Such a young man of substance, indeed he had a great deal to be happy and carefree about, although it must be said to his credit, he did manage his time, his leisure, his excesses and restraints, with considerable attention. Under no circumstances, the general opinion was, would he be persuaded to fritter his youth and his fortune away on folly or vice.

Branwell, eyes always keen and sharp on the uptake, mind drinking in any new scene for use as his *raw material*, was immediately enraptured by the naive Byronic stature of the young MacCraw. MacCraw was presented to him by the legendary pugilist, Black Spider Walton, and not without irony, as 'The King of Cuts'. Behind the spectacles, Branwell's blue eyes glittered and flickered, taking MacCraw in from toe-tip to hair-top, his mind licking words upon him for future literary reference. Eyes first, he worded. Strong, brow-hooded, lake-blue, Celtic eyes, one full of laughter, the other brimming with mystery and pain. His face was sharp and boldly angled, as if crisp-hewn of local yellow stone, framed with wild ebony curls that might have belonged to some Southern Sea buccaneer out upon the prowl and ambush. He was sharply and somewhat piratically dressed too - brightly striped red and green waistcoat with pointed front, a plain white shirt, black double breasted overcoat with tapering waist and cut just above the knee, trousers made full at the waist but longer than normal pantaloons.

'Pleased to meet you Mister Leyland, Mister Brontë,' MacCraw stuttered, trying to mask his own accent, but never being able to do so after imbibing. 'I hear you're a great sculptor, sir, and Mister Walton informs me that you're a worthy poet, Mister Brontë'

'Branwell, sir, or Patrick, as you please. Poet and artist, though alas presently employed, for crumbs mind, as skilful painter of portraits. Would you care to have yourself captured sir, for you cut a fine figure?'

There was laughter in the little fellow's eyes, and MacCraw, who tried to be casually aloof concerning his immaculate and well thought out dress, was not sure whether he was being ridiculed or not.

'Perhaps I would sir, if you're sincere, though I set no store by my own appearance.'

'King Of Cuts, hey?' glimmered Branwell, again with a friendly trace of mockery. 'Or perhaps, something of a regal cat?'

'Aye sir, but no rat-catcher. Nor a swordsman. It's of the hair the fellow's referring to. Though I profess myself to be a poet sir, after a glass or several of the brandy. By trade I'm a craftsman of a more human nature. A beautician and dresser of hair, gentlemen, at your service, though I see you've no need of my abilities yet on that score.'

'Ah, beautiful . And fond of Shakespeare too. You'll do for me, sir. What do you say, Joe?'

'You seem fine by me sir - glad to meet you. Any enhancer of beauty is fine by me.'

'A beautician and poet, Mister Leyland, though currently reduced by circumstances of place and time to a stylist of the wig and hair. Can I give you my card, gents, in the event that you ever desire an exquisite hair cut?'

In this teasing, playful vein, cards were handed all round, poet and painter, poet and barber, poet and sculptor, all pocketed in the event that any of them should want the other's service. The formality of meeting done with, the group of them were ushered to MacCraw's corner table, the acrobats willingly shifting round to make room. Brandy and water all round, cried MacCraw. And porter - more porter, sang Leyland. Potboy, potboy, over here, demanded Brontë. Heavily vessel-laden trays in due course arrived. The dark and delicious, tongue loosening brew. Here here! Branwell calling, raising his glass, toasting to friendship and immortality. MacCraw returning the toast, drawn into the mad, spinning wheels of them, overwhelmed by their crazy look and wild-charm, their audacious eccentricity, their amazing capacity to drink and drink more. Though little Branwell lacked bodily stature, his sheer life-energy and brilliant capacity for meaningful babble created a massive physical impression throughout the place, all in the room eager-eared for his next great jest or quip of wisdom, the boys and serving maids fighting to serve him and his table, the landlady grinning from the bar in only his direction. All present seemed to naturally love and adore him, for he gave off a warmth; he had a certain mysterious glow and a beauty that made a person or a crowd feel graced in his presence; and of course, he possessed that ridiculously comic, carrot-frizz of hair; a halo that despite its red chaos seemed appropriate, and of the utterly correct style for his unique being.

The afternoon wore on in the Worldes End room of stained glass and red velvet. Tales circulated the ebullient table. Branwell recited verse and rhythmic tales from Homer and Virgil. Spider Walton recounted, blow by blow, his great fights from around the globe, starting with his first scrap as a boy back in Zanzibar. Leyland told, in all sincerity, of his face to face meeting with Satan (in an opium induced trance, he conceded), and how he had exchanged his very soul for seven years of glory, and this was the fifth of them. MacCraw, for his part, entertained with his travelling adventures around some of the more obscure regions of Europe, or told wild stories of his youth in Ireland, and made his father's exploits in India and China his own. Luzio, upon the encouragement of his fellow Italians, passed around a box of peculiar looking 'Spanish' snuff, the tobacco ground fine but with visible traces of some powdery, white foreign mineral, that he swore would lift the spirits of the gathering even higher, as indeed it did. A tiny finger-pinch of the stuff blasted the head clear of alcohol haze or confusion, filling the mind's pathways with a thousand clear formed ideas about every single subject under the sun. All around the table were flushed and shining and beautiful and articulate and brilliant. They declared themselves bright comets streaking across the skies of History, and more brandy was ordered, though Luzio's wonderful snuff had quenched any real desire for further hard drinking. Tiny, simple jokes about the hairs on the chin-mole of the still beaming landlady or the veins on the back of a serving maid's ankle had all rolling about and guffawing with laughter. The tremor of a pursed lip or meaningful tilt of an eyebrow brought the table out roaring. Branwell, unable to contain his outpourings, would on the sudden, without prompt, launch himself up and recite a full metered and rhyming translation of some ode by Horace, or warble away with nightingale-sweetness some gentle bog-ballad of the Homeland, it emerging that despite his falsified accent, his roots were as deeply Irish as MacCraw's.

Leyland himself sat there majestic and noble, looking like some earth-fallen angel. He was the only one of the company who talked less as the afternoon flowed on, and proved to be much more a listener, and watchful too, eyes all around the wider company of the bustling tavern. Often his lewd gaze fell upon the pretty, slender women there, who in the main were dancers and actresses from the many theatres about. Generous he also proved, guaranteeing on his own account each new round of drinks called for by the table. Perhaps he really had been Devil-blessed, for he always seemed to have endless purse resources, ordering drinks for groups around other tables too, inviting the dancing girls over to squeeze into the spaces in and around them. The whole place became one great, revelling party, the astounding Spanish-snuff (of which MacCraw, being a man of interest in all manner of remedy and stimulant, arranged to buy good and expensive quantity of, along with a list of all the ingredients) going around the golden haze of the corner to further raise the spirits of the company.

With much song, reciting of poetry, and general bantering, the party at The Worldes End Tavern extended long into the summer night, the landlady happily closing her shutters against The Watch and constable as long as the room's company were willing to spend money.

It seemed a blink of an eye between sunset and dawn. As the day loomed forth beyond the stained-glass windows, the company disbanded and filtered away into the silent streets of the sleeping, Sunday town. Into the pinking flush of whispering morn, the three new inseparables stumbled - Leyland, Brontë and MacCraw - as if walking out into the promise of a New World. Over the last hours the three had raised many oaths of kinship, friendship and artistic allegiance. Now, linked against the natural inclinations of gravity by hooked arms, they staggered along toward the centre of town, laughing, jesting at the few stragglers out of other taverns of the long night as they passed. They deemed themselves untouchable by Law, invincible against Fate, and prepared to battle it out with Nature, all convinced of their future-bright Destiny. Immortal poetic fame and grand material reward, they agreed, were undeniably theirs - a simple, rightful blessing to bestowed upon them for no other reasons than they were of the Chosen, the Fortunate and the Gifted portion of humanity of that particular Age.

Warbling out song, rhyming lewd new lyrics to old tunes, they escorted the now leg-weary Branwell right along John Street to the greens market and then back along to the corner of Fountain Street, where his present lodgings lay. Here Leyland and MacCraw had to part from him, for he swore that his landlord was an abstemious, upright fellow who would not take lightly to having a band of rowdy drunkards reeling upon his respectable doorstep. Thus the trio was temporarily fragmented, though not before he and MacCraw had arranged to meet again at the same venue, and the three of them had sworn further oaths to recruit more shining-likelies to their band of Rhymers.

Around this point of letting slip loose Brontë, and laughing loud as they watched him waver up the cobbles of his street, MacCraw's memories of events began to falter and crumble within the very memory. He lay there in his bed trying to fix the flow of events. He was not certain whether he had already rolled up the happenings of several evenings in that glass-lit tavern room into one great night of it. He was sure that he and Leyland, still linked together for support as they stumbled down upon Kirkgate, had entered into fisty-cuffs with an equally boisterous band of wool-combing rogues. The drunken gang of four had voiced some objection to Leyland's 'dandiness' from across the road, and then to MacCraw's retorting Irish tones, declaring that they were Bradford's greatest dandy and Irish-bashers. He and Leyland, like faithful dogs to the horn, had bloody-knuckled it while brimming with unseemly zestful joy for the fray. Their enthusiasm for battle had somewhat vexed their more numerous antagonists. Already convinced that they were invincible, the new-allegiance had knocked the other fellows senseless, both being quick-footed and strong in the arm. Victorious and in glory went the duo, down toward Ivegate, and so to MacCraw's own place, for then, as now, he had made his dwelling above his Millergate Emporium.

Leyland, a resident of Halifax, thus temporarily cast ten miles adrift from home, after more but better brandy, had happily stretched himself out there on MacCraw's living room floor. The good-heart MacCraw, with only a churchless Sunday ahead, had in no way begrudged his fellow the sleeping space, and indeed had covered him over with rugs and blankets, propping his well-snoring head upon a soft down pillow.

By the next mid-day, when MacCraw eventually grogged his way down the stairs to his living room, Leyland had been replaced by a neatly scribed and rhyming note - which like all further notes from him, MacCraw had kept, and still had stowed along with Branwell's. Through that throbbing-murk of daylight, his new 'golden friends' seemed but a ridiculous and crazed hallucination, idled up by some distempered mind. Indeed, he would have accepted that they were mind-phantoms, had it not been for his pulsating head, his bruised knuckles, and the very real note that Leyland had left there for him upon the neatly folded rugs and bedding: -

> ' We burnt like meteors in
> The black of night
> Such flashing glory is indeed
> Our born right
> We are as bright comets
> With fiery tails
> To scorch the velvet thighs of Heaven
> We surely cannot fail
> Thank you, sincere FRIEND,
> For illuminating my good night,
> But pale i' this New Dawn have I

Taken homeward flight.
Until we meet again, kind friend,
I will not set eyes on you;
Until the bright day soon, MacCraw,
Must I then bid
Adieu!

> *'til soon*
> *Your good friend J. B. Leyland.'*

That very afternoon, brain still chattering-full of the previous night's optimism and still sparking ideas, confirmed now in his own mind that greatness through the high craft of bardhood was his destiny, MacCraw cleared a space amidst the clutter of his bachelor-dining table. He took up quill and clean paper, and with fresh memory of his luminous friends, he made his first attempts at what he came to call 'character portraiture'; a whimsical form of writing that he became somewhat famous for within his own circle. Surrounded by empty brandy glasses, plates of cold, gluey gravy, chop-bones and shriveled left over vegetables, MacCraw sat there scratching and scribbling, composing a likeness of first Joe Leyland, and then of Branwell. Both these portraits he could recall by the word to this day, or so MacCraw thought as he lay there in the flickering sleeplessness that very night of penning his 'Wuthering Heights' letters.

'A princely, noble poet was he...' he said out in the darkness. But halted there, doubting the phrasing.

'A noble, princely poet was he...'

MacCraw wriggled himself to a sitting position in the bed. He rubbed hard at his glassy, itching eyes. He lit his bedside candle, then a lamp, then consulted his pocket watch, which had set by habit upon the bedside table. Twelve minutes past two in the morning. Much earlier than he had expected. He knew he should have wormed back down into the warmth of bed and allowed sleep to come, but he could not resist his new impulse. Rising, putting on bed-stockings, he returned to the chest at the bottom of the bed, and beside it upon the floor he set his lamp. Strange shadows were cast upon the room, flickers of disturbing shade dancing around the walls. MacCraw bent forward and rummaged in the bedding chest, keeping an eye on the room's corners, a strange though not unfamiliar fear suddenly upon him. He fancied that he could see the shapes of people there in the corners. There they were, faces blacked out by darkness but their eyes probing him. Malicious eyes, full of foreboding and ill-intent. Sure they were there, and the figure of one tall, dark man in particular stood out. A spirit-fiend, no less, unleashed upon the world, to forever wander it, creating terror in those he stalked, murdering where he could. He heard whisperings too - one phrase in particular that he had heard uttered with his own ears; a phrase that would haunt him to the grave. *My hand... my hand...* the pathetic and forlorn voice wailed; a trembling, child's voice, full of terror. *My hand... my hand...* the mocking wind groaning it at the window as the bony white hand went rapping upon the glass pane. The shadow-fiend stepped out from the corner, arm raising, white skeletal hand thrusting out from the black cloak to point directly at MacCraw. Up from the casket he leapt, swinging to meet the pointing shadow that was stepping across the room toward him.

'Back there, you devil!'

But nothing. There was nothing there but air and empty darkness. Nothing there, but MacCraw's own skin was crawling, hairs prickling upon his own neck and scalp.

'Away with you, foul demon,' he shouted, still uneasy, swiveling a full circle with the lamp raised to ensure that he was in the room alone. He circumnavigated the chamber, checking behind cupboards and chairs as he went, lighting the room's gas-lamps to fill the place with as much light as possible. This done, he returned to the opened casket and went looking again for those stored leaves of his own precious memories. He was looking for his own work this time, since frustrated by doubts about the accuracy of his recollection, he wanted to read the actual wording of his ancient text. Into the bottom of the trunk he delved, shuffling notebooks aside here, pulling out ribbon-bound manuscripts there, scratching in all corners of the box until he came upon that bundle of his own single-leafed, string-bound collection of poetic writings. Back again in his bed, fingers trembling visibly, MacCraw undid the ribbon and leafed through the separate papers until he found the sought for sheet. Two of the same he'd written, one of which he had presented to Branwell as a token of friendship. Branwell had in great appreciative enthusiasm instantly dashed off three copies in his own hand, one copy each, he told MacCraw, for his beloved sisters. He would send them their copies that day to show how well he was thought of by his new Bradford friends. He wriggled with excitement, shouting phrases aloud as he wrote with both hands simultaneously, revelling in the flattering phrases.

MacCraw looked at his own first draft of the piece now, the sloping, drunken ink etched into the paper in the heat of the young mind's frenzy. There, back in the warmth of blankets and eiderdowns, the room's lamps all ablaze about him to keep his mind's demons at bay, he read the piece aloud once more to get the sense of it, and was greatly impressed at his own youthful word-smithery.

George MacCraw's Word Portrait of Patrick Branwell Brontë of June 1838

'A princely poet he was, and startling to look upon, too. A slender little fellow in a coal-black frock coat and sooty grey trousers, his silk hat propped upon the back of his head, brim framing a bushing blaze of fiery red hair. Wild hair. Hair gone mad, frothing out at the side like a fanning pair of Phoenix wings. He elegantly bore spectacles too, balanced precariously upon his noble bone-beak of nose. Sure eccentric he appeared, a scraggy black (though silk) neckerchief strung about his neck, with no great attention to precision. In his ivory-white and dainty hand he clutched a silver-handled rattan - for protection against enthusiastic huckster, street-urchin or robber-ragamuffin, or so he declared - which he oft' twirled dangerously about him, causing all to flinch or cry 'Duck!'. Cockesque, he strutted on the tips of his pointed black boots, availing to make himself more skyward amidst his more statuesque companions. There, genius assured, he preened in the furze and din of the jaw-wagged smoky room of the rainbow-windowed Worldes End Tavern. In short, the little startling swaggered like a man fresh from Life Street who prided himself on being one of the grander pedestrians. There was a contagious happiness and excitability about him. A bubbling nervousness he was possessed of, this little peacock, always fidgeting, always hurrying, grass-hopping himself from one subject to the next, eager to be here, there, everywhere and elsewhere; to be doing better otherwise. His face shone with inner sunlight, this star-freckled visage boasting sideburns bushy and red-frizzled, this face set with the most beautiful, clear, pale-blue eyes. Eyes that swam over and haunted man or woman alike upon his meeting of them. Haunted, haunting eyes - full of lifelight, but the backs inhabited by prowling, wounded cats and shadows. Eyes of the gifted, the beautiful, the damned - eyes of a clay and earthbound Heaven's angel. Anxious as a caged parquet.....beautiful .... gifted ... haunted... swan and ducklings...

star and candles... small and delicate and beautifully formed ... thus go my stuttering
impressions of one whom I met this last fateful night...'

Somewhere in the reading of this page, delicious sleep at last took its grip on George MacCraw. The paper sheets slid from his fingers, gliding to the floor beside his bed. In the light of his own bed-chamber, safe at last from shadow-fiends and haunting voices, he snored and slept soundly until the first street-noises of morning.

CHAPTER 5

If you are a busy, rush-about, working person and have not always the time to wash your hair, then buy and store some powdered orris root. This in fact makes an excellent dry shampoo. A little should be gently powdered into the hair from the scalp outward, rubbed into the scalp most lightly, then brushed through, thus removing grease, lice and stale smells. Keep brushing until all traces of powder have gone. The hair will be clean, healthy looking, as if, in fact, you had spent a good hour washing, soaping and rinsing it over the tub. If you have a drip of oil of violets to the mix the hair will smell most lovely, if perhaps a little on the side of the effeminate.

George Maquire
From 'Essays On The Ancient Art Of The Barber'
1841

Bradford, February 1861

Over the next few days - dank, dismal February affairs, where rivers up and down the country were frozen solid and people were able to walk across them without the aid of bridges - MacCraw awaited some call or written response to his 'Brontë' letter. Bradford days then were as dark and sunless as the nights, fog and filth spewed out by the mill chimneys obliterating all feeble attempts by the winter sun to shine through upon the town. Many folk in the valley bowl were taken ill with coughing sicknesses and festering skin sores, the very air poisoning their lungs and corroding at the skin of their faces. All talk was of the freeze, the foul air, and the forbidding darkness of the yellow-black sky.

'It's as if the eclipse has come early,' MacCraw would cheerlessly grumble to customers, by way of leading into a set-piece conversation.

'Eclipse? What eclipse would that be, MacCraw?' was the response he anticipated, his trade at this time being with a narrow-minded, illiterate lot, who read little and knew less.

'Due in March,' he would dutifully inform them. The subject did genuinely interest him, and he saw it as part of his duty as a barber to dissipate information on all manner of familiar and exotic topics.

'Sun's to be blotted out totally over half the earth. Some of the zealots about reckon that it's the end of the world on that very day. On the continent they go mad, fearing that the sun's gone out like a great snuffed candle, and they go through all kinds of ritual to ignite it again. I'd like to see it myself, if the weather's better by then.'

'Well, tha'll not see it from this smoke-hole, MacCraw,' was the usual retort. Which indeed was true, for even in the heights of summer over the last years the sky had not been visible for many of the hours of daylight.

'I know that. They say North Africa's the best place, or the Americas. I've a brother down California, so I might even get over there. Maybe. I reckon I'll make my way out to the moors though. Out Ilkley way. Or Haworth. Somewhere like that. And while we're speaking of Haworth, did I get to tell you about...'

And from here, obsessed with his theme, MacCraw would lead the conversation on to the blighted Brontë family, to his old friendship with Branwell, and to the wrong done to the fellow with the publication of his book. As he clipped hair, snipped whiskers and lathered up faces, he'd hark back to the glorious past, to the days before the town was a filthy, smoke-choked place, before the coming of the starving Irish and the hungry country folk, in the main boring his customers rigid with his nostalgic babbling.

On the Monday evening Trumper, the second lad, was scowling and sweeping up the floor as they made ready to shut up shop. MacCraw himself cleaned away scissors and hung up his best brushes, half a mind on his poor day's takings. They were both startled from their own thoughts from by an apparition which came rapping at the glass pane of the door, wanting to be let in. MacCraw obliged, unlatching and opening the door, a razor ready in his hand in case of trouble. A tall, gangling being stepped in through the doorway, looking exactly like a giant, colourful grasshopper. A green and red smeared human face bobbled on his long neck, his lanky carcass encased in multicoloured, grimy overalls. Stiff spikes of blue and yellow hair poked out like antennae from the rim of his grease smeared cap. The peffling, anxious looking fellow held out a long, filthy hand. He reeked of sulphour and vinegar - a nostril stinging stench, even to MacCraw's snuff-dulled nose.

'Mister MacCraw sir, please excuse mi appearance, like,' the creature rasped out between throat-rattling coughs. 'I've come direct from t' dye-house. 'Aven't had time to get home and clean missen up yet.'

From the voice MacCraw recognised him then. It was Joseph Snell, the father of his other, absent shop-lad, the ailing Jazeb.

'Ah, Mister Snell. You gave me a start there. Thought it was the devil himself stepping through my doorway. Come on in man, out of the cold. Sit yourself down there. Trumper, you get yourself off now. You've done enough today. We'll finish that in the morning.'

The lad, thirteen or so with a plump, red face and coarse, black hair, gladly put up the brush and struggled into his street coat. He'd had a long busy day with his mate off with the illness and was glad to be out of the place. He nodded anxiously to Snell, not quite sure of what to make of the colourful visitor, then bobbed away out of the door. With the lad gone, MacCraw turned to his visitor.

'A glass of brandy, sir? A little something to warm your toes and clear your throat. You sound a little tight of the lungs there?'

'Oh, ta, Mister MacCraw. Thank you. Don't mind if I do. Wi' a bit of water, if that's no trouble. I am a bit chesty, like, along with half the town. Seems like everyone's ailing. It's messy work down the dye house, sir. To tell you the truth, I never know what colour I'll turn out as the day goes on. Oh, thank you sir. Lovely. Cheers. Good brandy - by heck...!'

Snell made a great whooshing sound as the fumes of the distillation reached the depths of his caked lungs.

'Blooming heck!' he croaked. 'That's nice, sir. Now then. It's about our Jazeb. You'll know the lad's struck down wi' the illness?'

'I do, Mister Snell. I was sorry to hear it, as the lads were. I hope he's faring better.'

'Unfortunately not, sir. Not this morning, anyroad. Nor his little brother. Coughing and sick, both of them. It's desperate in there, man. Clacking away like looms, they are. I thought I'd better come and explain his absence in case you thought he'd quit on you and given up on his apprenticeship.'

Snell stood uneasily, cap in one hand, glass in the other. He had refused a seat, not wanting to blemish the upholstery with the fabric-staining grime of his occupation.

'I hope his absence isn't troubling you too much. He's desperate to get back. You know, Mister MacCraw, he loves this trade and working with you 'ere.'

'Ah, he's a grand lad, Mister Snell. He's learning quick. He works hard. He's reliable. I couldn't ask more from him. You've a lot to be proud of there.'

'That's it, you see, sir. We wouldn't want him to lose his place here. You know yourself regular work's not easy to come by. So what it is, I've come to offer my services. Cleaning t' shop up and that. I don't want no payment. I'll bob in each evening after my shift. Its just, I thought if I could help out sir, there might be a chance of keeping the lad's job open.'

MacCraw nodded thoughtfully, touched to his heart by the desperate father's concern and proposition. He finished off his brandy and set the glass on the shaving-mug ledge beneath the main mirror.

'Nonsense, man. His job's safe. Don't fret on that account. Me and young Trumper have been coping fine, though it must be said he hasn't the same inclination to work as your lad. But now I know he's off a bit longer than expected I'll take on a temporary lad, just until he's better. There's this Moorish lad from White Abbey I've used from time to time, he's a good lad. He'll stand in a while.'

Snell rocked backward and forward on the corroded soles of his boots, stunned, and just not by the brandy. Long used to exploitation and the fickle whims of those who employed him, he had been expecting a long, hard negotiation ending with the loss of his lad's employment, and he hardly knew how to react to such an abrupt and generous response.

'That's it? You'll keep him on then, sir?'

'I will. But on half pay, you understand, Mister Snell. The rest will go to the stand-in, for the short term.'

Snell's face buckled and bubbled like melting candle wax, green-rimmed eyes widening. Tears were forming in the corners of his eyes. He downed the remainder of his drink then let escape another great, lung-clearing whoosh of spirit-fumed air.

'Well, God bless you sir, that's great news! He brings good money in from you, and you'll know yourself how 'ard it is at the moment for a family to get by. If anything's going to make the lad feel better, it'll be the news his job's still open. He does so love the work.'

MacCraw took Snell's empty glass and set it beside his own.

'Do you know what's up with your lads, then? Not the typhus or cholera, I hope. They're not sprouting the roses, are they?'

'No sir, no spots or rashes, thank God. Just withering, and the coughing. It's just the air, I reckon. All the folk are coughing like consumptives down our yard now. They've not eaten so much as a bowl of soup between them all weekend. Like I say, I've not been back yet. Happen Jazeb's picked up a bit. If he has, and he goes on bettering, he might be fit by Friday.'

'Have you had chance to get a doctor to them?'

By chance he meant means, doubting that Snell could stretch his family budget to such a luxury.

'Ah, well, not yet, Mister MacCraw. You know yourself the cost of those fellows. We've had Old Hannah down though, and as you know she's seen more sickness than the whole set of doctors up at the infirmary. She's looked them over and prepared us some tincture and tea. She reckons it's but a passing bout.'

MacCraw hummed and rubbed at his whiskers, taking upon himself a professional manner now, fingers playing with his apron pockets.

'Hmm... coughing eh? And a touch of fever too. Was it coltsfoot, Hannah left you with?'

Snell shrugged, looking doubtful.

'I don't believe it was, sir, but then I wouldn't know for sure. Some tincture or other. I never thought to ask the name. Our Alice will know, like.'

MacCraw strode across to his rack of stone jars. He rubbed his hands clean in his apron, then lifted a jar down from the middle shelf.

'If it's coughing, Mister Snell, then it might do well for them to try this.'

On the counter there he rustled out a good quantity of dried dusty-green leaves into a brown paper bag, double folding it closed to prevent spillage, then holding it out to Snell.

'Fresh leaf would be best, of course, but it'll be a month or so before it's growing. Make a good strong, hot tea with it. Make sure the lads drink it down. Just a cup full, every three or four hours or so. It can't harm them to have too much if they take a fancy for it. A tip of honey or sugar with it might make them take to it better, if you've any. It's just the coltsfoot leaf, so it won't go against anything Hannah's given you. And as they pick up they can have a smoke of it.'

'Smoke it?'

'Aye. Just a little pipe.'

'Even the little one?'

'Aye, even the little one. There's no tar to it, and it's not habit forming. It's good for the airways, you see. Here, take it man, don't be hesitant on me now. I don't want anything for it. The stuff grows free on every bit of grass land and street corner here.'

'Mister MacCraw, I don't know what to say. You're too kind. God bless you sir. If only there were more bosses like you. Wait until Alice hears on your kindness...'

Through a chorus of gratitudes and compliments, MacCraw saw Snell back out into the dismal street, but not before handing him the few coins that made up Jazeb's wages from the last full week of his work.

'Don't send him back before he's fit,' he called down the street. 'And that's not me being generous sir - I don't want him spreading illness among me and my customers.'

'Right you are, Mister MacCraw. And anytime I can return the favour, you just ask me. Anytime.'

'Ah well, Joseph, that's nice to know. I may well call you up on that one.'

Snell waved his farewell then lurched away into the murk, clutching onto his little bundle of coltsfoot. MacCraw closed up and locked the door. He poured himself another brandy, took up Trumper's sweeping brush, then with vigour set about finishing off the hairy shop floor.

Over that next week 'zigzag' MacCraw took to drinking more brandy than even he knew was good for him. His temporary shop-boy, who they called Mufty, his actual name, Mohammed Mustapha Eladin, being too hard to trip off the local tongue, was sent round the corner to Conway's Grocers for a pint of brandy every afternoon. MacCraw was well down the bottle by the time they had shut up and swept the shop. He felt deeply unhappy and, despite his contact with the customers, extremely lonely. His rekindled interest in the Brontë affair had stoked up more memories than he'd expected. Caroline flickered in there every time he thought of Branwell or the book. Dear, departed Caroline. Even after all these years, he was still deeply missing her. Day in, day out, he was missing her, and his thoughts began to linger around the cruel, tragic manner of her death. In deliberate attempts to counteract the bleak memory, he found himself thinking back more and more on their sweeter times together, but always the blackest moment seeped through. An awareness dawned that once the business with Branwell was done with, he would have to make some big changes to improve his own life. A move right away from the place would be a sensible idea now; shut up and sell the shops; use his profits and savings to retire to the countryside, or to a new town; perhaps even up-sticks to another country. Though somewhat set in his Bradford and barbering ways he was not too old yet to take up a travelling life. After years of stasis it would be a joy to venture out and see some of the lands he had talked of visiting before his own inevitable passing away. Never too old to travel, never too old for change, he told himself in these mind-wandering moments. Never too old to pack up your wagon and move on. Travel; a move away; a ship out. Maybe a wife? That was the right way to be thinking now. Otherwise there was a good risk of lapsing into one of those slack-bellied, sour-mouthed, griping old men that he had always despised in his own youth. New Zealand was a great starting place for a man with some capital, so he had heard. Or South Africa with its warm, kind climate and easy living - many Yorkshire folk were heading out there to start a new life. Canada was said to be a country so vast that a man could buy a portion of land the size of Yorkshire for a pittance. There was his brother Eammon to consider, too - the last surviving member of his immediate family, and the only one of the whole clan that he had any contact with, though that was rare enough. Since the '40's, contact had been irregular and lacking in depth - the occasional missive, often months from the penning to the receiving. It was well over a year ago since he'd heard from him. Unlike MacCraw, Eammon, who called himself now Eddy Rawson, had maintained the family's wandering ways. The twists of fate in the new nation had seen Eammon make fortunes and lose them again within a year. His early letters read like an adventure-filled, picaresque novel. He had trapped fur, sold grain, traded guns and whisky with the native red men, worked with cattle, all this while travelling the vast nation up, down and sideways, the current carrying him steadily west with the waves of gold-rushing of the late forties. He had remade a lost fortune in the goldfields of California. According to his last letters of a year or so ago he was now comfortably off and well settled in a Mediterranean style paradise in the rapidly booming city of San Francisco. The place as Eammon described it sounded something like the merry little Bradford that MacCraw had been drawn to, back in his youth. To spend his last years in a sunny paradise, leading a simple, healthy life, eating fish, drinking wine, taking walks along a beautiful coastline of spectacular sunsets - that would sound an attractive future to any dissatisfied, grief tainted man of the world.

Travel would be fine, then, but here was the problematic matter of Caroline's grave, up there on the hillside in Undercliffe. He did not want the plot to lapse into disrepair, the angelic tombstone to crumble or topple in some winter storm, laying there forever uprooted, weeds growing up over it. For a small annual fee, he reassured himself, he could surely arrange the upkeep of the grave? This matter - the state and upkeep of Caroline's resting place - fretted him greatly. Every time he walked the streets of the town centre he would find himself gazing up the hill toward the spires and monuments of the great cemetery in Undercliffe, the Necropolis deliberately situated so that it loomed visible from all corners of the town. The place was even visible from his own attic skylight, and when morbid he would press his face there against the small pane, peering up the hill, fancying he could make out the white angel that marked his beloved's grave.

The unhappy, dissatisfied frame of mind persisted to dog at MacCraw. He could nor bear to be alone in the house on an evening. After his meal - eaten out or prepared and heated by himself using the new preserving cans that were a Godsend to a single fellow like himself - he took to going about town for a few jars of porter. Alone, like a shade, avoiding conversation and company, he began to wander around the tavern haunts of the old Rhymers, trying to capture memories and past incidents of those days from the fittings and corners of the places they had frequented. He would start out in The George, where the literary fellows - writers of dramas, poets, critics and the like - would meet to swap ideas and new tales. Just a gill there, for it was deserted and soulless now at that early hour of the evening, then along to The Queens. Here, in those past days, painters, sculptors and portrait artists would cluster with their paint-splattered hands and wild waistcoats, swapping details of brush-strokes, glazing techniques, great paintings they had seen of late. Branwell would often frequent the place, wittering and arm-waving, talking up his latest portraits, trying to drum up custom for himself. From there up to the New Inn, once home of the Philosophical Society. There, intense clusters of black-neckerchiefed, moustached gentlemen would lean together with the somber gravity of crows, discussing the morality of the slave trade, or the future of a mechanical industrialised society, or some vague nuance of the nature of life, often talking themselves, their fellows, the world and God out of existence and then back in again before the night was out. On such themes Branwell could rant and banter as well as the best of them, often underlining his line of argument with some apt and precise Latin or Greek quote of philosophical antiquity, using Socrates, Plato or Heraclitus as the foundation of his argument against a Supreme Being, the existence of Whom, now that he was removed from the fold of Haworth, he openly denied.

Lastly, on these lonely, wandering nights, the reflective MacCraw would end up round the corner from his own place at The Bull's Head. He found himself there alone the Thursday after posting his Branwell letter out to various newspapers, journals and editors. Then, as in the years of the Rhymers, Thursday night was music night. Musicians of all ages would gather, pale, sallow and morbid-faced in their baggy, ragged clothing. They would pluck at their battered banjos, piping or fiddling along on to whistles and clarinets, playing the night in turns, the music becoming merrier and more frenzied as the late hours approached. On occasion, when the mood was benevolent and the landlord thought it fit and profitable, a band of them would play on right through until dawn, often inspired in their stamina by a grain or twist of some stimulative potion that helped keep drowsiness at bay. There in the music of the Bull sat Barber MacCraw, comfortable with his tankard, his pipe and his misery. From the fire-clustered band a count went up; a tune began. A slow, drifting reel unfurled, filled with sorrow, longing and reflection. MacCraw recognized the core of the melody from his youth and childhood. Then the lyric had been about a girl reflecting upon her lost lover while walking a deserted beach on the Kerry shore. He found himself quietly humming along, drifting away with the snaking coils of his own blue pipe smoke, floating back always into that blurry haze of memories. He was glimpsed by those around him as the tatty, sad-eyed old barber from down behind the mill there, and was left alone to his wallowing, not even bothered by the hucksters or dainty night-girls. His pale blue eyes filmed over. Like some solitary harpster of his own mental regions he plucked upon memories, letting them string out to the fiddle, running past events together and into each other. Those long-ago, wild afternoons and debauched night times reeled out into one great and merry-mad party of remembered life. There, in the recollections, he was dancing and singing alongside little Madness Patrick Branwell and the burly, heroic frame of Lusty Joe Leyland...

All the Rhymers were there, croaking hoarsely in bawdy song. There was a pale, blurred crescent of whisker-fringed faces, MacCraw staggering the dance while arm-linked between Branwell and his painter-pal Robinson, Leyland leering away to the left somewhere, arm curled around the slender waist of a tavern-lovely. Mad, discordant music, rapid-full of twisting harmonies, jangled and piped out from over by the bar. Around the Worldes End table, tulip-purple mouths were twisting wide open in chatter and song, lips wet and gleaming in the lamp shine. Drink-fuelled eyes flashing, nostrils flaring, pipe smoke curling, snuff snorting, veins bulging, necks twisting, words blurring. MacCraw, a snuff-fiend from his boyhood days, and now with knowledge of herbal potion and invigorating remedy, pulled out his ever-generous box, watching his latest concoction do the rounds, fingers of men and women alike dipping in to try a pinch. The eyes around brightened, faces flushing, fits of sneezing and laughter erupting round the room following the snuffing of the stuff. Then Branwell - overcharged with liquor, snuff, and exuberance - bellowed out some rhyming couplet before leaping up onto the pot-cluttered table to set his shiny, pointed boots clicking into a jig, heels and toes a-tapping out the music's rhythm. Despite the frowns of Lizzie, the ever tolerant landlady, and the protestations of her harassed pot-boys, Branwell's heels went banging faster to the speeding reel and hand-slapped beat of the cheering crowd, until the pitch reached such a frenzy that he surrendered to oblivion and launched himself from the table as if into the flow of the music itself, arms outstretched, expecting to soar right up to the ceiling and Heaven beyond. He landed in the arms of his fortunately well synchronized fellows, his battered hat and spectacles flying loose across the room. Night after night Branwell would perform his table-top dance routine. Following his display tavern-wide cheering and wild applause would erupt for the arm-flapping jig, people mimicking it in every corner as the music picked up again. It was dance style that many copied but none could better, or put a sticking name to. Click and Reel. Jig and Bang. Clack and Jingle. The Branwell Waltz. None of those terms captured the frantic movements of that satanic stomp.

Later, in the same tavern, or perhaps on a different, steadier night completely, The Rhymers would settle in the more comfortable chairs over by the glowing coals of the fire. Renowned yarn-spinners would in turn unfold some bone-chilling story. These tales might be long or short, in plain narrative or rhyming verse, original or recounted from tradition, but always well told and articulately delivered. Faces of listeners would loom and bobble above black frockcoats in the darkness, the lamps dimmed now so that illumination was merely by the firelight and the very imaginations of the listeners. Pale blobs of faces, licked orange and yellow in flame and shadow, eyes hooded to darkened pools, noses cut into great beaks by the dim lighting so that the whole audience seemed to have taken on the aspects of gargoyles as the gothic-taled mood took its grip around the room.

At these events, Branwell was always much in demand. This storytelling to a fixed audience, much more than verse or song or life-like painting, seemed a situation where his true genius could shine through immediately. Spectacles glinting, reflecting the firelight in their lenses, wild hair bristling toward the smoke wreathed ceiling, he was relaxed and completely at ease, tale after tale streaming from his lips. Bizarre yarns of savage, moor-haunting ghost-hounds that would appear howling and yellow-eyed on dark nights to prophesise a family's ruination or a gory death. Stories of a ghostly, glowing shepherd who would appear out of the autumn mist. This fiend would transmogrify into a vicious, upright wolf, then snatch a baby from a mother's arms before disappearing over the moor, shepherd and child never seen again - until the next wolf's howl. Other yarns he wove, of the gytrash; of cruel and vicious faeries; of evil, black-eyed gypsies in league with roving witches; of ancient Irish family feuds that brought curses and bloodshed avalanching down the generations. Throughout these stories, Branwell's audience would be enraptured, leaning forward on their stools and chairs like a class of school infants, men and women alike gasping, trembling, flesh acreep with goose-pimples. And there in that room, before the flickering fire, the same family-damned tale would be recounted. The yarn of the mysterious darkling brought into a home as a child by a warm-hearted and unsuspecting family. The dark-hued boy, taken in on charitable, good intention, only to weave a curse throughout the family, bringing forth horror, death, destruction and damnation to pour down like black rain upon all who cared for, loved, or crossed him. That reworked tale of the blighted cuckoo-child who tainted those who tried to come closest to him. Many a variation of this he told. Always he painted a beauty and irresistible force of will into his mysterious stranger, as though each time unleashing some kernel of his own deeper self there into the telling. That very hero, if the grim fellow could be labelled thus, he created, moulded, fashioned, and refashioned, month in, month out, there around the story-telling fireplace in the Worldes End Tavern. Sometimes the man he called Rogue, sometimes Percy, others Northangerland. Gradually the very principle of the darkling was shaped into one magnificent, malignant being – and in the last tales, this being he called Heathcliffe.

There in The Worldes End, as the many forms and versions of the tale unfolded to the engrossed crowd, MacCraw often witnessed a strangeness come over the gathering. The faces would run and melt like wax, twisted with pools of shadow and their own inner-darkness so that they looked not like a human audience, but more a rustling cluster of demons. Often on those yarn-nights, MacCraw felt himself to be in the presence of Hell's own legion, the evil, cast-out lot of them sighing and groaning along with the horrific twistings of Branwell's tale, as if thrilled to be hearing the deeds and somber exploits of one of their very own incarnated in human form. Indeed, on more than one occasion, when the tales were over and the room somewhat returned to its normality, several in the company would swear, and on oath, that a silent stranger had come and set himself down in their company, head bowed, listening with intense concentration, only to have vanished before the tale had reached its grim conclusion. Just are there are numerous tales of Lucifer hoofing onto the stage at performances of the Bard's 'Scottish play', so it came to be reckoned that a genuine demon would slip in amidst the crowd there at The Worldes End to listen to Branwell. Complimentary though this might seem to some, MacCraw found that it greatly disturbed the ever-sensitive Branwell. He could recall one foggy, moonless evening, when poor Brontë, quaking and gibbering, could not be persuaded to step out through the tavern door. MacCraw, mingling and chattering in other company, was requested over by Lizzie to help the trembling wretch out of the place. Thinking that Branwell was having a fine theatrical jest with him, MacCraw succumbed a while to the nonsense of there being some 'dark-angeled fellow' awaiting out there in the snickets. Only when he playfully shoved his friend doorward and he then let out a high-pitched, piglet-like screeching, did MacCraw realise that no jesting was going on.

'But we must go, sir,' MacCraw gently pleaded. 'Look around you - the place is all but closed now.'

'Well then walk with me George. Escort me to my door. I swear sir, I'm fearful for my life, and I know not fully why.'

'Why Branwell, you're shaking all over, man. Come on now, take it calmly. What on earth is the matter with you?'

'It's him, George. It's him I fear.' Branwell pointed haphazardly into every dark corner and cranny of the emptying room. Around them tables were being cleared of pots, brushed, wiped clean, stools being raised up atop of each other so that the floor might be swept.

'Who, man? Who?' MacCraw looked about the room, for they were all but the last two in the place, the exhausted potboys busy clearing around them, frowning them out of the place.

'He was here again tonight. The stranger who creeps into our company. The Shade, George. The Shade! Even I saw him, tonight, peering on at me. Bob Storey swore just now that some fellow had come in and sat down behind him, bringing a dreadful chill with him too. Then the next moment, when Bob glimpsed over his shoulder to get a good look at the fellow's face, why, the man faded into air. He shimmered away and vanished before Bob's own eyes, like a melting vision.'

'Ah, come on now, Branwell. It's just the tales and the ale getting to them. Tales about tales. They're just jesting with yer, that's all.'

'But don't you see it, George. I've conjured him up. Years and years of imagining the dark fellow - I've conjured him up like a mind-creature. The Devil himself has picked up on my mould and sent the phantom out to haunt me.'

'Now that's nonsense. The drink's fuddling yer thinking, that's all. Come on, I'll walk with yer to your door and see you safe inside. Now come on. Goodnight there Lizzie; goodnight lads, 'night girls.'

MacCraw bundled Branwell out into the night, linking his arm, amazed that his friend was in such a genuine terror. As they clacked their way along Manningham Lane, Branwell could babble about nothing but the fiend that he had now unleashed, or so he believed, as a real and physical presence in the world.

'Don't you believe it, George? Don't you believe it? That the human imagination can yield forth all sorts of creatures and beings into the very fabric of the world? I tell you now, if you imagine something long enough and hard enough, it comes into being. And especially so if you accompany your black ideas with oaths and blasphemies, like I've done myself. I'm certain of it - we can make our thoughts into atoms; we can fashion our very ideas into matter.'

'Come now Branwell, calm yourself. You're nearly home now.'

'But do you believe it?'

'I believe no such thing. What's imagined is just that. Only what's real can be real.'

Branwell would have none of this sensible logic.

'But George, I've seen the fellow. Several times now. He tails me, I tell you. He tracks me through the streets on a night. On the moors too, I've seen him, when I hike home to Haworth. He stalks behind me, following me pace for pace. Watching me. Watching. Always watching. On nights like this he stares up at my window. Don't look so incredulous, man. I swear on the Rhymer's oath. I've looked down into the street in the earliest hours of the morning and caught him there, just staring up at my window. Oh, I'll have to put him away. I'll burn my book, that's what I'll do. I'll put the fellow to the flame before he gets the better of me. Burn it and bury it, that's what I'll do. He means me ill! He'll have my soul!'

Branwell's melodramatics, spluttered with much flapping of arms and flustering, were sincere enough, and the sincerity disturbed MacCraw that night. The fear, like some spreading, malignant illness, seemed to infect him also. He too leapt at shadows in doorways; his heart also pounded with dread and terror at every strange footstep through the night streets. He remembered, after seeing Branwell safe through his door upon Fountain Street, walking back toward the town with a creeping sense of dread. The streets were deserted. Yellow mist hung upon the sky and coiled down in sulphurous wisps through the yards and snickets, so that one moment all was clear down the hill ahead, the next all around was shrouded in a stinking, impenetrable fog, not a view of wall, window or doorway to be had. The clacking of his own boots on the cobbles and street paving echoed in the clear patches, but were quickly muffled whenever he stepped into the sinister fog. Gradually he became aware that there, to match his own footsteps, he could hear a fainter, echoing tread, almost in perfect time to his own. Peering back along Kirkgate, he fancied he could see the tall shape of a cloaked, hatted figure loitering back along the street.

'Halloah!' he called out. No reply came from the lurking stranger there. 'Hello there, sir. What's your business?'

Mist billowed down upon the cobbles, screening off all view of the street. MacCraw hurried on, making sure his footsteps were stamped loud, for a damned fear was chilling him to the very marrow now. At the top of Ivegate he halted abruptly. He was determined to put an end to the fearful matter before he reached the doorway of his own property. Behind him the footsteps continued a few steps, hesitated, then scraped to a halt. MacCraw froze, heart pounding, his breath rasping fast and harsh.

In his pocket, for protection against thieves and rogues or those out to beat upon one of the Irish, he habitually carried a brass knuckle-duster. This he now slipped upon his hand, curling it to form a solid, deadly fist.

'Are you following me, sir?' he called out bravely. As he expected, no answer was forthcoming. The street and night was utterly silent. Everything was still, even the fog no longer coiling now. The seconds dragged. His heart was booming. He seemed displaced, as though captured and frozen outside place and time, afloat in the yellow mist like some unfortunate insect embalmed in glowing amber. He had to break the grip of the spell, and decided that abrupt rashness was now his best strategy.

'Again, are you following me, sir? If you are, then the devil take you, but not before I thrash you first myself!'

He spun about then, bursting and howling back along Kirkgate, terrified but enraged, arm swinging, ready to land a deadly blow. He was determined to teach the malicious cur a good lesson of manners. But he ran into mist and shadow. Where he thought the footsteps had halted, back alongside the drapers and druggists, the street proved clear and empty. He ran this way and that, listening for movement, anticipating a blow. The doorways all around were also deserted - he checked every one of them, cursing for the coward to come out, face him and fight. Whether the fellow had fled, or whether the whole thing was some trick of his own imagination keyed up by the stories and by Branwell's behaviour, MacCraw never knew for sure. One thing though he was certain of - when he locked and bolted his own door that night a great sense of dread and unease followed him in from the street, breezing through the briefly opened doorway. A malignant aura of disquiet pervaded his shop, his house and his mind for weeks after, so that he too felt he was being hunted and haunted by some invisible, parasitic fiend from beyond the boundaries of his own physical world. MacCraw chose never to mention this night-time matter to Branwell, aware that details of the incident might disturb his friend's nervous temperament even more, causing him further mental distress. As for himself, the matter was never satisfactorily explained. As the years progressed he too came to believe that he was being hounded, his life blighted by a mysterious stranger who was a fiend conjured up from the mere force of human imagination.

There in The Bull the song ended and MacCraw was startled back into his real surroundings by the applause that erupted about him. He joined in with the clapping, rubbed his heavy eyes, clapped again, then necked down the last of his drink. The session was over, the musicians packing up, the potboy starting to clear away. He realised he had nodded off and slept through the set. Embarrassed that he'd dozed, he rose quickly and made his way out to the street. The memory of the fiend in the yellow mist from all those years ago lingered with him, and he thought back on it as he hurried along to his shop. From that time his sleep again became light and uneasy. His nights were littered with troubled dreams and the dreadful sense that somebody was stalking him, watching him, preparing to hunt him down. His once steady hand began to tremble on a morning; it was a real struggle to work the scissors on the first haircuts of the day. That dank February, many a shaved customer went away with a nicked chin, quietly cursing, determined to take their custom elsewhere in the future.

CHAPTER 6

From 'The Tale Of Barry Robb'
Patrick Branwell Brontë
1840

I was born in the parish of Saint Giles's in the Fields, in the year eighteen hundred and eight. My father was a soldier in the British service, and my mother, like myself of short stature, was an entertainer - a singer and dancer on the boards, and rare good at it too - right famous, she were, in some ways. My father was in fact an Irishman, from the country of Limerick, though my mother was of London, her family going back years in the shows and entertainments, and I aint exaggerating here when I say that Shakespeare was familiar with the family on my mother's side, and based one or two of his characters - the happy ones, like - on her forekin. My elder sister, not tinged with the family shortness, has been sentenced to four years, and another sister to five years transportation, both for stealing watches and other pocket articles, though on different occasions. Me, being different to look on, was never sent by my parents to school, but have learned to read a little by my own exertions. I've a little knowledge of writing but am better like this, at speaking out, than I am in writing down - my hand moves too slow for my head, if you understand what I mean. I've knowledge of arithmetic, but again, that's better in my head than it is on the page. I swear it, no man's ever taken me over coppers, or silver, and certainly never will over gold. I was sent out to get my living when I was ten years old. I was selling oranges in the streets from a basket, and mingling there, like you do, with all sorts of flotsam and whatever from the tides of the world, I was soon led into bad company. I sometimes played at pitch and toss with the lads from about the place, which trained me in gambling ways, and I often lost my day's takings by this means, which meant I started elaborating on great excuses why I'd taken no money to my ma', and though she saw right through me, god bless her soul, she just shook her head in pity, and covered for me with the old general, as we called him. By eleven I often remained out all night with the roaming boys, and slept in the dark arches of the Adelphi on straw with 'em. We met one lad there who was a pickpocket, who learned me to steal in crowds, me being small and quick handed like. About this time I was separated from my family once and for all, on account of me being apprehended in the act of removing a gentleman's wallet - I were committed at the Middlesex Assizes, and received six months' imprisonment. And this, don't forget, at the eleven years old. I hope I'm not boring you - please just tell me if I am, and I'll sit back down with my drink. Like I said, this ain't no story. This is the truth. I've come up here to escape all that. It's just, like, fun being with you lot, listening in and the like, and I've got a story to tell in a way, I suppose - so - shall I go on?

Haworth Village, September 1848

After that strange, phantom haunted night in the yellow mist, Branwell Brontë was never the same man again, or so it seemed to the more wary MacCraw. Upon many occasion of the Rhymer's meetings, he thought he glimpsed a darkening inhabitant who dwelt behind the cheery, cajoling facade that Branwell projected forth to the gathered company and the world at large. Indeed, it was as though two lodgers inhabited the same house and were always in to answer the door at differing times. Two dwellers, it seemed, inhabited his body - two minds and characters seemed seated within the single organ of his brain. One of these lodgers was bright summer sunshine, all joy and warmth, abundant with benevolent rays; the other fellow cold, bleak, as hostile and distant as the unglimpsed dark-side of the sterile moon. This dark tenant, MacCraw observed, more often emerged when he was alone with Branwell, or when the company was small - perhaps just the two of them and Leyland, or Storey, or one other. Boost the company to four and the morbid little cellar-dweller who reflected morosely on death, on a godless universe and on the grim mortality of disease-ridden life, would scuttle away downstairs. Down from the attic would come tripping the brighter fellow, full of cheer and fun and japesting banter.

That inner darkling of Branwell's, MacCraw came to realise, was rooted and nourished back in the harsh bitterness of the poor little fellow's childhood, that same susceptible time when all men's genius and demons are shaped up. Like many of the Age, the boy had witnessed his own bright siblings fall ill, wither, demise, then suffer prolonged, pain-wracked deaths. The little coffins of his sisters had gone into the gaping earth, along with that more substantial, and possibly devastating, casket of his mother's. Little wonder then that the fellow would dwell long upon the subject and theme of earthly death, desertion and the isolation of the human creature in the great, indifferent universe.

In those early Rhymer's days, Branwell more often than not maintained his charming, sunny-faced charade, his morbid, chuntering dark-self usually only putting an appearance in the small late hours after too much brandy or a pipe with a shred of opium. Sometimes its emergence would be sudden and inexplicable, some word or incident or shade of the room's lighting triggering a memory that clawed and clutched him back into the tragic confusion of a death-shaded childhood. When thus snatched by such a moment, he would usually clamber back out of it within minutes, though his concentration and conversation would be somewhat jaded for hours afterwards. When thoroughly morose, there was no recalling or cheering him forth from the quagmire of his darkest depths and feverish morbidity. At those times, bed was the only fit place for him.

To MacCraw it was evident that this dark mirror-self began to emerge as the more dominant aspect of Branwell's outer personality as he aged through the self-proclaimed futile and unfruitful life of his twenties, the inner fiend demanding more of an appearance in the wearying, outer, real world. This twisted, darker version of the poor fellow MacCraw came upon in The Black Bull at Haworth that evening after his venturing there in the company of Francis Grundy, the very week before Branwell's passing in the September of 1848. There in the snug of that hostelry he had witnessed the demon within man stare madly out upon the alien material world, the real Branwell of old sublimated by the fiend who had gripped control of his faculties to the extent that the person who initially appeared there before them was almost the exact human opposite of his self when back in the full-bloomed enjoyment of his Bradford days.

It was grim Friday evening in Haworth then, after their bleak wade upon the wild moor paths from the warmth of the Pack Horse hostelry in Keighley. Chilled to the core by wind and drizzle, Grundy and MacCraw had trudged their way up the steep cobbled hill of the little village's main street, and thus into the cheerful warmth of the Black Bull's snug room. They sat themselves before the blazing fire there and called the boy to bring them hot water and brandy. With the landlord they arranged for a good dinner to be served within the hour, booked a double room for the night, then had him send one of his potboys round to the parsonage with a message for Branwell. The hastily scrawled note was to let their friend know that they had arrived, and that they expected his company as soon as was convenient - within the hour if he should wish to dine with them. The landlord, a solid, white haired, ruddy faced gent who introduced himself as Roy Tucker, reluctantly, confirmed that Branwell was still welcome there, though he let them know that his reputation for non-payment of bills, and for outlandish behaviour, had made him an outcast to practically every inn and hostelry within Haworth and most neighbouring parishes. Tucker cheerfully bantered with his visitors and the few other drinkers in the place. Seeing that his out of town guests were intent on spending good money, he set them right with a free hot mulled wine to warm them through, for he could plainly see that they had suffered the weather. A few of the regulars declared that they remembered Grundy and MacCraw from their last visit there, which in MacCraw's case was all of eight years previously. Within minutes a sense of good cheer was about the place, and all within were relaxed and jovial.

They waited and watched the door. On occasion it creaked open, a figure came hastening in from the rain, and though they expected it to be Branwell it was always just some local fellow calling for a warming jar. The meal came, and was served in the fireside corner – piles of hot roast beef, pudding, and steaming vegetables, served by a squat, dour-faced local lass. When they were well into devouring the mound that had been set before them, they sent for the potboy who had delivered their message for Branwell.

'Who was it you spoke to, lad?' inquired Grundy.

'One o' t' misses, sir. Bossy one.'

'Miss Charlotte?'

'I dunno sir, bi name.'

'The eldest.'

The lad shrugged.

'Aye, sir, 'appen.'

'Well go again, my lad, this time for a sixpence.'

The same message was written out, and the lad set out again, this time instructed to hand the note only to Branwell, or to one of the servants. Within minutes the lad was back.

'Well?'

'Well, sir, no servants were there. It were one o't other sisters though. The little squinty one. She promised that she'd give him't note.'

Grundy sighed and tossed the lad his sixpence.

'What do you reckon?' MacCraw asked, perplexed by the situation, fearing he had ventured so far from his beloved Caroline on a wild goose chase.

'I don't rightly know, George. Like I said, he claims he's virtually a prisoner in the house these days. I'll tell you what though, if he's not here within the next hour, I'll damn well call up there myself. I'm not walking all the way up here for nothing.'

'I'll drink to that, sir.'

They toasted the last of their wine, called for more, and settled down to a pipe, chatting weather and local gossip with the regulars. Presently, just as they were giving up on the hope that their friend had received the note, the door of the inn was opened haltingly, closed again, then reopened. All the chatter halted. All eyes were upon that door. If ever a person had made an entrance by not even walking into a room, then this was it. Neither MacCraw nor Grundy were prepared for the spectacle of Branwell that, by inches, presented itself before them. Around the wood of the door emerged a mass of unkempt, bright red hair, wildly floating like clouds around the moon-white bulge of forehead that followed, for it seemed he was entering the place on the horizontal. Then in he stuttered, head jerking form side to side, haunted, hunted eyes scanning the dimensions and shapes of the room, but seeming to see nothing.

'Come on in, and close the door, would you Branwell,' Roy Tucker called from his bar. 'It's too cold to leave it open, and you know you're always welcome here, lad.'

In nervous jerks and halting movements, Branwell did as requested. He squinted around through his precariously perched spectacles, seemed at last to see his two old comrades at the hearth end of the room, and waved nervously, though rooted to the spot, is if about to bolt back for the doorway at any moment.

'Branwell,' Grundy called, just to confirm that it was indeed he. 'I'm here, and look who I brought up with me.'

MacCraw half rose, waved and sent forth a cheery greeting, though in truth he felt shocked at the sight of his old friend. Branwell began wavering unsteadily toward them, knocking into stools and tables, though out of nerves rather than drunkenness. He looked even more wretched in the lamplight as he neared them. His once flushed cheeks were jaundiced and hollowed; that once smiling, singing mouth was now collapsed in on itself. Thin, spittle-crusted lips went twitching as he tried to stutter back greetings. There was no flesh on the fellow at all, and he seemed but a skeleton propping up ragged clothing. Behind the spectacles his eye sockets were sunken like dark caves, the eyes at the bottom of their pits glaring with what could only have been the moon-glow of madness. In his trade and time, MacCraw had seen many addicts of various vices and concoctions, medicinal ones amongst them - laudanum, opium, alcohol, sheer lust - and it seemed that the Branwell here before him now was these and more rolled together into one. He and Grundy rose fully to greet their fellow Rhymer, ritually shaking hands and embracing him in the old devised ways, both taking an elbow and ushering him to their jolly corner table, seating him between them so that there could be no bolting back to the door.

'Hot brandies,' MacCraw called up to the bar. 'And another jug of your good hot wine. There's another fellow here needs warming, though he's not walked so far as we have.'

After a brandy or two, helped along with the warmth of intimate companionship, Branwell visibly returned into himself. His eyes brightened. His skin lost its unnatural yellow hue, the cheeks even flushing pink. His hands steadied. His whole disposition became less nervous. To MacCraw, it seemed he was watching a man remembering how to be himself.

'Well, it's so good to see you both. Heaven forbid, I thought I'd but fabricated up the two of you in past dreams and nightmares. I have so many of those, these days. Nightmares, I mean. Tell me, MacCraw, are you still barbering?'

'Unfortunately, I am Bran, though I hope to be out of it soon. I've a few plans afoot to escape me from that game.'

'And you Grundy - still in the engineering game are you?'

'Alas, so. But like George here, I hope to be out of it and furthering myself.'

'And what about you, Branwell?' As soon as he uttered it, MacCraw realised it was a blunder. 'Have you... erm, plans for the future?'

'Plans for the future,' Branwell echoed, then snorted. His eyes glazed over. He trembled his glass up to his quivering mouth.

'I do have plans, George, but they're thwarted at every turn. Plans of marriage to a fine lady. Her husband lives, though. Plans to pay my debtors who come brazenly to the parsonage door now. But I lack profitable employment. Plans to be a great novelist of our Age. Though it seems I'm to be cheated out of that too, now. Plans, my friends, are such vague and fickle things. They seem quite obscene to me, as a matter of fact. I plan to not plan, self-deceiving that I thus live some higher kind of life, but as you see by my sheer appearance, this is self-delusion now.'

Warmed up and started on the topic now, the poet babbled and chittered on his half nonsense while picking over leftover food from the dinner plates that had not yet been collected by the serving girl.

'Branwell,' Grundy attempted to intrude. 'I can soon order another dinner if you're feeling hungry.'

'Hungry!? Not me, sir. I barely eat, these days. Just picking over scraps, now. Just picking over scraps.'

He leered with a sly grin, every gesture and utterance seeming to contain hidden significance or reference external to the immediate conversation. It was clear from every utterance and movement that he was a man who was troubled to the core of his soul. Yet, contradictory as ever, the more he drank (and he kept insisting upon more brandy, though he knew well that the bill was not his to foot) the more lucid and human he became. He began to banter with the local folk around him, as if recognising them at last after some long journey, though he must have passed them at some point in the street outside during the same week. They were polite and tender in turn with him, knowing that he was one of their own out of sorts - a soul that needed greeting and handling kindly, not shunning and damning out of sight for alleged distant misdeeds. Try as they might, MacCraw and Grundy could fathom nothing of the recent events that had led to his alarming decline, other than his cryptic offerings about some liaison with a great beauty of noble birth, and of strange shaking fits that were creeping upon him on a regular basis. As had become usual in the late and declining days of The Rhymers, Branwell took upon himself a half-ranted monologue, with no ears for the banter, news or history of his long unseen visitors. And as in the past, his conversation tracked upon a singular, sombre theme – that of death. His own, he assured them, was certain and not far off.

'Which is why I called you fellows up here,' he announced. 'I'm dying, you see, as sure as I'm sitting here. But I need some security. Some confidence. She's burning the lot of it, you know. Page by page. Everything. Bit by bit. She's burning me up, heart and soul and body and all.'

'Who would that be, Branwell?' Grundy requested, genuinely mystified, an anxious frown clouding his broad face.

'Why, Charlotte, of course. You know she's published now? All of them are, though they think it's the big secret. Why, damn it, they're each all but famous, and all on the back of me.'

'But surely sir, she's your best friend,' put in a wary MacCraw.

Branwell stiffened, looking anxiously around, fearing he was overheard.

'Sir,' he hissed, 'she's my executioner! Sure, I'm confused, and doing myself no scrap of good with the stuff I'm indulging in, but I know when my draws have been rifled. Any writer, sir, as indeed you'll be aware, knows when his papers have been tampered with and rearranged. She uses me for firelights. If I was up early enough I'd catch her at it, but I can't rise of a morning. The thing squats on me, lads, and won't let me out of the bed. Sits on my chest, grinning down, whispering its loathsome theme to me. And while it won't let me go, little by little, day by day, my pile of papers is depleted. But I've taken precautions. I've hidden it away. And just in case he's waiting for me out there, I carry this...'

From the sleeve of his jacket he shuffled out a barbaric looking dagger, a great, crooked carving knife which he set on the table before them, his eyes fixed upon the blade.

'I'll not go easy with you...' he whispered. He glanced back over his shoulder, pale lips spittle-frothed. 'You damned fiend, I'll take a chunk of you with me yet...'

MacCraw was alarmed upon the sight of such a weapon and scuttled it out of sight beneath the table, fearing the landlord would spy it and evict them from the premises.

'You see, lads, I'm at the end of my tether with it all. He'll have me down soon and no mistake. I'm not long for this world. Sure, I may look healthy enough, after a drink or two, but mark my word, I'm dead before the month's out. So, I've sneaked a parcel or two away from her scratchings, and it's these I'll be giving on to you. One of you, tonight, or tomorrow, you must call up to the house. You must promise. Swear it now, on this hand. I'll be looking out for you, MacCraw. I rarely sleep. You must come - some security, for my name at least. Promise me now, lads, on the old oath of the Rhymers. You'll come to me and take away my packages.'

They would have promised, but Branwell was in full rant, attracting attention from all corners of the tavern, and neither of them could butt in a word.

'Just a few scraps of manuscripts and rags of old journals that I don't want her to set her hand upon. She'll do away with me, breath by breath, word by word. She'll scratch me out by the inkblot. Come Rhymers, swear to me. You both know that all I ever lived for was the word.'

In this shrill hysteria oaths were sworn, vows made, more drinks called for. MacCraw sensed that he was now part of some awful scheme - a preventative pawn in the merciless ruination of his old friend. Darkness seemed all about them - hooded, fiendish spectres seemed to be lurking in every shadowed corner of the inn. But once they'd vowed allegiance and assistance to him, the mood lightened. Branwell visibly cheered. Stories and tales of the fates of the Rhymers over the last years unfolded around the table, the talk moving comfortably away from Branwell's own plight.

'We came upon an old companion of yours this afternoon ourselves,' MacCraw informed Branwell. He seemed uncomfortable and suspicious with the news.

'Who would that be, George? What did he say of me? What did he want?'

'No, no - he said nothing. He wanted nothing of you. We didn't let on that we were coming here, and he didn't seem to recognise us.'

'The little fellow,' put in Grundy. 'You remember at The Cross Roads Inn, the readings we'd have there. And that midget - the swanky little London fellow.'

'Ah - you mean the real midget, not just little like a fairy.'

'Aye, the real dwarf. He used to tell tales of when he was a thief in his childhood.'

'I know him,' Branwell confirmed, though he looked decidedly uneasy with the information. ' Barry. Big Barry. Barry Robb.'

'That's him,' MacCraw said with a click of his fingers, remembering the name now. 'He was serving on at an inn we called at in Keighley.'

'No no, he wasn't just serving on,' said Branwell, as if aghast with their error.

'He owns that place. Lock, stock, barrel and spiders. He's more wealth than you'd think, and he's ruthless enough about his money, as I well know. I owe money here, and there, and everywhere, as I'm sure you gentlemen know - but to Barry I owe nothing. I made sure he was the first paid off down to the farthing. He's a bit of a limb breaker, you see. He's been known to snap a man's arm in two over a shilling outstanding.'

'Well, he seemed pleasant enough,' said Grundy.

'But he always made me feel uneasy,' MacCraw put in. 'There was an edge to him. A violence, I suppose.'

Branwell straightened up in his seat, drew in a sharp breath, then spoke in a voice that was not like his own.

'I was born in the parish of St. Giles in the Fields, in the year eighteen 'undred and eighteen. My father was a soldier in the British service, and my mother, like myself of short stature, was an entertainer - a singer and a dancer on the boards, and good at it too - right famous in some ways...'

Branwell had mimicked the London midget so accurately, with such perfect accent and baritone, that both MacCraw and Grundy had started and looked about, as if indeed the little fellow was in there with them, speaking, telling his tale again.

'That was astounding!' Grundy clapped as he spoke. 'I forgot you were the mimic. I suppose you do me as well. And MacCraw there.'

Branwell rattled out a couple more sentences of the dwarf's oft-told tale, switching between voices, doing Grundy, MacCraw and Big Barry in turn, seamlessly flowing between them, his memory of the story intact and precise, the whole room listening on in awe at the sudden entertainment their old companion was providing.

By ten o'clock all in there were warm-flushed and happily chatting despite the howl of the moor wind rattling the tavern windows. Following Branwell's cockney twanged impersonation of Big Barry, who all to a man knew on account of him being a ferocious and notorious publican, laughter now came easy upon the gathered company. Branwell, as in days gone by when Tucker used to summon him to entertain cultured travellers, was in full spout, bubbling snippeted tales and stories of his travels and adventures up and down the land, though in truth he'd rarely set foot beyond the boundaries of the county. His grimace, his mad-eyed death mask, had slipped away to reveal the vibrant charmer of old. MacCraw's own sadness about the eyes, etched there by the tribulations of his wilting wife, was also banished, and he shone with bright youth again. Grundy's harsh, self-imposed solemnity (for to him, life was all a very serious business) had ebbed away to reveal something of the rioter. In a haze of merriment at the pleasure of the reunion of kindred souls, the night meandered on cheerfully, the whole tavern company picking up on the spirit and joy of the occasion. MacCraw's last memory of the evening was of Branwell getting ready to leave. He was suddenly anxious again, with a hunted look in his eyes. He scrabbled about beneath the table, looking for the dagger he had brought in with him.

'Where've you put it George? Where is the thing? I daredn't leave without it. He's awaiting me out there, and no mistake.'

'What's that? Whose waiting for yer? Yer's not still fearing that imaginary fiend you conjured up?'

Branwell had located the fearsome blade and went tucking it into the waistband of his breeches.

'Fiend, yes. Imaginary, no. Well, lads, I'm off up the road, and let him come at me, the mood I'm in. Devil or not, I'll take him ear to ear. In the morning then, George. Out front of the church.'

Here he fixed MacCraw with his forlorn stare, and earlier oaths were glimmered upon by the hazy barber.

'I'll be up there as early as I can,' nodded MacCraw.

With that Branwell was away into the night, slamming the door of The Black Bull behind him for what turned out to be the very last time.

Despite not being able to recall getting himself to bed, MacCraw was up with the birds. He always awoke early in a strange bed, and anyway he'd suffered a night of fretful dreams crowded with hooded shapes and pale faces; dreams that troubled him in a niggling way, even though he could not recall the clear gist of them. He was fretful too about Caroline, feeling guilty with himself for having made such a night of it again while she lay at home alone, and sickly, in their bed. To rid himself of this brooding melancholy, he decided to take a turn about the village, knowing that it would be pleasantly deserted at that hour of the morning. Grundy lay in a blanketed hump in the bed close by, snoring away like a set of faulty bellows. MacCraw tiptoed about the room, collecting up his boots, coat and hat, dressing quietly so as not to disturb his companion. He left a message for Grundy with the kitchen girls who were cleaning the place and setting the fires going, then let himself out through the kitchen door. His breath clouded in the bright, crisp chill of a Haworth September morning. Yesterday's lid of cloud had been blown clear by the night's winds, the sky now blue and laced high up with faint feathery cloud, though the wind still raced north easterly, bearing a biting chill. The cold though was a small price for the prettiness of the morning. Sunlight had the world lit up and all beautiful again; it was enough to make a man glad to be alive. Down the steep and cobbled hill he strode, the stones gleaming green with moss, their attractiveness tarnished somewhat by the filthy side gutters which were choked with horse-dung and discarded waste from the workers' cottages. Some of the woolcombers had already set to labour, sulphurous wisps clouding up from behind the dwellings, poisoning the fresh breeze, the sounds of the bellows rattling like dry coughs from the basements of the houses. Momentarily - for the place and scenery were quite startling and refreshing to the town-dwelling eye - he wished that he was in the company of Caroline. She would have enjoyed the landscapes about. The stench here though, even so close to dawn, would have not been pleasant for his frail wife to endure. The air was tainted almost as bad as Bradford's, helped along no doubt by the festering middens he spied every few yards of the way, and the poisonous looking streams that foamed along with the course of the street. By the bottom of the hill the smell and dirt of the place had cleared a little. He beheld a stunning view over crimson and amber moorland, shaded dips here and there swirling with lilac mist. Like a good, handsome face shaved neat of dirty stubble, the grizzle and mist of yesterday had been scraped and cleared by the winds. MacCraw, inspired by the harsh beauty of his present setting, began to compose his own description as he strolled along - a description he promised himself, should he later that morning get the time, he would set fast in ink and perhaps share with the little gathering of Rhymers before they again parted on their ways.

'A golden morning of September - every breath from the hills so full of life,' he muttered, and was pleased with that, so continued. 'My darling Caroline's face, much like this landscape, shadow and sunshine flitting over it in rapid succession, but the shadows transient, melting away in loving sunshine...'

While thus poeticising, MacCraw worked his way around into the cleft of the valley, following a cart-track back up the hill that gave him good gazing over the landscape toward Keighley. With still an hour or so to whittle away before breakfast, he worked his way carefully back round, by various mire-filled ginnels to the narrow street that ran along the front of the church, and so up to the grim looking parsonage where the Brontë family dwelt. Smoke was already curling up from the house chimneys. MacCraw looked over the expanse of graveyard that stretched between the church and the house. Toward the far end of the yard two squat figures were shoveling out a grave, both dressed in blue hessian smocks, faces shadowed by wide black caps. Their deep cutting shovel strokes thudded a rhythm into the morning. Rooks were cawing in a screen of trees beyond the grave-diggers, a few of the more adventurous scavengers dipping and hopping along the trench edge, stabbing at unearthed worms in the heap of earth there. The men and crows ignored MacCraw completely as he approached the house. Though the curtains there were still drawn against the day he had no doubt that the servants would be up and busy in the kitchen. The sisters would most likely be scurrying around also, for in the good days, when he had visited and stayed there with Branwell, they were always industrious early risers. Years ago, without a second thought, he would have gone to the front door and knocked loudly there, confident of a cheerful, fussy welcome whatever the hour of day. But those times of light and laughter seemed to have slipped away from the grasp of that intense little family. In days of old, despite a heavy night of it, Branwell would have been up with the sun, his pen scratching over a page - refreshed with his own vibrant energy, bursting and brimming with ideas. Now, he'd most likely be in bed still, head heavy and dulled after his imbibing of the previous night. As MacCraw stood contemplating upon the dreary visage of the house front, a great black shape came slipping out between the gateposts. MacCraw's hairs bristled on his neck, thinking that the devil himself was sliding out to greet him. The shape rolled forward, snarling. A huge dog, black and shaggy haired, foaming at the fangs, came hurtling at him in a fury of barking. He did not wait to greet it with a chummy pat on the head, but in the instant swivelled on his heels and was away, striding over the stone flags, desperate not to make too close an acquaintance with those vicious looking teeth. He was down past the church and at the top of the main street when the harsh panting and foot-clacks of the thing closed upon him. At last, deciding that he could not out-run such a creature, he spun back round, walking cane raised, prepared to deal with the mad-hound in whatever way he must. He began to strike down with the stick, but checked himself just in time, the cane whistling past the pursuer's head. It was no black dog that confronted him, but Branwell.

'George! Stop man! Are you mad!?'

Branwell cowered there, wild eyed, in a terror from the nearness of the skull-breaking blow. His hair was upright and askew, and he was not yet dressed, standing there in the open street in his white nightgown and house slippers.

'It's you!'

'It is. Of course it is. Sorry about the dog there. Emily's pet... some stray she's taken in from the moor. He was just giving you a greeting.'

'A greeting! It would have had my throat out. I thought it was Lucifer coming to get me.'

'No, sir. The brute's as harmless as a baby. It's inside now. But thanks for coming, friend. I spied you from the window there. I've been up waiting the whole night.'

Branwell's nightgown touched down about his bare ankles. His pale, bloodless face with great black circles beneath the eyes; the hollowed, fleshless cheeks; the trembling, thin lips: all created the impression in MacCraw that this was but some fiendish, conjured spectre of his old friend that now hovered before him. Both stood a moment, breath rasping in nostrils, air steaming into the cold air. At his chest Branwell clutched a heavy looking parcel, wrapped in brown paper and tied up with white string. This parcel he thrust out to MacCraw.

'Here, George. The papers we talked of last night. I wrapped them up. Quick, take them, before she sees.'

The parcel was fumbled over into MacCraw's possession, and he tucked the heavy lump of it under his stick-bearing arm. Branwell folded his arms back about himself, shivering, eyes darting glances this way and that, then looking behind himself, back toward the parsonage. He turned to MacCraw, seeming humbled.

'My... my apologies. For last night,' he stuttered. 'Just a little queer turn. I get them frequently now. My health's broken. My spirit too. Anyway, I'm sorry if I've been an embarrassment. Say so to Grundy too. I'm so sorry.'

'But sir, you've no need to apologise on my behalf. You know me better than that. You were fine last night, so you were. I was probably much worse. I can't for the life of me remember getting up to bed.'

'Nonsense, man. I lost it somewhere along the line, and you know it. My nerves are gone. But anyway, quick now, away with you and my little parcel, before it sees the flame. I'm starving cold. I need to get back in before I perish now.'

The two shook hands there, Branwell's clammy and feeble in MacCraw's vigorous grip. Branwell winced and gave his hand a loosening shake when it was released.

'Mind my hand,' he moaned, flapping it about as though in great pain. He held the hand out toward MacCraw's face. White, trembling and effeminate, there were blue-black blotches spread over the back of it and along the wrist, bruises as round as sixpences spaced there, as though strong fingers had been gripping into the tissue.

'The devil takes a hold of it every time I fall asleep George, which is why I don't do much of that anymore. Pulls me toward him. Grips on tight and pulls me toward him.'

MacCraw, not really knowing how to respond to this, simply nodded and tucked the parcel tight under his arm.
'I'll look after this for you. You call down to Bradford for it whenever you want it back. You know where I am.'

Branwell's flickered a brief, sunny smile, his eyes brightening.

'I do know where you are, George, that much is true.'

He was about to add something else but at the slamming of a door from back toward the parsonage he braced upright like a startled rabbit. He gave a quick circle of a wave then was off back along the path toward his home, shuffling from view around the corner of the stone church. Laden with the parcel of manuscripts, unnerved by the whole encounter, MacCraw headed down hill, back to The Bull, ready for a good breakfast and eager for the cart back down to Keighley.

Not long after - weeks rather than months - MacCraw was to reflect deeply upon how the Will attracts the Act in this odd, scrabbling life. Two days after taking the parcel from his friend in the shadow of the church and the news reached him that Branwell was dead. Naturally, and more so under the peculiar circumstances of the visit, this news was a great shock to MacCraw. He attended the funeral, where along with a few other Rhymers, he was requested by Charlotte to stand on the back fringes of mourners. She made it plain that this was on account of them being of the deceased's 'degenerate acquaintances', whose habits and ways, she declared, had led her brother toward his decline.

In true, steady, atheistic Rhymer form, Branwell had passed-on blaspheming on his feet, denying God, swearing and cursing at his gathered family there, refusing to lie down or go gently while he had the will to stand. The details of this fierce last stand MacCraw heard from a reliable Rhymer acquaintance in the 'other service', at The Bull, after the funeral. He was to read a greatly different account of that death-bed scene in the hired and paid for words of others in the years that followed, and it enraged him to see his friend's life daubed down so unfairly and inaccurately by the bitter pens of those who had never even met him in the flesh.

CHAPTER 7

Cold in the earth, and the deep snow piled above thee!
Far, far removed, cold in the dreary grave!
Have I forgot, my Only Love, to love thee,
Severed at last by Time's all-wearing wave?

Sweet Love of youth, forgive if I forget thee
While the World's tide is bearing me along:
Sterner desires and darker hopes beset me,
Hopes which obscure but cannot do thee wrong.

No other sun has lightened up my heaven;
No other Star has ever shone for me:
All my life's bliss from thy dear life was given -
All my life's bliss is in the grave with thee.

PBB
Bradford
1838

From The Journal of Caroline Waterhouse
Little Horton Green
April 17th 1838

A most amusing day. The good Mr. and Mrs. W. and I were privileged to be invited to dine with the Kirkbys of Fountain Street. Like Mr W, Mr K. is an ale and porter merchant, though teetotal and pledged himself, and they are a family of the most sincere and devout nature. Of course, I have in these pages past dined there before, and though nice enough people, such occasions rarely demand much of an entry. Despite the usual solemnity and formality of such occasions, it is enjoyable for me in a flippant, flippery sort of way, purely because I get the opportunity to meet up and exchange all kinds of 'news' (some would say gossip!) with Maggie, their niece. M. is a girl of my own age, and who is in a position very akin to my own, in that she too is orphaned though fortunately cared for by two honest, caring and sweet Christian souls, who in their kindness of heart have rescued her (us!) from a fate of poverty and a grubbing life in the streets. Surely, I would have grown up an urchin and worse, were it not for the love of my generous guardians. Well, Mags and I enjoy an hour together on these visits, usually while 'the elders' (as we slyly call them) play whist or talk business, church and policy. Sweet M. and I always bestow little presents upon each other in a sisterly sort of way - ribbons, buttons, ear-rings, pieces of lace and such like. Well today - now it's night and the candle is my light - she greeted me in the reception hallway of their cosy residence and by her bright sparkling of eye and flush of cheek I could see that some excitement or other was afoot. As we all there exchanged greetings and pleasantries and doffed bonnet, cloak and coat. Maggie took me by the elbow and guided me aside toward the foot of the staircase, where she was all whispers and eye glances.

'We have a visitor staying with us,' she confided, although it was no secret as it turned out. 'A young man!'

Ah ha, thought I. So this is what such flushes and eyes are about.

'Oh, you must meet him Caz. He's wonderful. Oh, you'll laugh...'

'Vixen, you are smitten,' quoth I, seeing plainly the arrow shaft protruding from her heart.

'No no - not that, I swear,' she protested, over vigorously, thought I. 'It's not, although...'

Here, her sweet eyes made mischief with suggestion, but then 'the elders' were amongst us and our chatter fell to talk of schooling, church and other appropriate, more serious matters. We were led through into the drawing room and there settled, discussing the latest news of the young princess queen and the coming coronation, while Maggie played gentle airs on their sweet little corner piano. Mister K gravely informed us that a young man would be joining us for dinner, he hoped, although the gentleman was presently on a shopping errand in the town. The young man was painted with such mystery and solemnity that I imagined some dark, sinister stranger with a roving eye, beaver-side burns and a dagger at his belt. The fellow was lodging with them, Mrs. K informed us, as though that itself was something unsavoury, though town lodgers these times seem common enough in all manner of high and low folk. It now seems quite the norm in many households we visit. Mister K. informed us that the gentleman came well recommended, and indeed was the son of a good pastor, the Reverend Brontë of Haworth way, whom Mr. and Mrs. W. had met and declared had heard, as well as seen, much good. No sooner had they finished uttering the good family name when there was a great clattering and banging of doors in the hallway, with shrieks and giggles from the Kirkby's servant girl, followed by yelpings of pretend terror. Eyebrows raised and cheeks coloured all around the room, then the young man just mentioned made his most dramatic entrance into the room where we were all civilly seated. The young Mister Brontë, Patrick Branwell by name, came tripping and stumbling in on the most skinny, tight trousered sticks of legs that I've yet witnessed on a man. His slender arms were full of precariously balanced parcels and packages, his own pale brow and carroty red fizz of hair peeking over the top of his burdening pile. These he proceeded to tip and spill over the floor between us, all the while prancing about in excitement on the tips of his shiny black boots. The fellow was all abristle with nervous energy. He could not keep still! He was excited, shrilling like an infant on Christmas morning, rubbing his hands gleefully together as he nodded greetings all round to the gathered company, oblivious to any sense of formality about the occasion.

'See what I've got... oh, see what I've got!' he pleaded all round, then slid on his knees along the polished floor to his spilled pile of parcels, casting himself amid them as he began a frenzy of paper tearing and box opening. His enthusiasm was infectious though, and we all gathered around to see what he was to set before us. I was astounded to see even Mrs. Kirkby laughing at this exuberant spectacle, her usual face being one sturdily set against displays of any trace of emotion. Amidst squeals of his excitement and the conversation between the Kirkbys and himself, it transpired that Mister Brontë is something of a fine, upcoming artist, currently trying to set his course in the world by the painting of portraits of the gentlefolk of our town. He has been permitted to set up lodgings and studio in the rafters of the Kirkby household, and had that very day been on a shopping venture about the many bookshops and artistic establishments of the town to furnish his new studio. Brushes, palates, powders, ink blocks, pens, pencils and bundles of charcoal came flying out of the flappings of brown paper, the floor of the room, tidy to the last mote of dust prior to his entrance, now a chaotic littering of string and packaging. In between his tearing at parcels he recalled his manners, frenzied handshakes went all round, with a gracious kiss on the glove and sunny business-drumming compliments for me (...such beauty... exquisite... I must capture you eternally in paint etc. etc...). Then it was back to his child-play, passing around his new toys, bidding us all inspect them, explaining the use of each in turn. The whole atmosphere of the occasion was transformed and lightened by his vigorous presence - never have Maggie and I laughed so much, and so openly together, for he was all hilarious anecdotes, loud asides in mockery of 'the elders', open jests at the Kirkbys' expense and even mimicry, though such was his humour that none in the company was the least offended or put out, this being, it seems, his natural state and not some affectation or forced performance intended to flatter and woo his new crowd over.

I will add that in amidst his own packages was a little, carefully wrapped parcel for the flushing M., who was plainly most delighted and flattered with his attentions. As yet I would hesitate to say that she was 'in love', though for all I know that may well be the case, for who knows what passes beneath another's roof?

Although of a neat and well turned-out appearance, young Brontë's collar is somewhat high and of the old-fashioned style, his neckerchief huge and eccentric in its number of airy, silky folds. Overall he is of the diminutive though perfectly proportioned build that a suits a young woman perhaps more as a friend than as a master in love. He is about as tall as Mags and myself, which is to say quite short in fact for a man, and despite his vitality and blistering energy of presence he has a somewhat pale and overall unhealthy appearance - though I am told by Mr. W. that all the Brontë family look something like this, it being due to the hard-living in the mountainous moorland of these parts to the north and west of hereabouts. The picture of this location was set before us over dinner by Branwell himself. His conversation, stimulated perhaps by the dandelion and burdock drink for which he seemed to have a predilection, painted before us a wild, unwholesome place, full of brigands and ancient moorland beasts which, he assured us, still stalk the hills not ten miles from our bright little cradle of civilisation here.

So, young Mister Patrick Branwell Brontë. Not my own ideal for marriage stock and security, although my heart has warmed to him and I think, hope, I shall come to count him as a friend. Maggie is to sit for him in his new studio, as are both the Kirkbys in turn. Mister W. suggested that I too might be painted, in a bright and modern style, sometime in the coming months, and Mister Brontë was only too happy to agree, with more effusions of my skin tone and texture of cheek-hue Etc.

After a lively dinner, to the piano. To our surprise, after M. and I had duetted prettily a while, Mister Brontë himself took to the keys. His playing was truly wondrous - far superior to anything I could ever hope to be capable of producing. Without book or sheet to follow, he turned out airs of such graciousness, such melancholy tenderness, that I admit to the page I wept most freely, as did Maggie, Aunt A., with even Mrs. K. sniffling back a tear. A most refreshing and entertaining and moving evening then. Our cab had us back here home by nine, and I here to bed by ten, thus reflecting. I sit here with my candle ready to be blown, for the first time looking forward to dining with the Kirkbys again, and hopefully soon.

From Patrick Branwell Brontë's Journal
Fountain Street
Bradford
May 1838
Dear Maria,

Beloved sister, though the shadow of memory relating to you is never far from my feverish imagination, you were brought closer and almost, to me, in worldly flesh this very day, when one I met with shared not only the holy name you bore, but also a look of such beauty that would have surely been as yours, had you not earthly perished so young. A good, merry day it was. We (that being several companions and I along with our Charlotte, who has been over helping me copy our poetry for possible publication) went visiting a portrait of our new and very pretty Queen, Victoria. A world of new hope and prosperity, and of great Artistic achievement, surely awaits this nation with her ascension to the realm's throne. However, though certainly fine as the painting was, there was one there of the flesh whose beauty outshone the clumsy, restricting dimensions of a mere picture. This beauty, dear sister, I'll tell of later. Needless to say though, she only had real eyes for me and my shining face, and indeed I would have made a campaign upon her and plucked out her throbbing heart as mine to thus make her my own, had not my foolish. but beloved, companion declared to us all (the gathered Rhymers, that is) that he had fallen utterly and hopelessly in love with the maiden, thereby making it difficult for any other with a heart-felt interest to stake a claim. Poor fellow, his heart sprouts too close to his mouth. 'Tis that barber fellow I write of, the handsome one with black curls and a fine, woman-moving face. Being of a loyal, companionable nature, as well as a broad heart, I set aside my own designs upon the damsel to allow the barber a chance to express his feelings for her. Through the encounter with the fair maiden, which followed on our viewing of the aforementioned royal portrait, I set my irresistible gaze afloorward or averted sideways to the corners of the coffee house, thus further avoiding contact with the lovely's luminous gaze, though in truth she oft sought another heart-swooning clash of eyes with me. My barber fellow, now left with a chance to woo upon the lovely, was all bows, stutterings and perspiring brow, touching her gloved hand in a light finger-clasp as though it were some Angel's egg he was handling.

Following the encounter, in which Cupid must have let free a full quiver into the poor fellow's hapless heart, he had nothing but blabberings of unquenchable, undying devotion to the lovely, the whole evening afterwards; the impudent hair-chopper even swore that he would marry her, or die! (This, admittedly, after a fair bit of grog, though dear sister, my pledge remains close to my heart, and I'll be out of all this revelling soon). Ah, but here's the bitter rub for me, Maria. Upon seeking introductions with the damsel, her guardians, fellows of the Kirkbys with whom I here lodge and paint, (for she's an orphan of circumstances I'm not yet fully informed), endowed me with her name so that formal introductions might all round be made. I knew her already as a Caroline from a previous encounter here at the Kirkby's, but I knew not the heart-cutting middle name she bore. Caroline Maria Waterhouse. Woe fell upon me. Your own sweet name kerneled within her own. My blood froze and one of my fainting fits almost befell me. For a tortured flickering of a moment, dear sister, it was you who stood there in the full blooming promise of womanhood. It was you so radiant before me, unperished, having survived your bitter illness and blossomed on in some parallel life. Ah, Maria! In truth, it took me several good minutes to recover from this shock of the phantasy of seeing you standing there before me, full-grown from girlhood. Undoubtedly, I'll be seeking out further contact with this other 'Maria' - not for the seeking of love, you understand, but with her being an orphan under the care of elderly and strict-principled guardians, they provide good material and custom for my aforementioned venture into the field of portrait painting. Oh, but with her as my muse and material, I could create such a work!

Despite my own designs upon the heart of this maiden, you will no doubt be surprised to find that, upon sobbing entreaties and desperate begging, I have composed for my hapless barber friend the following accordingly sympathetic (Charlotte would say pathetic) poem. Before the night was out he forced promises from me, but not before acknowledging me the superior poet, that I would pen him a verse that might breach the heart of the maiden. This he'll copy out into his own clumsy, uncouth hand and thus send to her as his own heart's turn-out. This, I suppose, is well by me. He is a poet of a rough-hewn sort, but not able to sustain a romantic or cupid-verse. His is all raging against the machinery and industry and visible signs of poverty of this age, all material and politic. Luddite doggerel. Should he direct his pen to love verse no doubt he'd meander into railing against the cost of roses and the impoverished lives of those street vendors who are enforced to sell such flowers. His verse on love would dwell upon the enslaving symbolism of the enclosing matrimonial band of gold, and would turn upon anger rather than on joy. Thus I have penned this for the poor fellow:
Caroline, she with the startling eyes
>So clear and grey, such horizons
>Full of sunrise and morning promise,
>Of a future so blessed and golden.
>Kindness, generosity and warmth
>Shaped in the even features of her face,
>The promise of kindness and sweet caress
>In her subtle movement, her delicate grace.

Her tumbling curls - the darker shade of a promised night's depth
And deeply perfumed with a scattering of holy star-scent,
Her skin sky-clear, no cloud, no blemish on her face,
Lips possessed of the hue and softness of fresh bloomed roses.
Neck delicate as a blossomed flower's stem,
Your smile shining upon me was sunshine and golden...

Cupid has unleashed a bolt from his blind bow
And my heart is pierced by mine intended's arrow.'

That's all I have on it, so far, and what there is needs some fixing. I agree, it needs taming and recasting, but I feel it contains a kernel that can be shaped to soften and perhaps melt a young lady's heart. Now then, I must get back to work on it, for it's promised to MacCraw first thing in the morning. Doubtless, he'll have it re-penned and delivered by noon. Perhaps they'll be married by tea-time!

This is, Maria, to let you know that you are seldom far from the wondrous turmoil of my thoughts.

Goodnight, dear sister
Pat

From The Journal Of Caroline Waterhouse
Saturday May 1.th 1838

A splendid and moving afternoon in the town. We (my good guardians and I) ventured with numerous of others bent upon the same intention to visit the portrait by Parris of our new Queen, Victoria. This wonderful and lifelike painting is displayed on view to the public at Taylor's Bookseller, Stationer &c - viewable by lovers of all fine arts, or so Mister Taylor's splendid advertisement in the Observer read. In truth, there were many there much more in love with themselves and their own appearance than with the arts or our new Queen. All manner of the puffery-powdery local upperfolk were there in their finest dress and ridiculous bonnets, nosegays pressed close to their faces to blot out the stink and stench of the vulgar and lowly (or so they see it, my meaning here being the honest and hardworking merchant class of folk to which we too belong, but whom are well frowned down upon by these lacy puffballs) whom they were forced to mingle with in the chambers of the booksellers. Many more than were expected turned up to view the picture, it being on display here but briefly (until Tuesday, I believe) before continuing its duty around the patriotic north, thus giving as many as possible in these counties a glimpse of the splendor, grace and beauty of this much wondered after Victoria. With so many turning out and catching the frenzied, puffing, panting Mister Taylor and his scurrying assistants on the hop, as it were, the tail-end of the queue was forced to stand on the muddy rut of pavement alongside the establishment itself. The sight of the gathered glittering, powdered folk in turn provided great entertainment for the grubby mill and town's people, paupers, beggars, bun-traders, song-singers and all manner of queer life that the streets and rookeries of the town throw up. Much verbal bantering and exchange of humorous insults went on, or so we heard later from various sources. Constables were called out and posted along the street to ensure order, for there were rumours that a reformist gang of cut-throats was gathering to attack those of the class they openly despise - it was never far from anyone's mind, I think, that only a year or so ago there was violent rioting in these streets with many maimed and injured outside the Post Office. Fortunately for us, Mister W. knowing Taylor well enough through trade and being in the company of two 'worthy' ladies, we were spared that dangerous indignity of standing on the street amidst the common throng. We were ushered indoors, much to the grunts, clicks and tuttery of the unfortunates further down the line.

After being shown through into the outer shop, we queued with the others to enter the viewing chamber, and even in there we had to stand in line to await a closer view and inspection of the portrait. The viewing chamber, practically emptied of furniture save a scattering of chairs and benches for the ladies and elders to rest upon, was airy and spacious, though just large enough to comfortably hold the splendor of the painting. Corridors were roped off to allow free and fair movement of the queue. The portrait, in elaborately carved and hefty golden frame, somewhat over-ornate in my opinion, is indeed finely executed, as one would expect for the privilege of such a 'sitter', although here she stands sideways on, floating it seems in a heaven of clouds and sunrise, glancing out at us over her left shoulder, a lovely pink rose clasped lightly in her right hand. Indeed, She wavers there within the frame almost life-like, almost touchable in the apparent reality of the dimensions so captured upon the flat plain by the wondrous trickery of light, shade and colour applied by man. Victoria herself seems attractive, bud-faced, pretty even, though (is this treason?) I would hesitate to say 'beautiful'. There she stands - dignified, regal - our delightful, fresh-faced Queen (all of my own age! Imagine!), gracefully poised, a serene and gentle smile playing about her mouth, a kindly glance on her up-gazing subjects.

There in the viewing chamber a more human surprise awaited for us. Amidst the merchants, mill-owners, clergy and social small-fry of the town bobbed and bristled the lively figure of Brontë (Patrick Branwell), the painter who has had mention before in these pages. Well dressed and manicured, top-coat clean, hat poised not too rakish, he stood with a cluster of his fellows and associates. An agreeable looking group of the town's young men they formed, already before the portrait, heads craning upward so that the window and chandelier light had it seem as though they were gazing lovingly into the light of Heaven. All seemed grave and intense in adoration of their queen - though BB suffered from his usual inability to remain still in one position, tapping his feet, shuffling from side to side, raising his hand to mouth to shield the quips he made to his fellows. Two of those with BB cut fine figures, and were agreeably dressed, well turned out, if a little over-flamboyant with the big neckerchiefs and bright waistcoats, though that is the way of fashionable young bucks this year. All three, as they seemed to discuss the painting before them, were eyes up and down and over the queue - flicker-flashing eyes, as Maggie would say, no doubt looking for some paragon of virtue and beauty to compare to the divine example set there before them in the oils. When their eyes sought my face I held their gaze, determined not to be the nervous, quivering coy-mistress, for I believe that all women should stand up in their own right in this new age, even more so now that the nation has a young queen at the helm. None of Brontë's bunch dared to hold my eye for long, and both flushed, looking away, frightened to behold a bolder beholder. Of course, Branwell spied us out as his band were departing. He flitted over from his fellows to exchange greetings and stutter forth his unwavering appraisal of the painting. Then, after explaining what he would have done to make it even better, he was gone, bobbing to pauses at others he knew in the ever patient and patriotic line.

After our viewing of the aforementioned portrait Mr. W. treated us to drinking chocolate at Tim's Coffee House, which by those in the know is referred to as Radical Tim's, on Salem Street, an establishment of a somewhat blemished history that my wonderful guardians used to frequent together in their revolutionary, upstart days, when they (and somewhat to my astonishment when I consider them now) helped organise campaigns against the American slavery trade and the Corn Laws and the ill-effects of other certain Acts of Parliament upon the poor of this country. By all account Tim's back then was a thriving meeting den for all manner of revolutionaries, radicals, Luddites, drunkards, non-conformists beside others of more sociable, coffee-sipping intentions. Down the shabby, slippery stairs and into Radical Tim's we breezed, Mrs. W. boldly throwing open the door and leading the way, with no standing here upon formality or messy social etiquette. The place was of low ceilings, crowded and busy with serving boys running too and fro with their trays of steaming tea and chocolate, such newspapers and journals as requested by the clients rolled up under their arms and aprons. The air was acrid with steam, breath fumes, coal smoke and the fumes of tobacco pipes, an extremely unwholesome concoction of an atmosphere which I, with my heart-flutter and respiratory ailment, was loath to inhale. Indeed, I felt somewhat faint, but Mr. W. managed to procure us a table next to a street-window, and this small, dusty pane with some effort he managed to prise open, and with the wisp of breeze there I was just about able to withstand the place. We had not been there long when Brontë with the two afore mentioned friends came dancing between the tables across to us, leading along his somewhat wooden-stepped, reluctant fellows, along with an odd looking young woman. Introductions did the rounds. The woman, it turns out, was Brontë's own sister, Charlotte - a tiny, prim looking Miss, but with the most amazing, absorbing eyes of pale blue - certainly no beauty, but beyond her awkwardness, no dull Plain Jane either. His male companions were charming, polite, and pleasing to the eye. One, a huge, handsome fellow with big, warm hands, is said to be already, despite his youth, something of a famous sculptor, a Mister Leyland, of Halifax. The other claims to be a fully trained and expert beautician and apothecary, although really I found this difficult to believe, him being barely beyond the age of apprenticeship, being about twenty and two at my estimate. Branwell claimed that the fellow was also a great writer and journalist, soon to be published in various periodicals up and down the land, including ones local, and that we should look out for his name in print. The barber seemed uncomfortable with this, visibly squirming as Branwell babbled on, shrugging apologetically, as if to be a published writer was something to be ashamed of. The sculptor and our author were both what Maggy would term 'lookers', and of course they all directed many compliments and soft glances my way. All of us exchanged briefly our opinions on the subject and execution of the portrait, but the conversation did not last long. Aunt was overcome with a coughing bout, and I myself, though glad of company more of my own age, felt definitely faint and suffocated by the weight of my petticoats (horsehair is so hot and uncomfortable!) and by the general steaming, smoky atmosphere of the place. We thus quickly, but politely, took our leave. As we did do, with farewells and laughing glances, the eyes of the so-called beautician were burning upon me and (I felt) after me as we left. He is a tall, healthy complexioned, dark haired fellow with something of a mischievous shine to his eye that I confess here to the privacy of the page I found somewhat attractive. His tartan waistcoat, however, was really somewhat over garish, too gaudy, even accounting for what passes as fashionable at the moment. This impudent starer is young, as I say, and no doubt still finding his feet in the world of commerce - somewhat below the aspirations my good Uncle and Aunt have for me, and indeed my own, so I'll waste no more space or thought upon him.

And so, from Radical Tim's, a cab home, where now, after resting, Aunt and I feel much better and recovered. The drinking chocolate was delicious, as I recall, although I do not fully remember drinking my cup completely down, other stimuli and sensations of the busy rebel-den having distracted me somewhat. As a matter of fact, few ladies of modern tastes would care to sip chocolate before men, for fear that unbeknown to them they have acquired above their upper lip a smudge of brown moustache, and when they think they are holding forth with wit, charm and intelligence, are really something of a comic figure and subject of future ridicule!

Now Aunt W's footfalls sound on the stairs from below. I am for bed. My lamp goes out.

REFLECTIONS UPON THE ART OF SHAVING
by George Maquire, the barber, of Bradford.
The Bradford Observer, Thursday June 6th 1838

As a writer who barbers, or a barber who writes, it had never occurred to me to combine the two skills and produce an essay on the ancient art by which I earn my day to day living and sustenance. I must thank my good friend, the scholar and librarian Mister Archie Smithies, for suggesting the idea to me, and to him I dedicate this piece, as well as offering him a free shave and haircut the next time he honours my establishment with his worthy presence.

The reader might be surprised to learn that until the present time barbering was a well respected craft and means of livelihood, closely intertwined from ancient times with the arts of medicine, perfumery and all the skills of the grinding, powdering and potion mixing of the apothecary. The care of the external appearance of a man, and the well being of all that is inside, have long been the concerns of the skilled barber, and I myself in my apprenticeship from boyhood in my own home town, and in my expert training in Paris by Suleyman Kemal, a barber of ancient Turkish origin, was taught in these arts as well of those of mere hair clipping, nostril singeing, cotton thread plucking and everyday stubble shaving. Of the most fascinating historical and medical side of my trade I'll say little here, for that is the subject of a separate essay that will follow the publication of this brief tract, at the discretion and indulgence of this good journal's editor. Surgery and dentistry are now, as the reader is hopefully aware, outside the legal remit of a practicing barber, thanks to the meddling of various guilds, associations, organisations and the snobbish pride of those who wield the saw and scalpel rather than the scissors and blade. Of course, those who cannot afford the doctor or the surgeon will seek medical assistance by other methods within their means - and better, reader, from a well trained old-school barber than a high street quack or passing crocus. On shaving then, I will limit myself here on this occasion, for indeed from the practice of that art alone a discerning barber can learn much about the history, origin, health and lifestyle of a fellow man.

There are, it may surprise the reader to know, many different schools and methods of shaving, let alone the multitudinous methods of those men who prefer to shave themselves in the home rather than entrust themselves to the expertise of their barber. The wise and venerable Doctor Samuel Johnson was not far from the mark when he quipped thus: 'Of a thousand shavers, two do not shave so much alike as to be distinguished. That is to say, there are as many ways to shave as there are barbers, and indeed men. But while there are always particulars, there are recognised general superior methods to any form of handiwork, and thus it is with shaving.

My own method of cleaning up the stubble from a face might well be described as the

'Turkish School' thanks to the teaching of my aforementioned Parisian master. It is worth noting that a barber in the countries of the Mussulman, and particularly in Turkey, is still highly respected in the community, as well esteemed an established and trusted doctor is in this nation now. The Turkish method is sometimes called 'the slow method' - a derisory term created by those modern 'cropper' barbers whose sole aim is to get as many customers in and out of the chair as possible, and thus increase their own takings. Such barbers, the modern, quick-shave school who have no grounding or interest in the traditional arts, say to their customers things like: 'Oh, you don't want to go to old so and so - he messes about with the slow shave method. He'll charge you double the price for taking twice the time for exactly the same end product. Does a man in today's world have the time to spend forty five minutes over the lathering and shaving of his face!?' But reader, let me say, for one thing it is not the same end product, and in the long term the Turkish method will benefit the skin and face and well being of a man, be he pauper or Lord, so much so that he will noticeably age and wrinkle at a much slower rate than his fellows who go for the quick and instant ways in this modern and progressing life. It is my view that at least twice or thrice a week, means permitting, a man should seek out a shave from a good practitioner of the Turkish method.

The matter of shaving a face is not, in fact, a simple one, and there are many stages in the ritual that are distinctly separate but of equal importance. Preparing the face and man for the shave is really as important as administering the blade to the stubble. A client should be relaxed in the chair, the muscles of his face loose and manipulable rather than tense out or clenched in fear. The superior barber will ensure that his client feels comfortable in his surroundings and with his company, for of course two men in close proximity for the fifteen minutes or so it takes for the best shave have a bond and a relationship forged by mere physical juxtapositioning. The client must trust and respect his barber, for this is a man who will be pressing a deadly sharp piece of metal against his very throat! The barber thus must always endeavour to put his customer at ease, either through chatting amiably to him while at work on the customer beforehand or while lathering up the skin and whiskers. The superior barber is, of course, the one who knows something about everything, but professes to be an expert in nothing, and will always defer to his customer's superior, better informed and more intelligent judgements and opinions, be the subject weather, the growing of onions, or the possibility and likelihood of life upon other planets and other stars!

Eye contact between barber and client must be friendly, open, discreet, or if the customer prefers, not at all. Many a man, especially a stranger to a particular chair, is uncomfortable when holding his barber's eye. The expert barber will know exactly how long to hold a gaze, if at all, or where to put his eyes so that it seems he is busy looking at the area of his immediate work, and any meeting of eyes is completely accidental and incidental.

A good, clean, well maintained and well sharpened razor is of course essential for the best of shaves, though surprisingly this is not as important as the preparation of the customer and the lather. In some cultures flint is used effectively to shave the beard, as are shells, pieces of coral and the teeth of fish. Many modern, occidental customers would naturally shrink in terror if their barber set at them with teeth or stones, and the sharp open razor is as an effective and painless tool as any for reaping up the stubble from a face.

The next stage of preparation in the 'slow method' is to soften the beard (by beard meaning here any length of hair from an hour's new sprung stubble to a full bushy crop) with hot water, rubbed gently upon the face or applied through the hot, steamed towel. In some countries where the climate is adverse to the application of heat this softening of the beard is simply achieved through the application of certain oils and lotions, and this method I have employed to considerable success myself. In the far east, where facial hair and bodily hair in general is substantially more sparsely spread upon a man than here in the European climes, oils instead of lather are solely employed to soften and lubricate the beard upon the infrequent shave required by the men there. Perhaps with more experimentation into the value of certain perfumed and luxuriant ointments by innovative barbers, if such remain in this day of the quick-shave, oils for softening, shaving and the conditioning of the face afterwards might one day replace the use of lather and skin tonic altogether. In the meantime, the brushing and working in of the lather is a vital phase in the preparation of the face for the razor. A fine quality, soft brush should be used, and any barber worth his soap knows that badger hair brushes are by far the most superior, though these he may retain for use only on his best or favourite customers. The use of the badger hair brush is not simply because the appearance of such a brush is graceful and in fact beautiful, but also because badger hair has certain beneficial properties. This type of brush retains water, which is good for the lathering, and it is very soft upon the skin, yet remains tough and durable. A well made badger brush should last for many years if properly washed, hung and maintained after usage. Brush care and cleaning is a task delegated to the shop-lad or apprentice, upon with the sweeping of hair and brushing down of surfaces, but a good barber will always ensure that he looks after his own best badger brushes. Even within the best brushes there are grades of superiority, Silvertip being the most superior and sought after brush by a decent barber, and here I boast that I own three of these at the present time. With circular motions of the brush a good shaving soap should be worked up to a thick lather. This lather should be worked and rubbed into the beard, initially with the brush and then with the fingertips, and should in the final stages of lathering be worked against the grain of the beard and hair growth, for just like timber the face of a man has a grain to it, and this may well differ from man to man.

The shave itself should always be with the grain, or lie of the beard, and with a clean, sharp, well maintained razor. Those who shave against the grain of a beard will induce rashes, razor burn and ingrowing facial hair in their client, which can result in blistering, swelling, reddening of the skin, and potentially fatal infection. The modern hasty school pays little respect to the lie of the beard, for it is often quicker to attain a superficially smooth finish by quickly shaving against the grain - but in the long term this a folly that will result in a general blotchy appearance to the face, if not the worse aforementioned.

A good barber will shave over the main areas of the face with a steady hand and close concentration, perhaps plucking or pinching at the face to set the grain distinct from the skin, thus to more easily and effectively smooth off the offensive matter, that being hair. If confronted with a difficult, coarser beard he will shave over the most difficult areas twice or thrice to ensure uniform smoothness. This is more often necessary with men of Celtic, Iberian, Latin or Turkish origin - it seems that the men from these geographical areas are somewhat hairier and of a coarser beard than their other European counterparts. I would deduce that there is a climatic origin of this peculiarity, set long in the distant past, when hirsuteness was a natural protection against the harsheties of climate - although geographically this is somewhat contradictory, the tribes from the warmer regions of the globe seeming to be of a hairier nature than those of more severe climates within the temperate zones. No doubt there is a scientific explanation for this, and readers will perhaps inform me of this via correspondence to this publication. Generally, those of a more northern origin (English Saxons, Angles, those of old Viking, Scandinavian or Germanic stock) tend to be less hirsute than those aforementioned, and thereby more quickly and easily shaved to a satisfactory smoothness. An interesting, though some might consider vulgar, aside to this is the difference of the facial hair between the sexes. Of course all know that the fairer, more gentle sex do not have to suffer the stubble or the razor - but reader, this is a misconception. For of course, there are certain ladies who suffer the malady of manly facial hair - though the more cunning of these turn this to their advantage. We have all seen or heard of a 'bearded lady' at a fairground or travelling show, and I can confirm here that the majority of these 'attractions' are genuine. In my Parisian days I had the honour of attending and trimming the beard of a famous displaying lady - a mademoiselle barely in her twenties but with a splendid black moustache and beard that was of twelve inches and over. She was, this feature aside, a most elegant and beautiful woman, her charms and company much sought after by the aristocracy of that great city. She was in Paris exhibiting her unique charms, as she did so all over Europe and the eastern Americas, thereby earning herself a considerable fortune. She travelled under the French name of Mademoiselle Deveree, but was in fact American born, from Kentucky, I believe. On three separate occasions she graced my master Suleyman's emporium, calling in for her hair, hands and skin treating. On one of these occasions, to my upmost delight, Suleyman delegated the honour of grooming and trimming her beard to me. Mademoiselle's eyes danced with such merriment, her talk was hilarity, her scent was intoxicating - I confess it here, even in the heat of my youth I could not be repelled by her blatant masculine feature, and like half of Paris fell utterly under the spell and in love with this belle. I believe that she lives and displays still, and is in fact now a millionaire! But I digress, and aware of my editor, return to the subject in hand, namely, the razor.

After the actual shave the client's face is rinsed with cool water to remove soap and scraps of hair. Cold water is best used over warm as it closes up the pores on the skin, tightening the face, thereby again reducing the risk of rashes and soreness. The rinsed face is patted dry - never rubbed - with clean towels. Again, the after-work will vary greatly between barbers. In the Turkish or other 'slow' methods an astringent, usually citrus and alcohol based though witchhazel can be used, is applied with light dabs and gentle pats to cleanse and close up further the pores of the face, again reducing risk of skin rash. A light facial cream is then worked into the skin to replenish lost oils. Previously, I indicated that the relationship between a barber and his customer is an intimate, trusting one forced by proximity and touch, and should the superior barber have sensed during the shave that his client is tense, anxious or perhaps overworked during the shave, he will use the method of applying the facial cream taught by his own master, which is to say he will in effect massage the face of the client, manipulating certain muscles, blood vessels and nerves which causes the recipient to relax, to feel calmed and refreshed. With those customers he is aware will benefit from or appreciate further massage, there is a technique of manipulating the scalp and head, and finally the neck, which can be employed to induce a state of complete relaxation, so that the client leaves the chair not just cleansed and visually improved, but also visibly relaxed, invigorated and in a cheerful, positive frame of mind. As the Arabs are fond of saying, a man should step away from the barber's chair with a face glowing as brightly as a cheerful moon!

Reader, I am aware that I have gone on at great length about this facet of the barber's art, but in truth I have barely touched the surface of the topic - in a manner, I have merely prepared the soap and razor, with the shave and haircut yet to come! If the editor will indulge me, in the next issue I will inform you further of the ancient history of barberhood, back to Roman, Greek and Egyptian times, as well as presenting you with valuable advice on how to ensure and maintain healthy hair; how to prevent premature hair loss, and ultimately how to encourage growth on age-smoothed pates long thought to be barren and smooth. Aye, reader of the thinning crop, be heartened - there is an effective cure for baldness in the male, and this I promise to impart in a future installment in this series of articles. Until then, you may now leave the chair - adieu.

CHAPTER 8

To enrich the colour, enliven and stimulate growth of dark hair and as a protection and reversal of the thinning crown, extract the juice of red beet by cutting, boiling and reducing (1 gallon); a good handful of dried willow bark collected by the appropriate moon; the same of common spring nettle root and a gill of rosemary oil extracted from the leaf. Add all together. Stir until all is diffused and balances. Store in pots away from light. Apply the potion direct to the hair, leave for one hour, then rinse. Repeat twice or thrice each week. A flourishing, healthy head of lustrous dark hair will be your reward.

George Maquire
'On Hair, Its Qualities, and Good Maintenance'
Bradford Observer, 1840

Bradford, 1851

It was on a smoggy summer's morning - June 11th, 1851 to be precise - that the most heart-wrenching event in MacCraw's life had occurred. As he considered the tangling of the past, it seemed now that it was not just through pure chance that his wife's death been in connection with the handling of Branwell's manuscript. Even back then, in fifty one, MacCraw had realised that something was amiss with the publication of Branwell's cursed novel and the publicity surrounding it. Out under a false name anyway, on his initial reading of it, MacCraw had simply presumed that Branwell had invented yet another identity-masking nom de plume, as he often tended to do with work that was of a quality of which he was uncertain. Much had been written about the sudden emergence of the three Bells, the outrageous and provocative writers that were thought to reside somewhere in the barbarian north of the nation. Of the mysterious writer Ellis Bell and his novel, 'Wuthering Heights', most of the critics thought badly and were highly critical of the author for his vulgarity and uncouthness. One or two more discerning and deeper-living commentators had suggested that the work's raw uniqueness bore the mark of true genius. Then in the revised edition of 1850 Currer Bell, who MacCraw knew from past conversations with Branwell about the nature of his sister's writings to be Charlotte, had revealed that the actual author was a shy, demure, needle-working female. Critical uproar, and thus commercial success, had followed. Critics, reviewers and readers alike were astounded that the hand and mind behind such a black-spirited text was that of a shy, petite and reclusive female. In the more conservative sections of the press even more was being made of the foulness of the book.

The rumour went that the Bells, sisters now it seemed, were from the West Riding; their identity became a great topic of talk amongst the literary froth of the coffee houses and barbers' salons. Of course, some of these gossipers were former Rhymers, and it was soon generally acknowledged within Bradford and Halifax that Branwell was the actual author and not one of his sisters. Much of the talk was of 'the cursed family', and 'the cursed text', particularly as three quarters of the siblings had been wiped out within a year of the book's materialisation in printed form. MacCraw, even back then, had been appalled at the manipulation of the family's tale by the one surviving sibling of the tragic clan. In the shop, when the topic inevitably came up, he took to calling her 'that mean-mouthed Charlotte thing'.

He witnessed through literary magazines, reviews and novel previews, not to mention much later her outlandish, Branwell blackening biography, a careful erosion and editing of the historical past of the whole family along with their creative works. This blatant manipulation of the texts and the folklore of the family, particularly where Branwell was concerned, infuriated MacCraw. Even back in the early fifties, MacCraw had found himself stirred by his sense of loyalty to an oath-sworn fellow, as well as provoked by a sense of the injustice and maliciousness of it all. Once a Rhymer, always a Rhymer, as the oath ran. Back then, as now again, he had set out upon the path of colouring events in their true light, albeit in a semi-hearted, lackadaisical sort of way, for he was busy with upheavals, rises and declines in the patterns of his own personal and business lives. Despite relative wealth and success upon paper and in property deeds, he had been close upon bankruptcy at the tragic time of Caroline's death. While buying up and attempting to manage, simultaneously, a number of hair salons and apothecary shops around the West Riding, as well as run a family house out of town in Heaton for Caroline and himself, MacCraw had somewhat over reached his immediate funds. The shops, including his own on

Millergate, took in a weekly surplus of cash, but costs and out-goings were forever rising. Industry and trade across the country was only just beginning to stutter a recovery upon the decline of the terrible forties, and it was not a good time for raising capital. Men of new wealth and landed gentry alike were finding times difficult, bills mounting, accounts going unpaid, supplies and equipment awaiting to be paid for. In the mayhem of trying to set up a comfortable home and start up their own family of miniature MacCraws, he had lost sight of any literary or poetic ambitions, though on occasion he did still scribble doggerel. Odd scraps of verse, letters on current issues and small pieces reflecting upon his trade he still submitted to the local weeklies, where from time to time he found them published under his various pen names.

Somehow, between a hectic schedule of meetings with financiers, running around his shops and attempting to spend time with Caroline in Heaton, he managed to pen letters to Messrs Smith and Elder, a certain Mister Williams, and the original publishers the book, Thomas Cautley Newby of Mortimer Street, Cavendish Square, London. These letters, all to London addresses, he sealed hastily in his central business office, which was in fact the old living quarters above his first Millergate shop. The place was something of a refuge, where he spent a lot of time on his books, accounts and the other necessary paper work involved in building a little business empire. The 'office', as he begrudgingly tagged his old home, was his one quiet retreat from the frantic pace of his business life. Often on an evening, after pushing ledgers and papers aside, MacCraw would snort back a dose of his own snuff, down a glass of good shop brandy, and smoke a well packed pipe, all the while doodling on letters and ideas for articles. After an hour or so of indulging in his old solitary ways he would, with some reluctance, lock up the office and shop. Stimulated, but not intoxicated, having no desire to upset Caroline with his petty debauchery, he would walk or take a cab back to the relative splendour of Heaton and their new house.

The new place, as he called it, was at the bottom end of a pretty, hill-hugging street called Fountain Lane. Nearby was a small, friendly tavern, appropriately called The Fountain, where MacCraw soon became a warmly welcomed regular. The curved terrace of stone houses was walled and gated off from the main Heaton road. Across that road, beyond the top of Fountain Lane, a natural spring had been fed through a high stone wall into a rectangular horse trough, forming a mossy green pond, which bubbled over the stone trough lip with pure, drinkable water. The resulting stream was cleverly channelled under the road where it opened to light again, curling and gurgling down along the fringe of the street's common garden. Their own house, which Caroline had called Fountain's End, was larger and more imposing than the rest on the street, forming a neat, three storied rectangular block at the end of the terrace. It had a fine porchway, pillared front and rear entrance, French windows downstairs, a modern slate roof, and was easily as big as some of the detached villas that glinted in their large gardens further down the hill. The street's common garden was well kept by the respectable residents of the terrace. Lawn verges were abundant with flowers throughout the seasons, and a cluster of vegetable patches flourished at the fertile stream end, with benches dotted here and there to make the most of the garden's pleasing valley view. Despite the pleasantness of the area, the loveliness of the house and the friendly respectability of his neighbours, humble-rooted MacCraw could not get used to the spacious rooms and grand furniture that Caroline had been provided with by her aunt and uncle. Nor could he get used to the two live-in girls who kept an attic and helped Caroline run the place. He could never bring himself to call them servants, though his wife had little trouble with the term. He and Caroline had certainly been happy there in the first years of their marriage, and it had only to be in keeping with his own business ambitions along with her desire to move out of the mire of the town that he had leased the 'big house'. He never felt truly comfortable nor private in the big, echoing place with the girls scuttling about, and hence it was back there, in his cosy, comforting office above the shop, in the privacy of pipe and brandy, that his initial campaign of enlightening the world to Branwell Brontë's true genius and achievement was set upon. Of the actual wording of that first letter to publishers and editors he could not recall a dot, and he had long since lost his copy. The gist of the thing though was that, unless his old friend was acknowledged at least part-author of the original story and accredited thus on the cover of any future editions, he would mount a sustained national campaign, using every means at his disposal, to reveal the true authorship of the work, including the release of a handwritten manuscript of the full work, dated and signed by Patrick Branwell Brontë, that he had in his very possession.

To MacCraw's great surprise, him being used to waiting months before any publisher or publication responded to his own manuscripts and articles, his angry Brontë missive brought about a rapid and personal response. The following week there was an urgent knock upon his office door. Within, he was busy number jostling, and juggling figures, attempting to create a set of accounts that would persuade a party of German wool merchants who had established mills and storehouses in the town to give some financial backing to his county-wide beauty venture. He regularly attended the home of one of the merchants, Mister Franz Delius, cutting the hair of the whole family, as well as advising Mr. and Mrs. Delius on skin and hair care in the damp and smoky environment of their new home town. Mrs. Delius in particular, being something of a herbalist herself, had been interested in his various skin tonics and hair remedies, and even more so when he outlined his plans for setting up a chain of shops to assist ladies and gentlemen of the more genteel classes in the maintenance of their looks and general health. Seeing that his wife was so fascinated, and prepared to buy anything from MacCraw at seemingly ludicrous prices for the tiny size of the pretty pots and jars, Mister Delius also took an interest, although admittedly more of a commercially inclined one. Like any good businessman of the age, he was always keen to venture into a new and potentially rewarding market. Accordingly, once the trimming and pampering of the family was complete, Mister Delius had set MacCraw down in the luxurious drawing room and, over brandy and cigars, probed further about the venture and his future intentions. Suitably impressed with what the barber had to say and sell, confident of his good character and integrity, Delius had invited him to a formal business meeting with himself and a small number of other potential financiers that very week. Figures, projections, potential returns and long term intentions were all called for at the meeting, and though not too familiar with such detailed plans and fine figure workings, MacCraw had set himself to it with vigour, willing to do anything to secure some desperately needed capital. The sharp rapping at his office door jolted him up from a five year projection of returns on the leases of various shop properties he had invested in, and he slammed the ledger closed, as though all in there was secret. He composed himself and leaned back in the chair.

'Come in,' he called, downing his pen and reaching for his snuff box. The door opened and in hurried one of the shop boys, apron covered with drying suds and scraps of hair.

'There's a fellow downstairs to see you, Mister MacCraw.'

'A fellow, hey. What kind of fellow?'

'Dunno sir, but he looks important. A London fellow by the voice on him. Well dressed like, with a big black hat, and right posh. He sent this up. Says you'll want to see him.'

The lad handed MacCraw a printed business card: Arnold Friend, Literary Agent and publisher of Manuscripts, Bloomsbury, London. On the back of the card, in a hasty hand, were penned just two words - Withering Hands. MacCraw started up in his chair, spluttered, coughed, stood up and paced the room. He straightened his collar, smoothed his hair, then handed the card back to the boy.

'Show the gentleman up lad, and smartish now. Then fetch up a pot of tea with the best cups. Warn him to mind the loose stairs. Come on. Get to it. And change that filthy apron, would you.'

He took up his account ledgers and heaved them to the floor beside his feet, shoving papers aside, creating business space amidst his clutter of desktop. Time passed, with MacCraw sitting and fiddling pens and papers, wanting to look appropriately busy for the agent. Footsteps came shuffling up the stairs. MacCraw braced himself for the meeting, but it was his shop lad who again popped through the door, a clean apron on now.

'Fella's gone, Mister MacCraw, but he left this for yer...'
He held out a folded sheet of paper which MacCraw snapped from his hand.

'Gone? But why didn't you show him up?'

'He wouldn't come up, sir. He seemed to be awfully anxious, and in a rush, like. He were scribbling this by t'time I got downstairs, and he were halfway down the street by the time I'd change my apron. He said to make sure you got it.'

MacCraw nodded, waving the lad away. When he heard the door below close he unfolded the note and settled back in his chair, struggling over the tiny loops and swirls of a hasty, impatient penning.

'*Dear Mister MacCraw*

Meet me sir, and forgive me for my rudeness here, but I am in great haste. Meet me in the public eye, this Friday, at 11am, in The Chapter Coffee House I saw earlier beside the railway station. There, if your claims of late to certain publishing houses be true, you may hear something to your worldly advantage. Bring utter proof of your claim - the whole thing, and by thing *you know of that to which I refer. If this is possible, and you accept my proposal, immediate gain will be yours and the name of your friend deceased will be at last publicly attached to that which it belongs and previously owned, if you bear with my drift. Be there sir, and I will approach you, recognising you by the secret glimpses that I have already taken of your person, and by the parcel, that you should wrap in local news-sheet and bind with red ribbon to make your identification most definite. I will be in blue with a yellow waistcoat, and I'll bear a yellow carnation at my lapel, as might you. Forgive me for being so evasive and oblique, but in truth this matter runs further and deeper than perhaps you think. I will have ears for your story, a means for bringing it to the broader world, and a retainer sum for the guaranteed security of the papers you loan to me for confirmation of their validity. Further terms and arrangements can be made upon our meeting. Come alone sir. And please, I urge you, to ensure privacy over this matter - for others are interested in the business we may transact - destroy this missive now by putting it to the flame,*

Yours in all sincerity
Mister A. Friend of London'

To MacCraw later, in the retrospective blend and blur of life's memorable events, the arrival of this one object into his life - this fortune changing and life-altering scribble of a letter - seemed so important that he could not imagine how he had allowed the meeting with 'A. Friend' to pass from his own hands and control to Caroline. The only motivation that he could imagine for allowing her to set off alone to The Chapter House with one of Branwell's manuscripts was money. A retainer, security, reward. Suddenly it had seemed that there was much needed hard currency to be coined from his knowledge and possessions. He could think of no other reason why his wife should have set off with the parcel instead of him. The offer of instant currency, in the hand, must have been desperately tempting - a small sum on offer perhaps, but one that could go to paying off some urgent and pressing debt, to a furnishers perhaps, or even the local grocers in Heaton. Only with this mammonistic slant back on events could he see a glimmer of sense in sending Caroline to the strange meeting alone. That meeting with 'A. Friend' coincided unfortunately with MacCraw's arranged meeting with Mister Delius and his party of potential German backers into the beauty venture. At the very time he was supposed to enter the Chapter Coffee House with Branwell's manuscript, he had to be sitting round a polished table in the panelled office of a worsted merchant out on Leeds Road, bargaining for long term financial backing for his business projects.

That evening, while dining with Caroline at Fountain's End, MacCraw had been fretting aloud about the dilemma of his two clashing appointments, pushing the vegetables about his plate, stabbing at boiled carrots, banging and clattering his cutlery. Caroline tolerated his bad table manners and listened attentively to his witterings with loving patience. Ever much more practical and sensible than her husband, she smiled at him calmly, those lovely eyes so gentle upon his. She had the obvious solution.

'Calm down, George, my love,' she cooed.

He did the exact opposite, pushing his chair back, rising abruptly, pacing the room between the dining table and the bay window which overlooked the garden and the vegetable allotments beyond. She patted the seat of his dining chair, urging him to sit back down beside her.

'Come on, my love, sit down, and listen here...'

She murmured like a soothing mother to a fretting child, and he found himself complying, taking her hand in his as he returned to his table seat.

'It's all really very simple, dear husband. You go on the essential appointment that requires your presence alone. Let's consider it. Can I - as your marital partner whose interests in life, future and all things are as your own - can I go up to Delius's there, trim and manicure clients while discussing your projected business enterprises and displaying your knowledge of all herbs beneficial and beautifying?'

'No no, my love. I doubt very much that you can do that entirely by yourself. To my good knowledge you've never set scissors to hair in your entire life. And though you might know where each of them is located, you cannot comment on the value of the rents and leases of the properties in which I've invested my capital.'

'That's right, dear love. Well then, consider this. Am I - as a capable and reasonably intelligent young woman of an age enough to be wise in the worldly ways - am I able to put on a smart set of brisk-business clothing; my navy dress and jacket say; take a parcel that is of some weight but not so much that a woman alone can't lift it, tuck it under her arm, and with the parcel take one of the shop lads along with me for company to meet with our Mister Friend in a public place to discuss the matter of the manuscript that is collected within that parcel? A parcel, may I say, the contents of which I know well enough of by now after your years of chattering on about it to hold forth and debate its value as well as authenticity. Am I able, with my command of the language and awareness of appropriate vocabulary and manner, to converse with the aforementioned Mister Friend and inform him that the package I have is but a portion of the whole? That you, my husband, are otherwise engaged on important business, but will meet him that very evening after he has had chance to peruse and consider the contents of the package? There's no doubt that he'll be wanting to see more if the contents of his note are to be gone by. Am I capable of that little job, or am I not, my dear?'

'Well yes, of course you are my love, but....'

'But nothing, George. There, the matter's settled. Now eat up, you silly naughty fellow, or you'll not even be up to the clipping of a hair tomorrow...'

So obvious and simple. All she had to do was wear the yellow carnation at her lapel, have the red ribboned package under her arm, while keeping out an eye in the coffee house for the similar blossom bearing jacket of Mister Friend. Any conversations and transactions between them would be in a public place. It would be brief, a simple rearrangement of the appointment with MacCraw himself, with perhaps a handing over of a mere sample of Branwell's original papers. MacCraw took in the details of his wife's plan. He hummed and he hawed, scraping potatoes and vegetables from one side of his plate to the other. Under the doubled circumstances he could not really find a fault with the plan.

'But are you sure you'll be up to the nervous strain of it, my dear? You know you've not been too well of late.'

'Now stop that, George. You know well that I'm over my little ailments now. In fact, I've never felt better. And there's nothing more that I would enjoy than to have a little wander about the town with a splendid little mystery and adventure thrown in. Why, already I feel quite the heroine. True, I'll only be but a messenger; a dainty delivery maid. But I'd rather be doing that of a morning than sitting here listening to the gossip of the cleaning girls and staring over roses and a trimmed lawn, lovely as they may be, dear husband...'

With her natural sweetness and apt words, Caroline had soon won over her troubled husband. Before coffee, all was arranged. He would go to attend upon his potential investors, while she, along with one of the shop boys, would rendezvous with the mysterious London agent.

The next morning, a lovely sunny one with a powder blue sky and rare greenness of the trees and shrubbery, Caroline climbed up beside George MacCraw in the little hired gig, settled herself into the leather seat, and rode regally with him along Heaton Road. They passed the farms and small mill that had just been bought up by a Mister Lister, who it was said was planning to build the biggest wool mill in the country, right there on their own doorstep. Passing the pretty reservoir that fed the mill, both agreed that they must move further out of town if this were the case, Caroline insisting that any children of theirs were not going to go through their infancy in a neighbourhood where the polluted air was not fit for humans to breathe.

MacCraw took the bumpier but shorter Whetley Hill route into town, passing the Beehive Tavern and The Old Star, along John Street by the already busy vegetable market, and so to the top of Ivegate. Caroline was all the way smiling to herself and out at the world beyond their little gig. The morning was beautiful, the air even down White Abbey tolerable, she had an errand of some interest ahead of her, her handsome and still blossoming man beside her, and she at last, or so she suspected, was with child. She had been hanging on to this news, wanting to be sure, to be certain of her instinct and timing of phases. But now as the gig rattled on toward the main shop she thought that the time had come to break

the tidings. She leaned upon her husband, pressing against him, her mouth angled close to his ear so that he'd be sure to hear her.

'The next time you bring me into town, it might be better for us all if you went the smoother way,' she said. 'A bumpy hill like that - heavens! George junior will be feeling seasick.'

MacCraw picked up on her meaning instantly. He glanced sideways, met her laughing eyes, questioned for confirmation with his eyebrows, had his query confirmed with a sweet nod and turn away of his beloved's face as though she were suddenly embarrassed, then he was whooping. He was whooping and bellowing there at the top of Millergate at eight o'clock in the morning, his heart near bursting with the joy and the pride of knowing that at last the beautiful, wonderful, gorgeous creature beside him was carrying the stirrings of their child.

'Shush George - please! Calmly, calmly. I don't want anybody knowing but us. For the time being. Shhh, look out! Watch the road, you daft thing, watch the road...'

He took good, slow and careful control of the gig, fearful of a sudden that his jubilance might scare the horses and lead to them bolting, the gig overturning.

'Woah there, wooah my beauty...'

They pulled up outside the shop, MacCraw leapt down to still and tether the horses, then led his wife to the safety of the street with delicacy and gentleness, his face aglow with such a summer's grin.

Within the shop the youngest apprentice, who then lodged in the basement, was already busy with the back fire going and pots of shaving water set on to boil. Caroline was determined to make herself useful. Ignoring her husbands protestations, she put on an apron, rolled up her sleeves, and with great energy she set about tidying up the downstairs shop-clutter toward something of her own liking.

'But you must rest, love. Sit in the best chair there, or there's the beds upstairs.'

'Now shush, and don't be so silly George,' she chided. 'I'm with child, not mortally ill. I feel stronger than an ox. I know what it is to be frail and not in health. I've had enough years of being treated as some sickly invalid. I feel ... well, brilliant. Now move aside. Get on with your own work and leave me to what I feel I have to do.'

He had nothing to match her determination, and so stealing a kiss, left her and the boy to the tidying. He ascended the stairs to his office, sought out ledgers and accounts books, and when he was sure he would not be disturbed, slipped the inner bolt on the door, protecting against inconvenient intrusion. He closed the blinds against spying eyes. He lit a lamp, placed it on the mantelpiece above the hearth, and by its light slid out the ash-filled grate, as though about to set to a spot of his own cleaning. He reached into the cold hearth and rummaged a moment amidst the ashes and cinders there, pulling a metal ring that clicked the action of a mechanism he had long ago installed. A portion of the covered hearthstone rose up, and this he lifted out, giving him access to the heat-proof strong box that had been set in a hollowed space below the hearth. From this most secret hiding place, of which even Caroline knew nothing, he took out various packages of papers, setting them there on the rug before the fireplace. He selected one package of about six inches in depth, sifted through and divided it about half way, where the whole thing began to duplicate itself. Branwell, as MacCraw had frequently witnessed in his friend's Fountain Street lodgings, had been uniquely ambidextrous, often when writing doing so with a pen in each hand, producing two of the same document at the same time. This he had done with the doubled version of *The Withering Hands* that had been presented to MacCraw in

Haworth. The top, right hand copy, MacCraw now set on his office table, then replaced all the other documents and papers into the secret strong box. The grate was replaced, cinders pushed and scattered back to conceal the hideaway, and then with dusty hands MacCraw set about wrapping the manuscript in an old copy of The Bradford Observer, binding the whole thing with a length of red ribbon that he had bought from a street tinker the day before. All done, hands dusted, shutters opened, lamps extinguished, room as it had been before, he went back down stairs with the precious package, ready to place it under Caroline's stewardship.

The shop-lad was sent on an early errand up to the John Street market, with instructions to buy a bunch of fully opened yellow carnations - white if they had no yellow, and pink rather than nothing at all. With the lad out of the way, MacCraw slowed his wife down in her cleanings. He hugged her, and petted her. He marvelled aloud at her beauty; at her strength; at his luck in ever winning her hand. With Caroline's permission he looked and felt for signs of her swelling, though she told him not to be so ridiculous, for there would be nothing yet showing at this earliest stage. Within this bout of loving pampering, he tossed in instructions and of what to do with the paper package entrusted to her. He warned her about taking risks with her precious health in the cram and heat of a railway station coffee shop. His fussing and fretting she tolerated with good, scolding humour. She swore not to let the precious parcel out of her sight, and promised that when she opened it before Mister Friend she'd be certain to only to present him with the top quarter portion. In haste and mounting panic he went over more instructions - what do if the Mister Friend did not turn up; what to do if he tried to trick her out of possession of the package. By now the shop was opened and early customers were dribbling in and taking seats. With a lad out buying carnations, MacCraw had to chip in with the business.

Time soon passed, stubbled chins floating beneath his steady hand. The first lad returned with a good bunch of yellow carnations, one bloom of which was pinned carefully at the lapel of Caroline's blue street jacket. She was most pleased with the effect, and the rest of the flowers she set in a glass vase on the shop's newspaper table. As the place filled up with men, Caroline retired upstairs with the parcel. She sat in the office armchair, looking out of the front window on the busying streets below. The view there was quite pretty, the street curving away down toward Sun Bridge Road, half sunlit, half shadow, people popping in and out of the shop doorways, busying on their ways to markets or to work. She would come more often, she decided. She would sit there with tea and toast and perhaps a newspaper. As she filled with the life within her she would watch the street down there run through its daily phases, and thus be secretly entertained. Watching the toings and froings of Millergate, it seemed that within a blink ten o'clock was upon her. A lad brought her up a cup of tea. She drank this quickly then descended to the shop. Down there she simply had to laugh at her husband, for he was in a real flustering panic. Indeed, she had not seen him in such a jittering state since their wedding day.

'Calm down my love, they can only say yes or no,' she tried soothing, referring of course to the Germans. MacCraw was not to be soothed. He rushed up for his bag of accounts and ledgers; he rushed back down and grabbed up his barbering bag and his best top-coat; in between places he went babbling more instructions at Caroline and the apprentices, kissing the hand and cheek of his beloved as he rushed by and back again. As he pulled on his hat and arranged himself in the shop mirror he commanded that at least one of the lads escort Caroline across town to the railway station at a quarter to eleven, while warning them to make sure the water was piping, but not so hot that the towels would scald the skin of their faces. The scissors and razors had to be sharpened, all aprons clean, and not to forget now Caroline, just give the fellow the top quarter, not the whole parcel. Lads, don't be sparse with the lather, but don't waste too much soap or hair oil either. And no nicking or chin cutting now, but there's the alum block in the front drawer if you do, and all of you keep an eye on the cabinet potions - there are always thieving hands about on a Friday. Then this, and don't forget that, and sure to God he'd be late and bankrupt unless they all framed themselves and looked sharp to the business...!!!

Here Caroline, with a charming smile and gentle clasping about the right elbow, escorted her fretting, arm waving husband to the shop door, opened it, and with him still babbling thrust him out into the street. She closed the door behind him and put on the bolt. He stood there astounded, gawping in through the glass, and she with a little wave and a brush of the fingers plainly indicated that he should shoo... go on ... away! He knew she was right of course, and that he was fretting too much. He picked up his bags, bowed to her superior judgement, and remounted the gig. With a flick of the wrist he was away down the hill toward Sun Bridge, a final wave back to Caroline who had pressed her face right up to the door so that her nose was snubbed cheekily upward against the panel of glass. He steered the horses to the left at the bottom of Millergate and thus down the hill, trotting them down through the town centre, passing the railway station and the very coffee house where Caroline was due to meet the London agent within the hour.

CHAPTER 9

To Caroline:
Sleep Angel,
Sleep for a thousand years
To awake fresh born into new dreams;
Spring's flowers scattered on the lawns
Shall be your epitaph.
George MacCraw 1851

Bradford, June 1851

After MaCraw's frantic departure that morning, circumstances seem to have conspired against Caroline. The shop, though always hectic toward the weekend, was unusually busy, with all apprentices hard at it, shaving and trimming and clipping, keeping the water and the lather going, sweeping and cleaning up around the feet of the awaiting customers amid the snippering frenzy. Dressed, bonneted, royal blue dress lapel button-holed with her yellow carnation and three more fixed upon her bonnet for good measure, Caroline regally descended from the offices and entered the frantic activity of the shop. Eyes swept over her. Approving glances were raised above news sheet and periodicals. The busy lads nodded and bowed quickly before getting back to scissors or lather. She paused in the doorway a moment, seeing who might be escorting her through town. In a glance she took in that they were all far too busy to break off, and it would have been most impractical of her to demand that one of them come off the job just to see her along on what might well be a fool's errand. Confident and self-possessed enough to engage with a stranger on a matter which she was well informed, she decided to leave the shop about its natural business. There could be no danger or mischief in the venture. She knew what to look out for - the yellow carnation at the blue lapel - and she felt no sense of threat or danger in meeting a well represented literary stranger in a busy and public place. Thus, with a quick word to the doddering Alfred, her husband's elderly assistant who was second at the helm, she told him that she'd be back within the hour, and not to worry any of the lads about stepping out with her this morning. He nodded along to his mistress, barely even looking as his scissors rattled and clattered about his customer's unruly locks. He was not willing to cross the boss's missus, and as she pointed out, the lads were all hard at it. With the red-ribboned parcel under her arm, feeling useful and important, Caroline whisked her way out of the shop door, her best low-heeled boots briskly stepping her away into the bright, busy chaos of the street.

If only Caroline had been of a more suspicious and alert nature, MacCraw was to rue and bemoan so often to himself over his sad, aching years. If only she had been less generous-hearted toward others. For her own good, she really was too considerate of the good in folk, and not mindful enough of their potential for bad. From shop door to mortuary slab, he had been over the scene hundreds and hundreds of painfully imagined times. The parcel was beneath her arm. She looked so lovely in the blue dress with its fashionable bodice, buttoned to the waist, the turned down collars edged with the narrow lace frill. What heads she must have turned, pretty face peeking from beneath her wide-brimmed bonnet, the full skirt two inches above the ground to save its hem from street-mire as well as show off her fashionable boots. She was full of the world, no eyes out for threat or danger, utterly taken with the bustle of the streets - such a refreshing contrast to the quiet and solitary pattern of her day at the Heaton house. Her eyes danced on the children scrabbling and playing there in the gutters. Her friendly gaze absorbed the busy, bellowing traders and the women in ragged shawls clutching fraying baskets, some out shopping, others pattering about their wares. Caroline's bright eyes darted everywhere. She was all the while mindful of the mire and orange peel in the streets, taking great care where she placed her dainty boots. But even this danger of slipping and tumbling she enjoyed, glad to be participating in the dangers of the modern street. With just a little more suspicion as to the true nature of folk, along with some attention to the darker shadows and shaded doorways of the street rather than the open brightness of the road ahead, and Caroline might have noticed the tall, well dressed gentleman and the tiny lady, loitering there in the doorway of Conway's grocers at the top of Millergate.   He was a tall, gangling figure, dressed in tightly fitting striped trousers and a black top-coat, the brim of his hat not wide enough to cover the tip of his beakish nose. Apparently in conversation with his tiny wife, but actually watching Caroline leave the shop, he looked all the world like a famished raven that had just seen a lamb struck dead in a winter pasture. And if he was a treacherous raven, the odd little woman at his side was a stout, female blackbird. Shabby looking in her ancient shawl and dowdy brown dress, she too was keen-eyed, taking in every detail and movement of the street, and particularly now that the target of their observations was abroad. Even if Caroline had been all eyes-out for shady, sinister folk she might well not have paid great attention to this couple lurking there in the doorway. At a glance over her shoulder she might have seen them peel away from their window-gazing, considered a moment their ill-matching sizes, before turning her eyes forward again to the task in hand. She would not have noticed them come scuttling up onto Ivegate, almost keeping apace with her, though a little distance back. They were linked arm in arm as if a married couple, her stretching up, him leaning down to make the awkward junction of elbows. Though seemingly together on their jaunt, they never spoke, both gazing groundward, averting their faces from any chance watcher's scrutiny. Their eyes were fixed on the black heels of the package-bearing woman in blue. The pretty lady with the navy dress and jacket that some remembered seeing, later, when the story was up and down every street of the town. The tastefully attired lady with the yellow flower - some said a carnation, some said a rose - fixed at her lapel. The blue-eyed lovely, hair coiled up and cascading out from beneath her fashionable, face-exposing bonnet, the visage displayed there beaming and radiant, as though its bearer was in full enjoyment of the moment and the lovely morning.

Half way down the hill the gentleman broke arms with his diddy companion, tipped his hat at her as though bidding her adieu, then went striding faster, passing ahead of Caroline. He kept ahead of her in the busy shopping crowd on Tyrrel Street, making sure that he had her in view to his left, though not so obviously as to draw her attention. The shabby blackbird scuttled along behind at her own pace so that she too kept within yards of Caroline. Like a pair of wolves with vulnerable prey in sight, the assassins were closing in, one to the front right, one to the left rear - a calculated pincering manoeuvre. All three reached the bottom of the hill. Here the cobbled, mud-rutted junction of the several town roads was too busy and ajostle with the frenzy of the nearby market for the movements of the stalking couple to cause a second glance, everybody watching out for themselves amidst the tumult. Barrows and carts hauled by snorting horses trundled both ways along Tyrrel and Market Street, wheels rattling over the stones, the shouts, curses and exclamations of the drivers warning those ahead and around to look out, be out of the way, watch their step. Caroline, perhaps preoccupied with the mysterious business ahead, paid these yells and 'hey ups!' scant attention, being accustomed to them as a routine part of any shopping day. She paused at the kerb there, instinctively aware that the vehicles posed danger, but not unduly concerned, having crossed the same street hundreds of times before without mishap or incident. She strode on along toward the Mechanics Institute, peering ahead now to Bridge Street with the station beyond, craning her neck as if expecting the flower at the lapel of her counterpart to be visible even from here. Over the main road she went, pace quickening, looking all about her at the traffic. The dumpy lady, now almost at Caroline's heels, crossed behind her, eyes fixed on the parcel, then on the constable who was fifty yards along the road to their right, wondering if she had time to snatch and run and make a get-away in these crowds.

That seemed unlikely, so she held back, her companion some way off to the right now, keeping the quarry in sight with sidelong glances through the crowd.

A one-legged fellow with a squeeze-box was singing on the corner of the Institute; an old sea-dog with a naval cap set on the pavement before him, bellowing out with a grin on his face, singing so cheerfully of fruitless rovings and lost love in distant ports. A small crowd had gathered to watch him. Caroline stopped a moment also, fingering in her small, beaded purse for a few pennies to drop into the salt's hat. As the crowd watched this street entertainment, great carts and bale wagons rattled by inches away from the kerb, whipped and steered perilously and haphazardly by their indifferent drivers.

The local news sheets of the weeks preceding and following Caroline's death, of which MacCraw had recourse to scan and ponder when he was able to concentrate on such trivia, contained a dozen or so tragic cases of runaway or speeding carts and delivery wagons where pedestrians had been trampled down and crushed on the streets of the surrounding towns. Certainly, it was not just a local issue, but so commonplace were these accidents now that even when death or mutilation was the outcome, they barely warranted an inch of news space. Complaints about the frequency of such accidents and near-tragedies featured heavily in the letters pages of the local journals, where several of the irate and articulate of the district commented on the pressing need for some kind of policy or restriction and controls on carts and drawn wagons on the streets of the ever growing towns. It was a topic among the townsfolk of all classes - that along with the problems of the Irish, and of the excess of orange peel that littered the town's streets and pavements.

Upon a topical note then, after dropping her coins in the singer's cap, Caroline's boots clacked her away onto Market Street. The whole place was a frenzy of carts, barrows, wagons, pedestrians swarming between these, dodging relentless wheels. Caroline scanned about for a crossing gap in that wide avenue. Suddenly she started moving forward. There was a cry from somewhere up the street, a single warning yell, then people went screeching alarm calls, leaping back from the kerb. A bolting draywagon, its ill-tethered horses startled while the men were unloading full barrels at the New Inn, came hurtling down the hill. Surely, Caroline had heard those alarm cries? What could she have been thinking about? How could she not have heard the thundering rattle of the cart? The dowdy blackbird, at the moment the alarm cries went up, stepped behind Caroline, pressing forward against her, blocking any retreat. There was nowhere for her to step other than forward. Although none would swear to it on oath, one or two later muttered that perhaps a hand had gone up; a pale, gloveless hand, shoving MacCraw's lady in the small of the back, pitching her forward further into the street. The heels of her boots skidded as she went struggling for a grip or change of direction in the mire, but she skittered on directly into the path of the bolting horses. Within seconds all was over. A shriek pierced up from Caroline as the kerb-side horse closed upon her and mowed her down. She fell sideways. She wheeled on the road. She was like rag doll girl tumbling amidst the cogs and pistons of mill machinery. MacCraw had read of them, the mill-girls who were caught up by their dress or hair in the belt of some clacking machine, dragged in and smashed around like a toy until the machine could be turned off and the broken, shattered body released. That's how it must have been, but quicker, he hoped. Much quicker than an awful, shilling-a-day murder in the brutal mills. There had been an awful screaming. Above the town-din came a sudden clattering of hoofs and the iron rimmed wheels of the wagon cracking hard over stones. Then more screams and shouts from those who saw her stumble forward and fall under; shouts of warning; shouts of alarm. The sunlight gently smoothing upon street cobbles. The clear baritone of the cheerful sailor. Orange peel and cabbage leaves littered over rutted, drying mud. A yellow carnation somehow strewn upon a flat, crimson veined beetroot leaf. Legs and scruffy shoes, polished boots, a child's filth-crusted bare feet, the buildings suddenly tumbling skyward and cartwheeling over and over - ground, feet, sky, ground, feet, sky...

A moment of hush and still calm seemed to blanket the street, as though time had frozen; life's flux had halted and recent events could be undone or reversed. All was possibly going to be well and good. Then movement again, the wagon careering crazily away, weaving from side to side with the weight of the barrels. Oncoming carts lurched sideways as their drivers tried to avoid a head-on collision with the runaway hazard. The singing had ceased, covered over now by the screaming and whimpering of shocked bystanders as they looked upon the mangled woman who lay bleeding in the road. She was face up to the sky, eyes open, bright red blood trickling from her nose. The huddle of crowd closed upon her, circling, some trying to offer assistance, some crouching alongside her, pushing a folded coat beneath her head, trying to stretch her out and bring her round, patting away the unsightly blood from nostrils and ears with handkerchiefs. Others set about driving the press of anxious folk and morbid spectators back to give the poor lady some air. But of air Caroline MacCraw had no more need. Her soul had flown. A man of medical knowledge upon the scene could see that she was already dead. He pronounced her thus there in the street, covering her lovely face from the world with his own jacket.

Caroline's death had been brutal, but sudden. Many accounts of the tragic incident MacCraw heard over the following year, often varied, but always particular about two details. The first, to his gradual and lasting relief - Caroline had been killed outright. The gentle doctor from the scene, John Simpson of Heaton, who spoke to MacCraw that afternoon, who treated him for shock and monitored his well being for months afterward, and who for a time became a good friend, always assured him that there had been little or no pain for Caroline in her last moments. There had not been enough time. She had been dead even before the cart was over her. There had been no hope of reviving her from the moment the nearest folk had rushed to her aid. There were no profound or perplexing last words - no suffering or last gargling of breath. The life had been shocked out of her outright. Bitter, painful comfort to MacCraw at the time, but he came to realise that the lingering, painful death of his beloved would have haunted and scarred him even deeper. Better to be ground out in the chaos of a flaming moment, he saw, than fade and linger, ceasing a sad, slow spark at a time. Blood had been spilled of course - he saw the wounds - the wheel rut across her chest and neck, the side-skewed nostrils. But a clean death. The last word to escape her lips, according to witnesses, was a simple exclamation of 'Oh!' as the horse was upon her.

'Oh!'

He could practically hear her utter it, the varying qualities of her voice, the warm huskiness or the shrill, anxious edge, depending on her mood. He heard it in his mind a dozen, different, final ways.

'Oh!'

Fitting and suitable, he thought - more meaningful to him than any great expiring speeches. What other statement could be more apt or suitable when quitting this ridiculous folly of life? What else could there be better to say?

The second detail MacCraw had gleaned about the death was that there had indeed been a little, birdish woman at the scene. From the various descriptions he had collected it seemed that she had been attired in an old fashioned bustle dress and a deep-brimmed bonnet. She had been the first at Caroline's side after the fatal collision, crouching there, and although not directly giving assistance herself, calling for others to come and give help to the poor victim. This mysterious angel of mercy had bustled and fretted by while others checked for breathing or a pulse at the neck. Strangely though, none could recall the glimpse of her face afterwards, hidden in the shadow of crumpled bonnet as it was. In the confusion of cries and whimpering, of calls for medical assistance and ambulance carts, of attempts at revival and calls for the crowd to step back to give the victim air, the queer looking woman herself had edged further amongst the fringes of the crowd. According to some, she had gathered up a stained and trampled package from beside Caroline, something like a parcel of newspapers that had been ground into the mud of the street. Nobody had actually seen her scuttle away in the confusion, fleeing with the parcel clutched in her thieving hands, but by the time the constables had control of the tragic scene and they were trying to discover the accident victim's identity, the parcel had gone.

MacCraw's later attempts to explain the missing manuscript, when reason and some stability had returned to his shattering of a life, were confused even to himself. Some opportunist, he concluded, had plucked the package up from the street - some tinker or beggar, seeing the chance of perhaps a few penny's worth of paper. Or perhaps a child, seeing it fluttering there amidst the chaos, had gathered it up, taking the pretty bundle home for its mother to use as fire-kindling. Some months later, however, when MacCraw again tried to contact 'Arnold Friend' via the publishers Smith and Elder; Mister Thomas Newby; Charlotte Brontë herself and all others connected with the publication of Branwell's book, they denied all knowledge of his previous correspondence. The publishers categorically denied that they had ever sent an agent or representative to discuss purchasing the alleged Brontë manuscript of which MacCraw wrote. Newby went further, stating through a solicitor that his own house was not interested in examining any evidence or entertaining any possible notion that any person other that Ellis Bell (or, if he preferred, now that the world at large would soon know, Miss Emily Brontë of Haworth) was responsible for writing all or any off the publication first published by Smith and Elder in 1847 as 'Wuthering Heights'. Indeed and furthermore, upon correspondence with the afore mentioned publisher, Smith and Elder, both parties had agreed that any further attempts by George MacCraw of Bradford to discredit and dishonour one of either house's writers, living or deceased, would be vigorously met with legal proceedings. George MacCraw of Bradford, or indeed any other slanderer, would be libeled immediately upon attempting to bring the afore mentioned highly respectable and respected houses and authors (living or deceased) into question or disrepute.

Though incensed by this turn of events, MacCraw was in the midst of grief and had lost all interest in that now insignificant thread of his life's tapestry. Branwell Brontë, the missing manuscript, and who wrote what, when, why and wherefore was boxed away in the basement of his grieving, traumatised mind.

Months later, when the dust and haze of death had settled enough for him to see any sense in life beyond the immediate necessity of existing day to day; when the Heaton house was sold on and he had encamped himself back in the rooms above his Millergate shop; when the funeral was a windswept memory and his life outside the rigors of work began to take on some shape and glimmer of meaning; only then did MacCraw begin to sense some darker, more sinister aspect upon the face of the accident which had snatched his wife and unborn child away. But he consciously baulked from viewing the incident as 'foul play' - his own imagination back then would not allow him that. He refused to pursue the notion that there might have been assassins lurking across from his own shop doorway, awaiting for the bearer of a parcel to emerge, the give-away red ribbon and yellow carnation pinned neatly to the navy lapel. Surely, he could not have been set up so simply; so precisely? No life was worth a sheath of senseless, rambling pages. It could not be so ridiculous; her life; their lives. They could not have been extinguished over something as absurd as a book? 'Murder' was a term that his mind refused to coin. Still, he had the sense even then to keep the one remaining copy of the manuscript stashed away, along with other scraps of journals, note books and letters that he had retained. All were kept hidden in the hearthstone strong-box, along with his own most secret goods and papers. The box was padlocked. The stone in place. The fire re-lit and kept burning or cinder-filled, never an empty, cold cleaned grate. Indeed, it was a long time before MacCraw had recourse or inclination to prise up the hearth and open that box again.

CHAPTER 10

Feverfew is far too bitter to eat raw, and is best lightly fried, or the youngest, freshest leaves sprinkled sparsely in a salad. Particularly beneficial for those who suffer migraine and severe bouts of headache caused by the ferocious pace of modern living, a light tea of the leaves can also be of assistance to the ladies in their regular moon-led stomach cramps. Those of a certain age who suffer arthritic aching in the joints might also find some use for this common little garden plant. The herb though, like all that are beneficial to mankind, has its dangers, and may trigger of ulcerous swelling in the mouth. If this is the case, the user must stop taking it at once. The flowers, crushed and sniffed directly beneath the nose, can remove a lingering headache instantly, and generally invigorate the mental faculties.

George Maquire
From 'On Common Herbs As Medicines'
Bradford Observer, 1840

Bradford, Various Inns and Taverns, February\March 1861

Queer. That was the only word for it, now. Queer, it seemed to MacCraw in his late days of lone drinking and mental scratching upon past events. There was definitely something odd, something treacherous about the whole business. The darker, more-mystery hued the affair became, the deeper his thoughts probed upon the matter. Of course, he had realised at the time that there was something not quite right about the circumstances of Caroline's demise, but in the utter, soul-destroying confusion and turmoil that dogged him for years after her passing, he had never properly pursued the matter. Now, in his hazy hours of digging up and dwelling on past days, he began to catch a glimmer that there was something most sinister and malicious about his wife's accident. Only now, years later, as he babbled into his beer in the late hours at The Duchess on Sackville Street, did he tell Fish David, Apple Martin or any other tipplers who would listen, that he was convinced his dear wife had been murdered outright to conceal a secret away from the public world. Brontë this, he would mutter; Ellis Bell that. Branwell, better than the lot of them. That Charlotte - scheming, manipulative. Concealer. Murderer! The truth would come out, one day. She'd killed her. Her own kin too. Emily, killed. Branwell, killed. Anne probably, too. And it was all down to her. That Charlotte. He'd no doubt on it now. The little, tatty minx herself, or someone hired by her coin, had pushed own lovely wife, with child, to her death on the street. He was sure of it... sure... sure...

None in the Duchess snug had any idea what the old fool was chuntering about, but they tolerated him, as ever, with nods, pursed lips and grave faces. In these late bar hours he even talked himself into mortal danger. He had unleashed another Brontë letter upon the world, and was vexed by the notion that the same deadly machinery of that family's protection might be in motion again.

Yes yes yes, he muttered and mused to any ear that would listen. My very own life is in danger. The old fiend is unleashed. Aye, and there is a fiend. A Shade. Some dark fairy, drawn up from Hell. He's stalking me now; probably outside this room's very door. A great, tall fellow with black eyes that shine like glowing coals. I've seen him of late, peering at me in the streets. Aye, laugh then, but he's got his eye on me, and he's moving in closer and closer, like a wolf to the kill. I tell you, he's a fiend. You think he's not here amongst us, in this very room? Look about, man, look about. See him, there, shifting between shadows; there! In the smoke. He's here, man; he's in with us. Ah, well, let's be damned. Let's drink to him. To you, sir. To you, there, looking on at us. Aye, I can see yer, even if these wretches can't. They're laughing at me, but they can't see yer like I can, looking on at us. Yer plain as day, sir. Plain as day. You don't scare me, you know, damn yer eyes. Away and leave us to drink to our health in peace.

Here, MacCraw would topple forward, halting himself just before he propelled forward from the stool, rocking there and glaring into some empty space about the room, clamping teeth on his pipe stem, billowing out head-engulfing smoke clouds. By this point he was beyond the cards or domino game he'd engaged in, and not fit for more drink. The regulars knew better than to try consoling him by way of explanation or conversation. They'd tolerate him amongst them, and eventually one might help him to the tavern door. A few derogatory jokes on his condition might be made on his departure, a few laughs at his drunken expense, but no blame or judgement was laid upon him. Certainly, none would be round for a shave or haircut at his establishment the next morning, but other than that, his rantings and ramblings were instantly forgiven. Except, of course, by himself, grog-headed and remorseful the mornings following such insane outbursts.

CHAPTER 11

The scalp may be encouraged to sprout forth more luxuriant hair if a rinse of rosemary leaves is brushed into it once a week or so. This is particularly so
for dark haired folk, and thyme will work as well for all shades. Both of these herbs have antiseptic properties which will assist ease the itch of lice-bite. Make a good rinse by steeping a handful of either, or both, herbs in 1 pint of clean water. Bring the water to the boil, add the fresh herb and leave to steep until cool. Strain if you wish, then finger the rinse into hair and scalp until the hair is quite saturated. The rinse, which smells fresh and clean, is best left on overnight, before being washed away with a shampoo next morning.

From 'Essays On The Art Of The Ancient Barber'
George Maquire
1841

Bradford, March 1861

Awake again. A day. Another hateful, despicable day to plough through for MacCraw. And those memories - they weren't doing him any good. Thinking of her. Thinking of those what if onlys... what might have beens.

Grey, rainy light filled the room, darkening in the corners and around the bulky furniture. His head was banging, throat throbbing. The bedroom air was icy on the skin of the face as he poked his head further out of the bedclothes. It was difficult to breath through his bunged up, stinging nose. A cold, perhaps. Or too much of the old pop again, more likely. That wasn't doing any good either. He was only poisoning himself, slowly, corroding his body and his brain from within. He would cut down now, he vowed there - stop the poison completely before the month was out. Too much of anything pleasurable was no good for a man.

Coughing and horse-clatter rattled up from the street outside. From below he could hear the thumping and scraping of Trumper and Mufty, the shop lads, raking up the fire and banging the water pots, preparing for the morning shaves. A nice, hot shave, towels tight across the skin of the face, that was what he needed to perk him up a little. His own face felt flabby and exhausted, ill-fitting, and his scalp itched. He yawned and stretched his jaw wide to try and get a tingle of blood around the sluggish crannies and crevices. Growling in dismay and stomach-aching misery he went shuffling back deeper into the scant comfort of the bedding, happier to sit it out with bed-bugs than get up and confront the day. He felt so old this morning. The lines seemed to be burning there in his furrowed forehead. He stank too - onion sweat scent. Decrepit, disgusting, that vinegary tang that lingers about the elderly. He smelled too old, even for his years.

In this grim, deflated, black-dog mood, MacCraw knew that whatever the weather, he would have to take the day off, or the morning at least. Caroline was there, flickering and smiling in the fuddled corners of his mind. It was a long while - some months - since he had last ventured up to Undercliffe to chat to her at the graveside. Weeds would be creeping up fast by now - the angel figurine with its clasped harp and open prayer book could have toppled or blown over for all he knew. Certainly, he had been neglecting to tend the grave of his beloved, but that he would be putting right this very day. Trade was slack on a morning these days, and the lads below would be able to manage fine without him a while.

He tried to drift back into sleep but his mind could not be stilled. There was no comfort to be had under the bedclothes - just flashes of memory he'd prefer not to have illuminating that inner cavern. With a grunt, MacCraw launched himself up into the icy room, busying himself straight away, rushing about for his clothes, raking at the embers in the fireplace to get a blaze going, then gruffling down to Trumper for a strong coffee to be brought up. He would give it an hour in the shop, he decided. Once the day had got going he would take a walk up the cemetery. He'd be in and out within an hour, and then back down just in time for the potential rush they might have over the mill lunch breaks.

Once the fire was up in his room, and he was dressed, with a hot coffee and toasted bread thick with butter set before him, MacCraw sat himself down at his writing table with a very personal pile of documents, retrieved from the blanket box at the foot of his bed. Chewing toast and sipping thick, black coffee, he leafed through the papers. They were mainly Caroline's old journals and letters - intimate love letters to him, in some cases. Sometimes he smiled at the memory set in ink there; other times he frowned and his looked turned gloomy. Whenever he finished a single letter or a journal entry he would rise with it clasped between his fingers, walk the short distance to the fire, then float the paper mercilessly into the flames. This he did without regret in the main. There could be no one else interested in her papers now - there would never be any children or grandchildren intent on poring over their ancestor's musings and scribblings. He rarely read them or even looked at them himself anymore, and when he did they only caused him heartache for days. So, one last read of each, he decreed, then to the flames with them. A clear up, that's what was needed. An early spring-clean of matter and mind. Best for them, best for him. A purging by fire, in the Hindu manner. He knew that even if Caroline should be looking down over his shoulder from Heaven above, she would bear him no malice for these actions. She held no store by her 'twitterings', as she herself dismissed them. She'd suffered none of ill-fated Rhymers' desire of immortality through the written word. She had even tried to throw them out in the rubbish on occasions, only MacCraw himself stopping her, for he always instinctively valued and credited her well-crafted sentences. But now this world had no further use for them. One last slipping of the blade into his heart then; one last read of his beloved's fading blue words. And then to the flame with them on this grim and mournful morning:

From The Private Journal Of Caroline Marie Waterhouse
Saturday May 12th 1838
This is scribbled in haste. 2pm and we shortly go to Bradford for afternoon tea with the Reverend Heap and wife, the vicar of St John's. This morning, through Lucy, the girl who runs small errands for the cook and for Aunt W. (though she cannot be classed a maid as her employment here is neither fixed nor steady) a secret envelope, sealed with scarlet wax, was delivered to me. The girl arrived at the kitchen door, somewhat flustered, with a delivery of fruit that had not been ordered. She told the irate Mrs. Benson (our lovely cook) that it was in fact a gift sent by a Patrick Branwell Brontë of Manningham, and that she could deliver it into the hands of no one but Miss Caroline, and until the basket had been accepted by her in person the fruit could rot and perish in the basket. Thus I was called by cook to the kitchen to deal with the 'lunatic girl'. Smiles and courtesies (though she knew me well as her equal) she thrust the basket into my arms, all strange grimaces and twitching eyes. In confusion myself by now, I felt the smoothness of paper on the underneath of the basket, and realising that it was indeed some form of envelope, the game was suddenly upon me.

'Tell Mister Brontë thank you very much, and that indeed I hope to see him shortly,' I told her, and she, grinning and flushing now, was gone back to her busy day of calls and errands about the neighbourhood. Cook was all curses and blasphemies after her, but the charade was over, and I asked cook to calm down so as not alert my guardians to the strange happening, producing the envelope and waving it before her to show her what all the silly nonsense had been about.

'Ah, Miss, now I see. Letters from admirers. Why didn't she just say, the half-witted hussy? We've no need for that nonsense between us have we, my petal? You run along now and open it, Missy. No doubt you'll tell me of it later, if you want to.'

But I opened it there and then as she busied herself with her kitchen chores. It proved not to be from the Brontë painter himself, but from the flash-looking apothecary I mentioned just recently in these pages, a fellow who signs himself George Maquire. Indeed in thinking upon it, I have seen his shop notice about the town on walls and in the newspaper. The secret letter comes with begged excuses via Branwell Brontë, and its main contents form a poem, quite sweet and well executed, which I read with several dramatic flourishes to cook, and thus had her guffawing with laughter about the place. I simpered around like some faint-heart from one of the wonderful Scott's romances. We made much mirth out of the flowery metaphors, though I'll not divulge the words of it here. The thing is in a fine, neat hand upon good quality parchment, and though somewhat over-romantic, littered with heart-felt (so called) images of passion and wild declarations of love (for one who has seen little more than a blink of me - and then with my face besmeared with a chocolate moustachio!). Still, it is my first 'love letter', and despite my theatrics with cook I admit to flushing and trembling upon the receiving of it. I can barely wait to see Maggy to give her news of this development.

Now to hide this, and the little enveloped, heart-sworn poem within its pages, then to Reverend Heaps, where the tea is always weak, the cakes slightly dry, the butter spread thinly upon the bread, and where we have to endure hour upon hour of bagatelle, for that dreary game is a great favourite of theirs!

To the flame. To the flame. No mercy with it now. MacCraw hesitated with these leaves though, partially because they were so touching to him personally, but also, he convinced himself there, the excess of paper was smothering the coal and spoiling the fire. He gave the coals a good poking to stimulate the flames, the personal pages still held in his other hand. Once the tongues of yellow were licking strong enough he sighed deeply, and set the delicate pages upon them, then was back to the table before he should change his mind and try snatch them back from their eternal destruction.

Around ten that morning, after much painful reading and burning, and once all was set to in the shop which had no urgent need of him with business as slack as he'd expected, MacCraw put on his top coat. He went down the hill to buy some daffodils, then picked up the Shipley bound omnibus, not fancying the walk all the way up to Undercliffe on such a blustery day. He'd eaten a big enough breakfast, but anyway he took a little something to keep further appetite at bay, and to make the whole outing more pleasant and comfortable. A wind was up, blustering across from the west, threatening cold showers, but meanwhile having the beneficial effect of clearing the sulphurous smog that had been lingering over the bowl of the town for weeks now. For the first time of the year that he could remember he had a view clean across to the quarries at Bolton Woods and right up to Wrose on the eastern hill top. The omnibus clanked its way out of town, taking the road parallel to the railway line, and along where the old canal had festered. He nodded morosely to a few familiar passengers, but talked to no-one on the short journey. Staring at the passing streets, he wandered his own inner avenues, his self-administered medicinal compound ensuring that all excess emotion was pruned away. Physically, he was a little itchy, which he put down to the bed-bugs. Despite the sombre purpose of his outing he felt quiet, tranquil and easy within himself. The 'bus wound on the road, stopping now and then to drop off or pick up. MacCraw clambered out at Ingham's dye works and cut down Lionel Street. From there he took the steady climb up Bolton Road to the stone columned gateway of Peel Park. He had gone somewhat out of his way, but deliberately, for he fancied a nostalgic walk through the groves of the park, even though the trees were bare and a bit drab to look upon at this time of year. As he had hoped, the park was all but deserted. He skirted the ornamental lake and climbed the steps up to the top path. The times he had walked down here with Caroline in their days of courting! Pangs of feeling started leaking through the buffer of his tonic, and he stopped a minute at the lovely monument to Autumn, one of the stone carved maidens who depicted the four seasons along the length of the path. He took out his silver hip flask, raised it to the down-staring maiden, then took a good draught of the contents. Thus reinforced, he continued along the grove, past the empty benches and round the bandstand. The wind had dropped somewhat now, the trees almost stilled. Everywhere was deserted, not a soul to nod along to or pass the time of day with, and it seemed that he had slipped into a dream. He took a drink of water from the new marble drinking fountain, then carried along, leaving the park by the small southern gate. He crossed by the great brewery there, the smell of hops heavy and rich on the moist air. At last he entered the cemetery, and as ever was startled by the actual beauty of the place - always associating the location with past despair and grief, he inevitably forgot the actual loveliness of its situation once he had quit the enclosing walls. Between the avenues of tombstones there were spectacular views all over Bradford town to the south and east. Swivelling slightly, and with a crane of the neck, he could see the villages and quarries to the north, with the flat purple moor swelling and rolling beyond Ilkley and Haworth toward the darker rising foothills of the Pennines. The whole necropolis was perched upon the hill top and looked downright precarious, as though at any sudden gusting of a storm or shaking of the earth the monuments, coffins and old bones might go tumbling down toward the tiny spread of streets below. This was the cemetery where the rich or the ambitious left their dead to rest rather than risk them in the cramped, dead-crowded church graveyards of the town itself. Here, in this relatively new and fashionable out-post of the deceased, towers, tombstones, mock-monuments, miniature temples and impressive spires imposed a bristling, city-like horizon upon the skyline. As he worked his way through the temples and heaven-gazing statues which marked out different family plots, MacCraw mulled over the times he and Caroline had walked here. They would descend through the park on their way back into Bradford, as he had just done. Usually they were chaperoned by a varying brace of Caroline's aunts, but occasionally they had given them the slip around the busy park, then sought a little privacy amidst the new tombstones. These unhindered, unescorted times were the fondest times in MacCraw's own memory. Naturally, when sheltering there amidst the towering monuments, he and Caroline had sometimes reflected upon their own mortality, though with a playful gaiety, never really believing that one of them would perish so soon, and so stupidly. Neither of them was a stranger to death, and it was in the playful bandying way of those familiar with family bereavement and its consequences that they had toyed with ways of having themselves at last put into the earth. MacCraw had expressed an interest in a fire - a funeral pyre - like those the Hindus of India employed; or perhaps a great bonfire of his shell and all his worldly goods, if any were ever acquired, in the style of the great Viking warriors in their age. Caroline had been appalled at the savageness of such a disposal of a corpse. Burning to her seemed definitely heathen, barbaric, and she'd doubted that a soul could escape and reach heaven by such a brutal and sudden disposal. He had laughed at the quaint logic of this notion. Although even then of no religious persuasion himself, he respected the various beliefs of others, and particularly those of his beloved's family, with whom he had recourse to attend church every other Sunday, though largely out of his own ulterior, earthly motives. Church attendance for him was a path to the paradise of his beloved there on Earth, rather than to some hope of resurrection beyond this life. Caroline's delicate face had positively twitched with anxiety at the thought of her 'Georgie' being set ablaze.

'No, I won't have you burnt George. It's far too cruel, and illegal, surely. Even stuffed and mounted would be preferable. Then I could have you placed in a little glass cabinet and look upon you whenever I was missing you.'

'Hmmn! That's rich. Perhaps you could pop me on the parlour wall, next to the antlers.'

' Not a bad idea. Then we could hang hats on you.'

'Ha! And with a neat little plaque beneath. Here rests George MacCraw - hat-stand. Yet, do whatever you choose with my shell, my love. As long as you treat me kindly now, while I'm still in it.'

Thus they had joked on the theme, him never once considering that her beautiful, flowering life should be reaped in well before his own.

'Well, here would be good enough for me,' she had murmured, suddenly solemn, looking around her at the tombstones and memorials, at the lovely trees and the gorgeous view over the valleys. 'This place would suit me perfectly. I'd look down over it all like a sleeping angel. Just looking down over it all, and keeping an eye on you, my love. Oh, if only we can see when we are dead!'

She had become quite emotional then, tears pricking her pale blue eyes, shoulders trembling, and he had held her, perhaps too close, to try and offer comfort.

This little anecdote, minus the embraces, MacCraw had tearfully recounted to the Waterhouses in the trance-like shock of their first grieving immediately after Caroline's death. Of course, they were distraught over the loss of their beloved niece, and appalled at the brutal manner of her death. Though he lived in relative modesty, Mister Waterhouse was a man of some means, and he spared no expense on the funeral and burial arrangements. In agreement with MacCraw, Waterhouse purchased a family plot on the new western edge of the Undercliffe necropolis so that his niece's expressed wishes could be respected. The funeral had been lavish, with black coaches and horses bearing the coffin and mourners from Horton Green down through the centre of the town, bringing the whole place to a standstill, before climbing slowly up to Undercliffe. There, Caroline was placed in the ground in a silver handled oak casket, wreaths and flowers heaped and piled into the open grave. MacCraw had sobbed openly, as had the Waterhouses and many others. Beyond the graveyard, he had no real memories of that awful day. Some time later he paid for a marble plinth, on which was set the white angel. This angel was clearly a female, her wings folded, the beautiful but mournful face peering down upon the passing, fleeting mortal world of Man as she draped slender fingers upon the strings of a frozen harp.

MacCraw now stood looking up into the anguished, slightly weathered face of this very angel, feeling a hefty sadness, but none of the lurching, heart-tearing upheaval of body and mind that had struck him to a senseless, sobbing mass on his first dozen or so visits to the memorial. Clouds raced up beyond the angel's head and wingtips, the sky there a clean and refreshing wash of pale blue. Magpies were cawing around the trees, some bobbing through the air, beaks precariously loaded with straw and sticks, nesting already.

'Ah, Caroline, my darling,' he mumbled up. 'This petty, fleeting world. What do you make of it all now, eh?'

He placed the daffodils into the vase at the foot of the plinth. The lettering on the monument front, imbedded and highlighted with gold paint, was in need of a touch-up, having already faded, even within the few years since the passing of Isabella Waterhouse, beloved aunt of Caroline's, who had perished just three years before, peacefully, and in her sleep. He could see by the tidiness of the grave that old Mister Waterhouse had been here recently himself. They rarely had contact with each other these days, having exhausted all possible conversations about their memories of Caroline, and having not much else in common beside. If they met there at the graveside it was always a polite but hurried exchange, an awkwardness until one or the other departed, depending who had been there already, for neither liked to share their memories and moments there at the monument itself. MacCraw did his spot of tidying and rearranging, a kind of signalling that he too had been there on the site. He muttered more words up to his wife as he did so, as if conversing with someone who was really there; a little ritual of his whenever he called by the grave. He checked around and about him as he spoke, feeling somewhat embarrassed with himself for succumbing to this weakness, hoping that no other payers-of-respects were within earshot.

'I've just come through the park there,' he put to her. 'I suppose you were watching. I suppose you watch me quite a bit, and see me making an old, drunken fool of myself. Well, I trust you're guarding over me, my love. I know somebody needs to.'

He arranged the spread of daffodils in the vase, then scraped and picked out a few springing nettle leaves and goosegrass from the edges of the plinth.

'Well, it was quiet there in the park. No leaves yet. No buds to speak of. Spring's late this year, I reckon. The sun doesn't seem to get through that much.'

Straightening up from his weeding, he ran a finger over the lettering, checking for flaking gold, worried about the state of the paint.

'Snowdrops are still around, and the crocuses are peeping. Do you remember? You used to love the spring flowers...'

He saw the grave, brown earth and grassroots, the flowers heaped and piled and so beautiful, buried there now, closed off from sunlight, long since rotted. He wondered if any of their seeds had taken. Perhaps the shoots of bulbs were pushing through. A chain of flowers fanned through his memory - snowdrops, crocuses, daffodils, forget-me-nots, foxgloves, roses, willowherb, tiny lilacs. Especially lilacs. Caroline had so loved her blossoms, and on many a courting walk had made him inspect them closely. She'd had him poring over them with a magnifying glass, examining their veins and the lattices of tiny cells. He was aware of her touching game. She was trying to make him wonder at their improbable artistry, hoping he would come round to seeing the Divine craftsmanship of her Christian God in that intricate, mysterious design. She had never succeeded in that, but he had appreciated the awesome beauty that could be found in the minute particle as well as the whole thing itself.

'And the lilacs, Caroline. Do remember those lilacs that time?'

Those lilacs, in the heart of the park through which he had just passed, but back then in the early bloom of summer. The sky had been clear and blue, a hot sun dazzling, grass and leaves glowing an astonishing array of greens. It was the week before MacCraw had mustered up the courage, as well as clear statements of his strong financial position, and approached Mr. Waterhouse officially to ask for Caroline's hand. Though together and courting they were not yet officially engaged. Even having known each other a year or so they were still chaperoned, Aunt Isabella and her sister Estelle enjoying the May Day holiday with them. Well ahead of 'the elders' that day, Caroline and MacCraw skirted the fountain arm in arm. With a side-glance across his lovely companion's face MacCraw chanced upon the miniature rainbow; it dazzled there in mid-air when viewed from a particular angle through the cascade of droplets between the marble of the lower water font and the narrow circle of the smaller tier above. While enjoying this shimmering mirage they saw the shapes of elongated human figures through the screen of falling water - the arm linked figures of Aunt Isabella and her elder sister, rounding the row of holly bushes, sweeping toward them like two stately sailing ships in their skirts and wide brimmed bonnets, both top-sailed with yellow parasols.

'Quickly George, this way...' Caroline urged, giggling as she dragged him by the arm toward a bank of bushes. They moved through the foliage into shady green darkness, after a few paces coming to the high stone wall that marked the boundary of the park. Turning, they stood still there, backs pressed against the cool moss of the wall, trying to flatten themselves and hide in the shadows. Like children, they were tittering with excitement at their foolish pranking, shushing each other, silent a moment, then giggling again the next. Their eyes grew quickly accustomed to the gloom.

'Look,' Caroline whispered, picking out with her dancing eyes clusters of lilac flowers than hung rampantly like luminous blue fruit all around them, bees dancing about the open blossoms. 'Lilacs. God's work. How beautiful.'

'They'll spot us for sure,' hissed MacCraw, though he hoped they wouldn't, for moments of real privacy between the two were rare. Even here, hidden in shrubbery, he felt observed and was reluctant to be intimate. Her gloveless fingers found his, softly brushed then curled around them.

'Ssh!' she hissed. 'Here they come now. Be as the statues out there in the park.'

'But what about these bees?'

Shush! Or I'll sting you myself.'

And they were as statues, though grinning ones, trying to keep their faces straight and prevent them from buckling into laughter. The sisters did not see or sense them, but rustled by in a twittering of gossip, taking the turn in the path toward the bandstand. The two statues now edged along the wall a while, trying to remain parallel with the gliding aunts but unable to keep up with them. They came upon a hollow in the wall, a shallow arch set slightly back in the stones. It was a lost and bricked up doorway, perhaps to a tunnel or decorative grotto. This unexpected hide-away was concealed from the view of the pathways unless one stepped right up to the bushes and peered in close against the leaves. A sawn portion of tree trunk set within the archway formed a natural bench, and although covered in a cushion of moss it was quite dry and comfortable to sit upon. Here they retreated, sitting close to each other, delighted at their trickery, lips grazing kisses on cheek and forehead. They communicated in whispers, their conversation staccato as they broke off every few seconds to listen, fearing intrusion or discovery, for although they were behaving decently when compared to some, it would be disreputable for Caroline to be found in such seclusion with a young man. Naturally, this thrilled them and heightened their senses. Cheek against cheek, fingers entwined, each aware of the warmth of the other through their clothing, MacCraw felt quite feverish. Caroline began telling something of her days as a girl, in the city of Liverpool. MacCraw had no idea where the anecdote was coming from, or why, but listened intently without moving, for he could feel the warmth of her body against his, the buzz of her breath upon his cheek, and his passions were somewhat aroused. She spoke of her own mother, long deceased, and of whom she possessed just a few faint pictures in the corners of her memory. In the shaded light of greenery, amidst the glowing lilac flowers, her eyes bedazzled him; eyes shining, gleaming with tears at her remembered girlhood mischief. She was recounting an anecdote of another occasion when she had hidden away from the world. She had crawled into a coal-hole and watched the world of her neighbourhood from chinks in the grate. She spoke of the sense of power of one hidden from view but still able to see the world go on around. She had felt like she was watching from another world. Then they had started to search for her, friends and neighbours, her mother calling her name over and over. Her mother, she realised later, too late, had been frantic with worry. They had only lost father earlier that year; a naval man of rising rank who had died aboard ship and been buried at sea, so many thousands of miles away around the world. Her mother had nothing tangible of him, no corpse to recall, no burial place to visit. Just the memory of their times, and the letter informing her of his death. And now the nightmare grew - her daughter was missing. Oh, if only Caroline could have known how hurtful her prank was to be, she would never have dreamt of hiding herself away. The anguish must have been crushing her mother within. She had watched the neighbours and her mother from her little peephole, could sense the dread, could feel it tightening within her own stomach, but the worse her mother's fear became, the more she feared to move and reveal herself, knowing that she would be in trouble. Only when her mother broke down sobbing and wailing had Caroline come scrambling from her hiding place, wailing herself by now, filthy with coal dust, wracked with terrible guilt and shame. She had thrown herself upon her mother, begging for forgiveness, so sorry, so sorry... Caroline in the park hide-away with MacCraw had tears gliding down her pale cheeks at the very pain of the traumatic memory. MacCraw's heart had melted at the sight of those tears; he knew then that in a thousand years he would never love a woman so much. There in the shady bower he was completely snared. Caroline blubbered and sobbed a few more utterances, looking him full in the eyes. The trouble she had been in for the worry she had caused - her mother's chiding, but the sheer relief to have her daughter folded within her arms again. Her words became but a throaty murmur to MacCraw, who was all but lost in the splendour of her eyes - in the wet-petal beauty of her face. She smiled as her anecdote expired, though a certain, wistful sadness lingered in her gaze; a distant, vulnerable, wounded look. All talk ceased. Silence lingered. The sounds of the park beyond came filtering through - faint music, children shrieking with laughter, the yelping of dogs. With the silk handkerchief handed to her by MacCraw, Caroline dabbed away tears, then she eyed him somewhat quizzically.

'I'm sorry to get upset so. Anyway, we'd better emerge soon. They'll be round the parade and looking for us with the Peelers by now.'

He chuckled at this and clasped her hand. There was a pause. It seemed that all the world was silent, waiting, colluding, even bird chatter and insect drone falling to a hush. There in the green shade their eyes met and held. He would have crossed those few inches that barriered them apart to kiss and clasp her, but something held him in check. That permanent, stunting sense of being observed and judged on his behaviour and manners stalled him from acting instinctively. He had to judge his beloved's response exactly against any presumptuous rashness on his part. Her lips parted, moist. Lips trembling, he thought, in expectation of the one kiss that would change and merge their worlds forever.

'You... you...' he stuttered, mouth dry, words failing. Her fine eyebrows arched, eyes widening, questioning, waiting for him to expand on the utterance.

'You are so beautiful...'

There was nothing he could add. That was it. The sheer, summed up truth.

'Oh George! You're such a flirt and tease.'

'No, no, really, Caroline. You are. I mean... I'm not out to be the flatterer or anything. You are. Beautiful, I mean. So lovely and...'

Her laughter tinkled like music. She pouted her lips to a red, black-holed heart. Beyond them, beyond the screen of lilacs and shrubbery, he was aware that strollers ambled through the park, arm in arm; gents in hats despite the sun, the ladies with their angled parasols; children in holiday clothes in their ball games; dogs chasing the children; the crowd gathering and murmuring at the bandstand; musicians, uncomfortable in their jackets and starched collars, tuning their instruments. But none, he realised, could see or hear this moment. He could not allow his faltering courage fail him now. By the heart, MacCraw, he thought there. Do it by the heart.

'I'd kiss you, if I dared, and if you'd permit,' he said gravely, though with a slight grin now, for the moment felt right. Caroline's eyebrows arched again as she considered him and his statement.

'Well, would you now indeed, impudent young fellow?' Her neck came craning and trembling forward. 'Well then, you'd better kiss me, hadn't you?'

Breathless, he stepped forward, Caroline rising to meet him. He clasped her then, held her, drawing her to him at the waist, their breaths mingling, her trembling warmth merging with his. Mouths met there. Held there. The softness of her rosebud mouth. Her perfume was delicious as it pervaded his nostrils; a fragrant citrus and musk brushed along the silk ringlets of her hair and neck-nape. MacCraw felt as though sunshine and starlight were exploding within him, searing out from some vast inner core, his own heart so expansive and liquid as their lips parted, eyes held, lips met again. His whole sensual being was melting as he thrilled to the quick with the sight, touch and scent of this beauty. Her eyes fluttered, closed, lids translucent and lightly veined like the crocus petals she had made him examine that spring. She was smiling, as if she too was experiencing that same inner bliss.

'I love you, my Caroline,' he uttered. They parted at last. 'I do. I love you. I've no doubt. I love you.'

He surprised himself with the boldness of his straightforward declaration. She smiled simply, brushing aside a lock of hair that had tumbled across her pale, moistened brow.

'Well, seeing that I love you too, dear George MacCraw, you'd better get on with the business of proposing marriage to me then.'

This he did, down on a knee in a trice, there beneath the lilac flowers, her accepting only on the grounds that Mister Waterhouse's approval could be secured.

'Until then, it must be kept secret - swear that to me, George.'

'On my life, love, I swear it.'

'Now out of here, quick, for they'll be looking for us by now.'

They emerged from their hidden bower into the brilliance of sunlight, hastening back across to the fountain, perching themselves on the stone ledge on the shaded side, both thrilled to shaking with their vows, and with their declared and secret love. They sat close but not touching, awaiting the inevitable return of the elders, whom they suspected would reach the bandstand at the end of the avenue before deciding to double back in search of their missing ward. Indeed, within minutes the panicking aunts were bearing back down upon them, bustling, clucking and tutting, flapping all sails. Estelle immediately commented that the two were sitting far too close together for common decency.

'I was feeling faint, Aunt....' Caroline lied, fanning herself, trying to draw in her cheeks so that she looked sickly. 'You know how breathless I get...my heart was palpitating again. George sat me down here to rest. You must have both slipped by. He's been looking after me, and dared not leave my side to search you out.'

Aunt Estelle, who liked nothing better than gossip and scandal, looked askance along her nose at the two seated youngsters, believing none of it. With a triumphant 'Humph!' she reached down and plucked up a cluster of lilac florets which had caught in the lace of Caroline's bonnet, unseen by them both as they had hurried from their alcove.

'Hmm - the wind must be strong hereabouts,' she said, dangling the flowers before them both. 'Perhaps it's that which snatches your breath away so?'

Caroline reached up and took the tiny flowers between her fingers.

'Yes, we did look upon the flowers,' she said. 'George makes such an informative escort. He knows all of the properties and plants and the healing powers of nature, don't you George? He's already informed me that the leaves of the feverfew will be beneficial for my migraines, have you not, George?'

She dangled the lilac before his face. He looked gravely on, not quite knowing what to say, caught up in the game but not wanting to overplay his hand. He watched the pale purple crosses quiver there against such a blue sky, noticing for the first time that indeed the flowers were particularly beautiful, and it struck him that they looked so fragile, even as though they might melt like snowflakes in Caroline's dainty clasp. How could such beauty hope to weather out a cold spell or the scorching sun?

'Oh yes,' he mumbled. 'Feverfew for migraines, ladies, that's for sure.'

And lilac for true and faithful lovers, he'd wanted to add, though of course dared not.

'Well, shall we walk on? The band will be already half way through,' Mrs. Waterhouse huffily suggested. 'Are you fit enough now, my dove? You must help her George - come on, I'm sure you're not shy with the ladies - give the girl the support of your strong arm, just in case she faints away on us again.'

MacCraw noted her smile and that her eyes were wryly glinting as she suggested this assistance. She obviously had the measure of her young wards, though it seemed from the depth of her gaze that there was some approval in this potential union. MacCraw could have kissed her, and from that moment on the two of them had got on like the proverbial blazing house up until the very day of her own sad passing. Thus, temporarily rescued from Estelle's disapproving wrath, MacCraw helped Caroline up to her feet, the lilac flowers discarded there by the fountain. In the sunshine and brilliant greenery the four of them strolled along the main avenue of the park toward the crowded bandstand, MacCraw elated, gliding arm in arm with his heart's love, floating along through that gorgeous, now long-faded day.

CHAPTER 12

Notice To Emigrants
Steamers from Liverpool to New York
Depart twice every week
'The Queen' and 'Lady Mary' next week
1st Class to Portland £18 and 18 shillings
Cabin £15 and 15 shillings
Steerage £4
W. Searle and Co
15 Water Street
Liverpool.
The Bradford Observer
April 1861

Bradford, March 1861

The day after visiting Caroline at the cemetery, MacCraw took another break from the too-quiet shop to go on another little pilgrimage. This time he cut across town then set on foot up Little Horton Lane, determined to walk the whole distance for the exercise. He was heading up to Little Horton Green, retracing his steps from the days of courting Caroline up to the old Waterhouse residence, which had seemed a splendid place, big as a palace it had seemed then, just along from the Parsonage there. Walking up in the blustery, breezy morning gave him time for cold, hard thinking and reflection.

Peering much into that elusive kaleidoscope of the past over the last few bitter, winter weeks, he saw he had somewhat neglected his present and immediate circumstances. His drinking and other habits had come between him and the business of the shop. For too many hours of the day a 'closed' sign had been displayed at his door. He had over indulged in himself and vices, meanwhile, trailing alleys and ginnels, sitting misty-eyed in the numerous taverns and haunts of his 'Rhymer' youth. He had wandered the busy streets, sniffing out snatches of his own past; loitering about the corners where he used to meet with his literary fellows; lurking outside the houses where comrade poets and painters had temporarily held their lodgings; walking trails that he and Caroline had explored. He had been too busy reliving the physical geography of his past and 'golden' years to notice a real moment of the present. And here he was, at it again, wandering out to the little villa, Caroline's girlhood home, when his own shop was a tip and shambles.

As he passed between Horton Hall and the Union Workhouse he shivered, cold from within. The highest and the lowest in such a proximity; the richest and worst of the poor practically dwelling shoulder to shoulder, though never likely to touch, or meet. The fine hall was shielded from the street by trees, though he could glimpse the front and the upper windows through the bare branches. On his left, the workhouse was in plain view, and it was partly this that made him cringe and quake so. To end up there! – and it was possible. He was on a spiral, going down. To lose it all now, or to lose his mind, lose the shop, the business, his hands too shaky to maintain his basic trade. The chances of ever ending up residing in the grand hall were zero. But the workhouse ... he hurried on, not allowing the progression of thought and imagination to take him through those solemn green doors; through to the hard and awful life within. He scuttled past the church, along to the next street corner, and there it was - the old house.

The place was still inhabited, of course, though no longer by the Waterhouses. The garden was much wilder than it had been, the external decor somewhat shabby and neglected compared to its former glory days. Indeed, it seemed that the whole area of town there had greatly changed. He remembered clearly the day he had strode the same route in his best suit, bathed and shaved, black attaché case with papers and documents beneath his arm. The day he had come up to ask Mister Waterhouse for Caroline's hand, a week after proposing to her in the park.

How splendid the house and the area had seemed that day. He had been jittery with nerves and on fire with love. He felt sure Mister Waterhouse liked him, despite his roots, but whether he approved of him as a suitor – that was another matter entirely. The case was his trump card, so he'd hoped. The deeds and documents within showed his worldly worth and the potential of his businesses. How he had come by such wealth was hopefully of no consequence to Waterhouse, though MacCraw was prepared to explain himself if it came to it around the table. His father's ventures and trading exploits were not his moral responsibility. Silk, spices, timber, liquor, opium – all were as equally a valid commodity. And the medicinal intent of his father's venture, there was a humanitarian hint to that which MacCraw sensed Waterhouse would like. Mister Waterhouse himself dealt in liquor, bought it cheap and sold it on at profit, though rarely touched the stuff. MacCraw's father had done exactly the same thing, in principle. In his last years MacCraw's father had moved trunks full of opium from one side of the globe to the other. He'd made money. Good money. A fortune, in fact. Waterhouse could surely have no qualms about that. The family had been saved, the sons set up in good stead. That was the black and the white of it, and the rest he'd leave out. Ah, that day. He'd knocked on the door. The maid answered and he'd formally requested Mister Waterhouse on private and personal business. The cool of the hallway – how he'd insisted on keeping his jacket on despite the heat of the walk. He'd listened for signs of Caroline though he knew she was away with her Aunt in Leeds. Then Mister Waterhouse was there before him, tall and solemn looking, knowing exactly what the visit was about.

'This way, then, George...' He'd gestured him into the study, a room which MacCraw had glimpsed but once or twice in all his visits there. Into the cool interior with its smell of apples and furniture polish; the slow ticking of the clock on the mantelpiece; the impressive breakfront bookcases crammed with novels and ledgers; the reddish, gleaming mahogany table set with a fruit bowl at its centre. Into the business. And out again an hour later, MacCraw's heart positively inflated with joy and the thrill of anticipation.

'Ah, what a day that was.'

MacCraw spoke to himself on the street there, smiling like an idiot with the happy memory as he looked down the drive to the house.

'How things do change.'

He was looking about now, and beyond the house at the views over the town. Back then this had been a rural retreat with views over woodland and the fields of flourishing farmland; now it was densely populated, mills and terraced housing cluttering up the slopes and valleys. From the outlook of the villa it was as though a huge and hideous transformation had come over the whole town, with MacCraw barely noticing it over the passing years. Certainly, it could be argued that the town had flourished and mushroomed, with new and prosperous industry springing up everywhere, the housing being a necessary complement to such progress. But to MacCraw the whole aspect of the place seemed much dingier, bleaker and more filthy than when he had chanced his future in the area back in the thirties. The town now, he decided, was suffering some crumbling, spiritual and moral disintegration. The whole nation was, in fact. As though an invisible cancer was eating into the body of the kingdom. It seemed to him there could be no reversing of the diseasing process – there was no tincture, tea or remedy to restore the nation's health. Standards were declining. Structures were weakening. Morals, even slack in his own youth, were now degenerating into blatant and open decadence. Times definitely were changing, and for the worse, and too rapidly for him. *What'll become of it all?* he wondered. He had made his way back up to the church corner and he lingered there, looking down over the dips and smog of smoking hillsides. *This can only get worse, and bigger, and dirtier, with more smoke and more folk - and what then?* What would it all be like in another thirty years from now, considering the massive changes he'd seen in the same amount of time since his arrival here? House facades that he recalled as once being of clean, freshly hewn sandstone were now blackened with soot-grime; the dust coated greenery of the trees and plant-life was dulled away from the original brilliance of nature. The very people of the town seemed to be decaying too, even the youths he saw in the streets about more hunched, stunted, duller, more sordid, less polite, less enthusiastic, as though the very fabric of the life and the world about them was speeding into interminable decline. Times were harder. People were poorer. The streets dirtier. The night stars dimmer. The life, soul and substance of the people and place seemed to be withering and wasting like a universal consumptive.

'It's you, you fool. You're getting old!' he snapped out aloud, as though cursing to a passing horse that was pulling a potato wagon along the road. The driver steadied the horse, glanced queerly at MacCraw, then was past. MacCraw checked himself from spilling more thoughts out loud. He was becoming one of the babbling, muttering, bad-breathed old men that he remembered laughing at and teasing in his own childhood. He was, he realised, becoming a rancid and risible fixture of the town. He had allowed his roots to be tapped too deep. Perhaps not too deep to tear up though. Break away. Quit this damned smoky, fuming place, start again, afresh and renewed. As he hovered there, seeing himself as others probably saw him these days - the doddering ruin of a drunk swaying and staring on a street corner - he realised how much he was in need of a positive and cheerful influence upon the exterior and internal workings of his life. Complex and simple; he had to get away. Time for a change.

'Time for a change,' he muttered at a passing boy who was shoving his hoop down the hill. The little one smiled, nodded, then was away into his own game. MacCraw turned about, away from Horton Green, and began striding his descent back into the town.

CHAPTER 13

From 'The Tale Of Barry Robb'
Patrick Branwell Brontë
1840

'Like I said before, this ain't no story. This is the truth. I've come up here north to escape all that and be well rid of my thieving past. Some chums sent me up here with a bit of coin to get myself started in a respectable line, which is what I'm trying to do. It's fun being with you lot, listening in and the like, and I've got a story to tell in a way, I suppose - so - shall I go on? Right then. A bit more.

About that time, aged eleven or twelve, I learned how to swim, and was remarkably expert at it. Look at me, the shape of me - like a barrel, now, aint I? Barrel chested, or whatever. Truth is, I can't sink! Even when I stop swimming, I just bob along, like a little old cork. So, once I was released, I used to do a lot my jobs about the river - that being of course the old Thames. I'd take great risks, lifting watches, pocket books, snuff boxes handkerchiefs, whatever, from the tails of gentlemen's coats. If the alarm went up, off I'd head toward the river, and if chased, in I'd go - tide in or tide out, I'd take my chance with the water. And as you see, I'm here before you - I always made it to the other side. I worked about seven months at this, but the police were onto me, me being distinctive looking for a thief, even in London. I was followed about by secret Peelers, out of their uniforms, and caught in the act of thieving, my route to the river and safety cut off by a waiting party of them who battered me down with their cudgels. Up before the bench I went, and I was sentenced to three months in Brixton prison. I came out, and left home for good. My folk would have gladly taken me back, but I was in with a bad gang. We were making a lot of money - more money than I'd ever dreamed of. We had our own lodgings, warm and comfortably furnished, fine foods, wine, and girls and entertainments. We went to the theatres and dance gardens every night, and were really living the high life. Of course, we were funding this through our crime, running packs of pickpockets from a tavern and a lodging house down St. Giles, and doing our own work, shop lifting and night burglaries and the like.

About this time, I was engaged with two other persons in a house breaking in the West End of the Metropolis. On the basement of the house we intended to plunder was a counting-house, while the upper floors were occupied by the family as a dwelling house. Our chief object was to get to the counting house, which could be entered from the back. Our mode of entering was this: at one o'clock in the morning, one of the party was set to watch in the street, while I and another climbed up by a waterspout to the roof of the counting-house. There was no other way of getting in but by cutting the lead off the house and making an opening big enough for us to pass through. From below the signal was given to enter the house, but somehow a policeman on his rounds was out of time and saw our shadows on the roof, and he sprung his rattle. Our watchman and my pal on the roof both got away, but I was half in, half out the hole when the hullabaloo went up. I was as nimble as a monkey, and still am, as you can imagine, and I went leaping and scrambling about the roof tops, trying to hide from the policemen because others had arrived in the vicinity now, and were hell bent on capturing me, which of course, they did. But not without a fight, and I broke three of their heads before I went down in a scrum of boots and truncheons...

Bradford, March 1861

The Wednesday evening, after locking up the shop then snuffing and piping awhile in his room above, MacCraw stumbled off out for another wander to past haunts. Bye and bye, he found himself up in the snug of the Worldes End Tavern. This was a ruinous place by now, illuminated with bright, glaring gas lights, all the cheer and the leather and the polish of the wood faded, the chandeliers broken and cob-webbed over, the once beautiful stained-glass windows now begrimed outside with dirt, and inside so dusty that not even an indication of their former sunny-day glory ever glowed through. MacCraw was sitting there remembering times of companionship, past-pacts and dances, glimmers of brilliant, life altering conversations with all manner of artists, philosophers, performers and drunkards. He looked about at the inn's hunched, shabby crowd, wondering where the bright things and gilded youth about town of this upcoming generation gathered in the same manner now. Surely they must have their own haunts and roosting places, though come to think of it he rarely saw any sign of a creative crowd about town. Perhaps there were no poets or painters left in this mechanical age. Maybe society no longer had need of such people when there was photography and widely distributed daily journalism; when news of an item could be wired about the nation and half the world within hours; where there was machinery and the mass production of everything and more a living man could need. Where on earth though, he wondered, were the dancing beauties of the town? Where were the rebels, and the upstarts, the philosophers, the geniuses?

MacCraw was still sipping and musing on these and other things, chewing on his own lips and fingertips, when through the inn doorway sailed a familiar female figure. A slender, younger friend was floating along beside her. He watched her glide by in a rustle of skirts. A recognisable, startling woman. Gleaming black hair coiled down her back in a thick plait which drew the eye down over her voluptuous figure and sensuous movements. She glanced about as she crossed the room, eyes bright with inner fire. Certainly a passionate and sensual creature, though perhaps past her prime in terms of beauty and child-rearing years. This snaking, startling vision MacCraw recognised on the instant, and was somewhat surprised by his own very physical response to her presence in the room. It was Pot Mary – Apple Martin's delicious wife, Fish David's entanglement of late. She spied MacCraw directly, in an instant. Without even an angling of her head, Mary informed her companion with a side glance that here was their quarry. They passed through as though unaware of any soul in the room other than themselves, vanishing with graceful turns into one of the more intimate chambers within the premises. Just the glimpse of Mary sparked off a whole series of memories and mind-dawdlings in MacCraw, some very pleasant, others less so and guilt-tinged. He sat there clouded in his own pipe fumes, drifting through past spats and encounters with her, these too mainly back in his Rhymers days, when she had been little more than a lass, though one of the town's much sought after and sonneted beauties. This very place they'd both frequented then, and had eyes for each other, and embraces. Him being a man of his own trade with his own establishment and premises - well, they'd spent more than one night locked together within his rooms, and engaged in much more than poetic or philosophical conversation. Nothing other than the passion had come of it though, she being wayward and too full of her own beauty, unwilling to commit herself beyond immediate pleasure to the company of one whom she looked down on as a mere tradesman. Their liaison had passed naturally, fading completely once he had besotted himself with Caroline. Though he had never spoken to Caroline of his past cavorting, she had sensed something in her husband's manner whenever they passed Mary in the street or happened upon her in their circle of company. She had taken to referring to her as 'that lovely creature', whose beauty she recognised and commented on, though she had never managed to draw MacCraw on the matter.

MacCraw sat there alone in smoke clouds, dwelling upon past embraces and encounters with the still lovely Mary. Meanwhile, she and her young companion, her own daughter, sat a short distance away, though beyond sight or earshot. They were in fact discussing MacCraw in whispers, settling on how they would get the drunken barber up to the Old Star Inn. They were on a mission, directed and stated, spelled out clearly, and confident of success.

Mary herself had always vaguely regretted the rash choices of her passion-driven youth, but she was of Latin blood, and saw it largely as a duty to live for the feeling, for the moment, and from the heart. She had always forsaken future possibilities for short-term gratification. Only now, entering stouter womanhood, did she see that some choices had been unwisely made and decisions rashly taken. In her own daughter, Beatrice - the lovely young woman in her company this very evening - she had deliberately instilled a completely different set of values to those fleeting ones that had been her own. Beatrice, she had taken pains to ensure, was well primed and schooled to the advantages of the long-term-prospects in a man. Such future prospects, much more so than his looks or his turnout or his delicate turn of phrase, were the only thing of consequence in a relationship or betrothal. Beatrice, a beautiful, feline creature of eighteen, with the eyes, frame and face, and not least the know-how, to melt but the wisest man's heart, was worth any man's attention, and thus any man's gold. Only a man with a weight of coin behind him stood even a hope of as much as a glance from her. Thus, beautiful, worldly in manner, yet innocent in bodily fact, Beatrice was engaged and betrothed to the wealthiest and most powerful man within their spheres of reference and influence. She was now engaged to Barry. Big Barry. Big Bad Barry Robb, the dwarf, inn owner and landlord, and a criminal of countywide renown.

Earlier that same evening Big Barry had firmly instructed his fiancée and her approving mother on their evening's work. A task, he had set out for them - a mission of relative simplicity to any woman with a little art. They were to set the down-town barber, Zigzag MacCraw, at a table in The Star before the night was too long gone for any sort of sensible conversation with the blabbering old clipper. On a matter of pressing and urgent business he needed to speak with him, Barry had explained. It would be better that he arrived willingly in their escort rather than Barry have to send out a direct invitation. There on this mission in The Worldes End, Mary and Beatrice drank their spirits down quickly, ignoring the longing eyes of men about. At the nod from Mary they were up, and in a trail of skirts and perfume flounced back out into the main lounge, where MacCraw was still wallowing and glassy eyed. This of course was the opportunity. Starting, gasping, pretending it was the first time she'd espied her old flame that evening, Mary's formally poised face melted into a lovely grin, eyes sparkling, as though delighted from the heart to see him there before her. Foolish and lonely MacCraw, befuddled with drink and bewitched by surface beauty, was easily deceived, suddenly believing that his old looks and charms were about him; that he could melt the hearts of mother and daughter alike with a mere loping grin and raising of his eyebrows. Seeing their radiant greeting, he beckoned them both over, until on his call and with a bottle of good wine the three were soon ensconced in cosy chatter, familiar exchanges of smiles and shy glances, and shared memories of friends and times past. In with these MacCraw scattered comments and compliments upon the loveliness of Mary's angel-daughter, who sat smiling quietly and politely, listening respectfully, taking on the duty of pouring and topping up the drinks. For these ladies this was the work as good as done. It took little from there for Mary and Beatrice to have the much flattered and glance-pampered barber arm-locked between them, seemingly escorting them to their next port of call in this night – namely, at Beatrice's suggestion, The Old Star Inn.

As they entered the establishment of dubious repute, owned to the sawdust by Big Barry, the music and laughter seemed to enhance the glowing loveliness of MacCraw's good company, as though all humming, fuming and frittering within was for their convenience and entertainment alone. Even when MacCraw was joined at their jolly corner table by the familiar figure of the inn's owner, dressed dapperly in the latest styles and waistcoat, dripping with gold rings and chains about neck and wrists and fingers, the evening's conspiracy did not fall into place for the hapless barber. Two hefty looking companions, also extremely well dressed though with thickset, pugilistic faces, floated gracefully along behind the midget. Barry sat down at the narrow table directly opposite MacCraw. His employees moved around and stood behind MacCraw, one on either side, hemming him there like grotesque bookends. A serving girl appeared out of the bar-crowd and set down four full tumblers of brandy, then melted back away into the throng. Barry's women had done with their work now, his prey well baited into the lair, and at a winked signal Mary and Beatrice fluttered up like butterflies quitting the bloom. They bustled away toward the music room, where singers and a piano were enthralling the crowd with modern, hard played bawdy songs. At the departure of the women MacCraw seemed momentarily confused. He peered about through a sudden haze that seemed to have enveloped him. He peered forward through the mist at the diminutive figure he now found seated before him. Ladies gone. Lovelies departed. Sinister landlord now set there like a fleshy gargoyle. Notes of discord seemed to seep over in the distant piano chords. He realised that all was not well. He recognised the ever distinctive pot-lad of old, for he'd often seen him about his little business empire of taverns and music halls over the last years, and had even once or twice clipped his hair or whiskers in the shop. But now it seemed he was seeing the fellow with new, cleansed eyes and clearer vision. MacCraw was struck by the shocking expression on his face - the intense stare, the thick black brows, those glittering pits of eyes. Despite his stature he looked really strong - dangerously strong - which seemed odd and sinister in one so small. For MacCraw it was like being confronted with a horrific and menacing child; by something that was disturbingly cruel and against Nature. Barry's very physical presence made MacCraw feel strange within, and he felt as though he was coming down with a malady, his pulse sinking and slowing in the sudden unpleasant company. The very person, the very matter of the man, disgusted MacCraw to his core, and he could not exactly work out why. Something really was wrong.

'Good evening, Mister MacCraw,' Barry chirped at last, laying his hand as if fondly upon MacCraw's arm, patting him as though they were old and familiar friends. At his very touch an icy pang shot through MacCraw's blood. In the instant of that touch the lovely, rosy hue of the last hour vanished from the evening. MacCraw shuddered with a flood of dread, and he sensed that here he was in mortal danger.

Barry himself was totally sober, wits and faculties about him, as ever. He was straight in with the point at his guest, whose turn of mind he was well aware of, having partly engineered it.

'You'll remember me, Mister MacCraw?'

'Of course I do,' MacCraw slushed back thickly. 'I do believe, sir, our encounters go back many years now.'

'Indeed they do mister, indeed they do. As I recall, you used to think me something of a fool, on account of my ... well, shall we say my slight deformity?'

This sudden turn in the warm flow of the evening had completely thrown MacCraw, the soft comfort of feminine companions suddenly removed like cushions from a hard wooden bench. He tried to rake his wits about him, wondering what was on here with the dangerous midget.

'No... no sir. I never had you marked for a fool, nor considered you deformed. You always seemed too straight forward and content in yourself to be those.'

'Ah, well... a knave then? I recall that you were always a little wary of me and my, well, let's say my colourful history. You know I've been a man of straightforward violence, when the need arises. My manner and my ways have done well, though, MacCraw. Over these years I've set myself up nice and comfortable.'

'I've heard as much, sir. And I can see it. You've a good tailor. Good suit. Nice solid watch chain. And the rings, I see they're gold, too. Yes, you've certainly established a reputation.'

This was an insult, cleverly disguised by MacCraw despite his thick headedness. Barry smiled though, quite happy with it. The rings MacCraw spoke of were heavy weighted, one a set coin, another with a small protruding diamond in an upraised square of gold. He had other bulky rings on each sausage-like finger of the right hand; a vicious knuckle-duster of very expensive jewelry. A fist of metal, which had split open many a head and face before this night. As his business empire had grown, so had Barry's reputation for being ruthless and violent when it came to those who upset him, owed him money without effort of repayment, or in whatever way trod upon his metaphorical toes. Big Barry he might have been known as in relatively polite conversation, but Barry The Bastard perhaps better described him to those in the know of his brutal ways. MacCraw was by now quite fearful for his own well being. He felt chilled to the marrow, his neck and scalp hair prickling. The piano and song from the far room seemed utterly discordant now, voices braying rather than ringing in laughter or song. Visually too, things were awry, the gas lights reflecting hard blues and yellows from the faces around, drawing out the ghoulish shadow in them rather than illuminating and softening features toward the angelic. MacCraw, uneasy with the way he was seeing and feeling things, decided to come to the point of the matter then quit the foreboding situation before drink took him further into confusion.

'Is there a particular reason we're here in discourse, Barry?'

Barry laughed, shaking his head, the negative gesture slowing, halting, then he nodded. He nodded slowly and firmly, with utmost control. He raised his glass, urged MacCraw and his cronies to do likewise, and on a toast to 'old times and old friends' the lot of them downed the brandies.

'Ah yes, George MacCraw, I've certainly established my reputation, as you rightly put it. Believe it or not though - and you probably don't recall this, and I wouldn't blame you if you didn't - but a lot of my success over the years has been down to you. Which in a round about way is why you're sitting here comfortable now, and you've not been harmed as yet. You remember, years ago, just before Brontë passed on, and you and a pal turned up in Keighley at that a shack of a boozer I was running then...?'

Of course, MacCraw did remember it, and had dwelt back on it just recently, which made him feel all the more uncomfortable with his present situation. Caught in snatches from the corners of his vision, the brightness of people's eyes was also bothering him. Faces about him beyond Barry seemed unreal, like masks of frozen wax and dull glass. Closer in, he could see the pores and pigments of Barry's bulging face before him, the skin swirling and shimmering, unnatural in its clarity. His sudden persecutor went on.

'Well, I was little more than bar-boy then, though with a share in the place, and it always turned a profit. I had everyone believing I owned it outright, of course. Best building your reputation from the outset, I always reckoned. Oh yes, we were turning a profit all right. There's always a market in potions and substances, as you well know, MacCraw. But something you said back around then struck me as significant, and stuck with me from that day on. Property, you said. The future is in property. Strange word that, ain't it MacCraw. Property. Ownership. Bits of fabric, bits of things, bits of land. Buildings. Countries, even. Strange concept, property and ownership, least to a man of my thinking. But it did stick with me, and it seemed absurdly true. The future of this world would be in property. And from that day on, thanks to you, I strove to acquire it. Stuff. Items. Land. Buildings. Things. I scraped and I scratched. I acquired. I even stole. Oh yes, I stole, and I ain't ashamed to admit it. So you see Mister MacCraw, thanks to the odd word dropped by you all those years back, I owns this building. Also, I owns most of the souls in it, most of the places where they live, and half the buildings of this particular patch of town. Houses. Inns. Shops like yours. Wagons. A couple of fire carriages. All sorts, MacCraw. I've a wife deceased, another divorced, children scattered here and there, and half a dozen lovely girls at my beck and call, not to mention my lovely fiancée there. Young Beatrice. You know, Mary's lass. Ah – I see you didn't realise. Yes, she's mine too, MacCraw. I've my fine clothes, good food, good friends. In short, all in this life that a man, any man, might want, I have.'

Barry paused here, letting the silence swell between them. He clicked his fingers at a passing boy and within seconds fresh drinks were on the table.

'You've done well then,' MacCraw understated. He touched at his fresh glass with his fingertips, but just to push it slightly away. He felt peculiar as well as decidedly uneasy, and knew to leave further intoxicants well alone until this matter was resolved.

'But I've deeper interests too, MacCraw, other than the physical and material things of this life. You'll probably remember, like yourself I used to be a bit of a writer and yarn spinner. Back there, back in the thirties I'm talking about now. I don't bother with that no more. I ain't got time. But I do collect things associated with the old barding, George. Oh yes, I'm a regular collector. And one of the things I do like to collect is books. And the work before books. You know, words set down on pieces of paper, in print and in ink, that's what I do like to collect. Manuscripts, that's the word, isn't it. Books and manuscripts. Are you still a bit of a scribbler yourself, George?'

MacCraw barely had time to shake his head before Barry was on at him again. The fellow certainly could talk; he'd not lost that gift. As he half listened, concentration waning, MacCraw witnessed something odd across the room. Apple Martin and Fish David, heads swivelling, scanning over the crowd, had entered the inn together. Apple Martin, Pot Mary's cuckolded husband. Fish David, as MacCraw was aware, her latest liaison. The two spotted MacCraw and started to approach the table, then realised who he was sitting in company with. On a glance at each other they halted, turned heels, and headed away through the door into the music room, where at the last account, according to MacCraw's befuddled memory, Mary and Beatrice had headed. He wished he could see the scene in there, be viewing from the other side of

the door as the two fellows entered, both casting their eyes about for the same woman.
The dull hum of Barry's droning accent drew him back to the table. Suddenly he felt
annoyed. What was this? What was all this chattering nonsense? Barry had nothing
whatsoever to do with him or his life, and now he wanted to be away. He wanted away
from this ranting little runt of a thug. He wanted to be off with his own true old
friends where there was music and laugher and singing. He pressed his hands on the
wood of the table and attempted to rise, but was momentarily unsteady on his feet.
Two iron-strong hands gripped him upon the shoulders and thrust him rudely back
into his seat.

'What's this!?' MacCraw howled, swinging an arm back at Barry's rogue. A
swift slashing of fingers cracked upon the bone of his cheek, snapping his shocked face
back toward Barry. His cheek burned and he could feel stinging welt marks already
rising.

'Easy, fellas.' Barry crooned. 'Take it easy now, MacCraw. I tolerate no trouble
in here. And I'm not finished talking with you yet. You'll go nowhere 'till I've done.
I can see I need to be quick to the point now. So listen. Listen good. Like I said, I collect
books, and I collect manuscripts, and you'll appreciate the value of those, I'm sure.
And as I say, I have a lot of things, but there is one thing I don't have. Now, this
particular thing I don't have is, technically speaking, all mine.'

At last MacCraw, though confused and foggy, began to understand the flow of
the conversation that had been running about him. He reached for his drink again,
sipped on it, and listened, furious, helpless, appalled.

'It's a manuscript written by a mutual friend of ours. Well, a friend of mine, at
least. Indeed, I often saw him in coin, or a bit of this and that, when he fell short. Oh
yes, he ran up a good bill in my tavern back then. Now this manuscript, which as I say
is by rights mine anyway, I want to retrieve in its entirety. Our friend died well in my
debt, you see George. Up to the neck, you might say. A bar bill unpaid. Unsettled
gambling debts. The odd ounce of opium still owed for. You'll know yourself, he did
like a bit of a drink and a potion. But poor Branwell; he had no real money to call his
own. And now then, certain papers and manuscripts, as my two fellows here will
swear, even on oath in a court of law, well they were promised to me George. Promised
in the event of his death if bills and debts were still outstanding. Now, I can see you're
thinking, well why hasn't that little buffoon chased after these manuscripts before?
Why leave it till now? Truth is, Georgie, I didn't even know one of 'em was still in
existence until of late. See, it appears that at times old chum, you still can't resist the
pen and the post. You wrote a letter of late. Several letters in fact. A good mate of
mine, employed in the publishing world, which at the end of the day Georgie is run by
fellows of my sort in a different kind of round-a-bout way, drew my attention to your
letter. He let me know that you were claiming to have a manuscript of Branwell's,
which in fact belongs to me. In short, you have some of my property, George. You
have a very particular piece of my property, and I wants it back. And badly.'

All was swimming and confusion for MacCraw. The walls seemed to be
melting and no amount of hard-staring would freeze them back to solidity. Barry's
luminous and ridiculous face ballooned before him. There was no fixing the features
on it. It was like staring into a struggling fire, the features spluttering and dancing,
merging into one plume of flame them separating to harsh, startling solidity again.
Somewhere through this flux of confusion, MacCraw realised that some potion had
been slipped in with his drink just now, or into one of the drinks along the way with
Mary and Beatrice. Sheer brandy, no matter of what quality, could cause his confusion
to be so acute, his visual and spatial perception to be so disturbed. He had no doubt that

he had been drugged, or poisoned. There was nothing for it but to reach in the cavernous, suddenly cluttered and confusing recesses of his coats pockets, scrabbling about in them for his snuff-box, hoping that a short toot of his own snuff concoction might blast him back toward some sort of grip on the situation. Thus while Barry bobbled like a floating moon, faces were glass and smiles frozen, the music was a secret code that whispered to him of great and grave danger, with liquid fingers he managed to struggle open his silver box and sniff back there a decent snivel of his own snuff. Within moments the room fixed back into position about him. There, back there across the table, was a grinning, gloating Barry. The sounds and music hissed their way back toward some kind of sense and meaning.

'Aahh!' He sniffed another pinch, his confidence returning as the normality of the room restored itself. 'Sorry chum. I really don't know what you're talking about. Now if you'll excuse me...'

Again MacCraw attempted to rise and stagger out of the place, and again he was set with brutally firm hands back in his seat.

'Sorry Georgie, but you haven't outstayed your welcome just yet. You do know what I'm talking about. Exactly so, and precisely.'

A letter in MacCraw's own hand now materialised upon the dark table, hovering there, his own handwriting shivering and snaking like little angled worms above the surface of the paper. The top edge had been cut off so that no address of correspondence was visible, but MacCraw recognised it as one of the numerous missives he had posted out to newspapers and literary journals some weeks back.

'You can never trust the mail, Georgie.' Barry smiled, though somewhat wearily now. His fixed grin was slipping away at the edges, the lips curling cruelly, the eyes cold, without betrayal of emotion. Now he'd had enough of word games. Fixing MacCraw's eyeballs with his own, he broke direct to the crux of the matter.
'You have a copy of Branwell Brontë's 'Withering Hands', written by his own pen. Now then, he promised it to me, that story, in default of his debts. You have it. It's mine. I want it. Property, you see, Georgie. It's all a matter of property.'

But MacCraw, revived now through the fluxing haziness, was having none of this intimidation. He spoke brightly and breezily, feeling back with it again.

'Whatever Branwell gave to me, he gave it to me in trust. Possession, Barry, as they say, is nine tenths of the law. Even if there was such a document - and I may well have been making things up to stir certain debates and complacent minds, as I'm inclined to do from time to time - then technically and legally, as well as morally, that manuscript would be mine. If even there were such a thing, it would be stashed in a secure and secret place. In short, Barry, by threat, violence, death or whatever means you like, you can rest assured, you'll never have it from me. And certainly not by force.'

Barry frowned for the first time in the conversation. There was no trace now of real or pretend pleasantness about his face. He took up his drink and reclined in his seat, scowling at MacCraw.

'Perhaps you misunderstand me, Georgie. It's mine, and if you have it, I'll be having it back. By hook, crook or whatever, I'll have it. Your law and my law, perhaps they're different things. Me, I'm a Londoner. You - you're Irish stock, I believe. Two different ways and maybe two different laws. But by mine, you've got something that's mine, and something that I want back. ABC. That's how they spell it where I come from. By the terms of your real law, as it stands recorded down in books and in legislation, the nine tenths nonsense, well I've a dozen or more chitties still in my possession, signed by Branwell, saying that whatever material possessions he owns can be drawn and called upon in payment of his debts. I has 'em, Georgie, legally, sitting in the safe in my lawyer's office right now. Not that I ever expected to have use of them. In fact, as I recall it here, one of them explicitly states that in the event of non-payment of bills acquired due to services and refreshments provided by the barer of this tab, all written manuscripts of a literary or philosophical nature, published or otherwise, and rights associated with them, shall herewith revert to the bearer of this bill, etceteras etceteras, and all that in Latin too, if you like. Of course, all signed and dated appropriately, witnessed, countersigned by my own good self.'

MacCraw sensed himself helpless, physically and legally. He was sure that Barry owned no such tab, but would know just the man to fake one good enough to convince a crooked judge. The effect of his blasts of snuff was fading, the room again wobbling and swelling about him like a gigantic soap bubble, distances and perspectives warped, curves where there should have been angles in the corners. Laughter and voices faded and echoed as in a railway tunnel. Only Barry's face and voice remained singularly clear.

'So, ABC George. However, I've always had a generous nature, as you know. I've always stood my round in the tavern, and always looked after my mates and loyal employees. I do appreciate that you may have a sentimental and nostalgic attachment to the book that I want back, and I do recognise that you deserve some remuneration for being its caretaker all this time, so to speak.'

Barry grinned, baring yellow, horsy teeth. His face came pushing across the table right up to MacCraw's, his breath rasping, reeking of brandy and cigars.

'I suppose I'm making you an offer, my friend. Smoothing the way, as it were. And a ridiculously generous offer, on account of certain persons who have hired me being desperately keen to purchase my own property from me direct, and none other. One hundred pounds, Georgie. There, take that in. One hundred pounds, coins or paper, when you place that book on the table before me and give up on your letter writing nonsense. I won't ask you to accept the offer right now; not when it's plain you've a good amount of drink in yer. I'll give you a little time to think on it. Three days, in fact. It's a good offer MacCraw. A hundred pounds for nothing.'

The face drew back, settling in its right place above Barry's shoulders. With a click of the tongue he raised a chirpy wink.

'Right. That's it. Done. Off you go now. You think about it, though. Three days only. Three days to come to me here. If you ain't been, then my boys and me will be coming to you. Good night, sir.'

Arms linked under MacCraw's and he was hauled to his feet by the two thugs behind him. He could barely balance as he was escorted toward the door, the rogues quipping about how drunk he was; what a state to get in; how he ought to get himself off home to bed; how none seeing him like this would be down for a haircut the next day. Through the seedy, singing, laughing, dismal throng they escorted MacCraw, only releasing their tight grip on his arms once he was out in the street. Out there, out front, on the edge of a circle of gaslight, Fish David and Pot Mary were having a screaming, cursing row, her face a mask of fury, eyes burning, mad as a cat that might spring frenzied upon its foe at any moment. When they saw MacCraw and his escorts silhouetted in the doorway their screaming and language stopped dead. David stepped back away from her, cursing under his breath, spitting to the street as though ridding his mouth of a foul taste. The mask on Mary's face changed visibly, as if in fact she had picked up and popped on another face completely. She was soft smiles and glowing eyes now, gentle again, as earlier in the evening.

'Going home already, George? But we haven't even danced yet, and you promised.'

'Our friend's a bit worse for wear, Mary. You girls seem to have drunk him under the table.'

MacCraw's arms were released and he went stumbling over the pavement like a wretched, legless drunk. David, seeing the state of his friend, took his arm.

'Come on MacCraw, I'll see you down. I'm done here now, anyway.'

A black scowl from him to Mary. A snarl from her to him. A hearty cheerio from their host, Big Barry, with the two rogues grinning like clowns, waving in synchronised unison at the departing guests.

'They've tinkered with my drink,' MacCraw tried explaining to David. 'You bastards. You've tinkered with my drink.'

'Tut tut now Georgie, Not in front of the ladies. And don't forget, I'll be seeing you.'

'You'll not be seeing me, you little bastard dwarf. You'll not be seeing me, or the book, damn your eyes!'

'Come on George, away now, away,' urged David. 'You'll have the Blue Bottles on us with language like that.'

'By Friday, Georgie boy,' chirped Barry. He'd been joined now by beautiful Beatrice and snaked his stumpy arm up about her waist.

MacCraw would have hollered back more curses but indeed a constable was approaching them, whistling softly, swinging his baton. It was the fellow they called Duff, renowned for his brutality and by-the-stick law keeping. MacCraw, through his confusion and his rage, managed to control himself, walk along properly with the slight assistance of his David's crooked arm. The constable nodded as they passed, and as respectfully as they could manage they tipped their hats.

'Away along home now, gents?' questioned Duff, although in actuality it was a command, for he'd read the state of them from the street end.

'Aye, we are. I'll just see my good friend here to his door.'

Duff nodded with grave approval and passed them by, turning to cross the road and head along to Fountain Street, bypassing at a safe distance the doorway of The Star, for he could see a cluster there and wanted little to do on his own with that crowd.

'They've fixed my drink with some potion, David, I swear it on Caroline's grave. I'm never one to lose my legs, and you know that.'

'I do, George, I do. But anyway, you'll feel better when you're in bed at home.'

'It's the book. The book I was telling you of just the other week. Brontë's thing, remember? He wants it. Barry, of all people. The little gargoyle, he says it's his. He'll never have it. I'd rather die with it still hidden. I swear, I'll take it to the grave!'

The cold air, the constable, and the sharp fish-tang of his companion were working on MacCraw's senses, bringing him back toward sobriety. They clunked their way down through the silent streets. By the top of Ivegate he was able to weave and wobble unaided, and he heartily thanked David for his support.

'Come down for a last brandy with me,' he suggested. 'I've a good bottle in the cupboard. What do you say to a night-cap?'

David had his senses about him, and declined the offer. 'No thanks, George. I just want to get home to my own bed now. I've had enough of drink and trouble back there for one night.'

'You've done with Pot Mary, then, by the looks of things?'

David eyed MacCraw quizzically, unsure of how much he'd told the barber.

'Ah, you're better off without her, sir. She's one of Barry's now. She's a puppet. Her daughter there's to marry him, they were saying. They're all pulled by his strings.'

'I am better off without her, friend, but she's good company when she's good company. Now, George, goodnight. Get yourself on home.'

They clapped shoulders and parted there. MacCraw stumbled down the darkened pavement of Millergate, mumbling to himself, complaining to the empty street of his ill treatment. A mist seemed to be about him, with the street lamps casting long, menacing shadows through the gloom. He remembered his door seeming to waver there before him, and there was a snatch of a memory of struggling at the lock with his key. He thought he remembered entering the shop, collecting some money, then slipping back out again. Perhaps it had been a dream, but there was a mental glimmer of following the dark edges of streets and winding ginnels into parts of the town he usually dared not even visit in daylight. And then no more, though there was a nagging guilt. Had there been a woman? A young woman, with a soft voice and warm hands smoothing over his face. In through a doorway, up a narrow, unfamiliar staircase. No no – that, he assured himself, was just the stuff of drunken dreams. There'd been no night-journey. There'd been no lass. In through the door, and up onto the barbering chair. That must have been all there was too it. MacCraw awoke the next morning seated upright in his best barbering chair, still fully clothed, completely dishevelled, the door half open for all the world to see. He had no real idea of how he had got himself there.

CHAPTER 14

SONNET 1

On The Callousness Produced By Cares

Why hold young eyes to the fullest fount of tears;
And why do youthful breasts the oftenest sigh,
When fancied friends forsake, or lovers fly,
Or fancied woes and dangers wake their fears?
Ah! he who asks has seen but spring tide years;
Or Time's rough voice had long since told him why!
Increase of days increases misery,
And misery brings selfishness, which sears
The heart's first feelings: 'mid the battle's roar
In death's dread grasp, the soldier's eyes are blind
To comrades dying, and he whose hopes are o'er
Turns coldest from the sufferings of mankind:
A bleeding spirit oft delights in gore;
A tortured heart oft makes a tyrant mind.

Northangerland (P.B.B.)
1842

Bradford , March 1861

As MacCraw recovered that afternoon, set there at his living room table with a throbbing head, he grew more resolved by the hour to quit the town. He'd move on without leaving a trace or indication of where he had gone. Otherwise the rot that he was perceiving all around, rot and ruin that was now invading his own life, would pervade to the atoms of his marrow, wasting him to a sad and bitter death. A death by slow self-poisoning. That withering, wasting of flesh about the bone - that marasmus - was not for him. No, he'd not have that. He'd not go the way of Leyland and Brontë. He was a vital man; a living man. He would draw together and get a grip upon the strands of his own life. What he had glimpsed earlier in the week, on the slopes of Horton Green, now became a clear, life-directing vision. The time had come at last to leave this place. To leave it for good. No looking back, no coming back. Put his house in order, pick up his pack, and be on his way down the lanes and over glens. And at his age too - it would be no easy task. The very audacity of it made him laugh at the table there, with the fire lowering in the grate, the clock ticking on, the bought-in meat dinner he'd put out before himself setting into jelly and gravy, for despite his better instincts he had little appetite for food. He recalled one of the Rhymers – the boxer, Spider Walton, in fact - once telling him, with drunken ferocious certainty, that any real man could achieve any material objective, if he set it firmly in his mind to do so. And the course of a life could be radically changed at the drop of a hat. Ten seconds - that's all it ever takes to totally alter the course of a life, Spider had insisted. Ten seconds. Win a woman. Start a war. Set off on a journey. Put down roots. Ten seconds maximum to think and make the decision and totally alter the course of your life. Up the anchor. Trim the mainsail. Set her for starboard on the outward tide. The age of a man had nothing at all to do with such matters, as long as there was still some drive and vigour in the frame. There in his room MacCraw thumped a hand down on the table, sending his plate clattering, upsetting the glass of wine which spilled like blood over the dark table.

'America!' he said. That one word uttered, simply, decisively.

He was up and away from the table then, mess left, needing to pace the idea through. America. The decision made. He was going there. But then two things rankled in him as he circles the room. Two things, looming between the conception and the execution of his plan. Brontë's damned, troublesome, infuriating manuscript. And Caroline's grave. But nothing should stop him. Ten seconds. Decision made.

MacCraw ceased his pacing, sat back at the table and shoved his dinner plate aside. He leapt up again, stoked up the fire to a good warming blaze, shouted down to the lads that he must not be disturbed, gave the table top a good wipe over, then set out the implements of writing upon the table.

A letter he composed, short and to the point, to his brother Eammon, who seemed so unrealistically far away, residing in San Francisco, California, in the United States Of America. Without too many particulars or details he informed Eammon that he was intending to leave England once and for all, and to set himself up in some line of business across there. He had his trades, he had capital, and at only forty-four years of age, as far as could ever know, he still had a good few years before death or dotage. These years he sought now to enjoy in a little exploration of the wider world. He would, he stated, perhaps drop in on his brother within the next few months. Though he expected no charity, and there was no obligation to accommodate him. Whatever happened, it would be a delight to see his own flesh and blood again, as well as to have a personal and experienced contact upon that vast continent. He required no reply as such - perhaps a short missive sent upon receipt of this just to let him know that his letter had been received and that the way was clear and convenient, though depending upon the speed of mail these days he might well be on his way before such a reply was received. He would, he wrote there, be travelling under one of the old family names, although he would commit no more of that to paper and ink. Circumstance and particulars he would relate later, in the flesh. It was, he outlined, a sudden swell of sinister and life-endangering events along with his own dissatisfaction of his present life that was at last, thankfully, provoking him west.

The letter was written, sealed and posted within a single hour. Back up from the town's post office, regenerated and inspired by his plans, MacCraw made a pot of strong coffee. He shared the brew with Mufty and Trumper, then they all set about tidying the shop, which he now could plainly see had been allowed to slip into something of a degenerate and ruinous state.

Cleaning done, shop floor swept and scrubbed, shelves ship-shape, corners spicked and spanned, mirror polished, shaving mugs scrubbed, clean towels hung, chair leather and brass rubbed up to glassy shine, straps cleaned, razors hair-splitting sharp, oils, soaps and lotions made and topped up on the front cutting shelves, a last dust down, and the shop looked just about ready to be opened. By this time it was early evening, and the customers seemed to be doing their best to stay well away. Even though it had been a slack week, MacCraw decided to shut shop early, and it being Thursday he sent the lads off home with their full wages. He made up a packet of half-wage for little Jazeb Snell, who was still off sickly. In the morning, he decided, it would be completely back to business as usual, with bills and notices posted around town to draw the custom back in. It would be a vigorous, full sprinting, healthy business that he'd be selling and leaving when he slipped away from this town, not some invalid, hop-along concern, limping its way on wobbly financial crutches.

In the gleaming, soap-scented shop, MacCraw shaved and trimmed himself in front of the main chair, snipping down his frizzing sideburns, singeing away peeking ear and nostril hair. He went up stairs, put on a clean shirt and trousers, pulled on his sturdy black town-boots, then popped enough coin in his pocket to see him through a few drinks and a good dinner down at The Unicorn, where the food was always good. His simple intention was to eat well and have just a couple of porters to ease him back toward the clear headed sobriety that he would need to carry further through with his leaving preparations. After eating, he would pay a visit to The Snells; he would drop off the pay packet and have a talk with young Jazeb and his father. A serious talk. A termination of apprenticeship kind of talk. He needed to cut his losses now; be the hard and brutal businessman. But only if the lad was up to it. He wanted to be sure the lad was in some kind of health and recuperating from his illness. He wouldn't kick him while he was fully down, but his own house had to be put in order now. He thought well of the boy, and missed him about the shop, for though the other two were handy enough with the scissors and razor, they were on the lazy side, and little better than useless at keeping the shop in order. Jazeb had a natural inclination for the trade, including the old medicinal and potion mixing side. MacCraw had seen many apprentices come and go over the years, and he had no doubt that young Snell was one of his best to date. Still, MacCraw was determined to tell the lad that in the event of continuing ill-health he could only keep him on for two more weeks at half-pay. After that, if things were still not so well, then he would have to take on Mufty as full time lad and apprentice, this being a practical rather than personal matter. Illness or no illness, his business had to be seen to run along smoothly now that he intended to sell it on as a running concern.

MacCraw, shaved, dressed and determined, made his way out of the shop. He locked up and pocketed his keys. A check on his pocket-watch told him that it was going on for six thirty, so with plenty of time before Mister Snell finished his shift at the dye house, he made off up the street into the evening bustle on Ivegate. Had his mind been on his more immediate surroundings rather than future uncomfortable conversations, he might have paid attention to the two dapperly dressed gents who pressed themselves into the shadows of Dawson The Cutler's doorway as he hurried past. They seemed to be engrossed with a display of ivory handled kitchen knives there, admiring the quality of workmanship. One was stout, of average height, of average appearance; the other perhaps slightly on the tall and sinister looking side, though neither with anything too distinct or showy about their well tailored clothing other than the fashionably set angle of their hats. They watched the barber waddle up the street in the reflection of the doorway window. When he turned down onto Ivegate they spun from their peering and set off briskly after him.

As he picked over his meal in The Unicorn, comfortable enough near the fire, MacCraw struggled to remain relaxed about the task that lay ahead. To dismiss a boy who was sick and in impoverished circumstances did not sit easily with him. He was no stranger to childhood struggle and poverty. As a child, his own family's fortunes had fluctuated with the coming and going of his sea-faring father. Months, and sometimes years on end the family endured hand to mouth survival until, upon his father's return, with a small fortune stowed away in his trunk, they were suddenly catapulted into an oasis of luxury and good living. But the money never seemed to last long, the slow, prolonged impoverishment again creeping upon them as their father disappeared to sea on some new fortune-making venture.

Poverty he'd seen plenty of here in England, too. The black forties had been appalling in Bradford. He had witnessed the town mushroom in size around the valley centre; a chaotic, uncontrolled growth of building and population, with floods of refugees from the land's own countryside and from a starving, famine decimated Ireland. The town had been awash with the poorest dregs of the poor, hordes of them setting up ramshackle shantytowns on patches of wasteland or cramming themselves by the family into derelict cellar rooms, struggling against grime and sickness and starvation while all the time hoping to find some employment; some slender thread that would allow them to clamber up from starving, nightmare lives. Though no great Christian or humanitarian, in those blackest of times MacCraw had done what he could when and where he could to relieve the misery of certain families or individuals who he found within his sphere, and in particular he'd tried hard to help the Irish, for despite his past he could not turn his back on his own kind. Though it had been a trial to keep his own businesses and properties running and sustain his new married life, he'd given employment where he could, and had passed on small sums of money to help more than one family over a crisis. Hard work and perhaps good luck, if only in business, had seen him weather the turbulence in those years of upheaval. Due to peoples' vanity, despite the economic climate, he had always managed to literally cut a profit. When other small business concerns had gone bankrupt he had managed to save, and he had invested wisely in the railways. His ability to build upon his own initial capital, he saw now with hindsight, had been due to the fact that as beautician, hairdresser, barber or apothecary, he had always bought his premises and properties outright. No landlords or mercenary mercantile organisations had ever breathed down his neck as they awaited payment of a rent or a property securing loan.

'Ah yes,' he mumbled there over his sausages and potatoes in the snug of The Unicorn, dabbing at his gravy smeared chin with the napkin, catching himself before he continued aloud. Yes. Secure your property. Get yourself a secure base and strong foundation. And hard work, another key. Solid, hard, sustained work to promote and further the business.

But now, the job ahead – a sickly and impoverished employee. Poor little Jazeb Snell. Before the sickness had come upon him, MacCraw had seen a good, solid future for the lad. Several of his best apprentices over the years he had set up in their own venture, be it barbering or otherwise, sometimes loaning them a sum to set up, with little interest to repay so that they might get off in the world on a good footing. Success with these ventures had not always been the case. He'd seen good men and good businesses go under. He'd passed his 'failures' begging in the street and flipped them a coin too, even though they still owed him a good amount of money, though he doubted he'd ever see a farthing of it. He'd already considered Jazeb's future, and had been sure money sowed there would have been money well planted. Now though, with his altered plans, he would not be around to see the lad through his full range of learning in the trade. All that had been taught so far might well be wasted.

'Ah well, there's other true barbers who'll look at the lad,' he said out.

'Finished, sir?' the pot-lad inquired, presuming that MacCraw had called him over.

'Aye – yes. Finished, thank you. Take the lot away. Lovely. Thank you.'

He continued musing, lighting a pipe as the pot-lad clattered away the plate and cutlery. Whatever the outcomes with Jazeb, the thing could now only be resolved with a visit to the boy's home and parents. MacCraw did not like to call on people unannounced, but time and timing was of the essence now. So it was, dinner finished, gravy mopped up with bread, pipe smoked, another porter sipped down reflectively before the flames, MacCraw settled his account with the bar and headed out into the street to the unpleasant task that lay ahead.

CHAPTER 15

The general state of the surface of the streets of Bradford is respectable, but in most of the inferior and cross streets, chiefly inhabited by the working classes, the condition is quite otherwise. Few of those are paved at all; none of them properly. In some streets a piece of paving is laid half across the street, opposite one man's tenement, whilst his opposite neighbour contents himself with a slight covering of soft engine ashes, through which the native clay of the subsoil is seen protruding, with unequal surface, and pools of slop water and filth are visible all over the surface. The dungheaps are found in several parts in the streets, and open privies are seen in many directions. Large swill-tubs are placed in various places by pig-feeders for collecting the refuse from the families, for which they pay in some cases from 1d to 2d per week. The main sewers are discharged either into the brook or into the terminus or basin of a canal which runs into the lower part of the town. The water of this basin is often so charged with decaying matter, that in hot weather bubbles of sulphurated hydrogen are continually rising to the surface, and so much is the atmosphere loaded with that gas, that watch-cases and other materials of silver become black in the pockets of the workmen employed near the canal. The stench is sometimes very strong, and fevers prevail much all around. Taking the general condition of Bradford, I am obliged to pronounce it to be the most filthy town I visited.

James Smith, of Deanston
Report on the Sanitary Condition of Bradford, 1845

Bradford, March 1861

MacCraw had never visited the Snell household before, though he knew the address well enough. From The Unicorn it was back up the hill to John Street, then a short walk of half a mile or so through the old Black Abbey district which spread down the hill toward Thornton Beck. Though a short distance of a walk in his mind's working, it proved to be a walk into another, half-hidden world that though well aware of he rarely chose to venture in to. A dirtier and more wretched place he had never seen. The street running along the valley side was very narrow and muddy, the air about impregnated with loathsome, filthy odours that alone made him feel queasy. There were a good many small shops, but the only stock-in trade appeared to be heaps of children who, even at that time of the evening, were crawling in and out at the doors, or screaming from the lamp-lit interiors. The sole places that seemed to prosper amid the general blight of the place were little shacks of ale and gin -houses, illegal dens, and in them the lowest orders of Irish and local hustlers were wrangling, yelling, brawling, laughing and singing, all discordantly, all a cacophony. Covered ways and yards, which here and there diverged from the main street, disclosed little knots of shacks and tumbling down houses where drunken men and women were positively wallowing in the filth they found about them. MacCraw was just considering whether he hadn't better turn round and retrace his steps toward some kind of civilization, when he reached a broader street which branched off down the hill. This he took. The street went curling down into a labyrinth of other terraces. It was unpaved, and down the middle a foaming gutter forced its way, every now and then forming pools in the holes with which the uneven street was littered. Household slops of every description had been flung into the gutter, which in turn ran into pools, stagnated and crusted at the edges with waste. Heaps of ashes and discarded cinders were the stepping stones on which MacCraw picked his way by weak shop-lanterns. He passed clusters of women and children lurking about the little fires, leaning up against house walls or whispering morosely at the base of the few street lamps. He felt as though he had wandered amidst another humanity. All specimens were as ugly and undernourished as anywhere he'd seen in the city by night or day. The younger children gawked like rats upon MacCraw, who was thankful he had donned his boots as he picked his way by through the mire. They whispered and nudged each other, rattling up harsh accented comments about the rich gentleman, the fat rich gentleman, shouting after him a mixture of insults and pleas for spare coppers. All he passed were of the same, sallow complexion that glowed eerily and greenish in the gloom. These pallid faces, seemingly popped atop of rags and festering patched-up coats, bobbled and floated like diseased fish in a filthy pond. All here seemed small of stature, even the adults slight and spindly, some with warped backs and the bow legs typical of the lowest order of malnourished, ricket-ridden mill workers. The women seemed to walk awkwardly, deprived of any feminine grace, their chests thrust unnaturally upward due to the mis-shaping of their spines. They were, he knew, machine operatives, forced by their employment since girlhood to stand for long hours in unnatural postures as they scratched out their wages. Their very stature and posture was moulded by the machinery that they served; they were shaped and fashioned by the Age.

'Penny, mister?' A child popped before him, startling him, breaking his chain of thought.

'Away!'

'Can't yer spare a penny?'

'Away with you. Go on. Away!'

'Yah, yer miserable old gadger.'

A sudden swarm of children emerged around the first, their little gnomish faces twisted and angry.

'Yer great fat lump o' lard.'

'You old fat bastard.'

'Go on with you, you little rogues!'

Something whistled passed his ear and he hastened on, actually frightened by the little band of urchins. He didn't doubt that if he went down they would be on him like a pack of starving rats.

At last he came into the dimly lit clutter of Crown Street. Here were more tumbling cottage dwellings along with the ramshackle, makeshift huts and canvas dwellings of the rookery. A great slum had sprouted along every ginnel and patch of land around the Water Lane works. Here, along the edges of the mill works and one of the town's illicit slaughterhouses, the cottages were the oldest and the most filthy, the streets and beck edges littered with all kinds of vegetable waste and stinking offal. The very air was putrid, tainted with the smell of rotten meat and the spew of a dozen over-towering mill and dye house chimneys.

'No wonder the poor lad's sickly,' mumbled MacCraw, barely daring to breathe the thick, miasmic gas that passed here for air. He clamped his musk infused handkerchief over his suffering nose, checked with a stunted passer by that he was on the right street, and set about peering at the doors around him, searching for the house number where the Snell family had their dwelling. He approached the door of number twelve, the figures painted shakily in white on the green wood.

A wretched looking crone answered the door. She looked like a scarecrow woman of sticks flung into rags of shawl, skirts and headscarf. She peered out with a gleaming eye, birdishly jabbing forward, darting her head out beyond the frame while her body remained within. She peered down her hairy beak at him, nose angled up, seemingly puzzled and worried by the strange and well dressed gentleman at her door.

'Is Mister Snell about?' MacCraw requested politely.

'And who's asking? Who's asking?' she cawed, fluttering in her rags, hopping from foot to foot in the narrow opening.

'I'm MacCraw. George MacCraw. Barber. Employer of young Jazeb Snell.'

Here eyes picked him over and glimmered with recognition.

'Ah, the Mister MacCraw. The good hearted Mister MacCraw. I've heard all about you. So sorry, so sorry. You can't be too sure these days. We get all sorts knocking at this door. Come in, sir, please, do come in.'

This guardian of the hovel doorway was Jazeb's grandmother, Joseph Snell's own mother. She was unemployable other than child-carer and tender of the sick due to her great age and inconsistency of the mind. Muttering and gibbering of having heard of MacCraw, and his great business empire, and his generosity, and his kind heart, and his poor dear wife, and his own struggles and misfortunes of this life, she led him down a dark stone staircase and into their subterranean living area. The gloomy place had bare brick walls, and seemed little more than a candle lit tomb. The heavy air reeked of gin and cabbage. A window was set high in the bricks on the street side, but the small square panes that would have offered a view of passing feet at street level were covered with soot and grime, some of the little squares broken and stuffed with rags.

'The boys are doing much better now,' she croaked, hobbling across to a weakly lit fire place where a pot of coffee bubbled on a makeshift hob above thin flames. An oil lamp stood upon a leaning table, one broken leg propped up with stones to ensure it did not topple over. A couple of candles, smoking heavily, flickered out weaker light on a bit of a ledge above the fireplace, upon which a picture frame and a half completed embroidery of The Lords Prayer tilted precariously.

'Will you take coffee with me, Mister MacCraw? It would be a right honour. A great honour, you know.'

'No, thank you, mam, I won't have a coffee yet, thanks all the same. It's Mister Snell I'd like to see, if he's about. And young Jazeb, if he's well enough.'

She clicked her mouth and flapped her rags, put out that he wouldn't join her in a gin and coffee.

'Oh, he's much better now, much better, thanks all the same' she clacked. 'He's dozing though. Both of them are. In a nice, peaceful doze, they are. They're through there...' She nodded across to a doorway, an ancient, mouldy curtain serving as a door between the rooms.

'We have them down here because it's warmer, you see. Upstairs there's proper windows. Ruined, they are. Freezing, it is. So, we let the rooms, you see. To traders; decent traders, and gentlemen the like. Respectable folk, you know sir. All of them up there. Oh, aye, don't believe all you hear. Respectable folks. And renting out to them helps keep our heads above water, so it does.'

'And Mister Snell, would he be about?'

'Well he would, but he's at work, you see. And mother is too. She's on at the mill. Supervisor, you know. My lad Joseph, he'll be there at the dye house 'til the hooter at eight o'clock. He's not been the best himself, you know. A bit sickly and morbid minded. But we struggle on, we do. Oh, we struggle and keep our heads above water, Mister MacCraw. We're right good and experienced at doing that.'

She fluttered and clattered about around the fire place, moving empty, worn out pans from one place to another, checking the coffee pan, tipping some of the viscous black tar into a battered tin mug that MacCraw suspected was already half filled with gin.

'You'll not have that coffee with me then, sir? It's all I can offer, I'm afraid.'

'No thanks, mam. I'd like to see the lads, though, if that's at all possible. I'm no doctor, you know, but I've had a lot of experience of medicines. I've a knowledge of ailments. You never know, I might be able to help a little.'

'Of course you can see 'em, Mister MacCraw. Quiet now, though. They're dozing, you see. All warm and in slumber. Best medicine, sometimes, a little sleep is.'

Taking a good gulp of reeking coffee, she placed the mug beside the fireplace, then gestured for MacCraw to follow across through the curtained doorway. The room there was in darkness, but she took a taper and lit two stubs of candles which she set on a wooden shelf. The room was narrow, two rickety beds crammed close together and bearing their little sleepers within. A rough hewn stool, like that used by milkmaids on a dairy farm, was set between the beds, beside it a clay pot for phlegm and vomit. As his eyes grew accustomed to the candlelight he could discern the figures of the huddled boys, Jazeb and his younger brother Jonas, both deep in a grimacing, painful looking sleep. There was three or so years between the two lads, but now with their hair tousled and both husk-withered with the sickness, it was difficult to tell them apart. Jazeb he guessed was on his right, seeming here to have larger features, though that could well have been a play of the flickering light.

'Aye, that's Jazeb,' the grandmother croaked as MacCraw lingered over him.

He looked over the boys and around the drab little room. Between the beds at the wall was a low set fireplace in a rusty, broken grate, the grate full of cold cinders. On the slanting shelf - a strip of a crumbling plank fixed into its horizontal place by being balanced on nails - was a cracked drinking glass, the candles illuminating the space, and a scattering of glass bottles. A closer inspection of the bottles and their labels confirmed MacCraw's suspicions about the deep, shallow-breathed sleep of the two lads.

'Aye, they've had their medicine, they have,' she clucked as he read over the labels on the bottles. 'They've had their medicine. Sleeping now. Best medicine, a good bit o' sleep.'

'*Mother's Blessing*' one label boasted. '*Quietness*' whispered another. Laudanum concoctions; opiates blended with alcohol, flavourings and water. The very stuff of which MacCraw's father had cobbled together his fortune in his last years. Fine stuff for a bit of heavy, senseless sleeping, but of absolutely no use against true sickness such as had gripped the lads. MacCraw, knowing well of the properties and the value of the contents, was somewhat concerned, and his face communicated this to the grandmother.

'How much of this have they had?' he asked, holding out the only bottle that still held some of its contents, that being labeled 'Infant's Easy Sleep'.

'Oh, plenty,' she chirped, answering contrary to what he wished to hear, but as he expected. ' Well, as least plenty enough to set 'em on in a good slumber, Mister MacCraw. I swear by my medicines, you know.'

'Ah. I feared as much.'

She nodded moronically, grinning a toothless gap of mouth. Her own eyes were somewhat glazed like those of a dead fish on a market table, and he suspected that apart from the gin she'd probably been dipping into the medicines as well.

'I just give 'em enough to let 'em rest, mister. It's the only thing that puts them out of their spasms. We've got to get some rest too, you know sir. I've been nursing them night and day for weeks, you see. Now that terrible coughing - it keeps us all awake at night. That there's the only thing that settles them down.'

The guilty crone gazed off at the wall, as though troubled with herself, face dropping, looking suddenly so weary. She bit at her lower lip, rasping her bony hands together like dry sticks.

'I just want 'em to get well, Mister MacCraw,' she mumbled. 'I'm just doing the best as I can.'

'I don't doubt it,' said MacCraw, feeling a pang of sorrow for her now. 'And is their coughing no better then when they rouse from this stuff?'

'It's better than it was a week ago, but still as bad as I've heard in a set bairns for many a year. But there's sickness all about here. There's bairns dropping out of life like Mayflies. We can't afford other medicine, sir, and that's the truth. Nor a doctor. And there's no chance at the infirmary, is there? We do the best we can, and sleep's as good a medicine as I can give 'em, for now.'

Just as they were crossing back into the main living area, Jazeb stirred. He rolled in his bed, mumbling and trying to sit up, roused toward consciousness. He murmured up nonsensical phrases, speaking from his dreams, arms flapping then flopping out over the edge of the bed. MacCraw turned back and took up a spindly limb, allowing the clammy wires of fingers to curl about his own. With his other hand he felt the weak and erratic pulse. Suddenly Jazeb sat bolt upright, eyes snapping wide open, staring ahead as if in terror, then looking into his employer's face, confused that reality had intruded into the vague substance of his dream .

'It's Mister MacCraw,' he called out. 'It's Mister MacCraw!' His brow furrowed in puzzlement, unable to reason out why the barber should be in the basement bedroom.

'It is me, Jazeb. Now take it easy. Take it easy, son.'

The invalid snatched back his arm from MacCraw's tender clasp and mopped it across his forehead.

' Mister MacCraw. Mister MacCraw. Oh sir, you've not come to fire me, have you sir? I'll be back in tomorrow, I swear it. I'm fit again now. I'm better now. Look, I'm up. I'm up...'

The poor lad attempted to scramble up from the bed, eyes wide and black in his desperate, skeletal face.

'Relax, my boy. Back down, back down,' soothed MacCraw. He had to steel himself now, and either lie, or change his previous plan and intentions, having come there to terminate the boy's employment.

'Stay steady, son, and rest yourself. Your job's safe as long as you are. I just happened to be passing by this way and thought I'd drop in to see how you were getting on. The shop's hardly surviving without you, lad. How do feel in yourself?'

'Oh, I'm feeling very well, Mister MacCraw. Another day or two and I'll be on top form. I'll be back in. Please, Mister MacCraw...'

As if a sudden fit had taken on him, the lad darted looks about the gloomy room, his face fixed rigid with a mask of deadly apprehension.

'Jonas!' he called out. 'Oh, Nanna, Nanna - our Jonas!'

He was struggling to see round MacCraw to where his brother should be laying.

'Sh sh sh... calm now. Your brother's fine. He's sleeping. Don't wake him now.'

'He's fine, pet,' his gran assured, crowding back into the chamber alongside MacCraw. 'Now then, you get back to sleeping, lovely. Come on Mister MacCraw, let's be out of here now. Let the lads get on with their precious sleeping.'

'Do you need a drink or anything?' MacCraw whispered to his apprentice. The boy nodded eagerly, and MacCraw had the crone fetch in mugs of cold water from the urn.

MacCraw went through the curtain and stood before the fire in the main room, leaving the gran to fuss over and tend the boys, fluffing up their ragged pillows, setting them both a drink of water between the cots, tucking in their thin blankets to keep the draughts from further chilling their bones. When she had done he at last assented to a cup of the old dame's coffee, a brackish substance that tasted like tar, though it was better with a splash of brandy from MacCraw's own hip-flask, to which he also treated his host. They stood a while there in the bleak little room, MacCraw sipping at his tin mug, humming and nodding to her chattering and gossip. He was anxious now to quit the unwholesome place, and was just about ready to give up the ghost on Mister Snell when he heard the clattering of the outside door. The smell arrived before the man - a vinegary, sulphurous odour which wisped and ribboned its way down the stairs. In stepped Snell, banging and cursing, filthy, tired and angry after his hard day's toil. He stopped dead in his tracks when he saw they had a visitor.

'Mister MacCraw - excuse my language, sir,' he shouted, snatching off his cap out of politeness. 'I never realised we had company. I swear, I don't normally come in cussing like that, do I ma? There, you see sir. But I've had a bugger of a day, sir, a bugger of a day.'

In the gloom of the basement Snell looked a fearful and intimidating figure. He was caked in filth and dyes from scalp to toe, his overalls smeared with black oil, every pore of skin on face and hands covered with colour. He took the pint pot of freshly poured beer that his mother now handed him and quenched it down in a single slurp, washing away the grime that caked the inside of his mouth and throat.

'No need to apologise on my behalf, Mister Snell. I can see you've been hard at it. And please, do call me George. I can't be standing on all this formality, you know. I can see you're tired, and I daresay hungry too, so I won't keep you long.'

'He's already looked at the boys,' the old mother called over shoulder, for she was suddenly animated about the fire which she'd charged up with wood and coal, and was now bustling about with pans and packages, catching up with the preparation of the evening meal that she had neglected in MacCraw's company.

'He's looked at the boys, and they're sleeping fine.'

'Well, that's good. They were badly this morning, MacCraw. That stuff you gave me did ease them up a bit, but they've not had the strength to smoke any yet.'

'Ah, well, one stage at a time. Like I say, I won't keep you any longer. I was just passing and thought I'd call to see how Jazeb was getting on. I didn't realise the young 'un was sickly too.'

'I know, it's a bloody nuisance. Pardon my language, but both down with it now, along with half of the neighbourhood. It wears you out, sir. I'm just hoping that none of us get laid low. Have they been up at all, mother?'

'No, lad. Just sleeping. Best thing for them, ask mister here. Though Jazeb did wake up a while ago, he did. Not long back'

'A few minutes ago,' MacCraw confirmed. 'He seemed a little delirious, though his pulse is strong enough.'

Snell and MacCraw stood awkwardly in the middle of the little room. Snell's eyes had little circles of white about them where his skin there had escaped the dyes, making it look as though he wore a comic pair of spectacles. These circles widened as he looked into MacCraw's eyes.

'I fear, sir...' he mumbled, bowing his head, wringing his rag of a cap in his hands. 'I fear, if you'll permit me to be frank with yer, that you've come to relieve our Jazeb of his apprenticeship. Now, I can't say as I blame you, him being off a while now, but it'll be a blow to us. It's good money you pay him, and as you know, he loves the work. I've been expecting it though, this visit, like.'

Of course Snell had hit the nail on the head. But a few drinks on since his earnest departure from the shop, along with the terrible things he'd seen in the streets as well as the Snell household, and MacCraw had softened. His general plan was still running strong in the same direction - that of departure from the shop, quitting his home and the nation - but at this particular branch he had been derailed and wanted to alter his route somewhat. He shook his head, no no noing at Snell with his lips.

'No. I've not come here to give him the sack, Mister Snell. Far from it. I've said myself, he's a good hard worker, and he learns quickly. Beside, he reminds me a bit of myself when I was a lad. We all fall sick sometimes. I'm sure he'll pull through it. The fact is, ...' - and here he was thinking on his feet as his emerging plans took to the shaping of events - '... I've arranged for a doctor to drop by and give the lads a check over. A reputable fellow and a good friend of mine, Doctor Simpson. Don't fret, mam...'

The old mother had dropped an empty pan and muttered about the cost.

'...I pay into a fund and the bill will be mine,' declared MacCraw. 'I want the lad well, and his brother too. Let's get your family up on their feet. I want him back at work, quite frankly, so it's in my interest to see him well. No no, Mister Snell...'

Here Snell was head-shaking, imploring him to think again, for it was too much of them to hope.

'Now now, it's all arranged, I tell you. Doctor Simpson might as well look at two as one. He'll be here Monday evening at the very latest. Only promise me one thing, both of you...'

Under these fantastical circumstances they were ready to promise him the world.

'Don't be giving them any more of this muck now...' and here he held up the bottle of 'Easy Sleep' from which the old dame had been treating them.

'Anything like this is no use to them now. Let them come back into themselves now and the illness will take its own course. Keep them off such juice until the doctor's been, and he'll tell you himself that this will just perish them further. A tot of brandy two or three times a day would be better now - something to stimulate them and get their little bodies going again. And keep on with the coltsfoot.'

Promises were wrung out of them, and they were all thankfulness, amazement, bows, handshakes, though MacCraw was seeking none of that.

'You're an angel, sir, an angel,' Snell's old mother was murmuring. 'I've heard it from others, and now I've seen it for myself. God bless, sir, God bless.' She was trying to kiss his hands but he pulled away.

'Now now, mam, no need to be ridiculous. I'll be on my way, Mister Snell.'

He went squeezing between them in the little room, making sharply for the stairs. Snell followed, guiding his guest up to the street door.

'Remember to remind your good mother to keep them off that sleeping stuff now, will you Mister Snell. It's poison when it's over-used.'

'I will, Mister MacCraw, I'll see to it. And I'm sure the lad'll be back at work next week, doctor or not. He'll soon be strong enough to push a brush, at least.'

MacCraw, in a final act of goodwill, pressed the packet coins he'd brought with him into Snell's hand.

'The lad's wages,' he explained as Snell attempted to press the packet back on him. 'Half pay though, as I said before to you. No no, don't try give it back. It's to see him over until he returns. It's not charity, sir - don't get me wrong on that count. While the lad's in my employ he'll get his pay, or what he's due.'

MacCraw pulled on his hat and was back out into the mire of the street.

'Well, God bless you mister MacCraw. She's right, is mother. You're an angel sir.'

'Ah, stop it, will you; you'll have me blushing and weeping, man. We all have our flaws, Mister Snell, and I'm well aware of mine.'

'But I do owe you a favour sir. If there's anything I can ever do, I promise I'm at your call. You know that now for sure.'

'Well, I might well be calling you on that promise sooner than you'd think, mister. But for now, sir, goodnight. You get down to your supper and your family.' Snell nodded and winked a white eye. MacCraw went picking his way over the puddles and rubbish of the courtyard, waving back over his shoulder, barely able to see the ground before him in the evening's darkness.

CHAPTER 16

I enter upon this part of my subject with a deeps sense of the misery, the vice, the ignorance, and the want that encompass us on every side - I enter upon it after much grave attention to the subject, observing closely, reflecting patiently, and generalising cautiously upon the phenomena and causes of the vice and crime of this city - I enter upon it after a thoughtful study of the habits and character of the 'outcast' class generally - I enter upon it, moreover, as forming an integral and most important part of the task I have imposed upon myself.

Henry Mayhew
  Foreword to 'London Labour and The London Poor' Volume 4

Bradford, March 1861

Water was all about him. Freezing ocean water, glassy green, entombed him, yet his feet were embedded firmly in the mud of the earth. He could not breathe and the brine was burning at his eyes. Though frozen and immobilsed, he knew he must get himself up above to the surface to snatch a breath of air, or die. Worms and the slime of wet earth went creeping between his bare toes as he kicked and worked the ground loose from about his bootless ankles. Looking down, through the swirling green haze, he could see that his feet had in fact been planted in a freshly turned grave. They'd buried him already, and while still alive. And there was the headstone behind him; he could see it as he twisted and swivelled, drilling himself free from the murderous trap. From his mouth great packets of air unfolded into bubbles as at last he went rising up toward the surface and daylight. As his lungs clenched and imploded with the airless agony he at last broke the surface, croaked and groaned air, his eyes smarting with the salt and brightness of the blue above. His coat fanned out on the surface behind him, helping him keep afloat as he flapped his arms and kicked his leaden legs. For a moment or two, so relieved to have made it up for air, the panic in his guts subsided, but then came clamouring back as he saw his new predicament. The ocean about him was calm enough, but it stretched endlessly to each horizon, placing him directly in the centre of a vast grey circle. A tiny, smoking speck broke the flat of the horizon to his left - a steam ship, moving away from him. A tall, hatted figure stood against the railings of the ship's stern, waving at him; grinning and waving. The vessel, and his hope of rescue, melted from view into the dark horizon.

'You pushed me,' shouted MacCraw. *Save your energy now*, an inner voice warned. *Don't get excitable. You must remain calm.*

'You pushed me, you little bastard,' he screamed, ignoring his better self. He was lost. Worst than lost. Already the weight of his sodden coat was starting to drag him back down, and he struggled out of it, knowing now that his only hope was to swim. But which direction? Each way looked the same. *After the ship, you fool,* his voice told him. *It's your own only hope. Swim after the ship and there's a chance.* Already the water was icy about him, numbing him, making his thoughts and movements sluggish. Of all the ends, in all the places...

With a sore, throbbing head and bitterly cold feet, MacCraw surfaced from unconsciousness and dreams. He was utterly confused, sitting bolt upright, groaning out as pain stabbed through the side and back of his head, jabbing right down his spine. It was no ocean that he found himself in, but pools of mud and slime - in worse than mud and slime, for it stank. Trying to make some sense of the situation, he went feeling around himself, feeling for his hat, coat and boots. He was wearing none of these, yet he was most certainly not in a bed. After a few seconds of fruitless scrabbling in the mire, during which he succeeded only in making himself more filthy, MacCraw clambered to his feet. He steadied and supported himself on the stone wall of the ginnel where he had been lying. There was a crack of sky between the buildings, and beyond that a view of a sloping, slate house roof. The sky was already lightening toward day, and it was bitterly cold. *A long time since*, he thought. *A long time since I got so drunk so as not to make it home.* Then he remembered. He had not been drunk at all. In relative terms, he'd barely touched a drop. Pictures of Snell's house, and of leaving there, and the streets about came flickering through in memory snatches. He rubbed over the back of his aching head and around to the throbbing right temple. There was a bump there, and he tried to focus on the blur of hand that he held before his face. Blood on the fingers; his blood, wet, sticky, rust red. Quickly becoming sensible of his whereabouts, with more memories filtering back, he snatched up his crumpled hat then tottered along the ginnel toward the street opening. The corner of his eye was stinging now, and he fingered over it as he stumbled along, panicking, wondering just how badly damaged he was. He could feel the swollen, jagged edges of a laceration there. He'd been hit with something - some cosh, or perhaps a rattan end. He staggered into the open street, ready to cry robbery and blue murder, but the whole places was deserted. All were still abed, and he didn't fancy waking up this low neighbourhood with a hullabaloo. He fingered his waistcoat pocket for his watch to see exactly what time of morning it was, but of course there was nothing there but empty pocket. He checked his other pockets. The same. No wallet, no watch, no snuffbox, no keys. And damn it all, no boots on his feet even. The locket was still about his neck, thank God, but he was well and truly robbed and beaten.

Now that he was on the open street more of the night came back. He recalled leaving Snell's place, seen safely out by Mister Snell. Then he had been fine, clear headed, steady on his feet. There had been groups of figures huddled on the street corners and cluttered in doorways, but he'd passed these without problem or threat, absorbed in his own business and preoccupations, barely even noticing where his feet were taking him other than around puddles. He had been zig-zagging through streets, cutting up the hill toward Sunbridge Road while mulling over the fact that he had promised the Snells a doctor. Doctors were always busy men, his friend Simpson included. To arrange a call out for next week would need some notice. He'd been considering whether he ought to sort out the appointment that same night while the notion was still strong and fresh in his mind, his head bowed down, grumbling opinions on the matter to himself. He had scarcely been aware of the footsteps clipping up behind him.

'Excuse me sir, would you have the time about you?'

It was a familiar, southern lilt - Kerry or Kilarney way, though somewhat refined and Anglicised. He had swivelled round, expecting to recognise the face of the questioner even in the dim light of the single street lamp.

'I don't, I'm afraid,' he replied. He was not in the habit of taking out his watch in the middle of the street, and not at night time.

'Hullo! Is it George MacCraw there?' the speaker chirped, as though amazed at recognising an old friend in these streets.

'It is that. Do I know you, gentlemen?'

There were two of them; young fellows, well trimmed beards, features blackened out by the shadows of their hat rims. He sensed no danger from them - they were well dressed; hardly dandies, but not starving ruffians either.

'George! So good to see you.'

He had leaned forward toward the light to catch a better view of the fellow's face - and then nothing. No memory of a scuffle. A blow had been struck then, undoubtedly, and before he'd even got a good look at his assailants. And now the pain was ringing through his skull. They had caught him at least two good blows all right, taking him completely unawares.

'You're getting sloppy in your old age, and slow off the mark too.'

And when down they had emptied him from top to toe - every pocket pulled out, even his boots stolen.

'Bastards,' he cursed now, picking his way through the puddles, fearful of what chill he might have caught laid out the night there, and of what disease was seeping up between his frozen toes.

Out on Sunbridge Road a few carts were trundling toward the town centre, people emerging from the mist like pressed shadows, shuffling on their way to work or the markets. There was no sign of a watchman or a constable. Seeing no point in bothering these early shufflers with his predicament, he set himself in a likewise townward direction. He was not overly concerned about his missing pocket-contents, but the fact that his house and shop keys had gone sent pangs of worry shooting through his guts. The theft of his boots he bitterly resented. Comfortable boots, well worn in, expensively made to his own specifications.

'What sort of scum-of-the-earth would take another man's boots? And in this weather too.'

Big Barry, his own mind answered.

'Or those about his work.'

Muttering and cursing, MacCraw worked his way along to drier streets. As he approached the Queens Mill and his own street a feeling of dread and foreboding engulfed him. They had taken his keys. They had called to him by name. They had known him, and he could only presume that they knew where he worked and lived. His heart plummeted as he footed up Millergate and saw his shop door open to the street. Tears welled in his eyes. *Done over,* he was thinking. *I've been done over.*

The shutters were closed but with the door open he could see that no lamps were lit within. That someone had entered the place he had no doubt, and he went running up the hill despite his stockinged feet, great sobs escaping his lungs.

'If I get my hands on them ... if I get my hands on them...'

Without even stopping to listen at the shop doorway MacCraw rushed in, ready for the fray. He stood there panting, at a glance the shop room seeming deserted. He listened now, but beyond his own raspings he could hear nothing - no noise of rummaging or ransacking or footfall upstairs above. His intruders had been and gone. Still, he snatched up a razor just in case, then lit the shop gas lamp, listening all the while. A low, animal moan escaped his lips as the light came up. The room about him was in chaos and disarray. For the first time in many a year, George MacCraw sobbed and blubbered aloud like a great baby, sinking to his knees at the foot of his best barbering chair, crying amidst the wreck and debris there.

In a trance, he roused himself and wandered through the rooms.
Disarray. Chaos of clutter. Ransacked and violated. Drawers ripped out from cupboards, contents turned out over the floor. Shelves shoved clear of books. Shattered ornaments. Bottles broken. Jars smashed. He rushed up and down the stairs, from room to ravaged room, open razor ready in his expert hand, lantern in the other. He moved upon instinct and rage, rushing into his living quarters, seeing the same chaos there. The property had been ransacked from top to bottom, with signs of methodical but wanton destruction in every room. His bedding box too had been upturned, emptied and rummaged through, and as he now suspected, the few letters and manuscript fragments of Branwell's and Caroline's that he'd left there, the ones he had been waiting to read and burn, had gone.

'So that's it,' he muttered, checking beneath the bed, in the bed, around the bed. Gone though, every last leaf.

'So ... that's what the devil's were after.'

Heart thumping, he rushed back down the stairs and locked the door against the open street. Every cranny of the house was searched for the intruders, but they had long gone. Only when he was certain that he was alone in the house did MacCraw return to his bedroom. Outside it was broad daylight now, but he kept his curtains closed and the lamp lit. He knelt before his hearth, so relieved to see it undisturbed, still full of ash and cinders from the last fire there. He gathered up the cinders and ash into the bucket, removed the grating and the pan, then scrabbled about for the small ring that would release the stone. The stone came up easily, and there in the hollow beneath, undisturbed in its well chosen hiding place, was his iron strong box. Once again he checked the stairwells and corridor for intruders, then returned to his room and hauled the box into the open. He was certain now that it had not been discovered or tampered with. All his papers rested here, for he trusted no banker or lawyer. He quickly checked through them - his property deeds; his passports; bonds; share and holding details; a package of hard cash in notes; various items of gold jewelry. And crammed in with that lot, the brown parcelled manuscript that he knew the felons had been rooting for. Branwell's manuscript. '*The Withering Hands*'. The same sheets MacCraw had sat watching him scribble upon while waiting for his friend before making a wild night of it on the town. MacCraw sitting on the bed in the Fountain Street garret, studying Branwell's sketches and paintings while he waited.

'... just one more sentence, George, then I'll be out with you...'

'No rush, Branwell. You get on with it.'

'One more sentence, then this page is done...'

The sentences becoming paragraphs, paragraphs pages, and MacCraw had often sat there for up to an hour at a time while Branwell pushed on with the story that he was unravelling in ink - the same dark and sombre tale that he'd tell of and embellish week upon week around that fireplace in the Worldes End. The same story that was now at large in the world in book form, with another name and title upon its jacket.

MacCraw fingered and smoothed the old parcel. This was what they'd been after, all right. Well, now they had their scraps and their pieces of journal perhaps they would be happy and stay away. But by attacking him and violating his property they had shown their hand; proved his worries of the last weeks to be well founded. The game had been flushed out into the open, and if he was to be the quarry, then he would not go down to the pack without giving them a good run for it. MacCraw reached into the box for the last item, which lay wrapped in a red velvet cloth there at the bottom of the box. This he set on the floor beside the fireplace, then returned all the other items back into their safe house. The box he returned to its hollow, the hearth stone he set back in place, the grate returned, the cinders and ash scattered back there to conceal any trace or clue of the hideaway. This done, his hands dusted and rinsed with water from the jug, MacCraw tenderly set the velvet package upon his writing table. Carefully, as though unwrapping a new baby from the covering in its little manger, he opened up the velvet and peeled away the soft cushions of wool within. Gingerly, with one hand, he lifted out the gleaming weapon, which he set there on the table. It was an American model, a Colt 45, sent over in a parcel from the Americas years before as a birthday present from Eamon. In the accompanying letter his brother had maintained that no man there went without one; that it was a beautiful creature of a weapon, and was certainly superior to anything he'd ever seen imported from Europe. MacCraw had tested the gun in the fields around Heaton soon after its delivery, though shooting at nothing more than rabbits and birds. For over ten years now it had rested undisturbed in its bedding, only taken out from time to time for a check over, an oiling and a cleaning.

'Well my beauty, your day may well have dawned,' whispered MacCraw, handling the weapon delicately, checking the trigger mechanism and the revolving cartridge chamber, loading the chambers with the narrow cartridges from the packaging. When the gun was loaded up and ready for use, though with its safety catch mechanism in place, MacCraw took up his second topcoat from the hook behind the bedroom door. He slipped the revolver into the inside breast pocket, which was just deep enough to take the barrel length. He put on the coat and he could feel the weight of the weapon hanging comfortably there on his left. He felt instantly safer, stronger, ready now to face what the day, and more probably the night, might bring. Rebooted in his best black knee-length boots, clean shirt on, face washed, wounds self-cleaned and dressed with his own witchhazel and yarrow concoction, MacCraw went down and set about tidying up the ruin of his shop. He was still at the work when Mufty and Trumper arrived. They stared about in disbelief, shocked at the mess of shop and MacCraw's face. He mumbled an improbable explanation about a quarrelsome night over cards; the angry losers attacking him and wrecking the shop. He presented them with a shilling to share, telling them to go away a while and get some breakfast. They were to forget work for that morning and enjoy the town, though they needed to be back around eleven as the shop would be opening again bang on midday. They departed with shaking heads and confused looks, not knowing what to make of their boss and his troubles. MacCraw gave them ten minutes start, then securely armed with the revolver, and with his best hat, he stepped back out into the day. He was intent on calling upon the legitimate forces of The Law to make sure they knew the details of his assault and predicament. He was intent also on his own less legitimate settling of the ridiculous business, of which he would say nothing to the police.

CHAPTER 17

For problems with ingrown toenails, may I suggest an ancient and proven remedy. Take a good portion of the amadou, this being a hoof-shaped, triangular fungus that can be purchased through any decent apothecary. Prepare the fungus by cutting it into slices, which are then chopped and beaten, soaked in a solution of niter then allowed to dry out of sunlight. Insert pieces of the preparation between the offending nail and flesh of the toe, or press pieces against the inflicted area over a period of at least three days by means of bandages, poultices or tight stockings. Relief is guaranteed...

From 'Essays On The Art Of The Ancient Barber' George Maquire
Bradford Observer
1841.

MacCraw went down through Bradford to the Booth Street police station. An ugly, dingy building with small slits of windows and a sturdy, narrow door, it served as much as a temporary gaol as a base for the town's few constables, the tiny cells in its basement now never adequate enough to house the drunks and captured felons. The window frames and door frame were painted a dismal green, the door itself solid oak, four inches thick, with good strong bolts, locks and iron hinges. This was a serious, imposing door; not a door to be knocked on or passed through lightly. MacCraw had only had recourse to pass through it once before in his life – the very week of Caroline's death, when he had to go and make a statement that formally identified his wife as 'the deceased', and stated what possessions she had with her at the time of the tragic accident. He had little memory of that interview – it was a blurred fragment of an awful week. There had been a desk, with a police constable and a soberly dressed coroner, or magistrate, and a cramped, high ceilinged room that stank of sweat and sour breath. He had signed papers, taken away items of her jewellery and her bonnet, but he remembered little else. As he approached the station now he barely even recognised the building. There was another reason why he now hesitated in the street before that doorway. From childhood, experience had nurtured in him a healthy mistrust of all uniforms and law-enforcers. His earliest recollections of uniforms were those of the red-coats and customs officers as they gave chase and brutal beatings to the menfolk of their little seaport town. They had no value for life or community, loosing pistols off at suspects in the narrow, crowded streets, attempting to capture or immobilise them for some vague smuggling violation or other. Another time they had come in a great, vicious force at night, forcing families out into the bitterly cold street in their night-clothes while they went ransacking the cottages and hovels, smashing the furniture, tipping out the contents of drawers, boxes, trunks, in search of some booty or arms that they had been given the tip about. Like the rest of the fishing town's menfolk, his father, when home, had openly despised and verbally cursed all custom's officers, judges, jurors, Lords and Ladies, soldiers and constables of every army of the wide world over. The way he saw it, he'd growl, they kept him and his kind from making a free and decent living, and enslaved his own country to boot. Despite having tried to rid himself of all traces of influence of his tyrannical and barbarous father, MacCraw could still not easily cast aside his deep-rooted contempt for the law-keeping uniform. Still, he had an interest in their business this day, and thus he took a deep breath, touched at his smarting skull to give himself impetus, and pushed through that imposing doorway into the stench-ridden waiting chamber.

The walls of the station's waiting room were bare stone, the tiny windows on the shaded street side letting in little light, so that the place had the feel of a gloomy dungeon. A continuous wooden bench ran about the walls, and slumped in various places along its length, in varying degrees of receding stupefaction, huddled examples of the town's wasters, drunkards, vagabonds, night-girls and pickpockets, several of them chained at the wrist or ankle to the wall. The air was already thick with pipe smoke which billowed from the more conscious of the room's inhabitants, but this did little to mask the rancid stench of sweat, old beer and stale vomit. In one corner an old scarecrow of at least sixty years was hunched in layers of ripped dresses and shawls on an indeterminate colour. She sat swaying about with her behind on the slimy, cold flags of the floor. She seemed still drunk, softly crooning some grim ballad about a long departed, murdering lover. Seeing MacCraw enter she warbled louder and grinned toothlessly for his benefit, winking at him and licking her top lip, implying some sly proposition, the very notion of which made his stomach turn. At the far end of this ruffian-studded waiting chamber was the very office door that MacCraw recalled passing though on his previous sombre visit, and beside this was a set of panelled shutters above a counter. About the panels, pinned and plastered in haphazard layers, were bills and notices which described various wanted felons, listing their crimes and offering rewards for their apprehension. This was the business end of the room, and a brass hand bell was set on the counter of the shuttered hatchway. MacCraw strode across, rapped upon the hatch, then gave the bell a good clanking to let the officers beyond know that he was there on serious business. The room behind him waited, those awake enough all ears. A rustling and muttering burbled through from behind the counter, then the panel slid open to reveal a sturdy, brutish fellow seated in a wooden chair. An unbooted, unstockinged and hairy foot was propped upon the office side of the counter, sets of official ledgers, lawbooks and piles of pamphlets piled precariously on either side. Despite being bootless, the duty constable was in his impeccable blue jacket, his crested helmet and stout truncheon on the counter there beside him. Across the narrow office and behind him was a wall rack, rows of various birches of different thicknesses for meting out instant justice and punishment lined neatly within. Beneath the rack was another, this lower one containing an assortment of different weighted duty truncheons, designed to suit the day of the week, or phase of the month, or the particular and variable moods of the duty constables. To the right of the racks was the iron door, beyond it the passage that led to the tiny dungeon cells below.

Without even raising a glance, the foot-engrossed constable grunted and winced, his trunk bent forward over his propped up leg as he worked at his exposed yellow toe with a pair of rusty looking scissors. An ingrown toe nail, black and as thick as a claw, curled on the outer end of the big toe, and this nail he was trying to gouge free from his skin with the sharp point of scissors blade. More grunts and winces at the toe, then still without looking up, he grunted: 'Anything to report?'

MacCraw knew this toe-clipping fellow by sight and reputation; indeed he had all but stumbled into him when he had been worse for wear when leaving The Star a few nights back. Constable Duff. Or Big Duff as he was known about town, though none knew his exact rank, and his actual surname was Duffield. Big Duff had a large, balding head that was smooth to a shine on the top, with coarse grey hair fringing at the back. His misshapen and gleaming pate he usually covered with his oversized official helmet, but today, due to duty rotation, he was caught office bound. A pitted, pimpled nose, red and swollen by the tippling of spirits, seemed to hang and bobble out of his face like a precarious crimson fungi. All about him seemed swollen and over-sized. Large eyes, blue and watery, were deep set under a knobbly brow and shaggy grey eyebrows. Large red and yellow feet smelled unpleasantly of festering cheese. Large toes that at such close quarters appeared to be covered with hair, dirt and minuscule mushrooms. Large, thick fingers that looked powerful enough to poke a hole directly into a man's ribcage. And there on the table beside him was his large and trustworthy truncheon, his beloved Big Bob, with which he was renowned for breaking up fights and splitting the heads of those who chose to hinder him in his duty. Many a man had been on the receiving end of a law-abiding beating from Duff and Big Bob, or had been 'duffed up', as they expressed it hereabouts.

MacCraw, nose wrinkled in disgust at the odour of diseased toes, placed his hat on the counter. It was a clean, expensive top hat, his best, black silk, and its quality caught Duff's attention. He ceased in his toe digging for a moment and glanced up to see what kind of gentleman he was dealing with. He seemed impressed enough to close his scissors and swing his foot down from the counter.

'I'd like to report a serious breach of the law,' MacCraw calmly stated. Duff grunted and set about pulling on his woollen stocking.

'Street robbery,' MacCraw continued. 'Attempted murder, and burglary at my shop and own home.'

He leaned forward, turning his head-wound down to show Duff the dried blood and bruising there near his temple. Duff was impressed enough to emit a low whistle, and to begin putting back on his duty-boots.

'It's these boots that give me corns and crunched up toe-nails,' he complained to MacCraw. 'Cheap modern rubbish. Standard issue, you see. Get through about five pairs a year, and if I were paying for them myself – you know, good, fitting well made boots. Well, I'd have no wages left, would I? And even a policeman needs to eat, sir. So, standard issue it is. What did you say your name was again, mister?'

'I didn't yet. It's MacCraw. George MacCraw. I have the barber's shop and... beauticians place. You know, up town.'

'Ah... I see. Barber's shop. Hmm.'

'A reputable establishment, constable. I've been there without incident for nearly twenty years. No incident whatsoever.' MacCraw pointed this detail out deliberately, knowing well what reputation barber's shops of a lower order had with certain people, and particularly upholders of the law. In some quarters barber shops, whores and brothels went hand in hand.

'In fact my establishment is what you might call an emporium. I do a little apothecary and beauty treatment on the side. Perhaps you'd like to call up some time, sir. As I say, I'm something of a beautician, and I could recommend you something for those battered feet there.'

Duff was warming to this MacCraw, and indeed remembered him now. He had never had reason to arrest him for drunkenness or licentiousness, which set him apart from most of the folk he had dealings with, though he could recall seeing him late on in some dubious states and quarters. But every man was entitled to a little vice, that was Duff's opinion. A little discreet vice here and there prevented a great deal of open crime.

'You could recommend something, could you? Well, I think you'd agree Mister MacCraw, I've no use for beauty treatments, but I wouldn't mind putting my feet right. And now you mention it I do believe I have heard of your place, sir. Not that I was suggesting anything by you being a barber, mind. Shame you aren't a cobbler, eh? I'd be dealing with you over boots then. But go on though, off the top of your head, like. What would you advise for those feet?'

MacCraw raised himself up in his coat, pleased to be engaging in a medicinal consultation.

'Very simple, sir. Mustard. Common garden mustard in a nice hot foot-bath. A spoonful or two – powdered. Though you can use the flower fresh as well, if you happen to have any. Give 'em a real good soaking once a week. And maybe a sprig of rosemary in there, too.'

Duff nodded his huge head sagely, impressed with this prescription, for it sounded remarkably cheap.

'Well, mustard, eh? Happen I'll try it, Mister MacCraw. This very evening, I think I'll give it a go, Missus Duffield's pantry permitting. Thank you for that then. Now, that's me sorted out. Let's get on with you, eh?'

He grinned up a crooked row of yellow and blackened teeth. MacCraw grinned down, wincing in pain with the forced facial movement. All around, behind MacCraw, the detainees slept, or stared vacantly at the walls, only the drunken old woman making any noise, still softly mumbling her ballad. Seeing MacCraw and Duff grinning she grinned too, then crackled into crazy laughter.

'Shut up there, you old slattern,' Duff growled. Fearful of the menace in his voice, knowing that he'd cosh a woman without a qualm, she ceased with the laughter but soon resumed her crooning.

'Now then; robbery, violence, burglary. Out off towners, that's what it is Mister MacCraw. None of my villains behave in such a manner. I don't get much maliciousness on my patch. Drunks a plenty, like this lot. Cells down there are packed. Overflowing with drunkards, we are.'

Duff was already convinced by his own deduction, and was having no local villains capable of such violence and outrage.

'Drunkenness, licentiousness and a bit of family fighting, that's my main line of business, Mister MacCraw. Yes. My hunch is out of towners. Liverpool. Manchester. Leeds louts. Something like that. But let's fill the report form in, and I'll investigate. If they're still about, I'll get 'em. Nobody likes robbery with violence, sir, and I daresay within a few years we'll have the whole criminal fraternity stamped on, and stamped out, so to speak. Now then, let's take a statement. Eleventh, is it? Right then, Mister George...'

Duff had whipped up an official form from one of the heaps beside him, a mightily impressive looking piece of parchment, creased and crumpled, a little ripped about the corners, but printed in clear black ink, with a logical layout that inspired confidence in the upholding of the law. With pen scratching like a stick over dry stone, he neatly printed the date and MacCraw's name, wrote 'barber' in parenthesis, and began to question the victim about the alleged crime.

MacCraw was not put off by the fact that he was not invited into the privacy of an office to make his statement, and indeed it rather suited his purposes that all present and conscious enough to listen in the waiting area could hear every detail of the interview. There could be no quicker way of getting his story around town, other than hiring a cryer or printing up a run of bill posters, than telling his tale to a waiting room jammed full of gossips and tipplers.

'There's been threats on my life before this,' boomed out MacCraw. A few slumped backs around the room straightened, ears pricking up. 'For weeks now, persons I shan't mention aloud, though look, I'll write it here for you if you'll just hand me that – there you go, thanks – is that how you spell Barry? Well, they've been saying they'll kill me as well as burn my shop and home to the ground. I see you recognise the name, there. A well known villain, is he? You wouldn't think it by the size of him, but he's a brutal menace and a bully to boot. Hunting me like a dog, he's been. And for no reason other than a pile of old papers given to me by a good friend a long time ago...'

Here MacCraw proceeded to make a long and fanciful statement that poor Duff, with his labouring, scratchy pen dangling awkwardly between his big fingers, and his poor spelling and worse grammar, could barely keep up with. Every set of ears in the room was now twitching in on the tale of threats, crimes and bloody, murderous violence.

'And they said they'd be coming back for me...' MacCraw managed to slip in, several times, so that by the end and signing of the interview a number of the sobering drunkards were fidgeting, looking about themselves and door-ward nervously, expecting the gang of felons to burst in at any moment. All were anxious to avoid getting caught up in a violent vendetta that was not of their own making and none of their business, especially if Big Barry and his boys were in on it.

'... unless I paid out good money for what they called protection, though I can't see how clubbing a man senseless to the ground and robbing his home counts as protection now, can you sir?'

Several heads about the room shook sympathetically. Duff looked very troubled, chewing at the edge of his forefinger. He had read of such crimes, and such organisations of criminals, but always operating far away in the big cities and the capital. An intelligent and organised gang of hoodlums was the last thing he wanted operating on his own patch. By the time MacCraw was up and ready to quit the police station Constable Duff was agitated, itching to get off of desk duty and back out on his boots so that he could dispense some disorganising justice about the heads of the crooks who were threatening the stability of his town and county.

'I'll be up to inspect your premises as soon as Constable Blathers gets here and relieves me of this damned desk duty,' he promised. He slapped Big Bob hard down into his palm. 'Until then, Mister MacCraw, I suggest you go about your business as usual, and don't let these villains go putting the fear of God into you with their antics.'

'Well I won't worry myself so much sir, now that I know I've got the protection of yourself and the law behind me. Now good day, and thank you for your time.'

There was a firm handshake, Duff nodding solemnly. MacCraw donned his hat again, gave a regimental salute, and at last quit the loathsome place.

As he walked back up through town toward Kirkgate, MacCraw fingered the handle of the revolver, which nestled snugly in his deep coat pocket. This, more than all the officers and soldiers in the country, made him feel safe. With this marvel of engineering alone he knew that he had the real power to protect himself; the power to attack and to strike back with a blast of death. That was progress for you, he thought. Death in an instant from a safe and comfortable distance, with a bit of smoke and thunder into the bargain too.

On North Gate he called into Pie Ivans, and there over mouthfuls of hot pork pie and mushy, gravy smothered peas, he pondered and reworked his course of action. One eye was on the passing street and doorway, his hand always ready to snatch out his deadly protection. He would aim low, he promised himself, for the last thing he wanted was another man's death on his conscience. But he was not going to be threatened and beaten again, no sir, not he. He would aim low, immobilise. A sensible bullet in a living man was better than a rash shot in a dead one. But his meal passed without incident or provocation. He paid his bill and stepped from the steamy warmth of the pie shop back into the street. Across town to the Post Office he headed, and there paid for the privilege of sending a communication for the second time that week, this time a brief telegram. This wire-transmitted missive was sent a short distance up the riding to a good friend he knew that he could trust from times past.

'Rhymer in danger stop cursed book stop support needed stop tomorrow at the shop if you can stop MacCraw'.

This message sent and paid for, there was nothing else for it but to go back home, tidy up his wounds, then get on with the normal business of the chopping-shop.

CHAPTER 18

For cuts and wounds, Nature provides numerous remedies that may be used either directly in their natural state or in prepared poultice. Common yarrow is a great stemmer of flowing blood (as Achilles could well warrant!). Crushed or chewed then applied to the bleeding wound, the properties of yarrow assist the clotting of the blood, as well as proving to be a cleansing agent about the damaged area. For bruising or burns, and for helping broken bones heal quickly, there is nothing better in Nature or medicine than the wondrous and beautiful comfrey plant. There are all manner of preparations and uses from this plant, which indeed in some places is commonly known as 'bone-knit'. The leaves may be moulded into a poultice about a burn or wound, the beneficial agents thereby seeping directly into skin, blood and bone. A tea of the leaves may be prepared, best slightly sweetened with honey, the goodness then radiating through the fibres of the body, knitting together the snapped bone and healing bruising from within.

From ***The Healing Plants Of The Ancient Barber***
George Maquire 1841

Bradford, March 1861

The next morning it was fires and waters on as usual; coffee brewing; clean aprons all round; fresh, hot towels draping on the pipes; the shop scrubbed, polished and scented; shaving mugs washed to a shine; scissors ground; blades on razors death-sharp. The lads were sent scurrying this way and that under MacCraw's barked orders, earning in an hour their whole previous morning off. It was as though MacCraw was a barber possessed and invigorated with the very spirit of barbering. Even so, there were few customers in the place. Over the afternoon trade picked up a little; a sullen queue formed on the seats and benches more than once. As he trimmed and razored, MacCraw kept a watchful eye on his customers, suspicious and wary of those he did not know or of whom he had no trust. He did not doubt that he was being watched and followed – Big Barry had his minnows everywhere.

Early evening and things in the shop were starting to quieten down. MacCraw had just sent out for beers to wash the day down when Francis Grundy, as grave and imposing as ever of old, came pacing solemnly though the shop door.

'Francis! Sir! You came. Thank God!'

'I did. Of course I did, MacCraw. It's good to see you, sir.'

MacCraw clapped and jigged about the best chair, delighted and relieved to see his old friend at last, and to see him looking so well. He was greying at the whiskers, with a creasing of lines about his eyes and high forehead, but he looked to be in good health.

'You're looking good, Grundy. Thank God it's a man in full strength I see before me.'

'Thank you. I feel well, too. I see you're as busy as ever.'

There was laughter, much shaking of hands, patting of shoulders and loud Rhymer's greetings. MacCraw cast off his apron and gave his hands a good scrubbing to rid them of oil, hair and bristles. Leaving the evening running of the shop to the lads, he escorted his distinguished guest up the stairs to the living quarters.

Though the meeting of the two Rhymers in the shop had been expressed with joviality and warmth, to Grundy it was something of a shock to see his old comrade. Although he had expected MacCraw to have aged a little, the poor fellow looked wretched. He seemed wild and haggard, his once pleasantly flushed face flabby and yellowed, with blue bruising around the forehead. He had the look of a street-wreck who had not slept soundly for weeks. Though still strong in stature, he was thickening outward about his waist, and despite the hour already had the breath-smell of ale drinking. Worse, he seemed to have developed a slight but shocking stoop. And his eyes - once such flash-filled, spirited orbs that could bedazzle a room of men and women alike - they were now his worst feature. They seemed shrunken and deep set beneath bushy, unkempt brows. They were haunted eyes, with a dangerous glare of that familiar madness he had witnessed all those years ago in the inns of Halifax and Haworth. They were the mad eyes that Brontë had carried with him for that last desperate year of his life.

Once upstairs in the privacy of MacCraw's living room, set with a glass of brandy in his hand, Grundy felt freer to express himself plainly.

'It's nice to see you again George, though I wish it wasn't in such worrying circumstances. To be honest, friend, you look downright wretched. I hope nothing too bad is going on.'

'Not too bad, but bad enough, friend. I wouldn't have troubled you Francis, but to be honest, I didn't know who else to turn to. Leastways, not anyone who'd have even a rough understanding of what I was on about.'

'But that telegram, sir. This must be serious.'

'Aye. Serious enough to be life threatening, I suppose. Once again, it's that damned book. Branwell's. The Withering Hands. It's back to haunt me. Someone's after it again. I swear on Caroline's grave, they're out to murder me over it.'

'Surely not. It can't that be that serious.'

'Serious, and dangerous. But to me only, friend. There's no danger to you. You can back out of what I'm going to propose at any moment along the way, and I'll never hold it against you. Let me spell it plain – I only want you along with me tonight as a witness. I don't want you in any danger, nor doing anything rash. It's just I need someone along to observe events. A bit of moral support from someone in the know. But sit down. Maybe you'll have to drag me out of a scrape, if needs be. Sit there, in the fire chair there. Listen to the tale. Look at this. Look at my wound. Aye, wince. It's a good gash. That's how serious this is, man. Here, let me top you up and tell you a few things that have been going on these last few months...'

They settled down in the armchairs before the fire with glasses replenished, a plate of cold meats from Anderson's along with a basket of Fish David's oysters set between them .

'It's hard to know where to begin,' MacCraw mumbled. 'But I suppose it goes back to that morning in Haworth – you know, when you and me were up there for Branwell. That morning he gave me the manuscripts. This trouble happening to me now, it all started there...'

As the evening gloomed in, MacCraw unravelled something of the strange events of late. In brief, though it took a good hour and a few more brandies, MacCraw recounted his suspicions about the death of Caroline all those years ago. He rounded up with a greatly exaggerated account of his own beating. He added details of his robbed and ransacked house - and to finish off with a postscript, he told of his own visit to the police just the day before. A few omissions to the gist of it he deliberately made, such as the detail of the revolver that even now was tucked beneath his day jacket in the rear waits band of his trousers. When MacCraw had done the fire was low. He could see that Grundy was impressed with the gravity of the tale.

'There's not much the officers can do,' he said over his shoulder. His face was half shadow, half illuminated by flame, eyes flashing with firelight. 'And I could hardly start telling them about dream-beasts and fiends conjured into the world by poisoned imagination, could I now? I've reported it officially to cover my tracks, if you like. I need to thread them one tale before I can weave out another.'

He finished stoking, set down the poker then stood before his seated friend.

'As I said, all I need really from you is a solid witness and some moral back up. I want out from this, you see. I want away from here. I've a good plan. With just a little help from one two or friends I have trust in, I can pull this off. Are you with me, Francis?'

'You knew I would be, man. They've laid arms on you, now. Your fight is my fight. And don't spare me from danger, for I've news to you, too. Two months from now, and I'm to London. From there, it's aboard ship, to Australia. Aye friend - it's all arranged; transport, finance, and solid, well paid employment at the other end of it. I'll be gone from this land for quite some time, if not for good. So I've no fear of mixing in rough with your petty gangsters, nor them knowing my name. I doubt they'll come looking to the bottom of the world for me.'

MacCraw pursed his lips and whistled.

'Australia. Now there's a distance. Once last adventure then, friend. Let's shake on it; the old Rhymers shake.'

They shook hands firmly then, interlacing their thumbs in the old way.

At six thirty, MacCraw went down to help the lads tidy and shut up the shop. That done he sent them off home, then returned upstairs to his guest.

'We'll be needing this tonight,' he told Grundy, taking from his desk drawer a parcel of manuscript, wrapped in faded brown paper. He opened the parcel up and showed Grundy the top page. It was a hand written cover page; tiny, square lettered writing which at a glance might have been Greek, words here and there scored out or smeared illegible. Even after all these years Grundy recognised the page as distinctly originating from the hand of Branwell Brontë.

'*The Withering Hands*' read the title there, and beneath, by way of explanatory introduction, some carefully penned notes and a date, May 18, 1838. Beneath were the old Rhymer's initials – PBB.

'It's the book all right, MacCraw. You're going to give them it then? You're going to give them what they want after everything?'

'Perhaps I am - but look, sir...'

He fanned through the first few pages - all hand written too in the same neat, minute lettering - but beneath these top leaves there was nothing but page after page of blank paper. Grundy seemed a little shocked.

'Is this what he gave you, then? All that fuss all these years over nothing. Nothing but...!'

MacCraw laughed, but there was a catch in his laughter, and there was a sob too, for Caroline came to mind at that moment.

'Aye, nothing but nothing. This is to fool them, though. That's the plan, anyway. I copied these top pages down myself last night. Imitated his hand, so to speak. Took a while to get the shape of his writing, but nothing an old forger like me couldn't get to grips with. It brought me close to the fellow again, in a strange and personal sort of way.'

'Well! It's good job you've made of it, MacCraw. It could have fooled me.'

'It was taking forever though. I had to speed things up a little. Look here, closely, a few pages in and it's all mumbo-jumbo. Beyond the first two pages not more than a sentence makes sense. I just drew the shape of letters in rows. Random nonsense and artful gibberish. Now, the cover page here is real. The genuine article. But I think we can let that go under the circumstances. The rest of the real thing I've still got safe. One copy went of course, with Caroline. But Branwell, he'd duplicated it, you see. You know what he was like for doing double copies, writing with both hands at the same time. Two copies he gave to me. One Charlotte or her agents must have had a hold of. Probably destroyed years ago, put to the flame along with the others they worked from to make Emily's book. My copy is hidden, and I've a plan to stow it in an even safer place. But this here we'll take with us up to The Star. Now then, I reckon it's time for me to make my move. Are you ready, Francis? I don't know where this road will take us, but are you ready to give me that Rhymer-sworn back up?'

Grundy was indeed ready, and tipped back the last of his brandy before rising and straightening up his clothing. He could see clearly that he had to undergo a bizarre episode before this night was through, but he was resigned to the matter.

'Yes, sir, I am ready. Come on man, let's get this over with, and hopefully I can be back home to my packing by the morning.'

CHAPTER 19

'The elder plant is always a great favourite of the healer and the herbalist. The delicate flowers can be made into a tea, a light coloured though odourous brew, which proves soothing for jangled nerves. The leaves of the plant can be used in the manufacture of an ointment with which burns, hot wounds, and the puncture marks of blade or bullet can be soothed. Add a year-stored touch of liquid comfrey leaf to this potion and you have an all round skin, blood and bone mender. A rinse of elder flowers in warm or cold water can remove excess grease from the hair and leave it with a healthy, vibrant glow. As any barber knows, the flower blossoms best in May and early June, and once gathered can be dried then stored in jars for later use. The berries of the plant, of course, can be turned to an excellent wine.'

From
'Essays On The Art Of The Ancient Barber'
George Maquire
1841

Bradford, March 1861

Darkness had closed in about the town. Candles were lit in dwellings and shops, lamps burned on street posts and above doorways. People finishing work early began to drift homeward through the streets, some dropping in to the taverns or eating houses for a bit of refreshment and company after the long day's slog. MacCraw locked up, making sure that the shutters were tightly in place, the door doubly bolted from the inside. This done, and lights left on within to make it seem that someone was in the place, he and Grundy let themselves out into the dark from the kitchen door at the rear of the house. This back door was solid oak, the lock stout, and it would have taken some kicking open, even by a hefty man – a forced entry there would make plenty of noise and the neighbourhood would soon be alerted. They stepped out past the middens into a narrow snicket, which led them down onto Sunbridge Road. MacCraw was wound up to a noticeable state of nervousness and giddy excitement. He was tooled up for the work ahead - the revolver was back in his inner great coat pocket, the parcel of manuscript tucked securely at his chest beneath his waistcoat. Arguing that it seemed foolish to approach the place by the main street and front door direct, he had them approach The Star through a maze of ginnels and side streets.

'There's always a cluster of idlers and Barry's minikins on those front corners,' he justified to Grundy, who was anxious about the state his boots were getting in. 'Barry'll get word we're approaching if we go in through John Street. Down here - watch the puddle there, sir, watch the puddles...'

At last they approached a walled-in back entrance that led out into The Star's toilet yard. At the end of the snicket, hulking black even against the sky's darkness, loomed the back of the infamous Old Star Inn, which even before the end of the year, trying to avert notoriety, Barry would rename 'The Beehive'. This back side was part of the original building – an ancient coaching inn that had been set alight and partially burned down during a drunken riot almost a century ago. The new front that overlooked John Street had been grafted on to the old remains soon after the destructive fracas, for the owner back then, known locally as King John, had grown wealthy on his gin and ale trading. In the gloom the rear looked very ancient, with numerous slanting gable ends and huge zigzag chimneys out of which plumes of smoke rose in fantastic shapes, the clouds of black taking on, it seemed, the figures of beasts and giant, hooded and hatted men. The windows at the back, some lit by the light of lamps within, were old diamond pane lattices, the floors within those back dingy rooms sunken and uneven, ceilings time-blackened and heavy with massive beams into which were cut weird shelves and notches. The two Rhymers stopped there at the back beside the yard wall. Nobody usually entered the tavern this way, though some had been known to leave it by being bodily thrown over the wall for their indiscretions, and in various states of intoxication. MacCraw, however, wanted to come upon Barry and his company by surprise, even though he was not intending any action too rash or violent at this stage. He had furnished Grundy with an outline of his plans. To him they seemed reasonable enough, if somewhat unnecessary, perhaps a trifle excessive. Then again, he had not himself been beaten unconscious and burgled, so he accepted the somewhat dramatic flourish of his friend's scheme. MacCraw intended to go in this dubious rear way. Grundy would enter through the John Street entrance as a normal customer. He would then walk about through the various rooms and chambers until he came upon MacCraw in the rear Rose Room, where Barry and his associates were usually ensconced about their business. MacCraw was to settle himself at the table with Barry and his private company, set forth the business he had with them, and through a simple little act of destruction resolve the matter of ownership of the book, at least for the while. He would then up and walk out. Grundy was to stay in the background, unconnected to MacCraw unless things took a nasty turn, and then he would be there as a witness, or to provide some physical assistance for his friend's escape. It all seemed reasonable enough.

They stood at the yard wall, surveying the windows and chimneys beyond. MacCraw reached up and placed his hand of the flat top of the wall, preparing to haul himself up.

'Right, friend,' he whispered. 'Here's where we part, for now.'

'You certain you can get in that way, George?' Grundy nodded at the wall, a new six footer, knocked up two years previously beside a doorway over which was set an ancient and grotesquely carved porch. In this porchway in years past, when this profile of the place had viewed out over a valley of open fields, customers would have smoked and drank on a summer's evening, reposing on two grim looking high-backed settees set there in the stone walls. Now the doorway beyond these carved seats was bricked over and offered no way in. So, it was over the wall. With some effort and grunting, along with a push, a shove and a heave from Grundy, MacCraw made his scrambling, knee-grazing entrance to the place.

'You all right?' Grundy hissed out as he heard his friend drop with a clattering and skittling of bottles to the other side. There was a groan, and the sound of coat-brushing as MacCraw dusted himself down. As he did so he slipped the revolver from his inner pocked and tucked it neatly between his inner calf and the leather rim of his left boot.

'Aye, I'm fine, friend,' he hissed back. ' I'm in and ready now. See you inside shortly.'

'Right. I'm away to the front. Good luck, MacCraw.'

MacCraw had used these toilets at the back when patronising the inn over the many years, although he'd usually tried to hold out while there owing to the particular foulness of the facilities – those being a ditch and a few holes set against the yard's back wall, partitioned off with flimsy wooden frames to offer some degree of privacy. The doorway from there led into a narrow hallway which ran the length of the place in a series of uneven zigzags, eventually emerging through various other doorways into the main rooms of the inn. Other doors lead off here and there into the private rooms and smaller, less frequented drinking chambers. MacCraw counted the doorways, as he had done through necessity on hazy occasions in that warren before. He paused, took a deep, slow breath, drew the parcel of manuscript from beneath his waistcoat, then pushed quietly in through the fourth door on his right. The room he entered, The Rose Room, was a place of all manner of trade and transaction; a proper nest of vice and skullduggery. If a robbery was planned in the district, then it was in this room. If silver plate and cutlery was to be liberated from a local mansion, then its value, acquisition and safe disposal was deliberated here. If a man was hired to commit a foul deed – a beating, say, or even worse – then the handshake and oath of secrecy took place over these tables, followed, when the deed was done and proved, by the handing over of the agreed portion of coinage. If a woman or girl was sold on for usage, then it was in here that she was looked over, inspected, tested out, priced up and passed on, either for export or local tendering. In this room raw opium could be bought openly, by the chest full. Firearms were easily come by. Tobacco was practically given away. A cock fight, a bear-baiting, a ratting by dog or man, a bare-fister or any other blood letting form of entertainment could be arranged in this busy little chamber into which the cautious MacCraw now stepped. The room looked much like any other dingy back parlour in a large town inn – card and dice games unfolding gently, easy chattering in the air, a few solitary drinkers at corner tables staring down morosely into their drinks. A fiddle and accordion were twittering away to the dull clanking accompaniment of a piano in the far doorway corner, a gentleman in a top coat with a bluish, stubbled face presided at the jingling upright, a tumbler full of spirit upon the lid to aid the fluidity of his spiderish fingers.

The room was called ' The Rose Room' on account of its dull pink walls, its crimson furnishings and the beautiful picture of a large red rose which was painted directly onto the wall above the fireplace. There was a Latin phrase in black lettering beneath the rose, which Branwell Brontë himself was said to have scribed there. The dingy place was illuminated by sets of double gas-lamps, their light prevented from being visible outside by heavily barred shutters and permanently pulled red curtains. The ceiling was blackened and the room was so full of dense tobacco smoke that at first it was scarcely possible to see the back bar or the other door which led out into the front room of the inn. For its select clientele, The Rose Room was open all hours of the day and night and in there, it was said, the fire in the broad hearth had not been out for half a century or more. MacCraw's entry, with parcel tucked under his arm, caused more than one or two heads and sets of eyes to turn onto him and sum him over, but little more, for he was recognised as a local tippler from the area. In his time, he had attended to the beards and minor medical needs of most of the men in the room. As his own eyes grew more accustomed to the dinginess of the place, he became aware of the presence of the numerous company, male and female, gathered on his left around a long table. This little gathering was the very company he was searching out. At the upper end of the table, propped to the height of his fellows on a cushion or two in a narrow padded armchair, Big Barry sat gleaming and gloating like the King of Trolls. MacCraw picked his way through the gloom and noise to the bar, where a hairy lipped, black toothed hag served on. He was glad to see a good blaze was in the hearth along from the piano, and gladder still when he glimpsed Grundy across the bar in the main drinking room beyond. Grundy met his eye, nodded and slightly raised his glass. The business was on.

MacCraw ordered a brandy and hot water, leaving his coins in the withered hand of the server. Sure now of his bearings and back-up, he carried his drink and the parcel to Barry's table. Without any announcement or greeting, he sat on a stool directly opposite Barry and thumped the package down onto the table, ensuring that he had everyone's attention. That done, he calmly sipped at his drink, though his heart was clacking ten to the dozen. To the left of Barry, with his stubby arm about her waist, perched Pot Mary, her face softened and dazed with drink. On the other side, equally held in a lewd manner, was the lovely Beatrice, her eyes sober and aware, like a threatened cat's. A hardness about her mouth showed that she was not best pleased with this sudden intrusion by the barber. To the left of Beatrice was a hatless, gangly looking rogue with a scar right across his forehead, slanted from temple to eyebrow. Next around hunched a stocky, Irish looking fellow, who MacCraw was sure he recognised from his shop, or the streets around town. Other cut throats, vagabonds and whores of various degrees of prettiness and decrepitude were bunched and muttering about the table. MacCraw eyed around them, meeting each set of hostile eyes in turn, while beneath the table he eased the revolver out from his boot, setting it ready and out of view upon his lap. With his left hand he slammed the brandy tumbler down upon the tabletop. People started at the loud bang. The piano halted mid-tune, fiddle scraping to a high pitched squawk, the accordion wheezing its last chord. All the room was suddenly tense and silent, bristlingly expectant, aware of the potential for bloody violence. MacCraw spoke slowly and calmly, patting the parcel.

'I do believe this is what you've been after, gentlemen.'

Though he addressed the table in general, his eyes were fixed on Barry's in particular. All other eyes there were on him. Barry licked his thick slugs of lips and stretched back his shoulders, making a cracking, cricking noise of muscle and bone. Eyes swung from MacCraw to Barry, who clicked his tongue in the roof of his mouth. MacCraw smiled grimly and mimicked the same click. Barry looked decidedly uncomfortable, a little confused, possibly drink fuddled.

'Ah, my good friend, Mister George MacCraw. This is the barber I was telling you all of just the other day, my friends. Well, Georgie, welcome to our little company, and yes, you may join our gathering. Seat your good self at our table. Oh, I see you already have done so...'

A little ripple of snickering went about the table. The tension in the room seemed to ebb a moment. MacCraw sipped his drink again and held Barry's seemingly good humoured gaze.

'So, Georgie, you've seen some sense? Nice to see you've put your scissors aside and taken up postal delivery as a means of earning your living.'

The gathering snickered again, more easily and openly this time, relieved at Barry's ridiculing of the barber. In particular, the two tall fellows to the left of Barry and Beatrice laughed louder than the rest. MacCraw, though, retained his composure. When the laughter around subsided and all eyes had switched on him for his return, he retorted with open venom.

'No Barry, I've not seen sense. Far from it, in fact. It's not sense I've seen, you chump, but red. I'm seeing red. You see, I may appear to be calm, but inside you've got me raging as mad as a taunted bull.'

A single chortle of laughter erupted from the grizzled, stocky crone to Barry's right; the same fiend that MacCraw now reckoned had asked him the time before coshing him on the head the other night.

'Well, sorry to break up the great comical party,' MacCraw drawled, at which point his revolver slithered into plain view above the edge of the table. The barrel was pointing directly across at Barry's broad, unmissable chest. A collective gasp sighed up about the table. Barry paled, gleaming with nervous perspiration, but he remained rigidly still. Despite the unsavoury reputation of The Rose Room, the felons within were on the whole unused to seeing weapons of such extreme and immediate violence drawn openly in their midst. By unspoken rule, no firearms other than those for sale, and hence unloaded, were brought within those walls. There came a brittle click as MacCraw cocked the trigger hammer with his thumb. The laughter in Barry's eyes completely died, all trace of smugness melting from his thickset face.

'Now then, Barry, I'm sure you're well informed about your firearms, so I'm certain you recognise your predicament. Stay still there, the lot of you. Nobody move, or else this thing goes off and there's hell to pay. Oh yes, look fearful across there. And you, scar-face, stay very still. They've every right to be scared, isn't that right Barry? I trust you know what piece is staring in you the face, so to speak?'

Barry did not really care, satisfied enough that he was looking at something which could kill him. To buy himself time though he nodded, knowing well enough that MacCraw loved to talk. He might well blarney his way back to some sense and put the weapon away.

'Nice looking piece, Georgie. Go on then - tell us about it I'm sure we'd all be delighted to hear.'

'Well I will, then. Just so as to dissuade you pals from taking foolish risks. This, my chums, happens to be a Colt Navy revolver, one of the world's most deadly and accurate firearms. A revolving pistol, gentlemen. Open framed, as you see. Produced across in the Americas a few years ago now, but in as good condition as the day it left the workshop. Note the delicate hammer there, cocked and primed, as you see. A six-chambered cylinder, six bullets ready for the off, which in a round-about way means six of you dead or maimed before you even get close to me. Beautiful, isn't it? A cool, cruel work of deadly genius. A very fragile and sensitive trigger mechanism though. Could go off at the slightest knock or tremble or provocation. And here's me, all twitching and fidgety, and to tell the truth I don't give a damn about anything anymore. I'd shoot you all soon as look at you. So, stay still, fellows. Move away from the table, you ladies. No no, not to the door. Stay in the room by the piano there 'til this little transaction's done with.'

Mary, knowing which way her pot boiled, was up and away from the table even before Barry had wit to give her wrist a grasp, him fully aware that she had attachments to his immediate enemy from times past and might thus prove a useful shield or hostage in the sudden crisis. Beatrice and the other women shuffled aside also and stood rigid by the piano. All in the room were frozen by the deadly presence of the gun;. there was a mad-eyed look about MacCraw, and none wanted to be the first to take a bullet from him.

'Now lads,' he went on, once the womenfolk were clear. 'I swear, I've never been more on the edge, and all it takes is a finger flick and someone cops it. Now Barry, back to you, friend. All I want from you is a name. Somebody has hired you to hound me like this, and it may be that this person has caused me great harm before. I want to know who's so desperate to get their murdering mits upon the contents of this parcel.' Barry, like any decent merchant of night-time and leisure, had a predilection for gambling in all its forms; he loved his game of chance or cards. He had already studied the spread before him; had assessed the likely falls of fortune; had weighed up the odds and likely outcomes. He was still considering what to play and what to throw away. Already his dark queen, Pot Mary, had been moved out of the game for the time being, though at a grab she would prove to be a useful little bargaining piece. MacCraw there certainly looked deranged with his shiny revolver, but generally speaking he was a sensible, respectable, everyday fellow. A solid worker. A drunken dreamer. Certainly not a killer. So, the chances of him really pulling the trigger and splattering blood about the place were slim, and especially in front of womenfolk. He was nervous too, despite his outwardly controlled manner. Barry doubted whether the fellow had ever even fired a shot before. His hand would be trembling even now, his palm slippery with sweat. He probably would not be taking into account the arm throwing recoil of the weapon. So, the chances of MacCraw hitting him first time with a killing shot were comfortably slim. One misfired shot and his men about the table would be on MacCraw, seizing him by the arms to prevent further shooting, bludgeoning him to the floor, stamping him to unconsciousness for the outrageous intrusion. But Barry knew he did not have much room for a physical manoeuvre. He certainly did not fancy a bullet ripping into his arm or chest, or God forbid, his head. He had plenty of hands around the table; fast men, too, and without conscience. They'd crush MacCraw's skull soon as they would a beetle. Any one of them could take the barber; it was all just a matter of the timing. The papers that Barry wanted - though not for the price of his life - were set there on the table. The game then, it seemed, was just a matter of talking and waiting. Laying down words to secure time. And by his good fortune he knew there was nothing MacCraw liked better than to chew the cud. All this sang through Barry's head in a matter of seconds, and he played his hand accordingly.

'It weren't a matter of hounding you, Georgie. I'm not the sort of man who hounds people – you know me better than that. I'm direct. I'm up front. I'm blunt.'

The room remained silent, seemingly holding its collective breath.

'Not hounding, George, but retrieving property. Or trying to. I've merely been trying to recover something that by rights is mine, as I explained to you the other night out front there. Admittedly, someone might have offered a price to me for it, but then it's mine to sell. Now, in good faith, and because of the generousity of my little heart...' - Here the miniature fellow puffed out his barrel of a chest, causing a flutter of nervous laughter about the table - '... I did offer you a substantial sum of money for the return of my property there.'

'Stop the chatter now,' cut in MacCraw. 'Stop, or I'll shoot your damned teeth out. I want a name, Barry. Who's hired you? A Brontë? But it can't be one of them, now, can it? They're all dead, man.'

'Well, no. Not all of 'em, George. Most, I'd agree...'

'The old Parson then? I can't believe he'd put himself to all this trouble over a damned book.'

'Well, no, not directly. You're right there. He's no interest in all this. But there were marriages, Georgie, don't forget. One, anyway. And friends. And there's an estate. There's publishers. Books and writing is big business, Georgie. There's a future interest, too. Big money for many years. It's industry we're talking here, and you know how ruthless these industrialists can be now, don't you.'

Barry jabbed toward the parcel.

'I don't think you realise what you've gone and got yourself mixed up with here, Georgie boy.'

Barry shook his head. He tutted. He sighed. He wrung his hands together, great pink fingers like raw sausages intertwining and pulling free again.

'No, I'm afraid you just don't understand the depths you're into.'

In the lamp gloom Barry's face was gleaming like a glass mask. MacCraw clucked and tutted. He raised the barrel of his revolver, pointing it now toward the gangster's oversized head.

'A name, Barry. You've thirty seconds left, then I swear I'll blast you apart.'

Barry flattened his hands around his tankard on the table.

'I swear to you, Georgie, I've no direct name. I'm dealing with people who have connections with the family – with the publishers. Heatons. Nicholls. Smiths and Joneses. Browns too, if you like. Take your pick. You're up against them all, man. They've not hired me direct, you understand. Agents, Georgie. That's the method these days. People hire agents, and they hire other agents, and so it goes down the ladder until they come to the bottom, where they find the likes of me. I'm hired because they know I'll do the dirty work that they hint at, but haven't got the nerve to carry through themselves. Consider me a hired hand, George. But one who does his job and in turn gets well paid. All right, I admit, my men here did get a little carried away the other night when trying to retrieve my property. I hold my hands up to it. I asked them to give you a scare, and no more. But they're good ones, Georgie. They're keen to impress, like keen pups out to impress their master. Like us when we were young.'

'So you admit you had me duffed up, now?'

'Georgie - my lads were just being enthusiastic. They went beyond the call of duty, I admit. But that's no reason to bring irons into the matter, is it? A bit of a cosh is one thing. Deadly firearms – now that's another.'

There was a murmur of agreement with this about the room. Barry was making a good case for himself there beneath the rose.

'Retrieval, you say, Barry? Retrieval of property. Pardon me, but I believe the legal term is robbery. Thuggery. Attempted murder. That's why I find deadly firearms necessary, you chump. Now, this here...'

MacCraw slapped his hand down on the paper parcel, the sudden cracking noise setting a few round the room starting and ducking, thinking the first shot had been loosed off.

'... this here, along with the papers and items your bludgers here stole from me, was given to me by the hands of the owner and writer. Given, understand. Not taken. Not cheated in a game of cards or swapped for bar bills. Not wormed out by a cruel demander. Given, by the rightful owner, Patrick Branwell Brontë. Now look, look you here...'

MacCraw rose, revolver still aimed across the table. He tore back the brown parcel cover, pulled out a fistful of the top sheets then spun them across the table top to Barry. He collected the sheets up, inspecting them with gleaming, greedy eyes. They were the top title page and the first pages of half a chapter or so of the novel, in Branwell's distinctive handwriting. Barry's eyes bulged down at the manuscript as he skimmed through the opening paragraphs. A smile rippled on his bluish lips. Here at last was what he sought, and with it would follow a good reward.

'Oh Georgie, thank you. You'll get good chink for this. Johnny, the wallet...'

'Hang the wallet!' MacCraw growled. He moved around the table, sweeping the gun from side to side, holding all at bay, then in a swift movement plucked up the opened parcel, strode directly across to the fire and dropped the lot into the flames.

'No!' Barry shrieked, leaping up, shoving his chair backward, the sudden shout and clatter sending his scar-headed crony hurtling forward like a dog at a sharp whistle. The fellow went rushing toward the barber. There was a loud, snapping crack as MacCraw shot him low, the bullet thudding deep into his thigh. He stopped in his tracks, looked extremely surprised, then dropped to the floor, howling and writhing, hands clasping about his shattered leg. MacCraw snatched up a poker and pushed the parcel full into the centre of the flames, at the same time firing off another shot over the heads of the stirring crew, the bullet ripping into the ceiling beam just above the bar.

'Sit down, the lot of yer!' he barked, and they did, as one, in terror, none of them wanting the agony and blood spilling that they could see in their crony who squirmed and blubbered about the floor boards.

'He'll live,' MacCraw spat into the hush. 'Just a thigh shot, that's all. But the next one of you won't, damn you all. Six such bullets in a chamber. Two shots off. For those of you without reasonable arithmetic, that leaves me four. That's plenty of death or wounding before the nearest one gets to me, so you lads there, back right off to the wall. Let's all just relax a moment and watch the pretty fire.'

Petals of flame curled up about the edges of the paper, smoke rising thick and blue. Barry could not take this – it was as bad as watching good money burn. He pushed away from his seat and came waddling forward, bold and resolute. He would have to play his hand now and be ready to call the bluff rather than watch the valuable parcel perish.

'Sorry Georgie, but the playing about is over now. I need to deliver those papers there. I can't just let you burn them. You're going to have to shoot me, friend, and I don't think you're up to cold-blooded murder. You wouldn't kill, friend. And especially not a fellow that you've known from years back...'

He began to move forward, slow measured steps, eyes fixed past MacCraw and the revolver onto the papers which the flames were beginning to grip. Money burned for him there; good money, along with his name and reputation as a man who 'could do'. He banked on MacCraw not having enough nerve or madness to be able to put a bullet in him. He stepped around MacCraw, reaching forward toward the fire, then yelped like a dog even before he heard the shot or smelled the powder. His hand and arm were flung aside with the impact. He leapt back quickly, holding his hand up to his own shocked white face. A big, blatant, bloody hole the size of a penny gaped there in the middle of his palm. Through it he could see the flames, the fireplace, the sudden spinning room.

'You shot me!' he howled, gawping at his hand, not quite believing it. 'You mad bastard! You've gone and shot me.'

Barry slumped to his arse there before the fire, watching blood pump from his hand. Flames were biting deep into the papers on the fire now. It was too late. Barry popped his mouth open and closed, no words emerging. He keeled over backwards, fainting in shock. About the room erupted uproar.

'Big Barry's been shot! Big Barry's been shot!'

In moments the message rippled out of the room, around the whole inn and trickled out into the street. Big Barry had been shot. His henchmen, knowing that they had to salvage some credibility out of the situation, leapt up as one and rushed forward to assist their wounded leader. Others, the more fearful or cowardly, took full advantage of the sudden chaos and fled in all directions, shrieking and bellowing from the door into the main bar, clambering over the bar itself to seek shielding from the mad gun man. None now present expected MacCraw to leave that room alive.

The blue-stubbled rogue who had clubbed down MacCraw two nights ago was crouching with a glass of brandy at the fainted Barry's lips. From his crouch he leapt like a springing wild-cat, risking his neck as he lunged for the barber's revolver. MacCraw, himself somewhat stunned to inertia by the fact that he had twice dared use the weapon to shoot men down, was caught by surprise. His arm went jarring upwards, the gun flying from his grasp, clattering away toward the long-since deserted piano. It fell between the brass footpedals, a shot going off as the trigger mechanism was jarred on the collision, the loosed bullet burying itself into the body of the piano. There was a clonk of discordant music like a badly struck harp chord as piano wires were ripped and went twanging within. The heroic rogue hauled himself fully up before the disarmed MacCraw, two others, like well trained hounds, at his side in an instant, bracing for the affray, ready to pummel and batter the offending and outnumbered barber.

'You got a lick of this the other night,' the stubbled rogue sneered. He had slipped a leather cosh from his waistband and now slapped it into his palm. 'And I think you'll be tasting a bit more...' The weighted leather twacked loudly against his hand.

MacCraw considered the whole scene. The manuscript was well ablaze and there would be no retrieving it from the fire now. The revolver with three rounds left lay there, a few yards away, but far enough for him not to make it before he was cut off. Barry was coming round, stirring before the hearth. The first wounded fellow was still writhing and groaning. The felon with the cosh leered and took a pace forward, ready to smash the intruder down. People outside the room would be soon mobbing and braying, ready to put a stop to any attempted flight. Check mate, thought MacCraw. But he would not go down without a last fight. His hand was in and out of his coat pocket in a flash. A secret weapon came sliding out, silver blade hissing open, dazzling in the lamp and firelight. His best and longest cut throat razor he held there;

the ivory handled work tool and sustainer of his livelihood now a menacing and deadly blade. MacCraw knew it would be a brave man who stepped forward for a taste of cold razor steel.

'I'll shave your life,' MacCraw snarled. 'Very sharp, sir. Razor sharp. Take a step nearer – any of you, damn you – and I'll have your throat gaping open from ear to ear.'

The villains looked to each other, seeking in the glance of the others a hint as whether to rush the barber and risk a gash from the blade, or stay backed off and keep their faces in one piece. All it needed was a nod from one of them. MacCraw took up a sword fighting stance and slashed a zigzagging stroke of the blade in the air, his hand so fast that the steel blurred and whistled cruelly before their faces. It was the ever solid Grundy who now stepped in to the fray to avert any more spilled blood or splintered bone. In the moment that the blade finished its slashing Z shape, he bellowed out an order from the bar:

'Now hold it right there, the lot of you. Nobody move! You man, drop the cosh, now. You there, put the bottle down. I'm armed with iron here, I'm generous with my bullets, and I'm with MacCraw!'

All swivelled to look at the new and sudden threat, and none but MacCraw liked what they saw. Another fellow, well dressed and big too, pointing another pistol right at them.

'Now make way there so that my friend can step safely over here.'

Barry's crew shrugged at each other, agreeing with a look that the game was up. No point in going against more guns this night As they stepped back, MacCraw scuttled to the piano and scooped up his own revolver, re-cocking the trigger as he rushed toward Grundy and safety. Primed gun in one hand, opened razor still swinging in the other, he looked like some desperate and murderous bandit from a tuppeny flea-pit tale. With a nod Grundy signalled to the front street door. MacCraw nodded keenly, barely believing that he might be getting out of the room alive and without injury.

'My business is done here now,' he called back into The Rose Room, and loud enough for the whole tavern to hear. 'The damned book is burned to ashes. I've had a bit of revenge, and one or two men have got what they deserve. We'll be gone now. Come after us tonight, and you'll just get more of the same.'
A shrill retort came gurgling back at them from within The Rose Room's heart.

'You won't get away with this, MacCraw. You'll not live long for this...'

Barry had roused enough from his faint to realise both the book and situation were lost, along with a good deal of his dignity, pride and villainous reputation. To be downed and out stepped by a lush of a barber – he could hear the laughter now.

'You're meat, MacCraw...!'
He went spitting out insults and promises of retribution after his fleeing assailant.

'You're dead meat. Dead - you know that, don't you!? I'll not have a tatty, pissing barber ruining me ...you're finished... you're dead... you're worm-meat... you hear me!?..."

His words of venom continued echoing down the corridor but only the sound of the fury reached MacCraw's ears, accompanied by the banging blood of his own heartbeat. Seeing that they were still armed, people scurried aside from him and Grundy. The two fleeing Rhymers burst out into the cold air of the night and took to their heels away down the hill.

MacCraw was trembling from toe to scalp. Only when they were well away from the crowd and heading townward at a rapid pace did he replace the gun and razor in his coat pockets, though he kept his hand tight upon the butt of the revolver.

'Thank God for your support there, Francis. I was done for! I think it's fair to say you truly saved my bacon. I'm only sorry to have landed you in bother with the midget there.'

'Ah, nonsense, sir. I don't think the little fellow even saw me. Anyhow, he wouldn't know me from Adam. All eyes were on you there. Magnificent, you were too. Top form. A regular warrior. I never knew you could be such a barbarian!'

'Me neither, sir. I swear, I didn't go in there with the plan to gun anybody down. Things just fell that way. I'll probably end up swinging for this.'

'Nonsense again! From the look of the place and the crowd I hardly expect they're in a position to call upon the law for help. A surgeon's bill from Barry is the worst you might have to fear.'

'Well, I hope so. I never realised that you bore arms about yourself, though. When did you take to carrying that thing around?'

Grundy chuckled and pulled the firearm out of his pocket. He held out the lethal, brawl-allaying weapon as they passed beneath a gas lamp. MacCraw squinted down at it. There was no gun in his hand, but a pipe. Upturned, thick stemmed, huge bowled. Grundy like to inhale a quantity when he took a smoke.

'Tricked them, friend, just by the shape and suggestion alone. Faced them down with a solid made pipe. Though they do say these days, do they not, that smoking leads to an early grave!? Now come on MacCraw, let's get indoors somewhere. Your little criminal friend will be sending a carriage full of ruffians after us, for sure. We'd best lay low.'

Still in the thrill of shock at the blood spilling and danger, the two Rhymers hurried their way down ginnels and darkened alleyways toward Sackville Street. They fell snickering and chattering into the snug of The Duchess of Kent there. The place was busy, people chatting amicably as they drew on their pipes and pots. The two kept quiet their urge to tell and brag of their night's doings, but huddled themselves up in a quiet corner with rum bottle and water jug, where they recounted to each other step by step the scene in The Star as they remembered it. They ran and re-ran over details from each point of view, exploring Barry's wounded hand; the look of the villain's faces; the comical noise of the bullet pierced piano; the sight of the parcel lost to leaping flames. Over and over events they went, repicking a moment, focussing in on a look, a movement, a shouted phrase. From time to time they would break into their own retellings to swear and vow that they would stick by each other through this most dangerous of nights, and that each would ensure the other was safe that night to bed – or both to the grave!

CHAPTER 20

SONNET II

ON PEACEFUL DEATH AND PAINFUL LIFE

Why dost thou sorrow for the happy dead?
For if their life be lost their toils are o'er,
And woe and want can trouble them no more;
Nor ever slept they in an earthly bed
So sound as now they sleep, while dreamless laid
In the dark chambers of the unknown shore,
Where Night and Silence guard each sealed door.
So – turn as such from these thy drooping head
And mourn the *dead alive*, whose spirit flies,
Whose life departs before his death has come;
Who knows no Heaven beyond his gloomy skies:
Who sees no Hope to brighten up that gloom:
'Tis *he* that feels the worm who never dies,
The *real* death and darkness of a tomb!

Northangerland (PBB.)
May 1842

Bradford, March 1861.

Digging up a grave and robbing the coffin of its contents seemed easy in theory. MacCraw was able to research the subject in the town's Mechanic's Institute, which housed a good library that was accessible to apprentices, workers and shop keepers. He knew the Institute's Chief Librarian well - Archie Smithies, a wild looking man with a ferocious red beard and long ginger hair - a regular customer of MacCraw's back in the days of the Rhymers, before he decided to stop having his hair and beard trimmed at all. Although MacCraw was not technically a member of the institute he was allowed to slip in for a browse and a read from time to time, when he had the leisure or inclination, for which luxury wild-haired Smithies received a half price potion or box of MacCraw's own snuff.

Over two afternoons, a few days after his escapade in The Star, MacCraw went to the library and busied himself with books. Among the medical tomes, which were of interest anyway to MacCraw as an old-school barber, he recalled reading an extract by a Belgian scientist named Versalius. In times past Versalius had improved the world's knowledge on biology and physiology by opening up and dismembering recently deceased corpses. Like any decent medieval scientist he had an unquenchable thirst for knowledge, and with fresh cadavers legally hard to come by, he had taken to more sinister means to slake this thirst. He became a frequent nighttime visitor to the cemeteries of Louvain, and it was more than a handful of flowers or recently placed vase that usually came away with him. Apart from his notes, drawing and sketchings on the composition and workings of the human body, the good Belgian had been kind enough the leave behind details of how to quickly and effectively remove a recently interred corpse from its eternal resting place. His detailed instructions on how best to rob a grave now proved of great interest to George MacCraw; such skills would be essential to the next stage of his loosely thought through plan.

He located the relevant Versalius piece and read over it again, carefully and mentally noting the tools, implements and precautions he would need for the task. In his own mental perambulation of the matter he had created all manner of physical obstacles. Perhaps there would be a slab of stone upon the earth that would require moving; the ground would be frozen solid and iron-hard due to a sudden frost; people from the surrounding houses would be disturbed by the noise and would be out of their houses with torches and weapons to drive away the body-snatchers. Despite foreseeing numerous problems with opening the grave, MacCraw planned away. He could now glimpse a necessary and shapely ending to all his struggles rooted in Branwell's cursed manuscript. With the help of his long dead guide, and with his own flittering contemplation of the task, MacCraw gathered or bought the necessary implements. He had a checklist, in code, on which he scored a line through each time an item was acquired. Two spades; a good lantern filled with the best whale oil; good burning candles in case the lantern was too bright in the graveyard; a good sized canvas sheet; four ropes with hooks attached; a crowbar; a good sized sack into which to deposit the night's takings. A pick might be needed too, to break the surface if the ground proved to be hard. He listed one down, bought one outright, then crossed it off. A few items still remained on the list after two days of research and buying – vehicle and assistants being the most pressing of these. The actual fact of getting to the graveyard, in secret in the dead of night, would obviously be problematic. A common cart of some kind would be needed; a vehicle that would not cause a stir or attract attention by being out and about in the latest hours of the night. MacCraw had an ideal vehicle in mind - Fish David's fish wagon. It was a reeking thing, but solid enough; a cart with a hooped canvas cover, made for long road journeys and hauling weighty goods. Even the very smell of it went in the plan's favour - should it be stopped by night constables, MacCraw doubted that they would be inclined to make a thorough search through the boxes in the back.

Robbing a grave might seem extreme and repulsive to any whom he approached to assist him in the matter, but he was well aware that a good dollop of cash reward would grease the way, particularly with Fish David. On Joseph Snell he felt he could count, in return for financial reward above those few material favours he had already bestowed on him in simple kindness. If all went according to plan over the next month or so, Snell and his desperate little family stood to gain much benefit from MacCraw's escapades. Grundy had gone back up the valleys the day after the adventure at The Star, and he would not have broached this indelicate matter with him anyhow. His old Rhymer stalwart had already assisted him more than beyond the call of duty, and would have been unlikely to approve this next stage in the operation. So, Fish David and Joseph Snell it would have to be. He pencilled their coded names on his list, and determined to enroll the two of them that very evening.

Without his Rhymer comrade to hold the fort, MacCraw had to leave his premises vulnerable and unguarded as he set out again into the slimy, vice-riddled rookery, which surrounded the dye houses. Late in the evening, revolver loaded in pocket, MacCraw made his way down to the little cellar hovel of the Snells. He stepped much more warily this time, remaining continually vigilant, avoiding the clusters of men outside the skittle dens and drinking hovels, traversing the street away from dark openings or whenever groups of folk came jostling toward him. Steadily, he came upon the corner that marked the ginnel entrance to Snell's yard, and from there searched around for the most likely passageway that Snell would emerge through on his way up home from the dye-works. This time the discourse needed to be private, so he wanted to catch him on the open street rather than have to wait there inside the den of sickness. He stationed himself in view of the work's gate at five minutes to eight, but it was a long, cold wait. The work's hooter to mark the end of the shift sounded at quarter past the hour rather than directly on it. In effect, the men had worked fifteen minutes extra, for no extra pay. Factory and real time were known to be two different quantities of measurements of duration - a fact that had caused many disputes between managers and workforces up and down the country before now. Eventually though, the horn breathed its howling steam and the shift for those within was over. The gates opened. Workers emerged in a solemn, slow trudge, clouds of stinking mist and yellow steam billowing out of the interior along with them. Foolishly, MacCraw had expected to recognise Snell instantly upon the sounding of the horn and the exodus from the dye-house, but now found that he had overestimated his ability for differentiation of what turned out to be a uniform appearance in the stream of men. Hundreds of them poured through the high arched gateway, boots and clogs clattering over the cobbles. All had smeared, filthy mechanical's aprons and thigh length leg-shields, some with the luxury of a protective smock that had once been fresh blue or clean grey. All were hunched with weariness, some doubled over, ricket ridden, shapes altered by their years of hunched labour over one vat or press, or through running and ducking about some repetitive, bone jarring machine. Many wore floppy, wide caps with the hair tucked safely within; each face was smeared and coloured various hues, depending which vats and presses they'd been around. Out they streamed, indistinguishable as individuals, trickling away homeward or inn-ward into the maze of snickets that networked away up the hill. MacCraw had no choice now but to join the throng and hurry along back up to Snell's house to try and catch his man. He lingered there near the courtyard, hopping from foot to foot, swivelling this way and that, scanning over the faces of the thinning crowd. At last the familiar, skinny frame of Snell came gangling toward him, and Snell recognized the barber instantly.

'Well, Mister MacCraw, sir! You here visiting us again? Welcome, sir, most welcome.'

'Ah, Snell. Thank God it's you. I was waiting for you outside the works but I couldn't spot ya in all the other fellas.'

'Ah, well, we're all much of a muchness in that place, sir. I would shake your hand but it's a little grimy. Mine, I mean. It's nice to see you down here again, Mister MacCraw, especially after your unfortunate business of late. I've been hearing all sorts. But come on in, come in. The lads are up and about now, and Jazeb'll be delighted to see yer. I'll tell you all about your doctor fella's visit.'

Snell would have opened the door then and ushered his guest down the little staircase, but MacCraw hung back from the door and took his would be host by the sleeve.

'No, no. I'll not come in. But I would like to talk with you. Urgently. And privately. Somewhere busy where two fellows gabbing won't rouse any suspicion. Some inn nearby, perhaps, where we'd get a chance to chat a few minutes in a quiet corner.'

Snell never even hesitated, so grateful was he to the benevolent barber. Leading MacCraw by the elbow he steered him along the yard and up through the streets up to a rough and ready inn nearby. The Harp Of Erin was a ramshackle, leaning and narrow house of ill repute amongst the more genteel townsfolk. In truth, it was a friendly enough place. As its name suggested, The Harp was frequented by many an Irish worker anxious for a glimpse or taste of something of the homeland at the end of a shift. The place was always busy, full of noise and chatter with the scraping of fiddles, the air fugged through with pipesmoke, fire fumes and the delicious aroma of cabbage and bacon, of which there was always a pan on the go. It was an ideal place for a private conversation, as long as the noise and laughter of fifty other such chinwaggings going along nearby and around could be tolerated. Snell, a regular in this warm house when he could afford a few pence, found them a wall side table in the large back room, and after a yelled instruction to a passing potboy, four pint pots of dark stout were set before them.

'Now then...' Snell paused, sank half the contents of his firth mug in a slaking draft, then smacked his lips. '... work up a thirst, in there, sir. Damned hot. The fumes too... they get on your throat...' Down went the next half pint, followed by a comfortable belch. Snell settled into his stool, daintily scooping up his second pot, sipping at this one with a little more dignified reserve.

'That's better now. Well, as private as anywhere, this place, Mister MacCraw. So, what's all this scandal I hear about you being set upon in the streets around here? And fighting too, up at The Star. A right bad business, from what I heard.'

'Ah, it was nothing too serious, though it could have been. Out here, that is. I was set upon. Thugs and hoodlums. They gave a few whacks about the head to make sure I slept well. Robbed me. Left me for dead. And that business in The Star- ah, don't believe all ya hear. I'll tell you the truth of it later. But anyway, that business aside, I do need your help, Mister Snell. It's on a connected matter, in a manner of speakin'. Don't look so alarmed, man. I don't need you for violence; nothing like that. But I need a strong hand in a secret matter.'

'Then you have it, sir. Anything. I've already sworn myself to you for the help you've given us in the past.'

Snell raised his pot in an oath-binding toast, they clunked jars, drank deep, smacked lips, then MacCraw sat up straight with a formal, business-like look about his manner and face.

'I must swear you to secrecy on the matter, Snell. Life-long secrecy.'

'No worry there, Mister MacCraw. I'll swear it on the lives of my mother and my lads, sir. They're both getting stronger, as I said, so I owe you that much anyway. I'll take any oaths you want of me.'

'There's a risk.'

'Life's all risk, sir. Risk and struggle. It's the way I'm used to.'

'And it's night-work I speak of.'

'I work best at night, sir.'

'But there'll be reward, whether we succeed or fail.'

'I want no reward of any kind, MacCraw. I'm helping you out as a friend here, not working for yer.'

'Ah, well, thanks for that comforting assurance. Nevertheless, there's something that'll benefit you and the lads that's all part of the overall scheme. But let me tell you about it. I can't go into everything here, but I'll give the gist and outline of what we've got to do. Bear with me, though. It sounds like madness, but it's all worked out and thought through. I'll fill in the gaps for you later...'

MacCraw here leaned close to Snell's blue stained ear, his low voice mingling in with the general din of the place, the dye-worker's head nodding here and there, the colour smeared face frowning, gaping, clucking, sucking stout, lips now and then tutting at the barber's words. They ordered more drink, then their heads closed together again and the talk went on, with much nodding from Snell now as he took in the detailed instructions and strange logic of MacCraw's plan. All ended with agreement, with grim smiles, with vigorous handshakes and the draining of pots.

'I'm in, Mister MacCraw, though like I say, I want none of the rewards you mention. What you're offering – that's out of proportion to the favour.'

'Well, there's the deal, Joseph, as it stands at the moment. Now, I've got to get going to sort the cart out, and I daresay you're anxious to get back to your family. So, tomorrow night. About this time now, and outside of here will do nicely. We'll pick you up out front. Dressed in black sir, if you can. Dressed in black from hat to toe, or bring such night-work clothes along with you.'

Drinks and business finished, they scraped back their stools, stood and firmly shook hands, then headed for the street door.

CHAPTER 21

'David Of Bradford For Fresh Whitby and East Coast Fish. Cod. Haddock. Plaice. Herring - fresh, pickled, smoked. Oysters. Mussels. Crab. At your request, I will supply. Household and establishment deliveries undertaken - distance no object. Rawson Market, Bradford. David Of Bradford For Fresh Whitby and East Coast Fish.'

Haworth, March 1861

Night gloom shrouded them. A useful veil of mist clung about the lower valley. Fish David's covered wagon clattered along at a pace, appearing out of the fog like a mysterious ship, vanishing back into mist to the few souls abroad who glimpsed it, leaving behind a wake of reeking fish scent. Being a trader's cart, the bolted side-boards plainly stating its business, the vehicle attracted little attention as it lumbered through the towns and hamlets of the valleys. It was not unusual to see merchants on their way between places in the dead of night, though some might have wondered at a fish merchant travelling inland rather than east toward York or the coast.

None of the men aboard spoke much. David grunted now and then, muttered about the folly of such a night ride along such hazardous roads, but secretly he was pleased with the price of hire he had managed to draw out of MacCraw the previous evening. MacCraw had come upon him in the back room of The Duchess of Kent, had taken him aside and blurted out his wish to hire a cart and driver for a night. Already drink fuddled, the barber had come straight out with his business in hoarse whispering. David had thought it a mad man's scheme, but having heard of his old friend's troubles of late with Big Barry, who he himself despised, he agreed to assist MacCraw, if they could negotiate a price. MacCraw had come up with a price outright, and it was a tidy sum for a night's work that no sensible merchant could refuse, danger or no danger. Thus, David had been roped in and crossed off of MacCraw's list – the very last item to be scored through. All was now complete and in place; MacCraw had gone to bed nervous, but happy for once. At last, he could see a sensible ending to things – if he could stay alive long enough to see it all through.

A strange looking triumvirate they made. David was still clad in his fish smock and overalls, the obvious outfit while at the reigns of the wagon. MacCraw was dressed in baggy black barbering trousers and a dark, ragged coat that he intended to discard after the night's work. Snell, straight from the dye-house to his pick up outside The Harp of Erin, was still in his filthy work clothes, his visible skin completely dye-stained. To comply with MacCraw's request he clutched a bundle which contained a suit of black rags, all ready to change for the night-work when the wagon stopped rolling. MacCraw and Snell were sat on crates in the back of the cart, surrounded by a clutter of empty baskets, herring boxes and the tools for the night's job. Both were glad of the shelter from the cold, but barely able to breathe for the stinging fish-reek that smarted their eyes and nostrils.

Just after Keighley and on toward the Haworth incline, they parked up a while in the cover of a copse. When certain they were safe from view from any nearby dwellings, MacCraw lit one of the oil lanterns. Snell changed into his black outfit and boots while David, not wanting any identification with the strange matter beyond this point, removed the cart's trade boards, and slid them out of view into the back. The three shared a silent supper of bread and cold meat, washed down with a bottled ale that MacCraw had thought to bring along in a small hamper. He also had a pint bottle of decent brandy, and this they passed round for a pull to keep out the growing chill.

'We should be upon Haworth within the hour,' MacCraw reckoned aloud.

'Aye, and what then? To the top o' a mountain, I suppose? It's a heavy load.' grumbled David. He knew the limitations of his two horses, and he feared a steep climb with the weight of three men as well the tools MacCraw had put in the back would wear them out

'It's a rising road all right,' MacCraw conceded. 'But I can get out and walk along behind. You'd be best off staying in the back, Joseph, if that's all right with you.

Two of us on the street might draw attention, and you look a bit odd in the face with all that colour, if you'll excuse my bluntness.'

Snell laughed. The brandy was already cheering him. 'They'll have bright-faced dyers out here, Mister MacCraw. The company has a works in Haworth Brow. But I'm happy to sit in the back rather than climb a mountain. If it comes to it, though, I'll get out further up and give the old 'osses a push.'

'Hey - less lip!' David brayed. 'Good horses, them. Might not look much, but they're as nimble as goats. Anyroad, if I get too far ahead I'll wait for you all at top where it flattens out.'

It was agreed that David would drive to the quiet moor edge beyond the top village. He'd wait a little way out on the Colne road, that way avoiding rousing the suspicions of any late night wanderers or window peepers. They had another tot of brandy then hauled themselves back to their feet. Supper was over. They clambered back aboard the wagon and set upon their way.

It was somewhere past one in the morning when they passed up the hill through Haworth. Not a single window or lamp in the whole district was lit. Not so much as a cat's ghost prowled on the black streets. Nobody, it seemed, was around to spy on them. The mist had cleared from these higher grounds. Intermittently, a milk-silver moon flashed full through massive, brightly edged clouds, briefly illuminating the way ahead and the hills about. MacCraw marched up the winding road behind the wagon, legs burning with the exertion. He kept an eye about at all time for a watchman or a bobby, though he doubted that they had a night constable in such a remote region. He had no decent story to tell should he be stopped, and had determined to hide in shadow or shrubbery should he so much as sense another soul. Thankfully, he made the top unhindered, and at last came upon the wagon at the moor edge. The clouds were separating like black curtains, the moon leering down across the moors. Rasping for breath with the exertion of the hill, having been much younger and fitter the last time he'd ascended its winding route, he clambered up beside Fish David. A fringe of pines was pricked out against the moonlit blur of the near horizon. Wind hissed and moaned through the trees, scuttling its ripples across the bracken. Both David and Snell looked mad-eyed in this desolate moonlight, and to them MacCraw now seemed like an insane ogre sent straight from Satan's pit. For the first time of the long night all three were wary and fearful of what lay ahead, and of the supernatural consequences that their actions might unleash. Snell half expected some frothing barguest hound to bound howling from the trees at any moment, or a white-faced ghoul to leap grinning upon the cart. MacCraw saw the situation between them all, felt the fear that was running through his night's comrades. He rummaged back in the hamper and produced the brandy bottle, unplugged it, swigged, then passed it on to David. He saw that a speech to rouse the troops was in order.

'Brace yourself now, lads,' he wheezed around the bite of the spirit. 'Drink deep and get a grip. There's work to be done that takes a bit a mettle and a lot of bottle. We can't come this far to get strange on one and other.'

They swigged the bottle in turn, nodding, agreeing with MacCraw, but wanting the whole heathen episode to be over with. Of all nights, they wanted this one past so that they could get to their homes then wipe the deed from hand and mind. Another round of the bottle passed, then at last David broached the subject of their reason for sallying forth so far from Bradford. Although he'd agreed his price and taken money up front to go along with MacCraw's bizarre venture, he had thought it had been just the drink talking; he never actually expected him to be serious about going the whole way through with his plan.

'I do take it, George,' he wheezed, 'that you know the exact location of the grave you intend to dig up?'

MacCraw hummed, then nodded.

'Of course I do, David. I attended the funeral, after all. My memory of that day is imprinted strong. The grave is close to the south west corner wall, well away from the parsonage. I've enough memory to get my bearings. Anyway, his'll still be marked as well as the sisters.'

'And we'll be quick in there, will we?' Snell wondered.

'We should be quick, Joseph. I've read that the process takes no more than an hour, though you'll appreciate I have no experience of the actual work involved. It's as fresh a job to me as it is you. I hope. The ground's soft underfoot tonight. There's no frost. It should be quick work. Come on, then. Let's quit the chatter and get to it while there's moon enough to see by.'

As quietly as possible, David led the wagon back into the village. He tethered the horses in a tree fringed lane just around from the Parsonage house, silencing them with hay bags and blinkers. They were not far from the spread of tomb stones that the clergyman's residence boasted in its garden. Here some climbing was involved. Snell, being the leanest and nimblest of the three, went over the wall first, then lowered the tools, packages, canvas sheet, spades and lanterns that MacCraw passed over. MacCraw himself scrambled over next. David, too stout to even consider the climb, walked a little way down the lane until he came upon a wicket gate, and in a moment had joined his fellows. They stood motionless in shadows and shrubbery, away from the graves, waiting to make sure their actions thus far had not disturbed anybody in the village. Ten minutes or so passed, an eternity of night lurking, every sound and movement amplified through the dark. At last MacCraw gave the signal. Faces shadowed with lowered caps, clothing the colour of Death himself, they tip-toed in single file, quickly crossing the graveyard. MacCraw led the way to the far, tree-lined end. The breeze was rattling in the branches here, surging now and then like great gasps of breath, eerie and disturbing under their circumstances, but fortuitous in that it provided a welcome cover of noise when the canvas sheet was set down, and when their shovels at last went biting into the turf of Branwell's burial plot. This was a corner tomb nearby his mother's and sisters', his marker an unobtrusive and upright stone slab, simple and modest in design, the lettering that spelled out the brief span of his life already weathering with the rough climate. 'Aetas ipsa solatium omnibus affert' was inscribed beneath the dates there - Branwell, poet to the last, having requested this epitaph for himself, along with a translation: *'And all this too shall pass away'.*

The moon slithered in and out of banks of cloud, its brightness giving them enough light to work by without resorting to the lantern. Snell's anxieties had passed off a little now that they were on with the job. Their shovels went slicing and thumping, depositing a growing mound of earth on the canvas sheet which was set down so that the ground beside the grave would bear no tell-tale soil stain in the morning. His heart, he reckoned, was pounding loud enough, for those around to hear plain should they stop and have a moment's silence. Discovery at what they were about in a place as small as this meant certain capture. Snell knew that would mean imprisonment at least, and probably transportation, along with the eternal blackening of his name. He'd heard tales of robbers in the local cemeteries, digging up a recently interred corpses deposited by a family of wealth, stripping it of valuable jewellery and good clothing, then reburying the coffin without leaving a sign of disturbance. But this – digging up one long dead, and for no good reason – there could be no self-respect in this. Oaths of friendship and loyalty would not hold up in a court of law. Capture here would be further indignity and ruination for his poor family. Snell pondered all this as they took it in turns at the earth, two at a time in the deepening pit while the other stood resting, keeping look out and awaiting his turn.

David, far from the prime of life and good health, was soon exhausted with his digging exertions. His girth too was problematic – he was actually having difficulty fitting into the steadily deepening hole. In an exchange of whispers it was agreed that he should go back to the horses, make sure that they were settled and ready for a quick departure from the scene, then keep look out from the edge of the cemetery. As he waddled away Snell and MacCraw went even harder at the task. Within half an hour they were rewarded by the rattle of spade edge on coffin lid. They paused at the sound. Their eyes glittered at each other in the moonlight.

'MacCraw, I've just had this thought,' Snell hissed.

'What's that then?'

'Was he the last in here? You know, some families pile them one on top of the other.'

There was only a brief pause but in that silence, like stones dropping down a well shaft, MacCraw's heart and spirits plummeted. He'd not thought on this. Little Emily had gone soon after Branwell – but surely she'd been given her own plot and not placed in above her brother. And Anne, what of her? Scarborough, he'd heard. Charlotte had her own grave, no doubt about that. She'd not be crowded in until Doomsday with the rest of them.

'No no, he was the last in here, I'm certain,' MacCraw muttered, though he sounded none too convinced. 'For sure, he was the last. But shush, now. Let's to it!'

With bare hands he went scraping at the head of the coffin, the dark, dull wood becoming visible. To get this far and break open the wrong coffin! That would be a travesty. But there was no going back from here now. And it wouldn't be that tragic. The skull and bones though, they were important. They had to be those of a man. How could they tell, though, the doctors and the experts? The jaw? The teeth? The ribs, possibly. Did a man really have one more than a woman? The pelvis indicated gender, so he'd read; the woman's was wider for child bearing. But those Brontë's had all been such diddy things, and none of them as far as he knew had produced children. The pelvis he'd leave, though. He did not need every bone.

They dug the lid clear, both working at either end of the grave, taking care that their shovels did not bang too loud upon the wood. It looked like a narrow door set flat in the earth. Following Versailius's instructions, rather than exhume the whole casket they dug a clear space behind the head of the coffin to give MacCraw room to work in. He then ordered Snell to clamber up from the grave. Though grateful for his accomplice's assistance and company, he wanted to spare him the ordeal of witnessing a long sealed coffin prised open to reveal its grisly contents.

'Stand close by though,' MacCraw requested. 'I'll have need of a lantern in a minute, and I need you to pass down the package when I give the signal.'

Snell was happy enough with that, and it was with great relief that he clambered out from the pit. He lowered the oil lamp, which MacCraw lit then set firmly in the loose earth beside the coffin head. Shadows danced about the grave walls, light picking out broken, oozing plant roots, ends of worms and loose, glinting slivers of stones in the soil. Moths and other night-flies came fluttering toward the sudden light, clattering themselves upon the lantern glass, trying to extinguish themselves upon that cruelly luring flame. The poet in MacCraw sympathized with their blind plight. A light had attracted him toward it once, a dazzling brilliance that had drawn him in then all but destroyed him. Branwell the lantern, MacCraw the moth. He became morbid, imagining his own mouth crammed full of soil and small stones. He felt insects crawling upon his laid-out body, spines of legs twitching over his face, the soft mouths of worms probing at his skin, seeking entry into the meaty interior.

'Get a grip, MacCraw. Get a grip,' he muttered, fighting against the horror. He inhaled slowly on the putrid grave-air as he took up his hooks and crowbar.

'Well Rhymer,' he whispered, crouching at the head of the coffin, inserting the blade of a hook in the soil caked crack. 'We meet again, and as usual in unusual circumstances. I've something to return to you...' He grunted as he tried to force the lid, but the hook slipped toward him, gashing along the side of his palm.

'Damn and blast!' He whipped off his neckerchief and quickly bound it around the wounded hand, anxious not to get wet and diseased soil in the flowing blood. Again he positioned himself at the coffin head, this time with the crowbar. After much cursing and huffing and banging of slipping crowbar, he felt the blade slip in, and at last there was leverage. Down he pushed. There came a creaking groan of wood, then a loud snap as the lid of the coffin jerked loose. An audible whoosh, like a soft escaping breath with a miasmic stench of rot and death, engulfed MacCraw. The lantern was extinguished by that blast of exhaled coffin-breath. In the stinking grave-darkness MacCraw went gasping and retching, trying to cough himself clear of the stench; trying to gag away the film of dust that coated his mouth and throat. Startled by the loud noise, Snell rushed to the grave edge and peered over.

'You all right down there, Mister MacCraw?'

The stench passed upward over MacCraw, out of the grave, dispersing into the night like a tangible, fleeing phantom. MacCraw heaved his lungs and throat clear,

'I'm fine Joseph. A bit of dust, that's all. All's fine now. I'll just spark the lamp again.'

MacCraw composed himself and re-lit the lantern, the crack of open coffin gaping clear in the light.

'Nearly done here now. Pass me down the sack.'

Down came the empty sack, then Snell stepped back from the grave's edge, leaving MacCraw to get on with his morbid work. The barber again set himself to work on the coffin. Versalius, he recalled, advised that only the top end of the coffin should be broken open and the corpse hauled out and upward from the grave. This is what MacCraw now intended with the skeleton of his old friend, but in his fuddled planning he had overlooked the fact of physical decay. Versalius had been hauling out fresh cadavers for his studies. MacCraw would be setting his hands on a crumbling skeleton. A dozen or so years his friend had been bedded in the casket there; a dozen years for muscle to fade; for sinew to decay; for bones that once melded well together to slip and slide apart. Holding his breath to avoid breathing down more dust, MacCraw rummaged into the coffin, felt the chalky, domed object that he knew must be the skull, took a good grip, and began to haul his catch in. The dome rattled loose of any attachments, bolted free, and emerged as a very singular, staring object, leaving the rest of the skeleton behind.

'Damn!' he muttered, staring into the defleshed face of his old friend. Wisps of fine red hair still curled about the withered pate. Branwell seemed to be leering and laughing right at him. 'Oh, Brontë. Nice to see you, pal. Now, damn your eyes!' He tossed the skull unceremoniously into the sack, then again rummaged in the coffin, grasping about, dragging out a random handful of dry bones. These too were bundled, and this process he repeated several times, thrusting in right up to the shoulder, reaching as far in as he could before dragging out the twigs of bones. Once satisfied that he had enough material for his purpose, he gave the sack a good shake, called Snell back to the grave edge and handed up his booty.

'Bring me the parcel now, friend. We're very nearly done here.'

Snell handed him down the heavy package that they had lugged all the way with them, not even bothering to ask MacCraw what he intended to do with it. The parcel contained what remained of Branwell's pile of papers – the very ones handed to MacCraw not a hundred yards from the opened grave there, years before. This parcel was much bigger now than it ever had been, the bulk of it being wrapping and protection, secured so meticulously by the element-wary MacCraw. A layer of fine blue silk, then one of brown paper, followed by several layers of that very week's news sheets had gone around it, followed by two layers of greaseproof paper. Every seam and crack had been sealed up with candle wax to help keep out damp, corroding air. Around this inner padding had gone thin, overlapping layers of waxed leather, and finally a stitched coating of oil-skin cloth. The package certainly had some weight to it now. MacCraw intended it to last safe in the grave until Doomsday - or at least until he told the world, at a time when it was more prepared to listen, where the true, first draft of the book known as 'Wuthering Heights', safely rested. MacCraw pulled the coffin lid high enough to accommodate the bulk of the parcel then slid it like a letter into a mail box. It thumped to its resting place there, and at last he lowered the lid. As best he could, using a velvet covered mallet brought specially for the purpose, he hammered the loosed lid back into place. Snell was called back, the tools and extinguished lantern passed up, then MacCraw himself clambered up from the grave.

'Done, friend. All's done. Now lets fill it in and get out of this cursed place.'

Fish David rejoined them at the grave, and with the three of them shovelling at a furious rate, it did not take them long to get the disturbed earth back over the coffin. The canvas sheet was tipped out, the soil stamped down as flat it would go, then the disturbed turf was placed back as neatly as they could manage. The grave mound was still raised higher than it initially had been, bumped a little above the level of the graves about, but they had no time for fretting over that matter.

'No one will notice,' MacCraw assured Snell and David, who in truth couldn't care less and were already away toward the wall. 'I doubt anyone comes by this way much anymore,' he said then, more down at the grave than to anyone in particular. He collected up the lantern, his sack of clunking bones and a shovel, then was off after the others, glad to be away from there at last.

Dawn seeped like a pale stain upon the horizon as Fish David's wagon rattled back toward Bradford. MacCraw was hunched wearily beside David at the reins, sack of skull and bones pushed back and secured beneath his seat. Snell was snoring amidst the clutter and fish boxes in the back - some much needed kip, for in the hour he would be back at his toil in the dye-house. They had stopped just after Keighley to dump the canvas and tools and change their mud-filthy clothing. A few taciturn exchanges had been muttered between them, but for the most part the journey had been endured in a depressed silence. MacCraw was lost in his own reveries, meandering down the potential trackways that lay ahead once he had put the bones to the use that he intended. He and David struck up their pipes. Through wreaths of blue smoke they watched the weather develop. Drab as it was, they looked about the gloomy sky with grunts of satisfaction. The cold dawn-breeze brought a westerly band of cloud chasing up behind them, and within minutes light drizzle became a steady, drumming downpour of glassy rain. Grim to ride through, but good for the soil. Rain such as this would keep any but the most mournful people out of the Haworth cemetery, as well as helping to cover any tracks or traces that had been left about the disturbed graveside there.

The fish wagon clattered on through the grey smudged centre of Bingley. Beyond there they were joined with a thickening stream of traffic heading toward their business down at the famous new Salts Mill, just below Shipley. MacCraw watched with some approval as they passed the clean looking mill with its warren-streeted community, built by the river at a place that had already become known as 'Saltaire'. The great mill owner there, Titus Salt, was a humanitarian after MacCraw's own heart – a man rarely kind and considerate toward his workforce, treating them like real people rather than cattle. He had, built of good, solid stone, a controversial but humane mini-town to feed and nurture the needs of his magnificent new mill, complete with hospitals, schools, infirmaries and community halls. MacCraw watched the impressive mill and chimney stack until it dissolved into the mist and drizzle, wondering just how many of the new wealthy hierarchy would follow the good man's example.

The road wound on. Eventually, ahead of them through the drizzle, clusters of smoking chimneys and church spires began to emerge along the edges of the valley, a lid-like smudge of sooty smoke hanging malignantly above the town. The long, straight road was flat and glassy here, the going easy. In no time at all they were clattering along the mill lined edges of Manningham. As they passed the theatres and headed toward the town centre the smog about them thickened and yellowed, billowing out of the ends of streets, pressing strange, angular facades out of the nearest buildings.

'Well lads,' MacCraw said, knowing that their little adventure was drawing to a close. 'I can never thank you enough for your assistance this night.'
David clucked and nodded. He'd had his payment, the night was done, and he was back on his home turf. His thoughts were already of the day ahead, wondering how fish trading would go in such dismal weather and unhealthy atmosphere. Days like this, people tended to be off their food, and especially something with a bit of a tang or odour to it. Snell, roused now from his uncomfortable napping, sat looking ruffled and dazed at the rear end of the wagon, watching the streets jog by behind them. He felt as though he had just lived through a mad dream. His thoughts too came round to the weather, wondering about his boys, and how such a poisonous, foggy air might effect their recovering health. There was a whole days shift between now and the sight of them, and he felt twinges of anxious guilt at not knowing exactly how they fared. He was dropped off outside the dye house, his day shift there not long due, with just about enough time to gobble something hot from the corner chop house. MacCraw slipped him a few coins to cover his breakfast. On a final bit of stilted chat he agreed to call up on MacCraw over the next few days, then was away.

On route to the market, David dropped MacCraw at the bottom of Ivegate, then with a grunt and wave was on his own way. MacCraw watched the wagon out of sight, the sack tucked delicately under his arm, the loose bones surprisingly light. The streets were already busy, people trudging to and fro to work, to market, to beg, many carrying bags and sacks that looked just like his own. There was no reason why he should arouse suspicion, and he felt easy about the matter as he hobbled up the hill toward his establishment. He approached the shop warily and he went into his lately developed precautions, passing the window and door once without a glance, just listening, checking that the door was not kicked in or the lock forced open. At the bottom of the street he swiveled round to see if he was being followed, or if suspicious, lurking fellows had emerged from hidden doorways to watch him. All seemed clear. He re-approached the shop front, placed the sack down, then opened the door as quickly as possible while glancing about and behind him all the time, ready to grab in his pocket for the revolver. Once indoors, he locked and double bolted himself in. He hurried upstairs to check from the higher windows that nobody of a sinister cut or look was lingering outside. Reasonably sure that in the hour or so remaining before the shop lads arrived he would be free from disturbance, he gently set the sack down upon his living room table.

'Rest there, friend,' he said to the bones. 'Sorry to have to clatter you about and the like, but it's all for the best. Now, don't you be going anywhere. I'll be back to sort you.'

He rushed downstairs to stoke up the fire and set the water on. In the company of a good blaze he felt so relieved to be back in his little, humble abode. For a moment, comforted with his familiar surroundings, he began to doubt his long term plan. A glance out of the window at the smog and spluttering rain steered him back on course. He set about getting the tin bath up to his living room, preparing it for a double use.

CHAPTER 22

Kneel not and leave me: mirth is in its grave.
True friend, sweet words were ours; sweet words decay.
Believe, the perfume once this violet gave
Lives - lives no more, though mute tears answer nay.
Break off delay!

Dead, Love is dead! Ay, cancelled all his due.
We say he mocks repose - we cannot tell -
Close up his eyes and crown his head with rue,
Say in his ear, sweet Love, farewell! farewell!
A last low knell.

Forbear to move him. Peace, why should we stay?
Go back no more to listen for his tread.
Resume our old calm face of every day:
Not all our kneeling turns that sacred head
Long dear, long dead!

Go with no tear drop; Love had died before:
Stay being foolish; being wise begone.
Let severed ways estrange thy weak heart no more.
Go, unregretfull, and refrain thy moan.
Depart alone.

Lord De Tabley - A Leave-Taking.

Bradford, March 1861

Another fortnight MacCraw waited, sitting on his sack of scrubbed bones. He stowed them in the trunk at the foot of his bed, peeping in on them from time to time, but only ever in a morning. It proved a tense, nerve wracking, frantic fortnight, with him attempting to lead his barbering life as usual, and to appear normal in his outward manner. As best he could, he kept the shop open, though his own hand was often too unsteady to deal with the delicacies of razoring a man, and he had to let young Mufty take care of those jobs.

On the Tuesday morning after working at the Haworth grave, at about 8 am, a small, shivering, pasty-faced figure came nervously through the shop door and stood there at the fire-end of the room. For a moment MacCraw wondered what the child wanted at that hour; clearly it was not a pre-work shave, his white skin as yet untroubled by stubble. Then, on meeting his eyes, MacCraw recognised the lad. There he stood, little Jazeb Snell. Shrivelled by his illness, blue tinged rings of skin drooping beneath his pale blue eyes, Jazeb Snell had returned to work at last, and he insisted that he meant to stay there.

'I'll not be going home 'till mi day's work is done, Mister MacCraw,' he sternly declared up to his master. 'Mi dad says you saved my life and got me a doctor and all sorts of other good things. I'd work here for nowt, sir, if my folks weren't so short. I'm forever in your debt, Mister MacCraw. I know that, and I mean to make you the world's best apprentice any barber ever had.'

Seeing that the boy was sincere, and was resolved to stay through the day no matter what, MacCraw welcomed him back heartily. He sat his favourite lad in the best shaving chair, then knocked him up a blood tonic of angelica, sloe juice, dandelion root and a little powdered burdock. Tasty as this was, especially when heated and sweetened with honey, he had to urge his lad to get it all down, promising that he would feel the concoction's benefits before the day was out. As soon as the other two lads were in he ordered the lot of them a bought-in cooked breakfast from down the hill. They all ate, straight from the tray, a feast of steaming meats, eggs, vegetables, black pudding, mushrooms and fried bread, all washed down with plenty of tea. After this treat, and seeing their work-fellow back from the brink, they were all in good spirits. They set about work with a cheerful zest unusual for the time of year. As they worked through the morning, clipping and razoring, cleaning down the floor and surfaces, all chatted on to customers or sang the latest shanties and risky music hall ballads. MacCraw took care to give the fragile looking Jazeb the lightest of jobs that day and for the rest of the week, letting him rest with a cup of tonic or tea or meat stock every hour or so, trying to nurture him back into the rhythm of the place, as well as encourage back his sapped vitality.

For MacCraw, the pleasant return of his apprentice aside, it was an awful week. Every moment of his working day he expected the shop door to come bursting open to reveal Big Barry standing there, blunderbuss at his hip, blade between his teeth, a dozen piratical cronies armed to the teeth behind him, ready to slaughter MacCraw and every customer in the place. Every evening, after the shop had been shuttered, shut up, locked and bolted, MacCraw settled in the upstairs room behind the curtains, peeping down on the lamp-lit street, revolver cleaned, cocked and ready upon the table. He had set jugs and buckets of water about the place, for at the least he expected them to come and try burn him out of shop and home.

'The best armed are the bravest,' he would whisper there at the window. This was the trade slogan that had come with the gun. Vigilantly he waited, night and day, but nothing happened. Barry and his crew had not so much spat at the place by the Friday, by which time their inaction and silence was grating harder on MacCraw than even seeing them in the flesh. From shop-gossip and the talk in the taverns when he'd dared nip out for a sociable drink, it seemed that the town behind inn doors was humming with the rumour of MacCraw's outlandish assault on the loathed and much feared gangster. He heard several versions of the night's events, so exaggerated that they were not recognisable to the very man who had been gunning in the thick of them. He had shot Barry in a duel. He had shot him in the head. He had single handedly fought with a dozen gangsters before wrenching a pistol that was about to be unloaded into his head by Barry, turning the tables by gunning down half a dozen of them before setting the place on fire and making a daring escape through the front bar. The fight was over a woman – Pot Mary, it was rumoured. It was over a gambling debt. A lost haul from a robbery. A missing trunk of opium. Though there were many versions of the same tale, all ended with the same, neat conclusion: the heroic barber was as good as dead. The general opinion was that MacCraw should have finished the wounded villain off with a shot to the head up there in The Star. Having foolishly spared Barry, MacCraw's own grisly death was a certainty. It was just a matter of time, they deemed; simply a matter of time.

Barry and his leg-shot crony had both survived their injuries, having been patched up and bandaged by the best local surgeons. Both were said to be recuperating out of town in healthier air and a better atmosphere, on the advice of professional friends. With firearms involved in the incident, the local police force was likely to be interested in the case; indeed, it had been whispered on to Barry that a local constable, Duff by name, had a bee in his bonnet about a gang of organised criminals that had set up in the town, after receiving various tip-offs on their activities.

Big Barry was lying low, but he'd sworn that he would be back in town shortly, and that the barber would be tortured, butchered and roasted before the month was out. Chilling as these bar-ramblings were, they neatly suited MacCraw and his plans. He did little to discourage speculations of Barry's revenge, and whenever the opportunity arose readily confirmed that he had been threatened with death by Barry. For his bravery, he never left a tavern that week without many a handshake and a bought or promised drink, and with solemn, quiet good wishes for his safety in the future.

From inn visits and other excursions abroad, day or night, business or leisure, MacCraw would edge his way home through the shadows and side streets, hand on the revolver that all but lived in his pocket. He was ready to draw and shoot any man dead at the first hint of threat or provocation. But no provocation came, nor threat, nor insult, and by the Friday he was close to the very blade-edge of his nerves. He was snappy and irritable with the shop-lads, and short with the customers that he attended to himself. He was like a boil ready to burst – swollen, sore and inflamed. Sometimes, as he well knew, a boil needs pinching to provoke its own healing. In his nervous state he was ready to go seek Barry out and provoke him again; to prick the spot to bursting in order to bring events to a head. Common sense prevailed though, and he got on with his daily business.

Sleep in these troubled times was difficult, his head filled with worries and plans, plotting out details into the small hours, working over time-tables and routes and the criss-crossing of his various identities. He was busy criss-crossing about the county's towns too. One morning he was in Leeds, the afternoon in York, then over to Halifax, and as far afield as Manchester. He had stored and built up money over the years, his fortune tied up in his three different names, all supported by documents and legitimate registration, with running accounts in various banks about the county.

One thing he had learned well from his father's eastern enterprise was that there was no point in having just the one valid identity when half a dozen could serve you better. Other than the Millergate Shop, his two other Bradford properties, both apothecary shops, were also under his MacCraw signature. They had been under lease from him for years, and both leaseholders, content with the profits they were making and the fabric and situations of their premises, were quick to snatch the opportunity to buy them outright. His monies MacCraw set about raking together under one name, transferring an account here, cashing in a bond or shares there, closing down his tracks and accounts behind him, as the crooked path of his estranged family had long since taught him to do. He signed so many papers, in various names in differing towns about the county those weeks, that at times he hardly knew where or who he really was. At night his brain would be fizzing with problems and considerations, and more than once he resorted to a draft of laudanum to nudge him on toward The Land Of Nod. This remedy caused its own problems, leading to him possessing something of a jaded, haggard aspect the next morning, partly because of the dreams that manifested and unfolded in the depths of his opiated sleep. And what dreams they were. Such visions and dreams, the waking world seemed shallow and colourless in comparison.

Things got so bad that he feared to go to bed at night. Barely had he crawled into his blankets when the bones would come floating up from the bag in the trunk at the foot of bed. Real bones though - he could touch them, grip them between his fingers and feel the chalky hardness. The disparate bones would swirl about the room a while, separate and go their different ways, then a bright halo would form in mid air at the foot of the bed. This halo would become hair, a carrot, flaming mane, and the skull would float below until it locked into position like a boat docking on a quay. The other bones would converge then, ordering themselves to a man-shape, until at last a skeleton, complete and animate, pranced there in the room. Its hands of bone would jab and punch at empty air, whistling with their speeded movement, as though the skeleton was boxing with some invisible adversary. Then it would pause there at the foot of the bed, standing over MacCraw, ready in a pugilistic stance while inviting him to come and box.

'Come to the scratch, won't you?' it gargled. 'Blast your eyes, come to the scratch!'

Dust and skin and chunks of flesh would come raining from the ceiling, clustering about the bones and skull until, by the process of decay reversed, it was the semi-complete figure of Branwell himself who stood there at the bed end. He would be grinning and winking at MacCraw, chattering on as in days of old about some piece of prose or other he was working on, or some notion he had about the nature of poetry. MacCraw would be sitting up in the bed, contributing his hums and has and maybes to the conversation, when at the window would come a knocking, like a twig scraping upon the glass. The horrible, scratching knock would startle both of them to frozen terror, their lamp-shadows dancing on the walls and ceiling.

'She's here!' Branwell would mutter, those semi-decayed lips trembling in unspeakable terror. Then the rapping on the glass would come again, more urgent this time, whatever it was outside demanding by the urgency of the knock to be let in. Branwell would cross to the window, but it was as if MacCraw was seeing through the corpse's eyes. The curtain drawn back. The empty street, illuminated in patches by the corner gas light. Somewhere below they sensed rather than saw the figure, a slow movement of darkness back in a door well as it sought to hide itself completely in shadow. But the light would catch him just, edging him to the strained eye - a dark, sinister fellow, always tall, sometimes hooded like a monk, sometimes a dandy in a tall top hat perched at a rakish angle, nose and long chin jutting white against the blackness of the brim. Once MacCraw would have sworn that he was horned - not the little bulled horns of a Satan, but full antlers, twisting high up above the head, casting a lattice of shadows back into the doorway.

'He's here!' Branwell would say, jabbing a finger down toward the street and darkened doorway. 'You see him, don't you MacCraw - you see him, don't you?!'

The knocking would come at the window again, frantic now, a fist suddenly smashing through the lower pane of the glass. Both men would shriek with terror, the pale forearm and fist of a girl floating there into the room.

'Let me in - let me in!' a most melancholy voice sobbed. Branwell would be grabbing the arm, yanking it down cruelly on the broken pane, rubbing it to and fro until blood poured over the sill, but MacCraw had recognised the voice.

'Leave her be!' he would shriek at Branwell, throwing himself on the fellow's fragile frame and yanking him back from his harm doing. 'Leave her be, Branwell, leave her alone. It's Caroline. It's my Caroline, at last. She's come home!'

Caroline would be in the room then, elegant, pale and beautiful, standing with Branwell at the foot of the bed, both of them looking on most sternly at MacCraw. She was in her favourite green silk evening dress, hair pinned up, a black lace shawl about her glassy shoulders.

'He's not doing so well, is he?' Branwell would say to her. Caroline would shake her head, features grimacing to a frown of disapproval.

'No, he's not doing very well. Not since he let me go.'

Worse would come then. From afar faint music would sound, with a babble of chatter, as though there was a party or ball in an adjoining room. The two corpses, ghastly spectres by now, embraced delicately, then went dancing together at the foot of the bed, gazing and caressing as though they were lovers, their lips nearing, touching, meeting in a kiss that froze MacCraw's heart and lurched him up from the darkest level of his dream.

MacCraw would wake soaked through, shivering with cold, yet dripping with sweat as if in a fever. A tight vice of disquiet would be gripped about his ribs and stomach, and he felt absolutely forlorn. Hazily, he would struggle up from his pit of sleep, trying to nudge his mind toward clarity with a tot of brandy. Various concoctions of snuff and a pipe of strong tobacco would stand him in further readiness for the morning. Only after his morning's 'preparations' could he even consider breakfast, which through these last days was just dry bread broken and dunked into a mug of pungent, strong black coffee.

MacCraw's tense existence since his attack on Big Barry entered its third week. Still there was no sign of those he had assaulted, no direct word from those who would undoubtedly be seeking revenge. Though he was able to carry on with the furtive toings and froings that were necessary to tie up his business and travel arrangements, he never felt easy in the open street. No matter how busy it was around him on public transport, be it rail, omnibus or private hired carriage, he felt open to that attempt of assassination that he perpetually expected. MacCraw lived in mortal dread; an ever present, skin-prickling, mind-clamping fear. If there was a single word to describe poor MacCraw's mental life and inner turmoil throughout that desperate time, then it had to be *terror*. A darkness edged about all doors, as if the monster was waiting to slip in. A teasing darkness would shimmer about a stalking figure in the street like an un-holy halo - his persecutor was definitely there, but then at MacCraw's more penetrating glance was gone, melting into the thick of the crowd. The figure lurked in shop doorways as he passed, waiting with spiderish patience, stepping out behind him. Time seemed to freeze, motion stilled, noise was silenced and ice was upon his heart as he forced himself through a slow agony of turning to confront the fiend. It would vanish like hazy mist evaporating, even as MacCraw swivelled to the confrontation. Time would then jar back into action and movement, the street filled with ordinary and harmless folk scuttling and chattering again about their day's business. MacCraw would shiver and look about wildly like a mad fellow, before pulling himself together and heading back on his own way. At other times, when alone after the shop had closed, muffled, hiss-edged whispering would penetrate his living room from the street below. Big Barry and gang or the dark fiend? MacCraw would snatch up the gun, and a crucifix too, though he'd long been without that faith. When he twitched the curtain back to reveal his tormentors ... nobody. The wet street was empty. There was not even a shape sauntering away along the glassy cobbles; not so much as a fleeing shadow to give rise to the dread that churned within him.

Terror would nip on his heart in the strangest moments. In the shop, with a face below while he lathered it ready for the razor, those icy, bone fingers would grip him within. Round and about he'd glance, brush poised above the customer's chin, his wild eyes darting this way and that. Customer forgotten, he'd stand there looking out for Barry's assassin, or the phantom that he now knew stalked him, just as it had so murderously stalked down Branwell. His eyes would go swinging to the door, to the window, to the street. Of tall people he was especially wary, for as he recalled, Branwell's mind-conjured golem, the demon who had appeared long ago amongst The Rhymers, had been tall and pale. MacCraw would gaze down into the now unsettled face he was lathering, peering intensely into the eyes, making sure they were real and not formed of demonic mist. Naturally, the customers were a bit put out, and even frightened by the intrusion of the barber's maniac staring as he probed deep into their eyes.

'Are you all right, sir?' they would query, the bolder of them.

'I'm all right, sir. Are you, sir?'

'What are you looking at me like that for, man?!'

'Like what, sir! Like what, exactly?'

'Stop it, MacCraw, you're frightening me, you fool. Let me up out of this chair now. Away with that blade!'

And MacCraw, realising it was not a demon he was addressing, but a flesh and blood, paying customer, would back away, bowing, apologising.

'Sorry sir – so sorry. No, you stay there. One of the lads will finish you here. I'm not myself at all today. Just thought I saw something in your eye there. Jazeb, Trumper. Over here, one of yer. So sorry about that now, sir...'

MacCraw would cross the room to tidy a cabinet or knock up a potion, leaving one of the lads to get on with the business of lathering and shaving those customers that dared to stay.

Terror permeated his life. MacCraw's final week was overwhelmed by it, just as he realised now, Brontë's own closure of life had been. He recalled that ghastly, hunted look about Branwell's face the night he had inched his way through the door of The Black Bull in Haworth. MacCraw knew that his time had come to wear the same look, and perhaps for the same good reason. Murderers, cut-throats, demons and the Devil himself were out hunting him now.

When the shop was open but quiet or free of customers, MacCraw would be sitting there reading or musing when from the corner of his eye he would see the tall stranger halt before the shop window. The fiend would pretend to look over the packets and medicinal wares cluttered there, would seem to be reading the labels or contents of some bottle, but then the eyes – terrible, life-sapping eyes – would burn up from the display and into the room. Soul-drinking eyes, absorbing every nook and cranny of the room, searching out MacCraw, peering to the core of him. The eyes would swim over the shelves then focus and fix on MacCraw's own, drinking him in, stripping him back to his naked soul. MacCraw would at last leap up, certain that his moment of extinction had arrived unless he could shake off that consuming gaze. Death itself was upon him! He'd be up on his feet, calling to the lads in the back, shrieking out that Death was here – Death was here! And the very second he was about to flee the room screaming, the stranger peering in the window would straighten up to rustle past, as if all along he really had been a mere potential customer, seeking out some face cream or foot balm.

Terror. Its icy grasp would clamp around the very meat and blood of his heart, jolting him awake from nightmares in some unknown hour of the night. It was a though a ghoul had slapped its hand down on his chest to awaken him. He would feel utterly sick with fear, vomiting bile over the bedside, arms thrashing out in the darkness to keep the snapping demons at bay, driving them back into their world of dreams. They had been real, had been drinking at his blood and soul, and he knew that he was dying. They were killing him, night by night, sapping him away. He had never felt so mortal. He was a vulnerable carcass; a bag of fluid and sludge and bile; he was as much bone and dead meat as the pigs splayed out in the butcher's shop across the street there. Whatever sustained him – the quick, the vitality, the electricity – whatever animated the very carcass of a man, was in danger of being drained from him now. The spark of life that kept him, that illuminated his personal bubble of consciousness in the outer world, was under threat by demons, dream and real. He knew he was in danger of being snuffed out, as simply as a common candle at bedtime. He would lie awake there, panting, cold heart hammering, aware that life was such a ridiculously precious and vulnerable commodity, really as frail as a dragonfly's wing. And he, great lumbering, unthinking fool, had gone out of his way to jeopardise what he had left of his. Mixing and meddling with a bunch of cut-throats who set no more value on a life as they did a vase, or clay pipe, or jar of ale. How he ached and wished that Caroline was there so that he could share this realisation. Women, he reckoned, knew about the true value and frailty of a life, for were they not life-bearing vessels themselves, where men were just a mere means to an end? A huffing, puffing, vainglorious and utterly absurd means, full of their own value and worth, when if fact their real role was merely that of a seed pod. Individuals were meaningless and worthless; aspirations were simply distractions; noble designs were futile wastes of breath. He was sure that with these bleak thoughts and insights alone, the hounds of Death were closing in on him. He had heard before that as soon as a man realises the true value and meaning of life, then it is the time for his to be snatched away from him. But he'd not go without a struggle - not he, not George MacCraw. Thus, with such a whirlwind of thoughts, vague philosophy and general trepidation, MacCraw would drift back into sleep, and into those dreams of Caroline, Branwell and floating bones.

CHAPTER 23

Such a lore is being lost to us, day by day, as people squash themselves into the towns and leave their life and history amidst the fields and trees behind them. I can see a future without plants. Where the properties and uses of the very things that spring freely about us are forgotten and never used. If only people would look about them, and back to their parents, and see what they have in abundance from their God and for free. Being trained in my art rather coming upon it merely as a financial means to day-to-day sustenance, I was given a strong awareness of the uses of root, leaf, stem and herb. But I fear I am lecturing my readers, rather than informing them, and these essays are intended to do the latter. Here then, good reader, I list a few common flowers, shrubs and weeds (which I trust and hope you recognise to your sight and senses so I'll refrain from describing the appearance of leaf and flower) whose infusions I know have benefits to the hair and well being of men and women alike. Camomile flowers are commonly used to lighten hair that is naturally blonde, or to add vigour and shine to hair that has become dulled. Those who are greying about the top and temples might consider the infused flowers of the hollyhock, which adds a vigorous bluish tinge to the age-faded locks. Lavender is well known for reducing the excess of natural oil and greasiness in a head, as is a rinse of lemon, lime or witch hazel, these last astringents closing up the pores of the scalp thus stemming the flow of naturally excreted oils. Common nettles, parsley, rosemary and sage also have their beneficial uses, as incredibly does the scarlet juice of the beetroot, but these I'll examine in more detail in my next installment of this series (the editor permitting) when I once and for all reveal an age old and proven remedy for hair loss and baldness - a preventative and restorative concoction of natural elements, which rather than keep secret and make my own vast fortune with through patenting and modern mass production, I will share for no fiscal gain with the reader of these pages - my own belief being that what comes from Nature should come to all for free.

From 'Essays On The Ancient Art Of The Barber',

George Maquire, 1841

Bradford, April, 1861

MacCraw looked about his old shop for the last time. It was a Friday evening. The lads had cleaned up and cleared off home over an hour before, and he was left there alone, preparing at last for his quitting of the place. Despite all the vowing and promising of his youth, he realised he had become a creature of habit and routine, surrounding himself with tools, implements, bottles, jars and potions; things which gave the shape and substance to himself. His shop and dwelling were like the protecting shell of a tortoise, shaped and moulded to the life and body within. There was so much clutter and frippery that he ached to take with him, but knew he had to leave most of it behind. There were certain bottles and jars of mixed potions he thought were necessary to himself - rare perfumes bought from world travellers that he could not see how he could live without; lumps of valuable ambergris and deep-mined minerals hidden away in the corners of drawers; gifts of ivory handled razors, rolled in paper and put away for an imaginary future day; his first apron, Parisian, linen, that he now suspected would not even fit about his waist, still neatly folded away in the bottom of the shop towel drawer. This last item he had not even looked at in five years or so, though now he had a yearning to pack it in his leather travel bag. He resisted, and things he longed to take but knew he really should not remained in their places about the shop.

The best chair, the shop's oldest, its leather faded, cracked and crusted with years of polish and soap, MacCraw now stroked lovingly with his bitten fingertips. Despite its age 'the throne' had been well cared for, and was still clean in its deep and comfortable crimson. If it had been possible, MacCraw would certainly have packed it up in a trunk and taken away with him. The essence of his trade, even his life, had been ingrained within the thing. Set so solid there it seemed it had an existence; a life and identity of its own. The chair had been the first item for the trade he had bought, other than the brushes and razors he had acquired over his apprentice years. The very shop, the emporium, had been designed and set out around it, the other chairs on either side, though newer, now looking shoddy and minuscule in comparison. Every single Rhymer had been set there upon that leather for his beard shearing, hair clipped and skin toned for some engagement or special event. Boys had blossomed and transformed themselves to men either in that chair or working at it. One old fellow, a wool merchant well on his way to making a fortune, had even passed on in its comfort. At the time, MacCraw, thinking the fellow had but snoozed asleep peacefully, as overtired workers frequently did in the soothing softness of the leather, had carried on shaving. When the shave was done he'd not been able to rouse his customer for his brushdown and payment. He had been shaving a dead man! The story had made the newspaper, and somewhat macabrely had proved good for trade.

His beloved Caroline, still in her wedding dress on the night of their marriage, the shop closed and shuttered, had set herself there upon this red throne while they'd discussed their future over brandy and a shared cigar. There'd been such a shine in her eyes that night, face glowing with the love of her man and her life ahead. They'd embraced there, so passionately he almost blushed at the memory; from that very chair he'd scooped her bodily into his arms and carried her up every step of the staircase to the chambers above.

Within the chair's very essence the details and tribulations of his life were deeply ingrained, as though it was some great sponge, absorbing atoms and times and human memories. And now 'the throne' had a final role to play, its destruction being instrumental in his plan. MacCraw set it up carefully with his own recently worn clothing and the bag of Branwell's rescued bones. The bones he handled gingerly, laying them out like the yellowed pieces of a jig-saw, trying to mark out the framework of a man. The task was not easy. The bones he had snatched from Haworth did not form a complete skeleton. The individual pieces, now trembling like dry twigs in his hands, were not always recognisable to him. The skull, of course, he was sure of, but he had to set the chair's mechanism fully back before he could rest it in place upon the head of the seat, directly above the collar of his street jacket. Ribs were obvious too, and half a dozen or so of these he tucked inside the jacket. Over quarter of an hour or so he constructed as near a skeleton as his working pieces permitted, slipping tibulars down sleeves and a single femur up the leg of his laid-out trousers. Like a sculptor he fussed and fiddled about his work, creating a veritable scarecrow from the bone parts and his own clothing. The remainder of the bones, the scraps and pieces he was unsure exactly where to place, he scattered about the jacket top. At last, with his second best boots placed at the foot of the beloved chair, he was satisfied that his effigy was complete.

Up in The Rose Room of The Star Inn all was quiet except for the grunted commands of Big Barry, who was addressing his assembled troop of rogues. The room had been closed to the public since the shooting incident, only those with special favour, or with knowledge of the passwords, allowed through its bolted doors. There was the clunk and clank of metal upon wood as the tools for the night's work were set upon the central table. A crow bar, two large hammers, a pickaxe, several cudgels and truncheons, and a set of sinister looking metal spikes were laid out on the dark wood.

'We go in hard and we take down whoever's in there,' Barry drawled as the tools were set out. 'Don't care if it's a woman, child, whatever. They go down on the deck, you got me?'

There was of mutter of 'Ayes' and nodding of heads. There were six other men along with Barry about the table. The order had been strictly given that no women were to be allowed through that night.

'If it's women or kids, you blindfold 'em, gag 'em, tie 'em up and stick 'em in some cupboard. The men, bar MacCraw, you batter to unconsciousness before they even get a look at you. This is war, you understand. I don't care if you kills 'em, or whatever. They mustn't get to see you though. That clear?'

More nods and ayes followed.

'MacCraw you batter, but he must stay alive. Hurt him, but try keep him conscious, or close as. Don't matter if he sees you or not. He'll have nothing to tell and nothing to tell it with after this night's through. You get him up here straight away, and in through the back way. And then we'll deal with him in here. Tonight that little barber is going to learn all about pain...'

Barry took up one of the metal spikes with his left hand. With his right hand, still bandaged but some of its mobility returned, he took up a hammer.

'We'll pin the dog out and teach him what it means to....' - here he deftly placed the spike upright and with a single hammer blow drove it right into the table - '...hurt!'

There was a murmur of approval around the table. Barry winced at the pain the blow had caused through his hand, but he held onto the hammer.

'So, get your tools lads. The spikes and a hammer stay here with me. Clear a space in front of the fire there. That's where we'll pin him, right where I fell. Hoods and hats, too. Don't forget your hoods and hats, lads...'

By candlelight, MacCraw made a last nostalgic tour of the house. Each wall of every room he pressed his palm upon, as though touching hands with a lover or a friend, ritually taking his leave of the place. To each dismal room and cubby-hole he whispered a farewell, glancing over them for the final time. At first he felt some sadness, some nostalgia, but gradually he became numbed and immune to the burdening emotion that often comes with departure. Back down in the shop, braced and clear-headed, he set to his task with new gusto. He poured best whale oil over his effigy and the piles of private papers he'd set about and beneath it to make sure the blaze would take. He had avoided glancing into mirrors on his final walkabout, but now ready he breathed in deeply then set himself before the shop's front mirror. Slowly, methodically, with a steady hand, he lathered his face with soap that he had left aside from the day, all the time eyeing himself in the glass. This mirror he had brought with him from Paris, and before it he had spent the last twenty five years of his life. It was arranged so that a customer in the best chair could see his face while being clipped or shaved, if he so wished. The detachable mirror for showing the fellow the back of his haircut through that front mirror hung on the wall directly behind. This had the effect of creating a tunnel of mirrors, rooms and rooms in rooms, tapering off backward and forward toward infinity. At first he had liked this effect, and the discussions it provoked in his customers. Over time though he had stopped even noticing it, as had the customers. The mirrors had become just plain objects on dull walls. Those discussions on infinity, Truth and the appearance and reality of things had long since been nudged aside by gossip, or by silence. MacCraw now stood looking once again upon the multiples of himself. He took up his razor, wiped the blade, and set too, smoothly scratching the stubble and unruly growth from his cheeks and chin. As the soap cleared away he could not help but notice that he had a disturbingly haggard, sallow aspect. This was caused temporarily, he hoped, by the stresses and tribulations he'd been putting himself through of late. Shrugging his worrying visage aside, he shaved on, clearing the blade between smooth, sure strokes. He shaved methodically, in the right, slow way, eventually rinsing the razor, drying it and setting it aside. He took up a clean towel and gently began to pat his face clean of soap. As he gave his smoothed skin a final single wipe he stared hard on at himself, peering deep into and eventually past the black of his own eyes. The surface of the mirror seemed to ripple like a breeze-disturbed pond. His face flashed and shimmered, then faded to a mask of darkness. A tumbling, tumult of images and memory fragments were spilling and spinning there beneath the glass surface as he gazed beyond his own vanishing face. The deeper he peered into the shining pits of his eyes, the more the years fell away, so it seemed, with worry lines and creases melting, skin smoothing over, coarse grain softening, bags and creases and blotches falling away. Beautiful, he stood there, in that early flush of his twenties. He had never realised how handsome he had been, and he sobbed aloud for the loss, but got a grip, clenched back the emotion, and stared on. The eyes clear and shining, skin aglow with health, hair in thick, luxuriant and wild curls. All that was lost now; he could have none of it back. As the years melted from his face so the fabric of the room about him fluxed and fluctuated, scenes reliving themselves in the corners of his vision, rows of men, long dead or vanished from his life, sitting there on the waiting chairs, still blossomed in their youth, wanting the sprout of their growth stemming and tidying by his masterful hand. And there was Branwell among them, laughing and flittering, bespectacled eyes shining, never still, babbling and murmuring even with the blade at his throat, setting the room alight with his humour. There was Grundy, firm and stout, hair trimmed just so, whiskers always clipped down to the same length, never willing to test a nerve jangling potion but rather remaining in full control of his own faculties, recognising that in most men the fragile balance of these faculties was easily damaged by an excess of some herb induced euphoria or crystal tinkering. Leyland propped there easily, leaning his face into an upturned palm, an angel amongst men, and in fact of such a slow growth of facial and body hair that all ape seemed to have already fallen from his being. A parade of men spilled around him there in the spluttering light of the shop lamps. It was only when the shadows around him began to fill with the forms of women that MacCraw became truly afraid of his mirror-gazing and tried to tear himself away. He could hardly bear to confront the image and gentle smile of Caroline; the stern and drinking stares of Branwell's silent, judgmental sisters; that pitying gaze of his own mother as she had passed away on the sick bed with him holding her frail, clammy hand. As these women started to slip in to the edges of the vision he pulled up, stepped back, dragging his own time-weathered face back into the glass. He pulled away out of the mirror like a bather hauling himself from the waters of a delicious but treacherous lake. He moved back beside the chair, back into the brittle, stinking reality of the world, and at that very moment came a single sharp rap at the shop window. Two softer taps followed, close together. It was the signal. He had two minutes to quit the shop. He gave his face a final, quick rub with the towel then set it on the chair at the feet of his effigy.

From the bright doorway of The Star Inn a gang of silent, morose looking men filed into the street. All wore hats that seemed angled to cast shadows about their grubby faces; they scowled or snarled at anyone who so much as peered at them. They turned right into John Street, marching without word but seeming sure of their destination. One of them held a sack in his hand, another a coil of rope. Batons and bars were slipped out of sight beneath their jackets. The unmistakable shape of Big Barry appeared in silhouette in The Star doorway, a taller figure supporting his weight on a crutch came limping up beside him.

'Away, the lads,' Big Barry bellowed after the gang. One of them raised an arm and waved back without looking. He had a hammer in his hand. There was the rumble of laughter from inside the inn. Barry and his wounded companion went back inside to prepare The Rose Room for their evening's entertainment. Barry had already placed four iron spike tips in the edges of the coal fire – he wanted them white-hot by the time they had the barber spread-eagled on the floor there.

MacCraw collected up his luggage – a small leather bag containing the tools and implements of his trade, along with a large, black leather portmanteau. The bigger bag was stuffed with undergarments, shirts, trousers, stockings, waistcoats, half a dozen handkerchiefs, three neckerchiefs, essential toiletries, certain medications, snuff concoctions, best pipes, tobaccos treated and raw, a number of invigorating potions and their raw ingredients, a bottle of good brandy as well as the other scraps and fragments that make up a man on the move. He also had a well-crafted body- wallet, made long ago by a leather-worker friend when he had first embarked on foreign travels with Eamon. This he had strapped beneath vest and shirt about his upper torso. Held safely within the flaps and pockets were various papers, passports, deeds, and bankers' drafts in various names, with certificates of authenticity for each. He also stored here his surviving mementos of Caroline, including her daguerreotype, worked for him one evening by Branwell, along with certain letters and correspondences from their courtship days that he had not been able to bring himself to set to flame. In the lower pockets of his 'treasure-belt' he'd stashed a good quantity of gold coins and paper currency which would be considered anywhere a small fortune, along with a weighed pound of high grade Indian opium, rolled, flattened and placed between waxed paper sheets - good stable currency in any port of the world. In short, strapped about his abdomen was his entire worldly wealth, minus the sum he was bequeathing to the upkeep of Caroline's tomb in Undercliffe, and the one year's provision of monies split into fifty two equal portions that went along with the shop and premises. This last amount, still held in an account bearing his old name, was bequeathed via his latest will to his shop-boy, Jazeb Snell, under the stewardship of his father, Joseph, on the proviso that they ran the business legitimately for the period of fifty two weeks exactly from the commencement of the first payment, within forty days of the deceased and aforementioned, George MacCraw being interred in Undercliffe beside his late beloved wife, Caroline. By seeing them right for a year, he hoped, he'd see them right for life.

All done, all dusted, all set. MacCraw placed his bags by the back door then stood away from the best chair with a glowing lamp in his hand. On a deep intake of breath he dashed the lamp to the floor beside the chair. He watched the oil ignite. He watched smoke unfurl, flames lapping up through the papers jumbled there, fire seeping around the wood and leather of the chair. Flames began to lick over the clothing of the skeletal effigy. In seconds, soaked with oil as they were, the chair and clothing were ablaze. For the last time George MacCraw stepped out of his shop, closing the back shop door behind him, hurrying his way along to the back entrance and his bags. He'd forgotten something, he was sure, but there could be no going back now. Smoke was already creeping about his ankles and thickening behind him. He slipped out into the blackness of deserted ginnel, closing the outer door, locking it against any local hero who might try to force an entry and rescue the trapped occupant from the inferno. The hired gig awaited him there in shadow where the ginnel opened into the street. Joseph Snell, who had rapped out the window signal, was hunched at the reins, hooded and dressed from head to toe in black to disguise him from stray, passing eyes.

'Hurry up, sir. There's someone coming,' Snell hissed.

Without a word MacCraw tossed the bags into the interior of the cab, clambered in himself, and on the kiss of the whip they were away.

Round the corner, from Goodwing Street, a gang of silent men came striding purposefully. At the bottom of Millergate they drew hoods from their coat pockets, and these they draped over the caps so that their faces were quite hidden from view. In a sudden rush they charged up Millergate, then stopped dead in their tracks. Smoke was billowing out of the doorway that was their destination.

'It's on fire!' one gruffed.

'What the hell do we do now?'

One of them tried door but it was locked. A tall, stocky fellow whipped off his hood and took control of the situation.

'You three, round the back way, and make sure no one comes out that way – or if it's MacCraw, have him away, as planned. Keep your hoods on. You, back up to Barry, let him know what's happening. You, get your hood off. You can stay here with me, and we make sure no one gets in or out of there. If the police come, we look as though we're trying to make a rescue, and we'll have our friend away up the hospital for his treatment, so to speak. Right, to it lads!'

The shop shutters and blinds were closed, but as the hoodlums pressed up to the glass and peered in there was the unmistakable glow of flames from within.

Hungry flames licked and bit. Greedy flames went gnawing about the furnishings, eating into fabric, tonguing up curtains, licking along wooden fittings. Glass cracked. Jars exploded. Shaving pots shattered. Hanging towels and aprons puffed alight, devoured in an instant. The leather and stuffing of the chair hissed, expiring air as if softly groaning in dismay at its own death and imminent destruction. Flames danced over clothing and scorched onto the bones that were set within. A roaring gradually spread through the closed shop, as though the skull there in a bed of fire was bellowing out, screaming its last. Then came an audible whooshing up at the shattering of a glass windowpane and inrush of air which fed the flames to a frenzy. Fire had its firm and fatal grip upon the barbering room of George MacCraw's Emporium.

Snell and his silent passenger were well on their way out of town and ten minutes up the Leeds road before the shrilling call went up across the Ivegate neighbourhood:
    'Fire! Fire! Fetch the engine! Fire! Fire!'

CHAPTER 24

1 measure of castor oil
4 drops of vinegar of rosemary
4 drops of juice of fresh beetroot or two of pickled
4 drops of the juice of nettle root
1 oz of well dried mule manure
1 oz of used coffee grinds
1 grain of good luck by way of birth
all rubbed upon the required area daily or applied as a poultice there with fresh oats
rinse and repeat

Doctor Crossley's Patent Baldness Cure
San Francisco
1862

Liverpool, May 1861

Fortune is fickle; fame can be enduring or brief as a flash of lightning. As barber, writer or hero, George MacCraw had never really sought fame, despite all his huffing and puffing and spitting at Fate on his nights out with the Rhymers while still all but a lad. But for a while, an instant, he did create a little notoriety, when some details of his life, his history, and his terrible death fronted bold on the weekly local newspaper. Not many men get to read about their own death or to see the true opinions of his neighbours and his peers in print. Nothing MacCraw saw on the front pages disturbed or distressed him. His tale only made two weeks running in the publication. In the nationals, or even in the papers outside the Yorkshire borders, his tragic death made no impression at all. By the time he trotted up the gangplank to board the steamer in Liverpool, George MacCraw was already history. Only those immediately concerned with organising his demise would have recourse to scan back over the news pages for details of his life and death; only some future, accidental eye, roaming over the pages of a chance found copy of the Bradford Observer, perhaps lining a drawer, stowed in an attic, or used as carpet underlay, would come upon his briefly newsworthy death. MacCraw, like most, was not above vanity, and he kept copies of the editions, brought to him in his Liverpool hideaway by Francis Grundy as he made preparations for his own departure. After depositing his luggage in the cabin he had booked for the passage, MacCraw took out the papers and re-read the articles relating to him. Neither article was particularly well written or interesting in style, and he felt that much more could have made out of the mysterious nature of his death, along with the possibility that he may have been murdered, a victim of a feud with a local felon. Little was made of Big Barry's numerous reasons for killing him and razing his shop, and there was no mention whatsoever of the manuscript of Branwell's that he had offered to set before the very editor of the same journal. The rambling, unfocussed headline attached to the first story ran thus:

THE POLICE HINT AT POSSIBLE FOUL PLAY BUT HOLD SHORT OF A MURDER INVESTIGATION FOLLOWING LAST WEEK'S TRAGIC DEATH OF A LOCAL TRADESMAN AND CHARACTER OF THE TOWN

The severely charred remains of a man, believed to be George Maquire, known locally as George MacCraw, the barber, were today recovered from the burnt out lower floor of the deceased's trading establishment, located on Millergate, in the centre of the town. Mister MacCraw was a widower with no children or direct family in this area, and was believed to be about forty five years of age. The fire was extremely severe, and the deceased was believed to have perished while falling asleep in his own barber's shop chair and knocking over an oil lamp, thus provoking a blaze. There are rumours of signs that foul play and robbery may have played a part in the tragic death, although police have not yet declared that their investigation into the matter is a murder inquiry. A local constable has admitted that certain suspicious circumstances surround events leading up to the fire, and people have claimed a gang of armed hoodlums were in the area on the night. Details of these will be revealed in due course, once they have been checked and clarified by our investigators. Another constable at the scene of the ruined and charred shop the following morning said that at this stage in time police were not as yet hunting any individuals in connection with the fire, but will continue investigating the exact cause of the ferocious blaze. A full statement will be released with regard to their investigations into the death of Mister MacCraw and the circumstances of the fire later in the week.

Local residents have all spoken highly of Mister MacCraw, and he seems to have been
held in high regard by customers and neighbours alike. A sign of his compassion,
generosity and kindly nature is indicated by his apparent last will and testament,
which is said to bequeath his premises and goods of trade to a young shop apprentice
and his family.

The remains of Mister MacCraw will be interred alongside his deceased wife,
Caroline (ne-Waterhouse) MacCraw, in a ceremony next Friday, in the family plot at
the cemetery in Undercliffe.

After reading this and the other pieces relating to his death, MacCraw was careful to
stow the news sheets out of sight, not wanting to provoke any interest in his origins
should any cleaner or cabin boy chance upon them on his bunk. There was a bustle of
excitement in the corridors outside his room, then the ship's horn blasted the signal
that departure was imminent. MacCraw put on his topcoat and set out to watch the
proceedings from the upper deck. He went aft, where he reckoned it would be quieter,
for he didn't want to find himself in the sobbing, waving throng or endure their
excitement and undoubted tears at their own leave takings.

Green, glassy slabs of water churned over and whitened into hissing foam about the
stern of the great steamer. Gulls ploughed in and out of the swirling wake, diving at
fish that were turned up and made visible in the disturbance. The wind tousled and
ransacked through the barber's growing mane of hair, his hat sensibly left back in the
cabin, for he'd been sure that would be whipped away and into the sea if he wore it on
deck. George Crossley, as he was now officially named, stood at the rails staring down
into the waters, mentally toying over his new name. George Victor Crossley. Victor,
he'd be, to his friends. George just in case, for despite the world being vast, within the
circles of men it was always an unexpectedly small place. Best if he kept part of his old
tag, he had reasoned, just in case he ever ran into a familiar face. George Victor
Crossley. It had a certain, grandiose ring to it - yet was plain enough, and English
sounding. It looked right and appropriate written down or printed, as indeed it was, on
all his travel and financial documentation. A faceless name, sensible, safe sounding,
which had exactly suited his purpose. He was lost in thought, staring down into the
fascination of water, mesmerized by the movement and green flux of colour there. It
had been a long time since he had seen and sniffed the ocean. With one hand he
gripped firm on the iron railing, half-fearing that the momentum of the thundering
vessel might pitch him overboard with some sudden lurch or turbulence. That would
certainly be the last of him, bobbing and waving as a stranded speck in that vast
expanse of grey and greenery, the ship steaming on out of sight toward the Americas.
He'd be lost there, utterly anonymous in those awesome depths and breadths of ocean.
A man would expire out there for sure. He'd last ten minutes – fifteen at the most, he
reckoned, before the cold and exhaustion closed down all sensible faculties to let life
slip away.

He pulled his stare up from the foaming wake, frightened by the plunging urge
that had come upon him; a strange temptation, urging him to hurl his body headlong
into the sea. A half-recalled dream wisped through his memory, the uncanny sense of
a déjà vu creeping through him. His leather body-wallet was still strapped about his
torso - with the help of that weight, along with his new boots and clothing, he would
be dragged under within a minute. He'd disappear bottomward and no one would ever
know. On this ship there was nobody to miss him yet. No companion. No friend or
relative or parted lover to greet him on the other side of The Golden Door, as this one

way journey to the Americas was called by the Irish back there in Liverpool. Eamon would know he was coming, if he was still alive and the letter had ever got there, but he would not know when exactly. San Francisco was right across the whole continent, weeks and weeks away, so he didn't expect his brother to come and meet him, not even half way. Certainly then, it would be a long time before anyone noticed his absence or set about searching for him, should he go overboard. George Victor Crossley – that's who they'd not notice missing. That's who they might eventually scour the ship for, checking down the passenger list, asking if anyone had seen him since departure from port. The other fellow, MacCraw, was now officially dead and in the earth. George MacCraw, dead and buried, charred remains littered in a coffin and set beneath the turf with his beloved Caroline, his name and scanty details inscribed there below hers, the white angel towering over the clutter of tombstones and other monuments. It was a nice resting place; a nice view. At least of that he was sure.

He swayed with the lurching of the vessel, staring back at the smudge of land. Liverpool there was now indistinct; the outlines of spires and great warehouse buildings could just about be made out in the gloomy grey. To his own surprise, having heard that the place was a nest of thieves and fleecing cut-throats, he had enjoyed the hugeness and bustle of that great city. He had been grateful of the comfortable anonymity the sheer size of the place had forced upon him. He had spent the last month 'in cognito' in various small hotels and guest houses while tying up final pieces of business, sorting out his travel arrangements and transferring money to a reliable bank in New York. Those past weeks had been lived with the enjoyable sense of being a renegade. He had heartily enjoyed feeling something like a fleeing criminal or greatly successful fraudster, trying all the time not to communicate this giddy, childish excitement to the other guests and staff at the establishments where he had resided.

Twice in those Liverpool weeks he had met, as arranged, with Grundy, who though bemused by the extremity of his friend's actions and intentions, had agreed to help him to the last. Through Grundy he had received word from Snell on how events had unfolded since the shop fire. Overall, bar one or two hiccups, the plan had been remarkably successful. The news of his death was gossiped all about Bradford and the West Riding, for if nothing else, being riddled with mystery and intrigue, it made a good tale. Big Barry had been implicated, as intended, and questioned by the police on two occasions. Unfortunately for the plan, Barry had a strong and solid alibi for the night of the blaze. According to Grundy, he had been absorbed in a game of cribbage in the house of a local judge at that time, a game attended by several other decent men of standing in the town, all of whom were prepared to swear on oath of the publican's whereabouts on the night of the fire. Of the strange group of men who had been loitering about the barber's premises, Barry swore he knew nothing. No charges could be brought against him on this occasion, though Constable Duff, whose troubled feet had greatly benefited from the kind barber's advice, had tried his utmost to have the felon arrested, and had made it well known that from here he would be monitoring the gangster's every movement.

Some about the town whispered of a suicide. MacCraw had certainly not been himself in the weeks before his death. Several people who frequented The Star Inn were willing to swear on oath that he had in been of unsound mind and displayed definite suicidal tendencies. The rumour was that MacCraw had deliberately taken his own life in a manner that would implicate Big Barry for motives of revenge, following some trifling argument over his drink bill and gambling debts. Upon hearing this version of things, MacCraw actually regretted that he had not left more pointers and clues suggesting as much, for that would have tidied things up nicely. He was glad that the story was passing quickly from view, and the papers made as little of it as they did. A full police and newspaper investigation could have worked against him quite badly. Indeed, his greatest relief was that the bones found in and around the wreck of the shop chair had never been subject to doubt or question. They had been so badly charred by the ferocity of the blaze that the police had never questioned whether they were MacCraw or some other unfortunate victim. Seeing as how the barber was not around, and the shop had been locked until the firefighters broke down the door, it had seemed reasonable to assume that they were MacCraw's remains. No mystery-sniffing detective had come upon the scene worrying how half a skeleton was missing; nobody had been requested to suffer the horror of formally identifying the blackened remains. They were laid in a casket with a few half-burned items of clothing, boots, and a clean barber's apron from one of the damage free upstairs rooms, then the lot was planted in the earth with a priest's blessing and a little knot of mourners looking on.

Despite the vulnerability of his position while waiting for news of his case, MacCraw had enjoyed Liverpool life greatly. Though huge and slum ridden, like any great city, there was a vibrancy about the place that Bradford had lacked; the people even in the inns seemed more civilized, less taciturn. There was a great deal of living for enjoyment, even it seemed amongst the poorest folk. These bottom-of-the-pilers were, in the main, of Irish stock, though the lower caste was sprinkled with all colourings and racial types from the world over. This jumble of origins gave the city a thriving, cosmopolitan atmosphere much more in keeping with the ports of southern Europe he had travelled through in his youth, though of course the grey weather was much more gloomy. Such was MacCraw's enjoyment of those weeks that he toyed with the notion of settling there, perhaps opening an apothecary shop, or setting himself up in the import of medicinal plants and substances, there being from Liverpool a trade line to every isle and nation of the globe. At heart though, despite the daydreams, he knew this would be too risky. He was not so far away from Bradford for an unsavoury coincidence or happen-chance meeting with a familiar face; a former friend or customer who knew that he was supposed to be deceased stepping into his new shop or bumping into him in one of the busy thoroughfares. Besides, a ball had been set in motion and he was determined to follow its whole course to see which way the skittles would fall. This sea passage to New York was the next stage. He'd rest a week there, perhaps two, looking at the opportunities, taking in the sights. Then he'd head overland by train and wagon to the city of San Francisco. There, if his brother's written words of the past years were to be believed, a man like himself, with some initiative and a little capital, could settle for a life of good food, ocean views, easy living and gentle sunshine. There was not much more a man could ask from life than that, although he did have some creeping longings for the pleasure of a female companion that he had not yet addressed. All these years, he had never even considered remarrying, or being again in love. Now though, suddenly, it was a possibility. A possibility that not only thrilled him, but one that made him feel just a little bit frightened, in a tantalizing sort of way.

As MacCraw considered the possible futures awaiting him in the Americas, England became a smudged blur on the horizon. All thoughts of Branwell and his devilish manuscript he banished with the fading of that country. No more worries on it now - no more pressure to set the past to rights. One day, perhaps, in the distant future, the Haworth grave would be opened. The wrapped parcel of manuscript would be found, the package unearthed, the past revealed. But how long would such a country value its works of art? Its history? Its artists? Even fifty years on from now the book would probably not be remembered at all, the whole family of Haworth waifs forgotten, the inscriptions on their crumbling tombstones carrying the last word and memories of them into oblivion. But none of that or them mattered now. Here he stood, alone, cocooned in a sphere of grey sky and green ocean. Encompassed in nothing, yet moving forward. And it felt good. He felt good. A long forgotten flutter of excitement was bubbling through his stomach – the creeping, butterfly thrill that comes with distant travel and future uncertainty.

He stood there with knuckles whitened, fingers numbing at the ship's rail, watching the sky's light dim and the horizon close in about the vessel like an upturned, folding hand. The wind off the open ocean cleaved about his very bones with a sudden, penetrating chill. It was time, he decided, to head below to enjoy his cabin. As he swivelled from the railings a dark figure lurched from the nearest stairwell that led below. It was a thin man, extremely tall, dressed from top hat to boot toe in black. He stood out as sharp as a blade against the slanted green of seaward horizon. He came on toward the ship's stern with a determination that seemed deliberate and threatening. The fellow's face was pale and haggard, all deep set lines and sharp angles, mad eyes glittering like stars in the twilight gloom. MacCraw grabbed back onto the handrail as the stranger jerked awkwardly toward him. The dream... the dream! He remembered the dream now. The fiend's wild eyes blazed and came probing into MacCraw's face, as though he recognised the barber and expected a greeting. MacCraw was trembling with his back to the rail, teeth suddenly chattering, bowels churning. He was certain that at last he had met his assassin. He was all but ready to faint in terror, certain that the fiend would shove out and pitch him overboard as he passed.

'Evening, sir,' the fellow murmured, touching the rim of his hat and nodding politely. He passed by, leaving a waft of expensive cologne in his wake. No push. No shove. No murder. The fellow passed and stepped awkwardly along to the prow of the ship, gripped the rails, and stood there looking back into the ocean, just as MacCraw had been doing a minute or so before. MacCraw released his hold on the handrail and began wobbling on unsteady land-legs toward the stairs that would lead him below. George Victor Crossley, he became then, at that moment he stepped away from the tall, dark fellow. George Victor Crossley, born in the town of Bath, England, on the twenty first of December, 1817. Mister Crossley, making a First Class entrance through The Golden Door to America, travelling quietly but in style and comfort, as a gentleman of his standing and means should certainly do so. George Victor Crossley descended to his cabin to wash, shave and prepare for dinner. His old friend, George MacCraw, and all about him, at last, was done with.

Epilogue

AN ARRIVAL AT DARKWALLS
an extract from a work in three parts, entitled
'The Withering Hands'

by Patrick Branwell Brontë
Portrait Painter, Poet, Author
residing presently at Fountain Street
in the district of Manningham
Bradford 1838

From 'THE WITHERING HANDS'

From afar he had travelled, though now at last he neared those foreboding walls of his ultimate destination. Through the wide avenues and boulevards of the affluent city of Paris, and yet down many a dark and slimy alley of that great city's maze, he had meandered, disheartening numerous dark eyed maidens there, luring and netting them with his charismatic, animal charm only to thwart them in the trials of amour, casting them away like minions. Through this vengeful campaign against the night-softness of the female heart, his will and imagination led him always on northward, either in fact or in his mind striding one more furious, furnace fuelled step toward his darkest heart's destination.

Murderous intent, the black fuel that roared in that piston driven human furnace. Revenge, the bitter substance of that fuel. The winning back of the heart of his one true love, the fan that aired the furied flames.

Northangerland. Dark-browed. Blaze-eyed. Strong girthed. Northward Northangerland did stride, or rode, in many a bone-gnawing wooden cart. He always strove to travel on alone. Always, he inspired unease and dread, an inclination to avoidance in those unfortunates who were destined to share a carriage or tavern room with him - some grim but undeniably noble aspect of his savagely handsome face warding off those lesser, fritterish beings, thus sparing him the rudeness of snorting aside any attempts by them to chat or bandy petty road-gossip with him.

Northward and silent he travelled. Toward his beloved, sweet Caroline he moved, oblivious to weather, steep hillside, rock-face or treacherous mountain track. Onward toward Caroline and toward Darkwall, that great but solemn fronted house that lay upon the moor's edge. The house that was his by natural, moral and now legal right, for in the turmoil of her husband's debt spinning he had acquired the deeds to the place. Her heart, her hand, her house - his only intentions.

A coach brought him to the inn at the heart of the huddled town beneath the frowning shadow of the moor. There, in sworn secrecy to the landlord, he took rooms under his own true name - Heathcliffe Alexander Percy Northangerland. Three nights and full days he remained stowed there behind closed doors, sending out notes and sealed letters with dark eyed, burly servants who seemed to have appeared out of the darkness, for they had not arrived with him, and by their talk and manner were clearly not of the district. He ate his meals alone within the rooms, lurking there like a malign presence, pacing back and forth across the floors. He was waiting, it seemed, for a very particular message or moment.

On the fourth night, cloaked and armed with sword and pistols, he strode off without word of destination or intention to those at the inn who had harboured him. Upon foot he went, along the road that led upward from the little town. Ignoring sleet and wind, oblivious to all external stimuli, he marched toward the highlighted windows of a building beyond the town. As the houses and dwellings fell away by broken moonlight through fits of cloud, his memory of the way served and steered him. The furthest house, his destination, was one which stood on the highest level of pastureland, with large black walls and mossy porch, a plantation of gloomy firs, one clump of which - the oldest and the highest - stretched their horizontal arms above one gable like the very Genii of that desolate scene. Beyond this dwelling its long-built walls made a line with the November sky, and the path across them led to that interminable moor. No birds flew near the place now, by day or night, except common linnets, twittering by the hundreds on some wet, old wall. Despite its loneliness this house was of no common note in the parish, and many of the fireside tales of times gone, and surely after this night to come, took 'Darkwall' for their scene, and its owners for their subject.

Now, through the darkness, Heathcliffe could see that the house downstairs was well lit, the fires ablaze, the mistress of the place hoping to create a warm, if not loving, welcome for its long absented master. Caroline Thurston, suffering visible in the rippled perplexity of her unusual smooth-domed brow, was assisting in the busy kitchen, preparing a feastly supper for her expected husband and his 'companions'. Suddenly, to those within preparing the little feast, a clatter of boots upon cobbles was heard from outside. Doors and windows were rushed to. The night without pushed forth not the slanting frame of the wretched weakling, Thurston, but the projection of a man of such uncommon might and stature, attired beneath his opened cloak in short green frock coat, white cord breeches, a black, broad brimmed hat atop of his handsome face. A gasp! A sigh! A gentle moan was heard escape the lips of the trembling Caroline...

Heart thumping with giddy excitement, leg muscles aburn, aching with the unanticipated length of the homeward jaunt, Branwell rushed past the main door and lighted parlour window, going round to the kitchen entrance of the parsonage. In the kitchen at about this time, he well knew, his sisters would be there secreted and busy in their infernal business of reading and composition. He peeped in at the window to ensure that they were there without Papa or Aunt Branwell. Indeed they were, all hunched and huddled over books, though another was with them - a young woman of their own age whose face he could not discern, though her slender neck was pretty enough. He rapped hard on the cold glass then went to stand before the kitchen door, which was habitually bolted against night-roamers.

'It's me,' he called. 'Let me in - let me in!'

After a great fuss and scuttling the door swung inward, his three sisters' bonneted framed faces bobbling like sunflowers there in the doorframe. Behind them it was the lovely Mary Taylor who stood there, flushing and smiling without restraint. Arms reached out, hands grabbed, lips pecked his cold cheeks, the door closed, he was hugged, he was pampered, a seeming sea of sisters about him, uncoated, hat snatched, hair ruffled, ushered toward the warmth of the range, cake and hot tea set on the table before him.

'Branwell - you've not walked the whole of the way from Bradford town!?' exclaimed Charlotte upon sight of his muddy boots and breeches.

'I have too. And a great stroll it's been, though a little further than I thought. But quick sisters, a pen! A pen! And something to scribble upon. Such a story has found me out there on the hills.'

'You poor, frozen soul. Dear Branwell, warm yourself up before you think of writing anything.'

Mary Taylor said this, much bolder than her usual timid self, perhaps stirred by the earlier, teasing talk of Ann and Charlotte, who had all but married her off to Branwell before the year was out. She stepped toward Branwell, and half-pouting, tilted her right cheek to him, awaiting an informal, unconventional, kiss of greeting. An unusual, over-forward way, surely, to greet a friend or indeed a relative in public, but such seemed the way with this strange family, whom she would have gladly married into for her life, for she was convinced that they were geniuses, or angels, or fairies, to the last of them. But rather than kiss that offered cheek Branwell openly retracted from her like a snail recoiling for protection into its shell, while a strange frown clouded his usually sunny face. Such a dark and hurtful look that it cut Mary to the quick, in that very instant extinguishing all affection or marital ambition that had but moments before flamed so brightly within her. She could do nothing to contain her feeling.

'But Branny - you recoil!'

'No no - dear, sweet Mary. Not from you, surely. You catch me by surprise. I'm warmed to see you, but, I'm all worn out by the walk. And something's come up. A pen's all I want at the moment. Sisters, bring the writing box. Ink, Charlotte. And any paper - bags or sheets of it. At last, I've a story in a real voice. It's set itself into me upon the road. Let me catch it, girls, before it slips back into the eternal night-time...'

The sisters, somewhat vexed and astounded by Branwell's rudeness to their friend, hurried about getting quill and ink-stand and any loose sheaths of decent writing paper, seeing plainly that their wayward brother had a writing-frenzy upon him. In a blur of activity, amidst meaningful female glances (raising of eyebrows, slight pursing of lips and narrowing of eyes - for they all realised what a hash their good brother had made of his chances with a good and honest wife) a space was cleared on the kitchen table, a writing place created upon the homely wood. Branwell drew up a hard-backed chair and set himself down, stretching his arms, flexing and clicking his slender fingers, readying toward the pen. Charlotte, Emily and Ann formed a neat, neck-craning semi-circle behind him, keen to watch him flame-forth his inspiration upon the page, but aware that by stepping over-close they could become a distraction. The slighted, much confused Mary sat herself by the fireplace and took up the embroidery she had earlier been working on while chatting marriage with the sisters.

Even before a sip of tea had passed his lips, or the breath settled in his walk-wearied body, Branwell set his pen to the scratch.

'Why, what tale's this that's gripped you so, Branny?' Anne inquired as she watched ink flow and the black words uncoiling.

'It's one of the old tales, sister, but reworked in new voice. A modern voice. I realise it now - we must write for these times. We've been too long in aping the forms of old. A new voice. A modern voice. That's what we should strive for now. Word for word this poured into my mind as I walked just now - sentence, paragraph and chapter from start to end. Well, at least the opening of it. Now shush - if I can just get the gist of it while the heat is upon me...'

Emily, leaning calmly at his shoulder now, began to whisper-mouth the words that appeared there before her.

'One fine summer morning - it was the beginning of the harvest - Earnshaw, the sturdy master of Darkwall Heights, came clopping down the stairs of the great house, dressed for a journey...'

'Shush there, will you, Emmy. You're getting me all jumbled. Just give me half an hour of this, will you, and I'll be back amongst you.'

Thus snubbed, noses prim-tilted, lips pursed in tight lines of mockery at the great and famous Patrick Branwell Brontë, artist, poet, author, the sisters and Mary Taylor tip-toed from the kitchen and down the stone-flagged corridor toward the parlour, leaving their brother scribbling away at the kitchen table.

Published by East Coast Books,
108 Church Street, Whitby, YO22 4DE
Yorkshire, UK.

Also By Chris Firth

Miasma
Springboard ISBN 1 901927 01 6

Deserted, lonely, sad. Going slowly mad. A woman is angry; somebody will pay.
In this darkly humoured, compelling novel, Chris Firth leads into the murky world of Anna Fisher, exploring loneliness, betrayal, and the addictive compulsion to revenge.
A real page turner - a stomach-turning manual for anyone seeking vengeance on those they have loved.

'I really enjoyed (if that's the right word) this sinister tale.'
Barry Hines.

Electraglade
SNAP, Skrev Press ISBN 1 904646 00 X

**Stories selected by the Poet Laureate, Andrew Motion, and Anne Fine
for the Arts Council Writer's Awards 2000**

12 compelling, inter-woven science fiction stories that will make you re-examine your present, your past and the world's future. A parallel reality, a leap through time, or yesterday? Open up into the beauty and terror of the Electraglade - the future is now!

'He has created a quietly terrifying, yet totally plausible vision of our future world - the characters and action work well against such an exciting and violent backdrop'
Yvonne Hooker, Puffin fiction editor.

Both of these publications are available from
www.amazon.co.uk and
www.skrev-press.com

The Mulgrave Tales
East Coast Books ISBN 0-9536405-5-8

Strange and mysterious tales set in and around the ancient Mulgrave Woods, Whitby, North Yorkshire. Mulgrave Woods make a brief appearance in Bram Stoker's classic Gothic novel, 'Dracula'. Using the unique and atmospheric setting of these woods and the nearby coast, a series of magical and sometimes dark stories unfold. **Dare you go down to the woods today?**

'Delicious literary horror by the master of urban macabre!' – Whitby Gazette

More information about these books and the writer may be found at
www.electraglade.com